INVICTUS

By

BILL YANCEY

BRIARWOOD PUBLICATIONS, INCORPORATED

Copyright © 2003 William Yancey

First Published 2003
Briarwood Publications & Sassy Cat Books, Inc.
150 West College Street
Rocky Mount, Virginia 24151

All rights reserved. The use of any part of this publication,
reproduced, transmitted in any form, or by any means,
electronic, mechanical, photocopying, recording or otherwise,
or stored in a retrieval system, without prior consent of the
publisher is an infringement of the copyright law.

William Yancey

INVICTUS
ISBN: 1-892614-43-X

Cover illustration by
GINNY COVEY
© 2002
birdscapesginnycovey@juno.com

Manufactured in the United States of America.

Difficile est saturam non scribere.
                (It is hard not to write satire. Juvenalis, <u>Saturae</u>)

Invictus

William Ernest Henley

Out of the night that covers me,
Black as the Pit from pole to pole,
I thank whatever gods may be
For my unconquerable soul.

In the fell clutch of circumstance
I have not winced nor cried aloud.
Under the bludgeonings of chance
My head is bloody, but unbowed.

Beyond this place of wrath and tears
Looms but the Horror of the shade,
And yet the menace of the years
Finds, and shall find, me unafraid.

It matters not how strait the gate,
How charged with punishments the scroll,
I am the master of my fate:
I am the captain of my soul.

Dedication

This book is dedicated to my wife, Jerry Anne, who has blessed me with love and support, despite my many faults. It is also dedicated to the memory of a friend and fine physician (also mentor, father, grandfather, husband, flight surgeon, urologist, philanthropist, and gentleman). Very few people on this planet can fill the shoes of W. Landon Banfield. He is sorely missed.

Thanks

I would like to thank Pat Scanlon Aller, David Cattini, Jim Cloe, and Barbara Turner for their assistance in bringing my manuscript to print.

This novel is a work of fiction. The characters (with the exception of public or historical figures), incidents, settings, dialogues, and situations depicted are products of the author's imagination. Any resemblance to actual events or persons, living or deceased, is entirely coincidental.

Also by Bill Yancey

Elvis Saves

Chapter One
United States Air Force
July 1ˢᵗ

Doctor Spencer Dodd sat on the molded concrete bench in the courtyard of the minimum-security prison. The stockade sat in the center of the huge Eglin Air Force Base Reservation, which in turn occupied the middle of the Florida panhandle. The sun glared overhead, a never ending magnesium flare. It boiled the sweat from Dodd's brow, leaving a thin coating of salt and baking his dark brown, suntanned forehead. In his orange jumpsuit, immobile, he read the graffiti left on the sidewalk by previous prisoners also abandoned to roast in the reflections in the quadrangle of sand-colored barracks that comprised the prison.

A black bird circled warily overhead, catching Dodd's imagination. Wings make you free, he thought, unless perchance they are associated with air force blue. Dodd had always wanted to fly. His father piloted B-17s against the Germans in World War II and survived nearly fifty combat missions. After retiring from the air force, however, he never spoke of the dangers, only of the excitement. His son heard how to bomb an enemy into submission and how Earth creatures dwindled away to nothing as the huge bomber lumbered skyward with its load of death. An uncle, not a Dodd, flew Sabrejets in the Korean War and attack aircraft in Vietnam. The fighter pilot told Spencer of high altitude duels with Russian and Chinese pilots. Like gleaming swords, flights of attacking Mig-15s and defending F-86s, clashed over North Korea when propeller-driven, American B-29 bombers attacked the enemy's ground troops.

The raven swooped below the roof line of the building to Dodd's left, temporarily hidden. Dodd's mind wandered, following a feeder line onto a different track, into a mental morass. Vignettes flashed through his mind faster than he could have articulated them.

***

In Washington, D.C., in the office of the United States Air Force Surgeon General, Dodd sat at a conference table. A full colonel sat across from him. "You're AWOL; you know that, don't you?" the colonel asked.

"I was relieved from duty, Colonel. I do not show up on anyone's duty roster at the hospital for the next week. There is a rumor that I have been transferred from the ER to Primary Care. Officially, no one has told me anything, yet."

The colonel grunted. "This the chart?"

"Yes, sir," Dodd agreed.

The colonel flipped through the chart for several minutes, then spoke to Dodd. "He was treated like he had a seizure?"

"And died of a heart attack. One of the medics ran a rhythm strip on the monitor for fifteen minutes. The enlisted men tried to get my colleague to treat the ventricular tachycardia, then the ventricular fibrillation, then the asystole. Major Ventura kept pushing the intravenous Valium."

"Where's the cardiac monitor rhythm strip?"

"I think Phipps destroyed it," Dodd suggested.

"You have proof?"

The young doctor explained, "It was in this chart until he reviewed it, sir. I liberated the chart from his office last night, without his permission of course."

"So, the strip may still exist?"

"Maybe you should ask Colonel Phipps, sir."

***

Invictus

At about 0200 hours; a bloody-faced man sat in the emergency room stall, on the end of the stretcher. A giant of a man, he dangled an air policeman on each wrist bound by handcuffs. Bloody, civilian shirt, ripped from his muscled body hung suspended at his waist. The young man wore faded denims and sandals. Dried blood covered his face, chest, jeans, feet, and leather thongs. A laceration ran from the drunken airman's right eyebrow, downward and across the swollen, bloodied nose eventually ending at the left corner of his upper lip. A knife-wielding opponent had suffered mightily for making that incision.

The grizzly-bear-sized man took an instant dislike to the young air force doctor standing sleepily in front of him. Dodd nodded to the two policeman. Suppressing a yawn, he said, "I can't sew him up unless he gives me permission." He turned to the patient and added sarcastically, "It's too early in the morning for this crap. Next time, wait until reveille to pick a fight, all right?"

Effortlessly, the giant gathered Dodd's white coat and green scrub shirt tightly around the physician's neck with both hands. Yanked off their feet, the enlisted men swinging on either wrist struggled to reach their night sticks with their free hands. They shouted orders at the alcoholic, which he ignored. Indifferent to the bellowing men, the drunk pulled Dodd closer to him, staring at him with the one eye not swollen shut. "What did you say, Doc?" he asked, spewing hate, alcohol enriched breath, saliva, and blood.

Dodd smiled, in deep trouble of his own making, as usual. Acutely aware that the two air policemen were powerless to stop his murder, he replied, "I said," and paused for emphasis, "that you are ugly." The drunk's left eye popped open wide in surprise. "And you're going to be a lot uglier if you don't let me put a zipper in that mug of yours."

Slowly, a smile creased the lush's face. Dodd saw the

chipped central incisor; the split lip oozed more scarlet. The fists relaxed and dropped to the man's side. No longer restrained, the men attached at the drunk's wrists regained their feet. Dodd held his hands up, stopping them from hitting the man with their billy clubs.

"You know," the drunk said, "you're just crazy enough for me to let you sew me up."

***

Another night, almost dawn in the emergency room. The ashen face of a fifty-three-year-old man smiled at Dodd. Enlisted medics rolled the stretcher toward the front of the hospital and the elevator to the intensive care unit. Dodd followed, scribbling notes on the patient's chart as he walked. Intravenous solutions hung from every corner of the wheeled bed. A portable monitor, green face etched with the man's heart beat, beeped quietly lying between his legs on the white sheet.

An air policeman accompanied that patient, too. Dodd thought of the sick man as a political prisoner, a definition he knew to be incorrect — white-collar criminal fit better. Even so, many of the men he came in contact with from the minimum-security prison had been in politics, corrupt politics. Then, what politics were not corrupt?

He remembered Attorney General Richmond Flowers from Alabama. Dodd had been a high school student for a brief time in Montgomery. Flowers crossed a line; he backed the blacks in their struggle for civil liberties, defying Governor George Wallace's segregation policy. The attorney paid for his integrity, or foolishness, with a jail sentence for fraud. Trumped up as punishment for defying the establishment, or real? Dodd did not know. He recalled his disappointment when Flowers had been convicted, convinced at the time of his guilt. That occurred before Dodd realized his government consisted of imperfect individuals, some of whom do lie and cheat. Indeed, it was possible for his government to deceive him.

Invictus

No longer so naive, after two years in Vietnam as a sailor, Dodd now questioned everything his government, or persons representing that government, told him.

Regardless, Flowers spent time in a place like Eglin AFB, possibly in Eglin itself. Dodd assumed white-collar criminals sometimes made themselves prisoners of the political system. Many were failed team players who lacked enough political clout to redefine the team, to rearrange the pecking order in their favor, or to describe a new paradigm. Some, he assumed, had been martyred for beliefs not held by the reigning alpha dog in whichever pack they ran.

"Give me your bank account number, Doc," the patient whispered hoarsely.

Dodd laughed. "Why, so you can clean it out? I can assure you, there isn't anything in it. My wife emptied it by accident about two weeks ago."

The older man smiled through the chest pain. "No, so I can thank you for saving my life."

"You already did," Dodd said. He watched the elevator door scrape noisily shut, hiding the patient, the medics, and one policeman from view. The doctor turned to the second air policeman. "What's he in for?" Dodd asked.

"Bank fraud," the clean-cut NCO answered. "He used the bank computer to steal fractions of cents worth of interest paid by federal banks. The FBI found ten million dollars in his account, but they think he may have squirreled away a hundred million more in Switzerland."

***

Dodd stood at attention in front of the mahogany desk of the hospital commanding officer, Colonel Phipps. "This is the fourth similar complaint this month, Dodd," the CO growled.

"Sir, she's a drug addict. Her back exam was more normal than mine...."

"Then why would all these other physicians give her

narcotics?"

"Ask them."

***

He stood at attention, again, in the same room, on a different day. Phipps asked, "Why can't you just give them the amoxicillin, Dodd, like everyone else?"

"Where I went to medical school and did residency, sir, they discouraged the use of antibiotics for viral infections."

"You can prove this is a viral infection, Dodd?"

"Statistically, sir...."

"Statistics, my ass, Dodd! You cause me a lot of grief, son. Statistics state that I have more complaints about you than any other physician in my hospital. Are you too idealistic to give the patients good care? Are you a better physician than the five previous doctors who gave this mother amoxicillin for her son's runny noses?"

"Evidently, sir."

***

Dodd knelt in the ambulance at the head of the stretcher holding the dying Cuban. The young man gasped one last time and ceased breathing with a shudder. Through the back window of the ambulance Dodd saw a thousand brown faces pressed against the chain link fence of the compound. The ad hoc prison housed thousands of the Mariel Boat Lift survivors. Changing his field of vision, Dodd focused on the task at hand. He rammed the endotracheal tube home, deep into the unconscious man's trachea. Inflating the tube's cuff, he told the medic to start squeezing the bag that forced air into the patient's lungs.

"Half a milligram of epinephrine, intravenously. Get this ambulance on the highway. Now!" he barked. The faces at the fence receded in the distance as the Cuban returned to life.

***

"Christ, you're back," Dodd said to the patient. He

had trouble distinguishing the anemic man from his white shirt, except where most of his blood drained from the large, self-inflicted gashes in his brachial arteries. A red wave from each elbow washed over the stretcher, soaked the sheets and spilled onto the floor.

"Someone took my drugs. I was so depressed...." the patient mumbled.

"Hell, who gave you drugs in the stockade?" Dodd asked. "I told them you're an addict!"

"My good friend, Colonel Phipps," the man sighed; he passed out.

***

Rising above the roof line, the raven reappeared. That bird is as big as a God-damned chicken, Dodd told himself. How the hell can something that heavy fly without a jet engine strapped to its body?

"Captain Dodd?" a woman's voice called from the building to Dodd's right. "Captain Spencer Griffith Dodd?"

Dodd forced himself to stop staring at the huge black bird. He rose, stiffly, sore from having ridden the power mower for seven hours. If he had ever harbored an impulse to learn the game of golf, that thought died after two weeks of mowing the mosquito- infested greens of the Eglin golf course. "Yes, ma'am," Dodd answered. He walked slowly toward the small office in the adobe-covered building. Drained, he opened the screen door, and let it slam softly behind him.

Inside the small office stood Dodd's lawyer, Major Timberlake. "Spence," the major said. He held his right hand out to Dodd. "Sit down."

Dodd squeezed Timberlake's hand once, then sat in the uncomfortable, government-issue, wooden chair. He ignored the secretary. Timberlake slid another chair noisily closer to him across the dimpled tiled floor. He faced Dodd with a lap full of papers and smiled. "It's over. You're out," he said. "The Secretary of the Air Force has reviewed the case. You're a free man."

"Honorable discharge?" Dodd asked.

"With an addendum," Timberlake replied.

"That being?"

"Reason for discharge: Ineffective officer."

"What are the consequences of that?" Dodd asked.

"You probably won't be allowed to serve in the military, any branch, in the future. I'm sure you would have faced a court-martial had you not been a Vietnam vet. Being an enlisted man in the U. S. Navy saved your butt."

"That's a relief."

"Phipps wanted me to remind you that he is writing the recommendation the Air Force will use whenever anyone investigates your background."

Dodd shrugged. "In some circles, being hated by your commanding officer is a blessing."

***

Dodd walked across the golf course, taking a familiar short cut. His home and family waited on the far side of the sprawling complex. He needed time to think, and had discouraged Timberlake from either giving him a ride home or calling his wife for one. Across the road closest to him lay the farthest end of the approach to one of the runways. Huge, red towers on either side of the fairways, which may have been the original grass runways, held beacons for aircraft to follow when landing. In the distance, vast hangars housed military equipment and machines. Magnificent aircraft, F-15s and F-16s, flew overhead, took off, and landed. Clumsy on the ground, they also trundled along the taxiways. He knew he would miss them, and their pilots. Of all the personnel in the air force, only they routinely put their lives on the line. Support personnel supported — and played politics. And now Dodd was an ex-political prisoner. He had tried to change the bureaucracy. It, in turn, had reared up and squashed him and his career like a cockroach. 'There,' it said, 'we dared

you to speak your mind, to be an individual. Take that.'
Splat.

Preceded by intermittent rushes of feathered air that reminded Dodd of his mother sifting flour, the raven landed heavily, but not unexpectedly, on his shoulder.

"*Quid novi, Spence?*"[1] the bird asked.

"Same old shit, BeeBee. Do you have to speak Latin?" Dodd asked the animal.

"*Latinae loqui coactus cogor,*"[2] he replied.

"*Rara avis es,*"[3] Dodd told him.

"Feeling sorry for yourself again?"

"I guess so, BeeBee," Dodd agreed without looking at the bird. "A part of me says, 'Relax, things have to get better.' If so, why am I so depressed? Why do I feel like killing myself? My family would be better off without me. They'd have a couple hundred grand in insurance money. I could make it look like an accident."

"Then your family would have to face the world, alone, without your help. What kind of man leaves his family to fend for itself and to explain his inexplicable actions?"

"A depressed coward," Dodd answered, and laughed.

"Precisely." The bird invited the physician to speak, "Why, exactly, do you feel sorry for yourself? Maybe we should explore those thoughts."

"I really wanted to fly jets. I would have given both testicles to have 20/20 vision. That dream is dead, for good, now."

"Without testicles, fighter jocks are but airline pilots," the bird cawed with laughter. "Take it from me, Spencer, flying's not so great."

"Easy for you to say," Dodd observed, "and do."

Rocking side to side, from left to right foot and back again on the man's shoulder, the bird asked, "What happened? Couldn't keep your mouth shut again?"

Dodd laughed. "Haven't you heard? I have a personality disorder."

"The only person with a personality disorder is the air force psychiatrist, groveling at the feet of his commanding officer. 'Spinous Minus' might be his diagnosis. I'll give you two to one that the poor bastard got drunk after writing his report."

"Why?"

The bird explained. "He sold his integrity to the hospital commander. Not only did he dishonor himself by succumbing to an illegal order to label you with a nonexistent diagnosis, he dishonored the psychiatric profession. A Nazi's approach, or today you might say a Communist's. That's how they deal with dissent. You spoke your piece, lost your bonus, and spent time in the stockade for insubordination; but you got an honorable discharge and left with your head held high."

"The shrink can go back to work Monday. It may be difficult for me to find a job. I may have lost my livelihood. "

"You still have me," the bird said. "Never kick yourself in the crotch for telling the truth or remaining honest to yourself."

"Also easy for you to say. You don't have a wife to support, three kids to put through college ten to fifteen years from now, or a family to feed."

Tilting his head, BeeBee spoke more directly into Dodd's ear. He whispered, "Human childhood is too long by about seventeen years. If you can't teach the off-spring to feed themselves and how to get their own education in a year or two, you are investing too much in the progeny."

Dodd grinned. "Says the bird with hundreds of off-spring...."

"Later," BeeBee offered, departing. He thrust himself into the air from Dodd's shoulder so forcefully that the man felt sharp claws dig through the blue, cotton shirt, into his skin. With three strong flaps of his wings the bird disappeared through a gap in the pine trees.

Invictus

Chapter Two
Twenty years later
August 21st

From an altitude of two thousand feet above ground level, Southwestern Virginia University lay beneath the big black bird like a medieval city on a rocky plateau in mountainous terrain. Encircling the knoll that comprised the central campus, BeeBee saw (like a painting of a small English town in the Middle Ages) the patchwork colors of crop fields and dairy farms stretching outward for several miles. A seemingly endless national forest encompassed the fields. On the hilltop, buildings followed a plan ordained by SVU's founders. Massive gray stones, towers and turrets, at the ends of great monuments to human endeavor and education, made the university an impenetrable fortress. Impenetrable, that is, if the invaders came by foot and used nineteenth century weapons.

The founding fathers of SVU were the survivors of a much smaller college, the Southwestern Baptist Union, established in 1839, halfway between Pennington Gap and Cumberland Gap, in Fawsville, Virginia, on the edge of known civilization at the time. Twenty-five years later, all but two of the senior class of eleven students died defending Pennington Gap from Union soldiers. The northerners drove into Virginia from Kentucky, through the gap in Stone Mountain, intent upon destroying the Confederate military depot at Dublin and the railway bridge over the New River at Radford. Not content with killing rebel soldiers and civilians alike, the blue coats marched northward and united with Union forces then pillaging the

Bill Yancey

Shenandoah Valley.

The two surviving students, Jake Linkous and Rogers Price, although seriously wounded, recovered and led long, colorful, and profitable lives after the war ended. Toward the end of their lives, both donated their wealth to establish a college, a military school and fortress to defend Virginia in the next War of Northern Aggression. Ironically, this institution, Southwestern Agriculture College, owed its survival as a university to its sworn enemy. The land grant college system developed by the hated foe, the United States Federal Government, saved it from bankruptcy and guaranteed its continued existence.

For over a century, SVU's predecessor trained cadets to serve as soldiers for their state and their country in times of war and peace. The military school withered and nearly died, however, during the Vietnam War. The backlash of anti-war sentiment led to both demilitarization and integration of the college. Co-eds, blacks, and whites entered the institution as civilians; urinals were painted pink and life improved. After Vietnam, the state and federal governments poured millions of dollars into the renamed Southwestern Virginia University and it grew from a college of a thousand cadets to a co-ed institution of some thirty thousand students.

Rapid growth meant an increase in the demand for medical care by the students. The local physicians, previously two general practitioners who shared a horse and buggy, could not possibly assimilate into their practices the thousands of students at the university. So, the university hired its own doctors. The first director of student health services retired from a position in the federal prison system. He felt at home at SVU, there being no place to go and nothing to do, on or off campus.

Isolated in the far southwestern tip of Virginia, Fawsville sits nearly as far west as Detroit, a fact not lost on students driving there from towns in eastern Virginia.

There are no four lane roads, until five miles from campus. Still, thirty-thousand students manage to arrive each fall and stay until the following spring. The rigors of the location lend itself to the university having the highest graduation rate in Virginia.

The raven's magnificent eyes spotted the football stadium, then the practice field, and finally the lone human for whom he searched. Curling two feathers at the tip of his right wing, he stopped flapping and began a slow spiral, descent.

Dodd sat on the unfolded, portable camp chair. His feet hung in the air, legs crossed, one heel caught in the v-shaped notch of the chain link fence. A book lay open in his lap. His head bobbed, drowsiness clouding his thoughts. On the opposite side of the fence, on what was normally the varsity football team's practice field, football trainers moved equipment. One young man used a golf cart to tow a blocking sled from the grass. Two others lined the field with white, powdered lime. The junior varsity game between the SVU Black Bears and Tennessee's Crofton Military Academy Eagles would not start for another hour. Dodd tried to ignore the bustle. He read two more lines in the book. The rush of feathers and air startled him, but he woke quickly when the bird landed on his right shoulder.

"*Ave, animal bipes implume.*[4] What are you reading?" BeeBee asked.

"Teach Yourself Electricity and Electronics in Fifty Easy Lessons," Dodd answered.

"You tried to change professions once before," BeeBee observed.

Dodd nodded. He shrugged his shoulders and said, "All I learned was that I am a slow, non-intuitive computer programmer with that last foray into the real world."

"Well, you did find a job at student health, after taking two years off from practicing medicine," BeeBee commended Dodd.

"On the job for six and one-half years, the longest I've kept one. That's even a year longer than the time I spent running my own practice," Dodd bragged.

"*Tempus fugit.*⁵ You are to be congratulated, or does the book mean something?"

"It means I'm frustrated, again," Dodd admitted.

"You're going to prove that you are a slow, non-intuitive electronics technician too?" BeeBee asked. Dodd dropped his feet from the fence and laughed. The bird leapt from his shoulder. Spreading its wings, BeeBee landed softly on top of the football helmet lying near Dodd's feet. His talons gripped the Black bear logo, white letters 'SVU' within the bear's black outline.

"Quite possibly," Dodd nodded. "Actually, I have been thinking about Medical Informatics." He swatted at a fly. SVU's agriculture department and its associated manure made the campus home to the largest horse flies Dodd had ever seen. Their bite was less than benign, too.

"Boring."

"True," Dodd agreed. "Might be exciting being an informatics consultant, though. I know something about computers."

"The only excitement would be whether you would make enough money to eat or to pay the rent. You'd end up back in medicine again."

"I don't know. The state bureaucracy is becoming pretty overbearing."

"Is your new boss getting under your skin?" BeeBee asked.

"Yeah."

The bird surveyed the two junior varsity teams when they ran onto the field for warm up drills. "Great day for a game," he said. "I love the smell of crushed grass and clay. *Gramen artificiosum odi.*"⁶ BeeBee flapped his wings launching himself from the helmet. Dodd watched the bird soar gracefully to the base of the halogen lamps

Invictus

on the very top of the light post. BeeBee had an excellent view for the coming game. Dodd wished he could stay to watch, but he stood and began to fold his camp chair.

"Doc," a voice called.

Dodd turned to see one of the trainers on the opposite side of the fence. "Hey, Tony," he responded to the young Jamaican. "Time for the Anthem?" Tony had an angel's voice and frequently sang the National Anthem at the junior varsity games.

The boy shook his head. "No, I need the helmet." He pointed to Dodd's feet. "Fix it?"

Dodd grabbed the helmet by the face mask and lifted it over the fence. "Have Rob try this new chin strap, and tell him to wear his mouth guard." The trainer nodded catching the helmet. "I'll be in the training room after we close student health this afternoon."

"Okay, Doc. Gotta go. Catch you later." Tony sprinted to the far side of the field and the Bear's bench.

Bill Yancey

Invictus

Chapter Three
August 26ᵗʰ

Dodd had held lots of jobs. Everywhere he had worked, even in places where he had stayed for only a month, there had been a ditsy nurse. Joie LaFlamé filled that niche at Southwestern Virginia University Student Health Services. An artificial strawberry blonde and an ex-exotic dancer, she had experienced an epiphany one night. Her piano player suffered a cardiac arrest while pounding the ivories and watching her strip on stage. Although uneducated in basic CPR, she attempted to resuscitate the poor man anyway. Ineffective though her attempt had been, the wretch had died with a smile on his face. Now he tickled those eighty-eight keys in Hell, Dodd assumed. That would have been the proper punishment for foisting the large bosomed LaFlamé upon the medical world and Dodd in particular.

After the disaster of the musician's heart attack, LaFlamé decided that a career in medicine might assuage her guilt at not being able to revive the musician. Not one of her professors had the temerity to fail her for a single course. Women instructors worried about being branded jealous of her looks; men melted when she batted her eyelashes or shrugged her shoulders while crossing long, shapely legs. For the previous decade LaFlamé had been the bane of Student Health Services, capable of following only very, very specific orders and incapable of independent thought or action. Unfortunately, after ten years, her seniority almost guaranteed she would remain the head nurse and a thorn in Dodd's side until she retired or he went in search of another position.

Dodd had already surprised himself with his tenure as

student health physician, a job he held longer than any other, including the managing partner in a private practice. That lasted five and one-half years and ended when his erstwhile best friend and partner had pointed a pistol at him and threatened to shoot him if he did not start charging patients for recheck visits. Dodd acquiesced, then hired a lawyer and fled town. Eventually, he settled the suit for all the money he had invested in the practice and for having his name expunged from the documents enumerating the debt for the building and land on which the office sat. His ex-partner fired the office manager Dodd had hired, put his wife in her position, and went bankrupt within two years.

Now, sitting in his office in SVU Student Health, Dodd listened carefully to his surroundings. He was in an eight-foot by eight-foot cubicle staring out the window at the campus cop directing the morning motor vehicle rush through the intersection at West Jefferson Street and Washington Boulevard. Behind Dodd and across the hall, LaFlamé closed the door to the exam room, another eight by eight-foot closet. Her footsteps, those of the only nurse in high heels, started down the hallway toward the nursing station. Slowly, they stopped, hesitated, and then retraced their path to Dodd's office.

Shit, he thought, what now? He swivelled his chair to face the door. Her perfume arrived first, an overpowering musky fragrance that wrinkled his nose and watered his eyes. LaFlamé's head appeared in the doorway. Her long blonde hair swept across the opening, followed by the thirty-five year-old brick house that had only recently started to settle on its foundation.

Cosmetically altered smile and torso brightened Dodd's office. If only the wit were less dim, he thought. "I hope you didn't want him undressed, Dr. Dodd," she said tentatively.

"What's his problem?" Dodd asked, already knowing the answer to her question. He wanted *everyone* undressed.

Invictus

"He has an earache. Surely you don't need him undressed to look at his ear?"

Dodd counted to himself, knowing she watched him chew his lower lip. They had had the same conversation at least a thousand times in the past. "His earache might be from a cold, Joie; I may have to listen to his chest," he told her, again. She nodded enthusiastically, as if hearing these words of wisdom for the first time. "You took his vitals signs, right?" Dodd asked, guessing her response.

LaFlamé's eyes widened. "Damn," she said, "I knew I forgot something." She crossed the hallway and re-entered the exam room. Dodd heard her tell the student to remove his shirt before the door closed and blocked all sound.

The physician rolled his eyes and spun the chair, facing the window again. The campus cop held a bicyclist by the collar and was evidently explaining road etiquette to him. On the sidewalk next to a bicycle, a pedestrian writhed in pain. The campus ambulance sat in the intersection, lights flashing. "All set, Dr. Dodd," LaFlamé called.

Hating himself for suggesting it, because it meant that he would automatically be the pedestrian's designated physician, Dodd called to LaFlamé, "There's an injured student out in front of the building, Joie. Take someone with you, and a stretcher or a wheelchair. Bring him to the treatment room." Her high heels clip-clopped down the hall, turned the corner, and dissipated when she reached the carpeted waiting room.

Warily, Dodd extracted the chart from the plastic holder on the front of the exam room door. Quickly, he flipped through the tome, trying to find evidence that he had or had not seen this particular student in the past. Chart too thick to peruse carefully, he settled for scanning the summary sheet and flipping pages in search of his signature. Steeling himself, he glanced at his watch and noted the time, then gingerly pushed open the door.

On the flat exam table sat a long-haired, muscular,

tanned, student, totally naked. Nonplused, Dodd said, "I'll be back in a minute; put everything back on except your shirts and hat." Gratefully, the student grabbed for his underwear. Dodd made a quick trip to his window to check on the pedestrian, in time to see LaFlamé and an EMT from the student-run rescue squad hoist him onto the stretcher. His arm hung at an angle too improbable to be natural. At least he is conscious, Dodd thought. Then he returned to the exam room, looked at his watch one more time, and entered the room.

More relaxed, the student sat at the far end of the exam table. "Are you Mr. Peter Robinson?" Dodd asked the curly-haired redhead. The student nodded. "Good," Dodd continued, "that means I'm in the right room." The patient smiled. On gross visual examination, from a short distance, he appeared healthy to the doctor.

Sitting, Dodd continued with the carefully rehearsed routine. Over the years, he had learned a stand-up — actually a sit-down on a rolling stool — comedy act. It put him at ease to say familiar things, and since most of the students never saw the same doctor more than once a year, made them think it was spontaneous. But he had a second, back-up routine, for those who had seen him recently. That one was rusty. When flu season started, he practiced three or four and became fairly proficient at each. This being the first month of the fall semester, the routine was rough. Dodd had just returned from a month's vacation. "I'm Dr. Dodd; how are you?"

"Fine," the patient responded automatically.

"Well, then you're in the wrong room," Dodd told the student. He waited, watching the boy's eyes.

The look of confusion changed to amusement when the student recognized the joke. "Okay, I'm not too good," the patient corrected himself.

"Ah, then you, too, are in the right room," Dodd said. "We'll have to work on your lying, though. That's not a good way to start a relationship." The dazed look went away slightly more quickly with the second joke. I'll eventually have him eating out of my hand, Dodd thought. "Says here you have a sinus infection...."

"Woke up three days ago with a sore throat," the student explained. "Now my nose runs, my sinuses and ears hurt."

"Fever? Sweats or chills?" Dodd asked.

"I think so," the boy frowned, not knowing the answer.

"Did you take your temperature?"

"The nurse did. I don't have a thermometer."

Dodd reached for a handout. It hung on the wall in an acrylic holder with many others. "You need a thermometer," he said. "When you have chills, your temperature is climbing; when you sweat, it's dropping. You need to take your temperature when the chill stops or the sweat starts; otherwise, you won't know what your temperature is when the fever peaks. This brochure explains that and is a reminder to buy a thermometer." The student accepted the paper numbly. He hadn't expected a lecture. Dodd continued, "I can guarantee your fever won't peak while you are here, and if it does, these worthless electronic thermometers won't catch it. For instance," Dodd flipped the page in the chart, "we think your temperature is 96.4 degrees Fahrenheit, more than two degrees below normal and probably incompatible with a long life." Dodd smiled, sensing he had taught the boy something new. College is not all about classrooms, he reasoned. The student nodded. "Thermometers are three bucks at Lee's Food Market; you know, the place where all your friends buy their beer?" Again the student nodded.

"Moving on," Dodd continued, "stomach pain? nausea? vomiting? diarrhea? cough? nasal congestion? ear pain and sinus pain, you said? chest pain? short of breath? muscle aches? rashes? allergies? asthma? smoking? drinking heavily? taking any medications, drugs, or supplements?"

Nodding or shaking his head, the student withstood the withering litany of symptoms and responses. "Half a pack a day," he said in response to the question about smoking, before he realized he opened the door to another lecture.

"Thirty percent of smokers die of lung and heart disease," Dodd told the boy. "Your life expectancy is now ten years less than your friends who don't smoke. Once you quit smoking, it takes two years for your sinuses and lungs to recover from the damage you've caused by smoking — seven years until your statistical chance for lung cancer returns to baseline. You need to quit smoking."

Surrendering to the doctor's logic, the patient agreed. "I was planning on quitting. Next month I'm going to try out for the club soccer team."

"The Farmers?" Dodd asked. He referred to the club team that the varsity soccer team used as its junior varsity, or farm team — appropriately named for an ex-agriculture college, Dodd thought.

The student nodded. "I'll quit when practice starts," he said.

"Today," Dodd corrected. "No time like the present. Smokers get more infections than people who don't smoke."

Dodd stood, pushing the wheeled stool under the counter top. He slapped the end of the exam table. "Sit here," he commanded, "and we'll poke around and see what we can find." The student slid to the end of the bed. Dodd started his exam, continuing by rote. "How old are you? What's your major? Where do your parents live? Any friends sick? What, no friends? Oh, no sick friends. Since I cannot see through your head, you can't go to law school, and you have a heart. No good lawyer has a heart. Sit up. Open your mouth. Breathe through your mouth." (Added for the patient who breathed through his nose with his mouth wide open. One had to be *very* specific with teenagers.) Finishing the exam, Dodd asked, "Okay, which do you want to hear first, the good news or the bad news?"

"There's bad news?" the healthy student asked incredulously.

"There's always bad news," Dodd responded. "You apparently have a cold. The good news is that it won't kill you. The really bad news is I can't kill it; antibiotics won't work. It may last as long as two weeks. You are contagious. You may develop a secondary bacterial infection, so come back if you have a fever above 101.5, if it lasts more than two weeks, or if you develop much worse symptoms." Dodd pulled the stool from under the cabinet and pushed it between his legs mounting it the way Roy Rogers jumped onto Trigger. "I'll give you some acetaminophen, a decongestant, and some cough syrup. They won't make you well, but might make you less miserable. Drink lots of fluids, and get plenty of rest. Any questions?" He leaned on the counter surface to write the prescriptions.

"No," the bewildered patient answered, wondering how fast the truck that ran over him had been moving.

"Feel comfortable with that diagnosis and with taking care of yourself?" Dodd asked

"Yes. I think so," the student answered.

"Fine," Dodd added dryly, "hope *not* to see you later." He stood up, kicked the stool under the counter, and handed the patient his prescription sheet. "The pharmacy is up front, on the right when you leave." Dodd slipped out the door and looked at his watch. Seven minutes, thirteen seconds. Not a record, but not bad for the first month of classes. By the time the flu season arrived, he would have it down to four minutes.

"Dr. Dodd," LaFlamé called from the nurses' station in the middle of the hallway when Dodd returned to his office.

The doctor spun, turning toward the magnificent, brainless body standing thirty feet away. "Yes?" he asked dourly.

"Your patient that got run over by the bicyclist is ready to be seen in the treatment room," she said.

"Why does he have to be my...." Dodd interrupted himself. "Never mind. It'll be more interesting than seeing four more students with colds. I'll be right there."

Invictus

Chapter Four
September 6th

Chunky described Neal Abramowicz. So did corpulent, rotund, morbidly obese, and several other offensive adjectives. Detached mentally from the proceedings, Dodd watched indifferently as the student health center's administrator leaned on the long meeting room table with one meaty hand and slapped the polished wooden surface with the other. Abramowicz waxed on and on about something. His thick, deeply black plaits of curly hair, matted to his olive forehead by his perpetual perspiration, mocked the thinning, gray hair of the male physicians in the room. He reminded Dodd of Buddha, probably as much from his mixed American Jewish father/Filipino mother heritage as his immense size. Mild, chronic rosacea speckled his nose with bright red blotches. Dodd assumed Abramowicz dyed his hair black and his temples gray, knowing the man to be in his late fifties. He assumed that a lucky combination of genes helped the four-hundred-plus pound administrator retain his widow's peak and the thick rich hair others coveted.

Dodd could not quite force himself to pay attention to Abramowicz's rambling. He sat within the curve of the bay window in the conference room. From the second floor, it overlooked the intersection of Washington and West Jefferson, as did his office located directly below on the first floor.

From Dodd's perch, it appeared the coeds enjoyed the rare southwestern Virginian Indian Summer, courtesy of El Niño. On their way from the dorms to the recreational sports center at Sykes Hall or to classes, in various states of undress, they seemed much more appealing to him. He wondered why. Maybe their legs looked longer from this angle, he thought. Dodd termed his beauty analysis system 'the mile rule;' he graded women's looks from one through twelve. Every coed looked stunning at a mile's distance. Being higher up did mean he was farther away. Dodd's Holy Grail, a coed who passed the 2.578 foot inspection, eluded him. That distance equaled a mile divided by two eleven times. Dodd gave them scores: one point for good looks at a mile, a Miss January; twelve for passing the two foot test, a Miss December. There were lots of ones — maybe 15,000 on campus. In nearly seven years, he'd seen a hundred tens, Misses October. Twelves? Well, twelves were nonexistent. As Abramowicz rambled, several sevens passed in review about eighty feet away. Dodd could only wonder if they would turn out to be tens or fives.

Abramowicz's droning came to a close with, "Well, I have another meeting to attend on the other side of campus." With those words, he squeezed his bulk around the attendees and forced his obese form through the double door leading from the conference room. Dodd watched indifferently; thighs the size of mature oak trees rubbed together when Abramowicz waddled away, pausing briefly to allow his secretary to precede him. He wondered that the heat produced by that friction did not start a fire. After Abramowicz cleared the door, it swung inward silently and slowly; springs dampened the final thud when it shuddered to a close.

"Gone to kiss more administrative ass," the doctor sitting next to Dodd intoned.

Dodd smiled. He nodded toward the free spirit in the next seat. Clinton Massey held a rubber band in his mouth while he pulled tighter on his pony tail. Grimacing, the aging hippy struggled to cover the bald spot on his posterior scalp by seemingly tying all the remaining gray hair on his head — from his nostrils, eyebrows, sideburns and frontal

Invictus

scalp — into a pony tail over the shiny spot.

"You'd be better off shaving your head," Dodd informed Massey. "Certainly would look more natural."

"I don't want to look *natural* until it's my turn in the funeral parlor," Massey said between teeth clamped onto the rubber band.

Grinning, Dodd nodded in agreement. He asked, "What was lard breath talking about? I was distracted."

Massey winked, leer on his face. "Your dream girl is not out there, Spence. You're fifty-years-old. She's going to be thirty-plus. Besides, as a divorcé, you already know how difficult it would be to train another female. Haven't you realized that you are invisible to women under the age of twenty-five? Unless you are really unique, rich, wear a frazzled backwoodsman beard, shave your head, sport whole body tattoos or piercings, they don't know you exist. No Miss December is hiding from you. Miss January is always close at hand, however." Massey knew the grading system. Over the years, Miss January had come to represent the ugliest of those graded. Fortunately, no one else had deciphered their code. Massey finished positioning the fountain of hair over the empty scalp. He snapped the rubber band into place around the thinning bundle. Finally, he answered Dodd's question. "Neal said there are rumors about student health being privatized."

"Oh shit," Dodd said.

Understanding Dodd's negative reaction, Massey smiled. "Listen," he consoled the other physician, "it's probably a good idea. The first thing a big medical corporation would do would be to give us all raises. They'd even buy up our state retirement and give us a 403(b) plan worth having."

Glumly, Dodd disagreed. "Then they'd fire us, one by one, when they found replacements who better fit their corporate and management images," he said.

"True," Massey agreed.

"What else did he say?" Dodd asked.

Massey ticked off a list, easy to do because they had heard the same pep talk a hundred times in the past. "We need to work harder, see more patients, make ourselves look good to the higher echelons of the administration. He thinks they are looking for excuses to unload us. We definitely have to eliminate complaints, he said. President Furneaux is extremely tired of parents calling his office to complain about student health. Oh, and the budget has been slashed again, so we have to work with fewer supplies, cut down on outside tests and x-rays. Our continuing medical education budget is gone; you now have to pay for your own CME."

"Any good news?" Dodd asked despondently.

Massey brightened, sarcastic grin crossing his face. "Administrators are getting a three percent raise, as is staff," he informed Dodd.

"But not professional faculty?"

"No faculty, not professional, not administrative, nor educational," Massey explained. "We're at the twenty-fifth percentile, so the governor thinks that's good enough."

"Three quarters of the states in the union pay their university faculties more than Virginia does, and that's good enough?" Dodd asked incredulously.

Massey shrugged his muscular shoulders. "He doesn't want to get into a bidding war. Brain drain, you know."

"The governor's brain surely went down a drain," Dodd said sullenly. "How about the hiring freeze."

"Still in effect."

Dodd sighed; he said, "I guess it doesn't make sense to convince LaFlamé to quit. Even she is better than nothing."

"Any port in a storm," Massey agreed. "Any warm body. Of course, her body is exceptionally warm...."

Invictus

Chapter Five
September 18th

Neal Abramowicz sat behind his immense desk. The desk itself seemed to occupy more space than Dodd's entire office. The administrator's mammoth bulk dwarfed the mahogany surface, uncluttered by paperwork. Behind him, his flat screen monitor displayed the contrasting colors of some weird web site — remote camera scanning the distant empty beach of a nudist colony. In the corners of the web page, Abramowicz had saved grainy telephoto images of his favorite nudists. Seeing where Dodd's eyes darted, Abramowicz coughed. His faced flushed. He spun his stuffed chair and slapped at the power switch to the monitor, darkening the screen. As the video picture died, Dodd watched the red tide spread to the back of the man's wide neck. Stuffed too tightly into the shirt, his flesh sagged over the edges of the collar.

The view from the administrator's window overlooked the school's practice football field. The sound of shoulder pads clashing drifted into the room, along with clanging of blocking sleds. Dodd could almost smell the fresh grass and turf plowed up by the footballer players' cleats. He took a quick look out the window and saw a wide receiver gracefully pluck a spiral bomb from the sky. Girding himself, he stood next to the chair opposite Abramowicz's desk. The administrator rotated his chair to face Dodd and he nodded at the seat nearest Dodd. "Ah, just checking the monitor's capabilities," Abramowicz explained.

Not interested in the administrator's fetishes, Dodd dropped into the chair facing the desk. "You wanted to talk to me, Neal?" he asked.

Abramowicz adjusted his reading glasses, and placed a wide forearm on the desk. He leaned forward to read a single sheet of paper that lay on his blotter. Picking up the paper delicately, between his left thumb and forefinger, he answered, "Yes, Spencer. There have been entirely too many complaints about you."

"Really?" Dodd feigned surprise. "Who complained this time?"

"Let's see." Abramowicz said, placing his fat right paw on his cheek, squeezing his lips together and to the left. The result reminded Dodd of a tuna mouthing air bubbles. "The nurses, of course. Then, there are also some students: smokers, some who wanted antibiotics for colds, drinkers, etc. Three parents called the dean's office wanting your scalp."

"The usual suspects," Dodd agreed. "What are the nurses upset about now?"

"Eye exams."

"How can they possibly be upset about eye exams?" Dodd asked, stunned.

"They say it embarrasses students to fail an eye exam," Abramowicz clarified his statement.

Dodd began to chuckle. The futility of arguing with nurses numbed his brain; eventually the anesthesia reached his frontal lobes. He lost all ability to restrain himself. Laughing uncontrollably, he nearly fell from his chair. Finally regaining a semblance of composure, he suggested to the flabby administrator, "Tell them to have the students study harder for the tests." Mouthing the quip, Dodd lost his poise totally; he fell onto the floor. There he lay, rocking from side to side. "Embarrassed," he wheezed between guffaws, repeatedly, "embarrassed."

Abramowicz waited patiently for Dodd to cease convulsing and to climb back into his chair. "This is no laughing matter," he admonished the physician.

"I disagree," Dodd argued. "It's ludicrous. What about

their blood tests? Are they mortified that they might fail them too?" Dodd sobered, slightly, realizing that Abramowicz's expression remained glum. "If there weren't a possibility of the student failing the eye test, we wouldn't do it. How else do you know if his eye pain, blurred vision, or whatever is serious?"

"We can't be embarrassing the students," Abramowicz stated solemnly.

"Then do the eye test in private," Dodd suggested. "All you need is a room twenty feet long." Dodd let his head roll and his eyes search the office. "This room looks about right. You won't mind, Neal, if the nurses carted a student in here a couple times of day, would you? You'd have to vacate the premises, however, so as not to embarrass anyone. We'll hang the light box over there, next to your monitor. If you leave the nude pictures up, we'll be able to tell if they are malingering."

Ignoring the remark, Abramowicz asked, "Isn't there another way?"

"Sure, spend four to six thousand dollars for a desktop eye examination machine."

Curtly, Abramowicz replied, "We don't have the money for that."

"Then, embarrass the students."

"We can't do that."

Dodd exhaled loudly, baffled by the administrator's position. He said, "Then you'll have to make appointments with an optometrist or ophthalmologist for every student with pink eye, blurred vision, or eye trauma. Of course, the students will complain, since they will have to pay for the visit; it's not covered by their student health fee. They will be embarrassed somewhere else, though."

"Fine. That's what we'll do," Abramowicz decided out loud.

"That was a joke, Neal. If someone really needs an eye exam, they need it now."

"Then we'll send them to the emergency room at the hospital," Abramowicz proposed.

"So we can look stupid to the local medical community for sending minor injuries or people who need glasses to the emergency room?" Dodd asked.

"That's not my problem," Abramowicz declared. "I've already told the nurses to get rid of the eye charts."

"When?"

"Yesterday."

Flabbergasted, Dodd blurted, "Based on embarrassing the patients? Neal, you can't practice medicine without disconcerting someone. Hell, all the patients get undressed — at least, in real doctors' offices, anyway — and we ask questions about bodily functions. We touch forbidden parts of their anatomy, do unmentionable exams. *I'm* uncomfortable when I see *my* doctor. How can someone go to the doctor and *not* be embarrassed?"

Slapping the desk for emphasis, Abramowicz said, "We will not embarrass patients, Dr. Dodd. The eye charts don't go with the decor, either."

Dodd stood and screamed in frustration. "They don't go with the decor?" He slammed his palm on the desk. "Neal, this is a medical clinic! What decor do they go with, for God's sake? An ice cream parlor?"

Unrelenting, Abramowicz answered, "Optometry offices and emergency rooms. Sit down, please, Spencer."

Steaming, Dodd slumped into his chair. "You know I'm going to complain to your immediate boss, don't you?" he asked Abramowicz.

Abramowicz showed his palms to Dodd and tilted his head, to indicate what Dodd chose to do did not matter to him. "He already knows that you are a troublemaker," he said. "That reminds me, Spencer. If you don't like working here, why don't you leave?"

Suppressing the urge to strangle Abramowicz with his ugly tie, Dodd leaned forward in his seat. He gritted his teeth, in an effort to keep from screaming at the bloated, beached whale. He spoke in a whisper, far more threatening than a raised voice. "Because, you asshole, if I leave, then you win and those students who are truly ill or injured lose. I'm going to fight you and your asinine rules. They may find pieces and parts of my carcass on the field of battle, but I'm never going to surrender. I'll see you demoted first. I've quit before. The guilt of abandoning my principles stays with me. I'm not interested in letting idiots like you run me off any longer. I'm tired of trying to find the one medical practice in the world where people do things rationally. Eventually, I'll educate everyone here." Exhausted, he slumped into the chair.

Unfazed, Abramowicz added, "Or alienate everyone."

"At least I'll die content," Dodd suggested.

"We also need to talk about a complaint from a student."

"That being?"

"Tyler Charles...."

Dodd interrupted, "Is upset that I jumped him about smoking. His wife set him up, Neal. She wants him to quit. So, she made his appointment with me, knowing I'd blame his bronchitis on the cigarettes. What else?"

Abramowicz nodded. He continued reading. "Another student said he came in for nausea and vomiting, and you gave him a lecture on drinking."

"Could be any one of a hundred students," Dodd allowed.

"Does the name Stone Garrette ring a bell?" Abramowicz asked.

"Only if the ringing bell means drinks are served," Dodd observed. "Mr. Garrette is an alcoholic. He's been a student here for seven, maybe eight years. Every year he drops half of his academic load because he has been too drunk to get to class."

"Does Garrette *Hall* mean anything to you?"

"That a relative of his went to school here, too, or likes the place, has money, he donated some of it to Southwestern, and we named a building after him. Look, Neal, the kid's a danger to society. And he's no longer a kid; he's twenty-four-years-old. It's time that someone got him some therapy."

"His old man's upset," Abramowicz said.

Eyes locked on the administrator's, Dodd shot back, "Tough."

"He'll be here for the homecoming game."

"They'll both be drunk at a tailgate party is my guess."

Pressing his fingertips together, Abramowicz elaborated, "The president of this institution wants more money from him. The board of visitors wants him to leave here happy. They don't want you upsetting the old man."

"Well, I'm not going to the homecoming game. We'll never meet."

"Wrong," Abramowicz said. "You will apologize to him in person."

"For what?"

"For accusing his son of being an alcoholic."

"My ass."

"And it may well be." Abramowicz said, eyes gleaming with the thought. He asked Dodd, "Aren't you being a little too paternalistic?"

"Neal, do you know the number one cause of death for people under the age of twenty-five in the United States?"

"I have a feeling you are going to tell me."

Dodd fell into lecture mode. He said, "Accidents and violence following the ingestion of alcohol. The campus cops, the local cops, no one enforces the laws concerning alcohol consumption in this town. One could almost conceive of a conspiracy to allow underage drinking. The kickbacks alone could be worth thousands of dollars. Why don't the state troopers sweep the dorms looking for

Invictus

alcohol the way they sweep Interstate 81 for speeders? Could it be that the state profits from the tax on alcohol?"

Abramowicz tried to change the subject. "Stone Garrette is of age," he said.

"His problem started when he was seventeen."

"Doesn't matter," Abramowicz argued, flicking his right hand toward Dodd. "From now on, you don't mention drinking to him. And, in two months, I want an apology to his old man or your resignation."

Dodd stood, facing the portly administrator. Abramowicz remained composed. He smiled diabolically, believing he had Dodd cornered. "I'll think about it," Dodd said slowly. "Let me have your suggestion in writing, while I cogitate on the matter."

The smirk faded from Abramowicz's face. He jabbed a fat finger at the list in front of him. "We have more to talk about. Why don't you address students by their first name; it's friendlier."

Dodd had heard the same complaint from the nurses. Evidently, they commanded Abramowicz's ear. He explained, "I think it shows more respect for the student to use Miss, or Mister, unless she or he requests otherwise. It also distinguishes between all the Bills and all the Smiths when I say, Mr. Bill Smith."

"I want a *friendly* clinic...."

Dodd interrupted. "When did polite respect become less than friendly?" he asked.

The glower on Abramowicz's face darkened. He changed the subject, realizing he had lost the argument. Accusingly, he told Dodd, "You have an unacceptable complaint rate."

"So, what's an acceptable complaint rate?" Dodd asked.

"Zero," Abramowicz stated flatly.

"What planet do you live on?"

Abramowicz leaned back in his chair, turning it slightly

away from Dodd when he spoke. Dodd recognized the position, his usual posture when telling small white lies. "No one ever complains about any of the other medical providers: doctors, nurse practitioners, or physicians assistants."

"If that's true," Dodd replied, " and I doubt it is, you better make certain they aren't passing out illicit drugs. You live in Fantasy Land, Neal." Dodd spun on his heels and marched out. He didn't look back. Abramowicz sputtered.

Dodd walked silently past the receptionist. He took the back stairway to the first floor where he retrieved his leather jacket and briefcase. Feeling the pockets for his wallet and keys, he strode out of the building. "Dr. Dodd, Dr. Dodd," LaFlamé's voice called after him. "You still have a patient to see...."

Without looking back, Dodd grumbled, "Let Neal see him. It's time to find out if an MBA and a doctorate in education are as useful as an M.D. degree." He pushed open the electronic door. The slight push activated the motor; it swung open electrically. "Hadn't been for him, I would have seen the patient already. Besides, I wouldn't want to embarrass the poor guy...." He left LaFlamé standing in the hall holding the chart.

"Oh, okay," LaFlamé said, mollified. She turned and walked to the nurses' station. Dodd heard the page: "Dr. Abramowicz, you have a patient in the medical clinic." Then the door closed tightly, sealing in the chaos.

Dodd reached his car, three rows deep into the coliseum parking lot. The bumper sticker next to the parking permit read, "*Sona si Latine loqueris.*"[7] He had left the top down on the ten-year-old, blue Miata, daring the gods to rain on it, birds to crap in it, and the students to drop flaming cigarette butts onto the upholstery. Some day he would buy a tonneau cover for it, he reminded himself for the one thousandth time. The raven lay on its

Invictus

back on the folded black vinyl top, feet in the air, feigning death.

"Oh, knock it off!" Dodd told the bird. "I didn't cave in."

"But you thought about it," BeeBee said, rolling over and standing on his feet. The big black bird hopped into the passenger seat. "*Nolite te bastardes carborundorum.*"[8]

"Or, *Non carborundum illigitimi,*"[9] Dodd said. "That's pidgin Latin. Have we managed to corrupt you, BeeBee?"

"Whatever," the bird said. "Classical, scholarly Latin, or not, it sounds like Latin. Either way they translate the same way. Why humans have more than one language, I'll never understand." The bird rocked forward slightly and spread his wings to catch his balance when Dodd slammed the sports car into reverse and backed quickly from the parking spot.

"You do well enough in Latin."

"It was my first language. As Caesar said...."

"Yeah, yeah," Dodd interrupted the bird, "and you played muse to Edgar Allan Poe. If you're so great, why did you let Brutus stab Caesar. And can we blame you for letting Poe die prematurely?"

"Brutus surprised me, too," BeeBee admitted. "How was I to know that E.A.'s stray kitten had rabies? Besides, there still isn't a cure for rabies. You doctors are slipping. You can prevent polio, but not cure rabies," the bird razzed Dodd. "So, if you don't give in, what are you going to do?"

"I'll think of something. *Aut inveniam viam aut faciam.*"[10]

"You could kill him," the bird suggested.

Dodd contemplated the suggestion. Nodding his head, he replied, "Find me a rabid, feral cat and I'll stick it in his office one night." Changing his mind, he shook his head. He gunned the engine to kick the sports car in front of a slowly moving truck. "No, I couldn't do that. That might violate the Hippocratic Oath; I'll check. I could wish he were dead, but the last time I did that the object of my disaffection died. I felt guilty for years."

"Can't you get him fired?" BeeBee asked.

"His nose is so far up his boss's ass, he gets nosebleeds when the man farts," Dodd explained university politics to the bird.

"Get them both fired."

Curious as to how that might come about, Dodd asked, "How?"

"Get yourself hired as the boss."

"You mean," Dodd interpreted the suggestion, "go along with the privatization. Find out who's going to win the contract and offer to run the place for them?"

"Something like that."

"I'll think about that, too," Dodd said. He shifted into fourth; the Miata left the confines of the campus and its twenty-five mile per hour speed limit.

Invictus

Chapter Six
September 30th

"Ow!" The young man's knees flexed involuntarily.

Dodd looked at the student's face, contorted with pain and anxiety. "Sorry," he said. "Does it hurt here, too?"

"Not as much."

"If I let loose?" Dodd asked. The student grimaced, but said nothing. "Okay," the physician continued, "You feel warm to me. Have you had sweats and chills?"

"Some, but the dorm is hard to regulate. We have the windows open and the air conditioner on."

Dodd nodded and reached for the chart. He grinned. "Must be how buildings and grounds saves money," he said. On the progress note were written the patient's vital signs. The medical assistant had recorded his temperature as 95.8 degrees Fahrenheit. "I think you might have appendicitis, Mr. Dawson," he said. "I'm going to send you to the laboratory. They're going to do a blood test and a urine test to help us make the diagnosis. Then we'll decide what to do with you."

"Is appendicitis serious?" the patient asked.

"Only if we don't do anything about it."

"What needs to be done?" the student asked, voice wavering.

"Nothing, for now," Dodd replied. He tried to reassure the teenager. "Don't eat or drink anything until I tell you that you can, okay? Wait here for a minute," the doctor said, leaving the room. The boy nodded, scared but unwilling to display his fear. Dodd went in search of a nurse.

A plump, licensed practical nurse awaited him at the

nurses' station. She sat in front of the computer screen, which displayed the schedule. Doodling on a crossword puzzle, she sipped her coffee. The waiting room bustled with students coming and going to the clinics. Dodd saw no other staff. "Jan," he said tentatively.

"I'm on my break," she replied crisply, without looking up from the newspaper.

Dodd waited for thirty seconds, fuming. On the screen, he saw his schedule; it was double booked. No other nurses emerged from any of the other exam rooms. Trying to remain calm, he tapped the nurse on the shoulder. She flinched visibly. "You touched me," she whined.

Curtly, Dodd informed her, "Break's over. There's a student in my first exam room. He needs to be taken by wheelchair to the laboratory. While you are there, I want you to retake his temperature with a glass thermometer."

She eyed Dodd, angry at him for interrupting her, "Can't do it," she said.

"Take your break some other time," Dodd told her. He explained the urgency to her, "He may have appendicitis."

"Not that," the LPN said, rising from her chair slowly. "We don't have any glass thermometers."

"Of course we do," Dodd said. "There must be fifty of them in the treatment room. Just take his temperature with one of them. Don't use that worthless electronic thing. Write the new temperature on the chart, please."

She argued, "Dr. Abramowicz collected all the thermometers. He told us we would no longer be using them."

Frustrated, Dodd lost his temper. "Fine," he snapped at the LPN. "Take the patient to the lab. I'll talk with Neal." Dodd left the nurse standing at the computer. Scowling, he walked quickly to the treatment room, ignoring everyone in his path, even those who said good morning. Inside the treatment room, he pulled open the drawer that

Invictus

usually held the thermometers. Empty. "Crap!" he exclaimed.

Wondering what possessed Abramowicz, Dodd ascended the back stairway to the administrative portion of the building. There he found Abramowicz hobnobbing with a much smaller and older man he recognized as the director of recreational sports. Dodd waited patiently for the administrator to finish buffing the polish on the other campus administrator's bald head. When it appeared likely that Abramowicz would talk to the other man through lunch and dinner, Dodd finally lost his patience. "Excuse me, Neal," Dodd interrupted, "we need to talk."

Mobilizing his great bulk, Abramowicz rotated slowly in Dodd's direction, imitating a Zeppelin turning to port in a strong wind. When his mass had shifted enough that he could see Dodd, he spoke, smiling for the benefit of the other man. "Oh, Dr. Dodd," he said with a lilt in his voice, "just the man I was looking for. You know Boyd Carleton, Director of Recreational Sports?" Dodd nodded.

Abramowicz glanced at Carleton. "Will you excuse us, Boyd?" he asked. Carleton nodded. He gave Dodd an evil look, squinting with one eye through the ancient, wrinkled face. Dodd wondered what kind of attachment the old man had for Abramowicz. Meanwhile, the director of student health had waddled halfway across the hall in the direction of his office. Dodd had no trouble catching him.

"Sit," Abramowicz commanded Dodd, pointing to the chair in front of his desk. He continued plodding toward his own chair. Eventually arriving at the stuffed chair, he sat heavily. The seat springs squealed in protest. "Tell me why I shouldn't call the police and have you arrested for assaulting a nurse," the administrator demanded of Dodd.

Stunned, Dodd asked, "Who? Jan?" He explained, "Christ, Neal, I tapped her on the shoulder."

"Assault and battery then," Abramowicz decided.

"Bull."

"Then you overstepped your authority as a physician. Who told you to assume that you were her supervisor? You are not the nursing director. All directives are to go through the proper chain of command."

"I told her to take a patient to the lab."

"You tried to end her break," Neal explained the LPN's point of view.

"What is this?" Dodd asked. "Does she belong to a union? I thought she was a state employee, an LPN employed as support staff in student health?"

"She is. But she is entitled to breaks."

"I don't get breaks," Dodd countered.

"You are paid a heck of a lot more than she is."

Dodd felt the anger welling inside him. He forced himself to remain calm. "I'm a physician, for Christ's sake. I went to college and medical school, completed a residency. She just barely got out of night nursing school after getting a GED."

"You don't need to put down the help."

"You're right," Dodd agreed. "But I *do* need some help. "*If* they start helping, I'll stop putting them down. When are you going to tell the nurses and nursing assistants that they are here to make my life easier, not to add to my burdens?"

"They are people, too," Abramowicz babbled.

Tiring of the political correctness and the administrative nonsense, Dodd changed the subject. "Fine. Let them make diagnoses. I can't even get them to take temperatures; which reminds me, where are the glass thermometers?"

"Health and Safety says we can't have them any more."

"What the hell does that mean?" Dodd asked.

"There's mercury in them. Mercury's poisonous," Abramowicz said curtly, as if the physician had never heard of heavy metal poisoning.

Invictus

"Not in that form," Dodd explained. "The poisons are compounds, like methyl mercury, not elemental mercury."

"Regardless," Abramowicz dismissed Dodd's argument. "Health and Safety doesn't want to clean up after a mercury spill if we break one. They have banned mercury thermometers from the campus."

Skeptical, Dodd asked, "Are you nuts? You let them do this? Didn't you question the stupidity of such an idea?"

"We have electronic thermometers...."

"That are inaccurate if not used precisely as described by the manufacturers. Did you know that we have patients downstairs that radiate heat and their temperatures are recorded as two to three degrees below normal?"

"So?"

"It takes skill to use the electronic thermometers. Our RNs had some skill. You've run them off, replaced them with less expensive LPNs and medical assistants. The one RN that remains is worthless. She and the LPNs never get close enough to tell if the patient is sick," Dodd complained, volume in his voice rising as he spoke.

"That's an exaggeration," Abramowicz said, flicking his wrist to shoo away the thought.

"Maybe," Dodd agreed, "but, there's a kid in the lab — at least, I hope he's in the lab by now — who I think has appendicitis. How do you think the surgeon at the hospital is going to respond when I tell him the boy's temperature is 95 degrees? 'Hell, Dodd,' he's going to say, 'appendicitis is an infectious process. Don't you think the patient should have a fever?'"

"That's his problem," Abramowicz suggested glibly.

"No," Dodd said, finally losing his temper, "it's your problem. In my office I have a rectal thermometer for large animals, like horses and cows. One of the agriculture students gave it to me as a joke. If you don't come up with a glass thermometer to take my patient's temperature before his blood test is done, that's what I'm going to use on him. And if you think failing eye tests embarrasses students and upsets administrators, then imagine what this kid's parents are going to say to President Furneaux after he has to sit on an eighteen-inch-long thermometer."

Abramowicz's jaw dropped. He finally stammered, "You wouldn't do...."

"I will," Dodd corrected him. "And when I'm done, I'll probably be mad enough to use it on you, too. You do know the difference between rectal and oral thermometers, don't you?"

"Sure, one is red...."

"No," Dodd said leaving the office. "It's the taste."

Invictus

Chapter Seven
October 2nd

The conference room smelled of warm bodies, underactive deodorant, and cheap perfume. Dodd squeezed into the last chair. He sat between Clint Massey and Joie LaFlamé, breaking up their game of footsie. The fragrances intensified, bringing tears to Dodd's eyes. "Excuse me," Dodd said tripping over LaFlamé's leg and falling into the seat with an ungainly plop. She gave him a big smile and made a kissy face. Dodd turned to Massey, "Your girl friend is on the make; are you losing your touch?" Massey grinned. Dodd continued, "What's this required meeting about? No one told me. They locked the entrance doors downstairs, and there's a sign that says we open at nine instead of eight."

"Seems we humiliated a student," Massey explained, trying to get his shoeless, sock-covered foot up LaFlamé's leg to her thigh. In the process, he nearly broke Dodd's ankle.

"Ow," Dodd said. "What happened? Did he fail his eye test or some blood test?"

The person standing at the front of the room stopped speaking and stared at Dodd. Directing her comments at him, she spoke with a lisp. "Are we all settled there?" she asked. Silently, he took note of the woman's size and other visible characteristics. The woman was a rotund dwarf, maybe four feet nine inches tall. Abramowicz's dream date, Dodd told himself. She had a high, piercing voice. Devoid of the usual jewelry, instead she sported bright orange hair, a necklace tattoo, and a nose ring through her right nostril. Dodd thought he saw the flash of light reflected from her tongue dumbbell and thought he heard the clack when it struck her teeth while she talked. Her pronunciation left many words undecipherable.

Embarrassed, Dodd held up his hand meekly. The speaker recognized him, mutely pointing in his direction. "I apologize for interrupting," Dodd said. "Also, I spent two years on the flight deck of an aircraft carrier during Vietnam. I have lost about fifty percent of my hearing to jet engine noise and loud rock music. Can I persuade you to speak up, and to speak a little more slowly?"

Massey covered his face with both hands. Dodd thought Massey sobbed; he turned his head and looked at LaFlamé. For the only time that Dodd could remember, the nurse's mouth hung open but nothing emanated from her vocal cords. Dodd shifted his gaze back to the front of the room. The dwarf's orange hair now clashed with her own bright red face. "Smooth," Massey said, "really smooth."

"What?" Dodd demanded, turning toward his colleague, than back toward the speaker.

A sudden flurry of bodies being pushed aside announced the departure of the bowling ball-like woman. She bulldozed a pathway through the crowd standing around the table on her way to the exit. In her wake, Dodd saw distorted faces. She elbowed and kneed an opening through the meeting attendees, but he couldn't see her. Suddenly, the room was very quiet. "What?" Dodd repeated, staring at Massey. Massey continued to laugh, head lying on the table. Finally, Dodd picked him up by his pony tail. "What?!" he shouted.

Tears rolled from Massey's eyes; he attempted to mouth an answer, and failed. Abramowicz saved him the trouble. The administrator spoke to Dodd. "One of your colleagues insulted a deaf student last week. Mrs. Lyndhurst is here to give us some pointers on dealing with hearing challenged students." Abramowicz then addressed

Invictus

the woman seated next to LaFlamé. "Dr. Summers, would you mind asking Mrs. Lyndhurst to return to the conference room and continue with her observations?"

Persia Summers, a thin, over-dressed, black psychiatrist, sat two seats away from Dodd. She lifted herself daintily from the chair closest to the door. After she smiled sweetly for Abramowicz, she made an ugly face at Dodd and turned toward the exit. Elevating her chin and nose into the air, she departed the conference room in search of the deaf students' advocate. Immediately, the room fell into a babble of noise. The nurses, technicians, doctors, and other staff began to chatter among themselves.

Eventually, Massey ceased laughing. "Jesus," Dodd told his friend when Massey finally opened his eyes, leaving his head on folded arms. "This is a political correctness class." Massey nodded, eyes bright, tears reflecting the sunlight from outside the windows. Dodd continued, "How many deaf students are there on campus? Who embarrassed the patient?"

Massey lifted his head from the table and spoke in a whisper. "A.J. did it. Like you, he is a bull in the political correctness china shop. You could hear him a mile away, even with the exam room door closed. The less the student understood, the louder he yelled. When one of the nurses heard him ask the patient if she spoke English, she ran into the exam room. That embarrassed the patient even more. Neal told us that there are twelve deaf students and about thirty hearing impaired students on campus."

"Because A.J.'s an idiot, we all have to listen to a lecture on getting deaf people's attention?" Dodd asked. Massey nodded, again. Dodd continued, "Hell, don't tell Neal there are three hundred Chinese students enrolled here; we'll all be learning Mandarin before the year is out. Next year, we'll have to greet the Japanese contingent in their native tongue. The trouble with political correctness is that once you start, no one knows where to stop.

Everyone has sacred cows they think have been skewered. I fully expect some blind man to sue for the right to pilot a passenger aircraft for American Airlines some day."

"Visually challenged...." Massey suggested.

Dodd retorted, "Blind. Deaf. The only challenge some of these people suffer from is a lack of assertiveness. Assertiveness-challenged fits better. They can't speak for themselves so they hire lawyers. They could always adapt to the world as they found it. If they'd just say they were deaf, instead of expecting everyone to automatically know, life would be so much easier. You don't see left-handed people demanding to have two door knobs, one that turns clockwise and the other that turns counterclockwise, on every door, do you?"

"Not yet," Massey offered.

"And you have all the answers?" Summers asked Dodd loudly. She returned to her seat after having escorted the teary-eyed Mrs. Lyndhurst back into the conference room.

Dodd leaned around LaFlamé and whispered his response. "All the answers? No. But I do have one. Be polite and be direct. Don't expect people to read your mind. That would certainly make political correctness obsolete."

"Okay, Mrs. Lyndhurst," Abramowicz interrupted the angry tête-â-tête, "you may proceed."

"Jerk!" Summers blurted at Dodd.

"Certainly not very politically correct of you to point that out," Dodd replied, "Maybe I'm manners-challenged."

"We don't have to be politically correct to white males," Summers replied, springing from her seat, voice rising loudly enough for everyone to hear. She stood and reached around LaFlamé, trying to grab Dodd's collar. "You stole the...."

"Dr. Summers," Abramowicz interrupted her, pleasant tone of voice out of place in the midst of an argument. "Please have a seat. We'll continue this conversation with

Invictus

Dr. Dodd another time."

Snapping her head away from Dodd while raising her nose at the same time, she smiled wanly at Abramowicz. "Certainly, Neal," she said in the voice she used to calm psychotic patients. Then she sat in her chair, serenely, as if the incident had never occurred.

"How can she do that and not break her neck?" Dodd asked Massey. He added, "Oh, and sign me up for insensitivity training." Massey's eyes filled with tears of laughter, again.

Bill Yancey

Invictus

Chapter Eight
October 15th

In his office, Dodd kept a small refrigerator. Inside he cached the lunches he made at home and brought to work. Most of the time he ate in his office between patients. Occasionally, he forgot, being too busy to stop. On rare occasions, his dealings with Abramowicz made him so nauseated that he could not face the prospect of eating. On those days he either took a long walk at lunch, or read a book sitting in his camp chair near the practice field.

In the building early one morning before anyone else except the janitorial staff, Dodd dropped his soft leather brief case onto the chair in his office. Opening the refrigerator door to deposit his lunch, he immediately noticed something amiss. Someone had removed the six pack of beer. Probably the same person had smeared blood inside the tiny fridge. Tilting his eyes downward, Dodd spotted red drops on the floor at his feet. Searching the floor outside his office, he found a trail of blood that led from his office past three other offices and to the door at the administrative stairway. Stepping back into his office and closing the door, Dodd pulled a paper towel from the holder next to his sink and ran some water across it. Quickly, he wiped the refrigerator and the floor inside his office. In the hallway, he continued cleaning until he had obliterated the bloody trail between his office and the next one.

After rinsing his hands and throwing away the paper towel, Dodd picked up his phone and called housekeeping. "David? Good morning, this is Spence. Say, someone spilled blood on the floor in front of Dr. Massey's office. Suppose you could take care of that for me? Just a little. You won't need the moon suit, but you should still be careful about infectious diseases. I'd recommend a Mark Three Swab with afterburner and microwave ray gun. Thanks."

After hanging up the phone, Dodd left his office. He followed the ever diminishing drops of blood to the stairway entrance. There, the red trail faded, becoming much less noticeable. Cautiously, Dodd pushed open the door. The floor in the stairwell was also clean. Looking carefully, he saw a blush of red near the hand rail. He followed the trail up the stairs. At the landing on the second floor, Dodd scanned the doorknob on the door to the administrative offices. Nothing. Searching, he found a trace of blood on the railing leading to the attic. "Damn," he said to himself. Opening the door to the second floor, Dodd made certain no one approached the stairwell from the administrative offices. He slammed the door and looked over the railing at the first floor below. No one used the stairs. Quickly, two steps at a time, he ascended to the attic level landing. Pulling out his keys, he shoved the key to his office into the lock. It did not turn. Yanking that one out of the doorknob, he pushed in the key to the building's front door and twisted. The lock clicked and released; the handle turned. Dodd let himself into the attic space. He closed and locked the door behind him quietly. Sarcastically, he reminded himself to thank Neal for being such a tightwad that the locks shared the same key.

Surprisingly well lit, and airy, the attic in the building was also spacious. The climate control tower, which housed the heating and air conditioning units for the building, made up the central one third of the third floor. A metal roof leaned inward to meet the tower, but there were few visible supports. Dodd could see twenty feet to the apex of the building, and thirty feet in all directions. Before him squatted an immense, galvanized steel sheathed air-handler.

Invictus

Green and blue high- and low-pressure steam pipes, six and eight inches in diameter ran from the corners of the room and into the huge metal box that filled one half of the room. Air ducts hugged the walls and the ceiling; they fanned out in every direction.

The architects had divided the attic into thirds. The two main walls gave support to the roof. Small, half-sized doors led between the rooms. On his first visit to the attic, Dodd had been amazed at the openness. He had asked about using the wasted space. A building and grounds employee said no. Design engineers told the university that the third floor had not been constructed to withstand any load. The health service could not store old charts or x-rays there without jeopardizing the ceiling to the second floor. No one ever went to the attic, except to work on the climate control system. No one, that is, except Cody Gray.

Pulling open a metal, half door in one of the main walls, Dodd bent over and ducked through the small hatch. Inside the second huge empty chamber, he walked in nearly total darkness, feeling his way with his hands outstretched in front of him. Eventually, he bumped into the far wall. Exploring the wall, his fingers found the seam to another small hatch, this one also metal with sharp edges and closed tightly. He tapped softly on the steel. "Cody, it's me, Spencer Dodd," he called. "Are you in there?"

Dodd heard a rustling and a scraping. The door vibrated, echoing as someone released latches on the opposite side. The hatch swung inward, revealing a plush suite. Dodd crawled through the opening. It slammed shut behind him. Dodd stood upright in the spacious apartment. He turned to face Cody Gray. Kneeling, the young man leaned against the metal hatch, trying to re-lock it with his one good hand. Medium height, thin build, and blond, the lad's skin seemed pale in the artificial flourescent lighting. Dodd allowed the student to work at the sliding bolt for several seconds and then gently pushed the young man to the side. "Here," he said, "let me do that."

"Thanks, Doc," Gray said, slumping to the floor, and pushing back his long hair.

Dodd flipped the second latch and turned his attention to the boy. Blood-soaked gauze covered his right arm. More blood oozed from near his elbow, soaking the gauze in ever darkening scarlet. "What happened?" Dodd asked.

Gray explained the accident. "I was dropping a fiberoptic cable down one of the air ducts last night. I lost my balance. Sheet metal is sharp."

Dodd's eyes searched the apartment for supplies. The desk, made up of a half sheet of plywood and plastic five gallon cans, supported the computer and monitor. A cinder block and pine board bookshelf held only books and paper. On the inflated bed, which rested on the carpet remnants from Abramowicz's expensive decorating and the last clinic upgrade, Dodd saw gauze and adhesive tape. "Let me take a look at that," he said pointing to Gray's arm.

"It's a mess," Gray declared.

"So was my office and the hallway downstairs," Dodd informed Gray.

"Sorry," the student apologized. "I didn't realize I was leaking at first. I cleaned up everything up here. The cable, microphone, and camera are hung up somewhere in the air ducts, but I can deal with them later."

"Lie down on the bed," Dodd instructed. Gray inched his way from the doorway to his bed on his hands and knees. Dodd helped, supporting Gray as he crawled. He saw the red, toy periscope that penetrated the perforated vinyl soffit in the false dormer, several feet beyond the bed. Reflected in the first mirror, Dodd saw the practice field outside and below them. A pair of binoculars hung by a plastic strap on a nail near the overhang. "You watch practice much?" he asked the boy.

"Every day," Gray answered weakly. "Over the

Invictus

internet, I sell information about who is injured to the bookies in Vegas. It helps them set the point spread." Gray winced when Dodd unwound the unprofessionally placed bandage. The blood had begun to clot; it clung to the gauze and the wound. Pulling on the tape yanked hair from Gray's arm, reopened the wound. He gritted his teeth.

As Dodd removed the bandage, a spurt of blood leaped into the air, describing a Newtonian parabolic arc and splashing onto the carpet. "Whoops," he said, maintaining an even voice so as not to alarm the boy, "looks like you got a small artery here, Cody." The physician pushed clean gauze over the wound and re-wrapped it with the kling. "We need to sew you up. That means going downstairs, unfortunately. Did you pay the health fee this semester?"

Wanly, Gray shook his head. "No," he answered. "I couldn't afford it. I changed my status in the campus computer from full-time to part-time, even though I'm taking twenty-six hours. You don't need to pay the fee if you're part-time."

"How can you take twenty-six hours?" Dodd asked, impressed. "That academic load would kill a horse."

"It gets me out of here sooner and costs less. Some nice people recommended me to the dean via email." Gray smiled; his dry lips cracked. "Of course, if they ever find out that they recommended me I'm in big trouble...."

"I understand," Dodd said with a smile. He had been a poor student once, also. "Have you ever paid the health fee in the past?"

"Yeah, why?" Gray asked.

"It's enough to get a chart made. They aren't retired until you graduate. We need a chart to work on you. We also need to go. Can you walk?"

Gray nodded. "With help," he said.

Dodd finished securing the bandage around Gray's arm. He stood and then pulled Gray to his feet, holding one of the boy's arms around his own neck. Dragging Gray to the door, he undid the locks and crawled through the hole. Once through, he pulled Gray after him. "Sorry, I'm not helping much, Doc," the boy said.

"No problem," Dodd panted. "My lumbar discs are never going to forgive me, however. This will cost you big time later. That reminds me; you took a six pack of mine. I hope you didn't drink the whole thing. Alcohol makes bleeding worse. And if you took any aspirin for the pain, you may never stop bleeding." Dodd lugged the young man through the darkness to the first door, its outline lit by sunlight streaming through the climate control tower.

"Just Tylenol," Gray muttered.

"Thank God for small favors," Dodd intoned. He repositioned Gray and opened the door to the stairway carefully. One of the nurses shuffled through the second floor door when he peeked through the crack. "Okay, here we go," he said after she disappeared. Wrapping one hand around Gray's waist and leaving the boy's arm around his neck, Dodd grabbed the hand rail with his free hand and tried to move quickly down the steps. He felt like he were in a three-legged race, with his feet tied inside a potato sack and carrying three hundred pounds. Sweating profusely, the two men reached the second floor landing. At that precise moment, the door burst open and Neal Abramowicz's bulky frame squeezed into the stairwell.

Startled, Dodd said, "Neal!"

Abramowicz exclaimed, "Spence!"

Dodd recovered more quickly than Abramowicz. "Quick, call the nurse," he ordered the administrator. "This student passed out in the stairwell."

Surprised, Abramowicz stammered. "W-W-What's he doing on the second floor, Spence?"

"Damned if I know," Dodd lied. "If it didn't clash with your precious decor so much, maybe we could put the signs back up. You know: medical clinic, laboratory, x-ray department, records, stay out of the stairwell, etc. This is the third student I've found on the stairs this semester. And beside that, he's bleeding and he's heavy. Get your ass in gear and find me a wheelchair."

Embarrassed, Abramowicz shuffled quickly down the stairs yelling, "Nurse, nurse!"

"Sit," Dodd told Gray, lowering him to the cement deck. "In fact lie down and lift your feet onto the steps. Bend your knees." While Gray stretched out on the floor, Dodd bent over and placed his hands on his knees. He tried to slow his own breathing and heart rate. "If I have a heart attack, Cody, I'll never speak to you again," he said.

Also exhausted, Gray remained silent. His skin color matched the pale walls. The nurse eventually came and together they heaved Gray into a wheelchair. She wheeled him through the administrative offices to the elevator, then to the treatment room on the first floor. Dodd followed, short of breath. His arthritic knees and back screamed at him for being so foolish. On the way to the treatment room, he stopped in medical records, gave them Gray's last name and last four digits of his social security number, and asked for his chart.

"Is he a patient?" the medical records secretary asked.

"No," Dodd lied. "I'm reviewing the record for Friday's Quality Assurance meeting."

"Okay," she said, handing him the chart. She filled out the pink slip to put in the chart's place in the metal cabinet.

Bill Yancey

Invictus

Chapter Nine
Evening of October 15th

Cody Gray and Dodd walked slowly up the stairs toward the third floor landing in the student health center. "Are you sure the building is empty?" Gray asked.

"Positive," Dodd answered. "In the whole building only one light is on. You can see it under Abramowicz's door. I knocked; no one answered. How do you feel?"

"A little tired," the boy answered. "Two bags of intravenous fluids works wonders, though. How much blood did I lose?"

"Not much. You had a vasovagal response...."

"A what?" Gray asked.

"A fainting spell," Dodd explained. "You cut a small branch of the brachial artery. It looked like more blood than there really was. If you'd been an inch more medially, you would have bled a lot more, possibly fatally. It would have been tough to explain a body in the attic."

Gray laughed. "Would really have been a mess if I had fallen into the air shaft and bled to death."

"Not to mention the smell after a couple days." Dodd chuckled. He pulled open the door to the attic and held it for Gray.

"Coming in?" Gray asked. Dodd did not answer. "Come on, Doc. The least I can do is thank you with one of your own beers. Hey, what else do you have to do? Your wife took the dog; the kids are grown...."

"Okay, okay," Dodd gave in. He closed the door behind him, locking it with his own key. Quietly, he followed Gray through the dark antechamber and to the door leading to the apartment. "What did you do all day?" Dodd asked locking the second door behind them.

The student ran through his itinerary, "I went to class, and spent some time in the library. Did some surfing on the net in the media center; read my email." Gray walked toward the small refrigerator in the corner of the room. Stopping next to the bed, he peeked through the red plastic periscope. Grunts and groans sounded from the practice field below: the varsity and junior varsity did calisthenics in the twilight outside. The field lights came on while Dodd watched Gray survey the scene below. "Hey," the boy said, "looks like Jackson Forrest is warming up. If he plays, then we will be three point favorites against East Carolina this week. Have to tell Benny the Mooch." Gray detoured to his computer and flipped it on. While it warmed up, he continued on his way to the icebox. "Man, I'm starved," he said.

"Why didn't you say so?" Dodd asked. "There are two lunches downstairs."

"Were two," Gray corrected. "I ate one last night." Gray tossed a can of beer at Dodd. "To your health, Doc."

"Yours, too, Cody," the physician replied. After popping the top to the can, he tilted his beer toward Gray in a long distance toast.

Dodd sat in the bean bag chair next to the bed and surveyed his surroundings. Gray's living quarters bested many on, or off, campus. The single room measured thirty feet by forty feet, with padded carpet — albeit no section larger than six-foot by six-foot so it was easily transported. Gray had salvaged furniture from all over town, from dumpsters and yard sales, when abandoned by students at the ends of the semesters. Without outside help, the student had wired the apartment for electricity, telephone, video, and ethernet. What more could a geek like Cody want, besides a degree? Dodd thought. "How long have you been here, now?" he asked as the young man sat on his inflated bed and opened a brew for himself.

"Fifth semester," Gray replied. He chugged half the can without stopping. "One and one half more and I'm out of here."

"Got a job lined up?" the physician asked.

"Sixty grand a year to start, working for DoD," the young man replied.

"Department of Defense?"

"Yep. Going to program cruise missiles."

Dodd nodded. Pilots were becoming obsolete. Even had he been a young man, and the laser eye surgery worked as well as advertised, he would not have been able to fly jets — the competition was worse than that to get into medical school. He finished his beer in one guzzle and belched.

The computer flickered to life. Gray stood and walked to his desk. He pressed key combinations on the keyboard. Seating himself on the cushioned five- gallon bucket, he typed for several minutes while Dodd watched. Bored, the doctor went to the refrigerator and retrieved a second beer. He pulled the tab and handed another to Gray. Gray continued to type with one hand, sipping the brew. He smiled. "Fifty bucks from Benny for the tip on Jackson."

"Does it pop out of your phone line?" Dodd asked with a smirk, knowing the money would not.

"No. It's a credit. He adds it to my winnings."

"You're not addicted to gambling, are you?" Dodd asked.

"No," Gray explained, "I only bet on sure things. I paid this semester's tuition with my profits."

Dodd tilted the beer can toward his young friend, again. "Touché," he said.

"I'd like to start a web business in my spare time, Doc."

"Wouldn't we all," Dodd said. "Amazon's stock is worth billions. It hasn't made money yet. I should have gotten an MBA; maybe then I'd be able to explain that phenomenon."

Gray continued his thought, "I've got a great idea for one."

"Well," Dodd said, returning to the refrigerator for a third beer, "run it by me. If I laugh too loudly, you'll know you've got something. I have absolutely no business sense. Ask my ex-wife. Or her lawyer."

Gray watched Dodd walk unsteadily to the bean bag from the refrigerator. Dodd sat heavily, sloshing the beer onto his clothing. He chortled, "You know it's illegal to have alcohol on campus, don't you?"

"Only if you get caught," Gray suggested. "Almost every small refrigerator in the dorms has alcohol in it. Besides, that's why I steal it from you. Who can you complain to?"

Dodd snorted, "Tell me about it."

"So, Doc," Gray asked, hoping to slow Dodd's consumption of his stolen stock. "Why did you and Mrs. Dodd get divorced?"

"Angels," Dodd said somberly.

"Angels?"

"Well, angels in the bathroom," Dodd explained. "I had to take a dump and there was no place to sit."

"You're going to have to explain that," Gray enticed the physician. He typed briefly on the keyboard, putting the computer into hibernation. Leaving his plastic bucket seat, he dragged a second bean bag chair closer to Dodd. There he settled gently, trying to avoid bending his right arm.

Slurring his speech, Dodd continued, "We were at my mother-in-law's. She has two bathrooms, one in the master bedroom and one for guests." Dodd leaned back in the seat; the styrofoam beads squeaked under him. He put one hand over his eyes trying to recall the scene. "I went into the bathroom. She had covered every flat surface in the entire room with angels or seashells."

"Even the toilet?"

Invictus

Dodd nodded. He continued, "There was padded angel cushion on the seat. It wouldn't stand up on its own. I had to squeeze into the room. There weren't four contiguous square inches of flat, empty surface in the whole bathroom. You couldn't lay a toothbrush diagonally on the counter next to the sink."

"Stifling?" Gray asked.

"Suffocating," Dodd said, staring at the ceiling. He began to list the objects he saw in his mental picture: "A miniature Christmas tree with shells for ornaments, a ceramic candle holder, a seated ceramic angel, a heart-shaped, woven wicker basket filled with seashells and q-tips, a spiral shell dangling on a pink string from a brass holder, an angel-shaped hand cream dispenser, an angel-shaped soap dish, a ceramic seashell soap dispenser, matching seashell cups, a plastic angel-decorated paper cup dispenser with a matching toothbrush holder, a dangling stained glass angel hanging from another brass holder, a conch shell tissue dispenser, and that was just the counter around the sink."

Astounded, Gray asked, "There was more?"

Dodd rambled, made more loquacious by the liquor, "From the ceiling hung a basket of dried flowers. There were three curtains on the shower, outer fabric, middle satin, and inner plastic. She put a small table in the room and covered it with a conch shell flower vase filled with artificial flowers and knitted angels. On the top of the toilet there was a cloth cover, two huge clam shells, a ceramic conch, and two glass containers filled with smaller shells. The window also had three layers of curtains. On the walls hung three ceramic angels between the tub and the window, a huge wreath of seashells, angels holding a wall mirror, and two mounted seashell collections. Inside the tub, she had more stuff: all the soaps, shampoos, and oils Alexander the Great found on his trip to India. The trash can had angels painted on it. There was an angel-decorated, wall-mounted towel rack and shelf. On that shelf she had conch shells and a star fish."

"Jesus," Gray said, impressed as much by Dodd's memory as the list.

"Imagine an entire house decorated like that," Dodd said. "There was absolutely no flat surface to sit on, to lean on. My wife wanted me to spend weekends there when we traveled to Wilmington." Dodd breathed out heavily. "Whew. I felt like a bull in a china shop. My stress level was so high when I left there, it's hard to explain. It was such a relief to get home and sit in a completely empty room."

"How did that lead to the divorce?" Gray asked. The computer beeped in the background.

"Shortly thereafter, my wife started collecting frogs, wooden ones, plastic, ceramic, all kinds. After she filled one small table with them, I mentioned her mother's house to her. Every journey begins with the first step, Confucius said. That was step numero uno. It was all downhill from there." Dodd smiled. "It would have happened anyway. The kids were gone. We were drifting apart. Pisses me off that she kept the dog. Guess he liked her more than me anyway. I was never home. She ran her computer business from the house. Hell, he didn't want to leave home and go to a cramped apartment with me. I do miss the dog, though."

The computer beeped again. Gray lifted himself from the floor and went to the monitor. He sat on the bucket. Fingers danced across the keyboard, too quickly for the intoxicated Dodd to follow. "See this?" he asked pointing to the monitor. It's a remote camera."

Dodd looked up. The view of the parking lot did not impress him. "Abramowicz watches a remote nudist colony," he mumbled.

"This is our school. I've tapped into the security cameras. I was thinking about putting up a web site that

Invictus

students could check any remote cam they wanted, on school grounds or anywhere else in the world that we could capture. Advertisers might pay me to run the site if enough students visited it."

In a haze, made denser by alcohol, Dodd opened his fourth beer. "You know, someone wants to rent out driving time on a moon rover. They're going to use a web site and let people on Earth control the contraption remotely. They think that will make them lots of money." He belched, again. "Too damned expensive for my tastes. Be a lot cheaper to drive go-carts. Hell, you could have virtual and remote races. If that worked, you could scale up to NASCAR, or model airplane races. Even real airplane races for guys who are exceptionally talented. At least that's semi-affordable. Oh well, what do I know? Where did you leave your fiberoptic cable and camera?"

Gray turned back toward the monitor. He typed some more commands. A gray scene filled the screen. "Here's the camera. Nice shot of the inside of an air duct. Let me turn on the microphone. We might hear the air exchangers doing their job." He tapped several keys and reached for the volume control on the stereo speaker hanging from the sides of the monitor.

A high-pitched, female voice, loud moans, filled the apartment, "Oh. Ah, ah, ah. Oooooh,"

Dodd's somnambulism dissipated rapidly. His head jerked upward; his hand almost crushed the beer can, squeezing more suds onto his clothing. "Who's that?" he asked.

"Sounds almost like someone getting laid...."

Dodd shook his head. "Not in student health," he stated flatly. "Where's the microphone?"

"Near as I can tell, it's caught in the air duct over the administrative offices."

Dodd laughed. "Abramowicz didn't answer his door. The light was on. Can you record this?"

Bill Yancey

"Want to get names?" Gray asked.
"Just to embarrass him, if I can."
"You don't like him, do you Doc?"
"I don't like any bureaucrats, or politicians, for that matter."
"Why?"

Alcohol scrambled Dodd's thoughts, although he thought he articulated them well, "The power plays, the politics. Listen, 'yes' is a bureaucrat's only commodity. He sells it to the highest bidder. Without his approval, his underlings are stymied. He knows it; so, he squeezes everything he can out of them before he'll grant his approval. In China, and some other countries, this leads to graft. Communism limits the way a man can achieve great wealth, so they take bribes. They wield their power to improve their lives. In countries where corruption is punished, this power to deny leads to moral depravity, not easily proven in court. Just to show that he wields the power and to denigrate his subjects, a bureaucrat will subject his employees to unspeakable horrors. They have to listen to his jokes, agree with him on other matters, even do his bidding. Many times they compromise their ethical standards to achieve their goals. Some only surrender to the logic of the end justifying the means; others their dignity. After a while, everyone is compromised...."

"And Abramowicz?"

The drunk physician made a sour face. He vented his feelings about the administrator who had recently been appointed his supervisor. "He's an officious asshole," he said. "He's a brown-noser. The Peter Principle hit bull's eye with him. He has absolutely no interest in student health other than as a stepping stone to his next job in the administration. If he becomes the next vice president of student affairs, that's a step down from the jerk who's there, but still a step down. My only hope is that he stumbles. If

Invictus

he screws up in a big enough way, he may even take his immediate boss with him."

"Then you take over?" Gray asked.

"Nah," Dodd said waving a nearly empty beer can at the boy. "Who'd want that job? Kowtow to a bunch of political assholes who have lost their drive and direction, and think of nothing but screwing their secretaries. Screw that." Dodd chugged the final swallow to his fourth beer.

"Do you think Abramowicz is gay?" Gray asked.

Dodd shrugged. "Could be," he said. "He's definitely effeminate. Of course, once you cross the threshold of three hundred pounds, you tend to lose your secondary sexual characteristics. Fat men look a hell of a lot like fat women, and vice versa. Just like very old men look like very old women. I once saw a picture of a one-hundred-year-old man and his one-hundred-twenty-year-old mother in a geriatrics textbook. They looked like identical twins. Your age and your bulk can hide certain sexual features or distort them. Sometimes, fat makes it impossible to tell a person's sex."

Gray thought about what the physician had said for a minute. "Yeah," he agreed, "I guess you're right, Doc. Personally, I think he's gay."

"Well, so was Alexander the Great and so are lots of talented people. Hardly matters. I certainly wouldn't want to run a man out of town because of his sexual preferences. That's probably inherited. Even his weight is probably genetically determined, a mutation of the leptin gene for instance (not gluttony or sloth, or psychological problems). Either is definitely an unfair attribute to pick on, like the color of his skin, his religion, or his sex for that matter. I'd much rather stick it to him for being unethical, incompetent, dishonest, or stupid, something he should have been able to control. Sometimes I lose my preferred perspective, however."

"That's the second time you've mentioned Alexander

the Great tonight," Gray observed. Do you like him?"

Dodd shook his head. He frowned. "I hate the bastard," he said. "My dad worshiped him. My heroes were Batman and Robin. Father threw Alexander in my face a lot as a kid. Every time I tried to give up at something, he'd say, 'Alexander the Great never gave up; he conquered the world.' Did you know the Gordian Knot was on a donkey cart? It held the cross bar that attached to the animals." With those words of wisdom, Dodd fell asleep in the bean bag chair, leaving Gray to tidy up.

Before Gray slipped downstairs to use the bathroom and the shower in the psychiatric holding room, he scanned all the security cameras in the building to insure Abramowicz, or whoever made the noises, and his guest, had left the building. While Dodd slept peacefully, Gray showered, changed his bandage dressing and stole Dodd's lunch from the refrigerator in his office. After returning to the apartment, Gray spent several hours doing homework on his computer. Before he turned out the lights, he threw a blanket across the supine form of Spencer Dodd snoring in the bean bag chair.

Invictus

Chapter Ten
October 29th

Dodd finally decided that if the nurses would offer to help, he'd accept. Of course, he knew they would not. He held in his hand an example of their commitment to undressing patients. The note read, "Patient refuses to remove pants." It referred to a patient he had seen earlier. The woman had suffered a serious knee injury. Dodd had wasted ten minutes waiting for her to extract herself from her tight fitting jeans, because the nurse had refused to explain why it had been necessary.

Standing in the hallway, he saw three of the slackers talking and laughing in the middle of the clinic, near the nurses' station. Out of sight, around the corner, he knew two or three more sat, working crossword puzzles, surfing the internet on the computer meant for making appointments, reading, or eating. Thank God it's almost time to call it a day, he told himself, pushing open the door to the exam room.

"Afternoon," he said to the patient, not looking up from the chart. "Are you Mr. Dalrymple?" He scanned the chart for a chief complaint and vital signs. On the note the nurses had been directed to use solely for upper respiratory infections, impeccable nursing penmanship indicated that Mr. Dalrymple suffered a left wrist injury, and his temperature was 96.2 degrees. Dodd looked up from the chart. He groaned. The patient sat on the exam table, completely dressed. He wore a sweat shirt. Someone, evidently without medical training, had wrapped his wrist and hand in an ace wrap and hung his left arm in a sling. Frustrated, Dodd spoke to the patient through clenched teeth. "Football injury?" he asked.

"Yes, sir," the young man answered. "I ran into the goal post upright last night. Didn't hurt too much until this morning."

"Are you on the school team?" Dodd asked. The student weighed less than one-hundred-fifty pounds.

"No sir," the patient explained, "some of us sneaked onto the field after practice ended. In the dark."

"I don't suppose you were sober?" Dodd asked. "That would explain your anesthesia until this morning." The student shook his head. The physician nodded, too mad at the nurse to say anything. He seethed silently undressing and unwrapping the injured arm. He took care to avoid hurting the patient too severely. The blue discoloration and massive swelling of the wrist left little doubt that at least one bone snapped in the collision with the metal goal post. "We'll need an x-ray to see which bones you broke and how badly you fractured them," Dodd said after checking for nerve, artery, and tendon function. "Take your arm and this form to the far end of the building. After I see the x-ray, we'll decide when you need to see the orthopedic surgeon."

Numbly, uncertain if Dodd's anger had been directed at him for showing up ten minutes before the health center closed, the student left the exam room. "Yes, sir," he said meekly, cradling his arm and sliding gingerly off the exam table.

"See you in a little bit," Dodd said, watching the boy trundle down the hall. Once the patient disappeared from sight, Dodd lost his temper. He threw the chart across the hall into his office. It bounced off his desk. The plastic clasp gave way and twenty sheets of paper scattered throughout the office, under his small desk, into the trash can, and into the far corners of the room. "Crap," Dodd said to himself, angry that he lost control.

Striding into the room, he lifted the receiver to the

Invictus

intercom and dialed #0. He thought he addressed the nurses station, #1 on the intercom. Instead, he spoke to everyone in the building via the ceiling speakers. Overhead, he heard his own angry breathing, then his voice. "Attention all nurses. Attention all nurses and medical assistants. As of 8:00 a.m. tomorrow, all nurses will be required, repeat *required,* to undress at least one part of every patient they put into an exam room. Any nurse not undressing at least one extremity of any patient will forfeit one article of his or her own clothing. Strip poker rules will apply. This is Dr. Neal Abramowicz." Catcalls answered the announcement. They radiated from the center of the clinic. Dodd heard squeals of laughter from other offices and exam rooms.

Feeling better, Dodd slammed the receiver onto the cradle. He got onto his hands and knees and began to collect the pieces of Dalrymple's chart. Back to his office door, which he had left open, Dodd could not see the crowd that collected behind him. A brassiere — a forty D cup brassiere — fell to the floor next to his right hand. Startled, Dodd stared at it. Behind him eight nurses and technicians laughed loudly. They scampered out of sight before he could turn and recognize any of them. The herd thundered down the hallway giggling and laughing. Dodd smiled to himself. Maybe they would remember for a day or two, he thought.

After stuffing the brassiere into a lower desk drawer, he stretched to retrieve the last page of the chart from under his desk. Heavy footsteps shuffled into the doorway behind him. Shit, he thought, trouble. "Dr. Dodd," Abramowicz said.

"Yeah, Neal," Dodd replied, not looking up or making an effort to stand. Rear end high in the air and leaning on his elbows, he began sorting the chart into the correct order and fitting the pages into the manilla folder.

"I'd rather talk to your other end, although some of

the nurses have mentioned what a perfect ass you are," Abramowicz said, chuckling at his own joke.

"Better than imperfect, like yours, Neal," Dodd replied. He stood and turned to face the rotund administrator. Pointing to the chair near the door, inviting Abramowicz to sit also, Dodd sat in his desk chair. He laid the chart on his desk, upside down to preserve the patient's anonymity.

Abramowicz eyed the chair. He squeezed his bulk through the door and overwhelmed the ancient, armless, wooden structure. His immense body hung over every edge of the seat. Dodd subconsciously rolled his chair away from the administrator, backing it into the window in order to give himself more breathing space. With Abramowicz's rotund physique inside the small office, there was little room for much else. "Now," Abramowicz said, relaxing a little. The edges of his body oozed over the frame of the chair, hiding most of it from Dodd's view. Dodd wondered how long the wooden structure would hold out before it collapsed. "I have to remind you to restrict your announcements to clinic information."

"That was clinic information," Dodd protested.

"*Official* clinic information," Abramowicz corrected himself. Dodd nodded. Abramowicz's reputation did not include his having a sense of humor.

Irritated, Dodd asked. "Anything else?"

"Two things. I've decided to implement an appointment system, and...."

"I have to respectfully disagree, Neal. We have an appointment system. We see two appointments each hour and one to three walk-ins per hour depending upon how much time we have left over."

"It's going to be appointments *only* starting next week," Abramowicz clarified his statement.

"What about the walk-ins?" Dodd asked.

"They'll have to make appointments. All the machinery

Invictus

is in place. They'll learn eventually."

"Why are we doing this?"

Abramowicz rolled his eyes, indicating he talked to a physician who knew little about efficiency. Administrators knew about efficiency, he reminded himself. He continued, "We have too many complaints about the two and three hour waits. This way, we can regulate the flow."

Dodd made some quick calculations in his head: eight hours, at three patients per hour, for each of six practitioners, equaled about one hundred forty-four patients per day. "Okay. It'll work," he said, "but only if you force the patients to get up in the morning for the early appointments. Three patients an hour gives us a better total than our current one-twenty per day average."

Running the scenario through his mind, Dodd continued, "You have to remember, though, that we have an impotent triage system. Students triage themselves by the length of their wait. Really sick or injured kids will wait two hours. Those with colds and minor injuries won't. In no place on the planet has social medicine not been overwhelmed. Our system is a form of social medicine. There are no disincentives for coming to see us, except for the wait. Once they've paid their fee, everything is free. The only way you can insure the really sick people get seen first is to institute some sort of triage system, too. Some patients will have to be turned away; you will have to make damn sure they're not the sick ones."

Oblivious to the rejoinders and pleasantly surprised by Dodd's attitude, Abramowicz asked, "You won't object?"

"Right now, I'm seeing thirty patients per day, on some days, and some of my colleagues are lucky to see twelve. Why would I object to cutting my patient load to twenty four and increasing theirs?"

"I just thought you might," Abramowicz stated.

Dodd shook his head; he shrugged his shoulders perceptibly. "If it's done right," he said, "it'll make my life easier, Neal. I don't object to being more efficient. Of course, you understand that no matter how good it looks on paper, if the nurses can't put the patients in the rooms by their appointment times, then the system bogs down. There will still be complaints. If the medical assistants can't do some of their work with a second patient, concurrently while the docs are seeing the first patient, then the docs may still be waiting on the nurses to do their job. There will be no increase in efficiency." More problems came to mind as Dodd thought over the prospect. "Appointments are a way to structure wasted time. If a patient takes less than that allotted, those minutes are permanently lost. Docs in private practice double book for that reason. I don't know if the nurses will be willing to keep one step ahead of the practitioners."

Not listening to Dodd's arguments, Abramowicz waited for the opportunity to spring the second announcement on him. As Dodd finished expressing his reservations, Abramowicz thrust a stack of light blue, gray, and white papers into Dodd's hands. "Here," he said.

"What's this?" Dodd asked.

Abramowicz rubbed his hands together gleefully. He seemingly bubbled with joy. "New lab and x-ray requests, other stuff, and new progress notes," he said.

Dodd flipped through the pages. "Neal, there are only three colors here. How are we going to tell the reports from the requests? We have twenty different colored pages now. This is going to be a nightmare. Some of this stuff is disposable; some isn't. The wrong stuff is going to get tossed and other wrong stuff is going to end up in the charts. This is stupid. Whose idea was this?"

Abramowicz beamed, immune to criticism. "My idea. Those are the school colors," he pointed out. "When the alumni see the charts, in blue, gray, and white, they'll be impressed. Dean Waters loved the idea!"

Irreverently, Dodd said, "The alumni are never going

Invictus

to see these charts. They contain confidential information, you idiot. In addition to that, I'll be forced to spend an extra ten minutes with each patient, trying to find the correct piece of paper to use."

"I disagree," Abramowicz argued. "When we give tours of the student health center to alumni, prospective students, and their families, they will all be able to see the edges of those charts in the chart racks, and they'll all be in the school colors."

The x-ray technician, Frank Ramey, squeezed an arm into the room between Abramowicz and the far edge of the door. In his hand he held an x-ray film jacket. He handed the films to Dodd. From the hallway, he said, "Janitor's fracture, Doc." Dodd grabbed the x-rays. The arm slipped away and disappeared. Ramey's footsteps receded swiftly; the tattooed, long-haired, multi-pierced, hippy genius retreated from the imposing presence of Abramowicz as quickly as he could.

The administrator turned too slowly to catch Ramey. "Ramey, I wanted to talk with you about your dress.... Can never catch that man," he observed. "He's always in the dark room or x-raying someone."

"That's his job," Dodd said. He pulled the films from the brown envelope and, spinning his chair, held the acetate in front of the window. The sun hung low over Cumberland Mountain in the west. Enough orange photons reached through the atmosphere, the window, and the acetate to excite the neurons on Dodd's retina. He saw one of the worst Colles' fractures he had seen since leaving the emergency room in Richmond.

"What's a janitor's fracture?" Abramowicz asked.

"I'll show you," Dodd said. He stood, squeezed past the man out the door, and led the administrator to the treatment room. There, the patient, Dalrymple, waited, seated on the stretcher. The nurses had departed, after leaving out some plaster and a bucket of warm water. David

Evans, the evening housekeeping worker, mopped the room, straightening the mess left by a busy day of vomit, bleeding, and tears. Dodd snapped the x-rays smartly into the view box on the wall near the stretcher and flipped the toggle switch to light it. "Dave," he called out, while Abramowicz stared dumbly at the x-ray, unable to decide which extremity, much less which bones had been x-rayed. "What do you think?"

"Nasty radius fracture," Evans said, nonchalantly, glancing at the film. He returned to swabbing the floor.

Abramowicz looked at Evans, startled, then to Dodd, puzzlement growing deeper on his face. Dodd explained, pointing first to Evans and then to the shattered radius, "He's the janitor. This is a bad fracture. QED, or *quod erat demonstrandum*:[11] a janitor's fracture. Even he knows that, and you don't. Never underestimate the help, Neal." Dodd turned his attention to Dalrymple. Abramowicz attempted to slink out of the room.

"Before you go, Neal," Dodd called. "Where's my nurse?"

"Hourly wage personnel have been ordered to avoid overtime at all costs. Budget constraints, Dr. Dodd," Abramowicz smiled, enjoying a measure of revenge. "If you came to staff meetings, you'd know that."

"If we had some support staff, I'd come to the meetings," Dodd replied.

Invictus

Chapter Eleven
October 31ˢᵗ

Dodd wore aluminum foil molded to his head and fashioned into a point at the top. From the very tip of the structure he had designed, a two-inch-wide piece of paper spouted. It hung down, nearly touching his shoulder. "What type of Halloween goblin are you supposed to be?" one of the nurses asked, when Dodd arrived in the treatment room.

"A Hershey's kiss," he replied. "Did Mr. Harper and his broken ankle get a ride to the orthopedic surgeon's office?"

"Roommate took him," the licensed practical nurse said brusquely.

Oblivious to the nurse's attitude, Dodd said, "Good. Anything else going on?" He spun on his heels and noted the three empty stretchers and empty suture room.

"Other than the petition to have you shot at sunrise, I can't think of a thing," she replied. Six months pregnant, and immune to jabs from Dodd because she practiced sensible nursing and did not mind working hard, Virginia Strahan smiled when the physician made a face. Seated at the nurses' desk in the treatment room, feet propped on a stool, Strahan knitted booties with her arms folded across her huge belly. Her fourth child could look forward to warm yellow feet.

"I meant," Dodd explained, "are there any patients who would benefit from my expertise?"

Strahan stopped knitting. She looked Dodd directly in the eyes. "As you can see, there are no patients at the moment. I doubt if any of them would benefit from your criticisms, anyway. That is your expert field is it not?"

Dodd smiled. "I try. We critics are an unappreciated lot."

"You can say that again," Strahan restarted her task; knitting needles clacked repeatedly. "What, exactly, was your problem last night?"

Dodd stopped for a minute and thought. He leaned one elbow on the edge of the counter facing Strahan. "Last night?" he asked.

"See? You don't even remember what the fuss was about. However, the nurses are never going to forget. Do you pick those words at random, or do you intimidate people on purpose?"

Puzzled, Dodd asked, "I haven't a clue. What are you talking about?"

"The charts?" Strahan asked forcefully, reminding him of the tirade.

"Oh, yeah, the charts," Dodd acknowledged. He hit his forehead with his palm. "I hope I'm not getting Alzheimer's like my dad." He watched Strahan's fingers dance. Magically, the socks grew longer. "My ex-wife did that once."

"Knitted?" she asked.

"Was motherly."

"The charts?" Strahan repeated, ignoring the insult to his ex-wife, Sherry, whom she knew and liked.

"I just left some charts on the floor in the medical clinic," Dodd explained innocently.

"Threw them on the floor?" she asked. "That's what I heard."

"No. Just laid them gently. Actually, I dropped them from waist high to make a point," Dodd admitted.

"And that was?"

Enjoying the verbal jousting with the nurse, Dodd answered, "I'm too busy to take them to medical records."

She gave him the nurses' interpretation of his motives.

Invictus

"Too busy or too important? Too arrogant or too egotistical?"

Exasperated that the staff would read that into his actions, Dodd explained, "It's bad enough that I have to do vital signs, undress my patients, track down thermometers, eye charts, and other equipment for special exams, etc. I refuse to take charts back to medical records at the end of the day."

"You can't leave records lying around," she stated.

"The runner from medical records can take them back."

"They leave at 5:00 p.m." She explained the situation to Dodd, as if he had never heard the excuse before. "No overtime allowed with the budget crunch."

"We close at five. Lock the doors. Take them back tomorrow. It's not like people break in here to read patients' charts," he stated.

"Confidentiality is a big issue."

"So is locking the doors at night," Dodd added. "Uh-oh."

"Uh-oh what?" she asked.

Dodd smiled cruelly. "Neal's outside," he whispered, nodding toward the small windows in the electric doors. "It will take him a couple minutes to figure out how the door works. If I stand here, apparently out of the way, but with my heel just in range of the electric eye, it will never open. What do you think, should I let him in?"

Strahan laid the knitting onto the desktop. Dropping her feet from the stool, she stood and pushed Dodd in the chest harder than he thought a pregnant woman should exert herself. Losing his balance, he stumbled backward two steps. As he did, the red light on the electric eye winked out. She pushed the chrome plate that activated the door. Both sides of the double door swung inward, giving Abramowicz space to enter the treatment room. Cheerfully, she greeted the director, "Good afternoon, Dr. Abramowicz. Can I do something for you?"

Abramowicz flashed a smile. He took her hand and stroked it gently. Dodd hated the smoothness with which the fat man spoke, complimenting Strahan. "No, thank you, but I appreciate the offer. I'm looking for Dr. Dodd."

"I guess I'll leave you two alone," Strahan said, adroitly stepping between the two doors and into the hallway before they automatically swung shut behind her.

Abramowicz positioned his huge body facing Dodd and blocked Dodd's exit from the treatment room. "Spencer," he growled.

"Nice to see you, too," Dodd replied. "Is this going to take long? I do have patients to see."

Placing both hands on his hips and leaning forward, Abramowicz reminded Dodd of a nanny about to spank a wayward child. "You have to change your attitude, Spencer. I can't have you ignoring the rules. It's demoralizing to the staff."

"Not as demoralizing as stupid rules," Dodd argued. "Which nonsensical regulation did I ignore this time? There are so many I lose track of the ones I've broken recently."

"Don't be flippant," Abramowicz said. "I'm talking about leaving the charts in the clinic last night. You are supposed to take them to medical records."

"Why can't medical records pick them up?" Dodd asked.

"They go home at five o'clock."

"Have one of their staff stay late and return the charts. We may lock the door at five, but we certainly don't stop working then."

"No overtime allowed," Abramowicz stated flatly.

"Have someone come to work an hour later and go home an hour later. The mornings are less busy anyway."

"I can't get the medical records staff to agree to that," Abramowicz complained.

"Fire them," Dodd suggested.

Invictus

"Spencer, Spencer," Abramowicz patronized the physician, "these are state employees. Like you, they are nearly impossible to discipline or to fire."

"I forgot," Dodd said drolly. "I guess you'll have to quit then, because I'm certainly not going to take records back. Next, you'll want me to pull or re-file them. That's bullshit, Neal, and you know it."

Rattled, Abramowicz looked for a compromise. "Can't you leave the charts in your office and lock the door?"

Emboldened when Abramowicz faltered, Dodd asked, "Why would I want to? Then I'd have to fill out a chart request form, in triplicate for each chart. Another one of your stupid rules."

Angry, Abramowicz bellowed, "We can't leave charts in the clinic!"

"Why?" Dodd asked, "Do you think someone lives in the attic and comes down at night to read charts? The doors are locked after we leave. If you don't think the building is secure, then you should hire a night watchman — never mind, there's no money for that." Their voices rose with each exchange. Neither man was aware of the congregation in the hall.

"I was serious about you having to change your attitude, Spencer, " Abramowicz said, trying to return to his original statement. "You're just not a team player."

"The word *team* presupposes a team, with a coach, a game plan, a captain, and a sensible division of labor depending upon the sport. We have none of the above," Dodd answered angrily. "Look," he explained, "you took psychology in college; you'll understand this. I grew up in the same house with an autocratic military officer, who questioned everything and everyone. The only way I survived was to doubt everything; question every order. Everything had to be precise and exact, and done to perfection. Not giving one hundred percent meant failure, even if I succeeded. Consequently, I'm abrupt with people.

I never lived up to my father's expectations, so I'm insecure and I tend to criticize. So, some people think I'm rude." Dodd caught his breath.

"I don't see where that has any bearing...."

Dodd interrupted. "Bear with me a minute, Neal. You, on the other hand, are overweight, grossly obese, a heart attack waiting to happen. You have unresolved issues concerning your mother and food. You have your own insecurities: you worry about what people say behind your back; you want everyone to like you. Consequently, you can't make a decision without a consensus from those affected — like having someone in medical records come late and stay late. You might be a nice guy, but you're a lousy leader. I can at least make a decision, unpopular or not."

Abramowicz's face clouded and turned red. Dodd continued, "If you don't stop stuffing your face, you're going to have a heart attack. If I don't stop making people unhappy, I'm going to lose my job. Would you like to take bets on which one of us successfully modifies his behavior first? The chances of you changing your lifestyle in order to save your life are ten times the probability that I will change my attitude in order to placate you and save my job. You'll never quit eating! Does that explain my demeanor and the fact that it isn't going to change?"

A snicker filtered through the crack between the double electric doors. The sound startled Abramowicz. He rotated his immense mass slowly toward the laughter. Before he could press the button to open the doors, Dodd saw the tops of the heads of several crouched persons running for cover. The door opened to an empty hallway. Abramowicz pirouetted heavily toward Dodd. "You'll pay for this impertinence," he growled, waddling out the door in search of easier prey.

After the door swung shut, Dodd ranted, "*Absconde obesito illegitmo! Non gradus anus rodentum!*"[12] After

Invictus

several minutes, his seething cooled. Returning to his office, he noticed someone had taped a sign to his door, "Doesn't play well with others," it read. He smiled and left it up, on the door: a warning to the *others*.

Bill Yancey

Invictus

Chapter Twelve
November 1ˢᵗ

At 7:30 a.m. on a Friday morning, the only pleasant thought ricocheting inside Dodd's skull had to do with the nearness of the weekend. Unfortunately, that also meant Monday was not far behind. Mumbling, "Mornin'," to the much too cheerful housekeeping and pharmacy crew who greeted him on their way to a support staff meeting, he slipped into his office. He dropped his brief case into a chair, and checked his email. A note from Cody Gray read, "Thanks for the medical care. The wound looks good," and ended with, "There are some disturbing things happening. We need to talk. Don't trust the confidentiality of your email."

Dodd doubted that Gray suffered from paranoia, but hated people who panicked. He gave Gray the benefit of the doubt and typed a reply, "Tell me about it when we check the wound next week." The remainder of the email had to do with parking for the upcoming football game, faculty senate minutes, or long lists of jokes or inspirational material that had earned new leases on life because of the internet. Most of the stories should have died natural deaths years before, but because there was always one more person who might not have read them, they made electronic rounds, sometimes ad nauseum.

The usual cast of characters awaited him in the conference room for the practitioners' staff meeting. A.J. Watson never arrived late for any appointment. Small, wiry, and bald, the retired navy doctor reminded Dodd of Don Knotts when he played Deputy Barney Fife from the mythical Mayberry, North Carolina — highly excitable about the smallest of things, and picayune about the interpretation of any protocol, policy, or regulation. Not keen on persons who thrived, or even survived, in military medicine after his experience with it, Dodd gave silent thanks that A.J., unlike Barney Fife, did not carry a gun. At one time or another, each of his colleagues would have died for some minor transgression. "Morning, A.J.," Dodd said, sitting across the table from him, in his usual seat away from the table in the middle of the bay window. Dodd observed the campus cop directing traffic. This morning a dark-skinned female motioned to the drivers. Apparently the job rotated among the officers. Whistle in her mouth, arms flailing, hands covered with white gloves, the well-proportioned officer reminded Dodd of an aviation bosun's mate on the flight deck directing the aircraft to the elevators or the catapults. In his memory, Dodd heard the engines of A-4s, A-6s, and F-4s whine in preparation for sorties over North Vietnam.

"Good morning, Spencer," Watson replied, interrupting Dodd's revery. He then began a detailed rambling about the reliability of the glucometers when used in the clinic by various nurses. Dodd listened for a while. His eyes began to glaze over when Watson's dissertation started a second chapter on the statistical significance of the errors found in a study done by the Mayo clinic. When Watson's high, squeaky voice paused to catch his breath, Dodd suggested he send a memo to everyone concerned via email. He knew the small man hated to use his computer. Watson shuddered at the thought, but quit talking. Beady eyes cast themselves about the room looking for another victim. Watson rather liked walking office to office, telling the same dull story over and over again, until each practitioner had a vision of how nice it would be to choke the little man. Email, at least, Dodd thought, could be trashed without reading it.

Dodd turned toward Clint Massey. The hippie

Invictus

physician also sat in the alcove of the bay window, long legs stretched to the conference table, where his rattlesnake-skinned, cowboy-booted feet rested on the polished wood. The world traveler's leather Australian cowboy hat lay across his eyes; he pretended to catnap, avoiding Watson's presence until a quorum appeared for the meeting. Elbowing Massey, Dodd spoke, "Good Morning, asshole."

"Morning only," Massey said, pulling his feet from the table and sitting up. "Good is subjective and individual, as is an asshole."

Dodd chuckled. "Didn't get laid last night?"

"None of your business. And it was your fault."

"Meaning what?" Dodd asked. Other doctors, nurse practitioners, and physicians assistants began to fill the room, one by one, as the friends talked.

"Joie doesn't like it when I defend you," Massey said.

"Then don't. I certainly don't need your assistance."

"She — hell, all the nurses get so damn mad at you they can't see straight," Massey explained.

"Maybe if they'd do their jobs," Dodd suggested, "I'd leave them alone. Six years is a long time to learn that you are supposed to do vital signs on every patient for every visit, even hang nails...."

Massey held his hands up in surrender. "Don't lecture me; I agree with you."

"Tell her to find a real job, then."

Massey chuckled, his grin revealing surgically repaired dentition. "And work for a living?" he asked. "Actually touch patients? Have *real* physicians to deal with? That'll never happen."

"Nurse bashing, again, Spence?" the woman across the table next to Watson asked.

Dodd turned his head, unaware that his and Massey's conversation had been less than intimate. "Not exactly," he informed her. "So, please, don't run to the nurses with horror stories of how mean old Dr. Dodd rants and raves about them. I have no difficulty letting them know my feelings. If you haven't noticed, I'm not shy. My therapist does have me working on being more direct, however."

Dodd then eyed Hilda von Weintraub suspiciously. He half expected her to pull a tape recorder from the pocket of her shapeless dress and play it for everyone to hear, then threaten to play it for the nurses. Von Weintraub hailed from the deep north woods of Minnesota, German genes itching to start and finish a war victoriously. At worst, she could have played linebacker for the Minnesota Vikings, short neck and stocky build flattening running backs with abandon. She never lost the Canadian-German accent, or the tendency to pronounce W's as V's, or S's as Z's. Massey called her 'the Nazi,' behind her back. Despite her mannerisms, Dodd liked her; some of her ideas bordered on wacky, but she gave color and varying viewpoints to any conversation. For some reason unknown to Dodd, she had hated him always.

An itinerant physician, von Weintraub had worked at SVU student health for many years, probably with the original director. She had held positions part time, full time, nine month, and yearly there, for longer than Dodd had been a physician. On the side, she also had worked in many of the regional hospitals in Tennessee, Kentucky, North Carolina, and Virginia, earning her another nickname from her colleagues: 'the migrant worker.' Her empathies ran with the hills people, the common man, the undereducated, the downtrodden, and any perceived underdog within her sphere of influence. She championed the nurses, not because she thought they did a great job, but because they were mostly women, dealing with mostly men and, as such, needed her protection — a woman equal to any man: a female doctor. Somehow her logic made sense to her, as did her need to regulate every aspect of the life of any patient fortunate, or unfortunate, enough to

Invictus

be assigned to her care. Some of the lonely, underachieving freshmen who lacked the ability to assert themselves survived the huge university with von Weintraub's help. Other students decided that one mother was enough, that they had left home in order to cut the apron strings. Those students avoided her like the plague.

Von Weintraub also ran her own small, medical practice as a sideline. She continued to follow a small number of, Dodd assumed, mostly mousy, unassertive, patients who needed her opinion on everything, from when to pee to which vitamins to take. Everyone knew this because she left her office door open. When she talked on the phone, invariably her voice rose until she practically yelled at the person on the other end, barking orders like der Fuhrer. "Zo, vat time do you take zat pill?" she'd snap at the patient. The practitioners learned to ignore her conversations. At times, patients left the building to avoid listening to them.

"Zo, you don't think the nurses do a good job, Spencer?" von Weintraub asked.

"Not so much that they don't do a good job, well maybe that. When was the last time you washed and waxed a rental car, Hilda?"

Surprised by the question, von Weintraub asked, "Vat has that to do with nursing?"

Dodd explained, "The nurses have no ownership, here. Individually, they are not responsible for anything. As a collective unit, the nurses are responsible for lots of stuff, but if something isn't done, they shrug their shoulders and say, "*Someone* didn't do it." I think if each were assigned to three or four specific rooms, and to a single doctor or two, things would be different. They couldn't duck their responsibilities, but then they could take pride in the fact that their rooms were always well stocked and that their physician saw more patients, or allowed them to do more medical procedures than some other nurse's physician."

Bill Yancey

"You don't like the collective work ethic?" von Weintraub asked, looking at Dodd critically.

Dodd shook his head. "I thought the Cold War settled the debate over which system, capitalism or communism, was more effective. Unfortunately, the Commonwealth of Virginia, or at least this institution, still practices the losing method. It's also true for the practitioners. When we see a patient, there's little chance we'll see him next time he comes in. Why worry if you got the wrong diagnosis, if you don't have to deal with the complications? Educate a patient? Take responsibility for him when he is a collective patient and not my own? Why would I spend my energy on someone else's patient?"

"Which is something we have to talk about," Abramowicz said, interrupting. Dodd looked up. The remaining physicians and health practitioners in student health, and the administrator and his secretary, had entered the room while he debated von Weintraub. Abramowicz waddled to the head of the table. His assistant, Ms. J.P. Jones, closed the door and sat rigidly at the distant end of the table. She pulled a stenographer's tablet from her large purse and immediately began transcribing her boss's words.

"Concerning privatization," Abramowicz continued, "the administration is looking into several possibilities. The first, of course, is to do nothing. We will continue as we have for the last twenty-six glorious years. In times of monetary stress, ideas are always cast around about the wisdom of capitalism and privatization, as Dr. Dodd was saying." A chorus of guttural boos filled the room. "There may be other options...."

"Like?" Dodd asked.

Abramowicz stared out the bay window and across campus. His vision included Burroughs Hall, the main administrative building, wherein sat the president of the university. The presence of that building, his eventual goal, gave him strength. "Maybe a joint venture, an exclusive contract with a health maintenance operator," he said.

"Oh, terrific," Massey joined the fray, "from the frying pan into the fire. Managed care is killing our colleagues in private practice. We have two applicants a month hoping one of us will kick the bucket. They are clamoring to ditch salaries twice what ours are, to work our hours and have fewer HMO hassles."

"Or, maybe," Abramowicz continued, "an arrangement with the university similar to that which they created with the bookstore. They turned a failing government bureaucracy into a profitable enterprise and kept most of their original staff, although those employees are no longer paid by the state and are easier to discipline and to fire. The bookstore gives excess profits to the university. There are some benefits to capitalism, again, as Dr. Dodd pointed out and Dr. Massey has seconded."

Dumbstruck, Dodd sat with his mouth open. "Say, something, dingleberry," Massey said, poking his friend in the ribs, "or close your mouth. Steven Hawking may investigate that chasm as a newly found black hole."

"Crap," Dodd finally said. He shook his head. "I don't need the aggravation."

"What do you mean?" Abramowicz asked. "You shouldn't be aggravated at all. You won't be involved in this process, unless of course you are fired when the new operators take over." Abramowicz beamed, pleased by the thought.

"Someone has to organize our bid." Dodd said.

"Our bid?" von Weintraub asked.

Dodd eyed Abramowicz, carefully. He rose from his chair slowly, not taking his eyes off his huge opponent. Standing in front of the bay window, he raised his right hand, pointing four fingers at the beefy administrator and then turned his head, nodding at each individual practitioner. "You don't want him doing it, do you? He's the first guy we get rid of, unless he writes himself into the contract. Hell, take his $100,000 per year salary and divide it among us. That's ten to fifteen thousand dollars more for each of you, even if we change nothing else."

Abramowicz coughed. "Who will deal with the administration?" he asked.

"Who cares?" Dodd spat. "When I was the managing partner in my private practice, we didn't have a bootlicking, blowhard scrounging up business for us. For the life of me, Neal, I can't imagine what your role would be. Good capitalism demands that you produce or that you get sacked. What could you possibly do that any one of the practitioners couldn't do better?"

"I can administrate!" Abramowicz bellowed.

"I can find a nurse with an MBA to do that, be the clinic manager, oversee nursing and billing, and for half your salary," Dodd countered. "In fact, I can think of five people she could replace without overworking herself. And I know just the woman to do the job. Just by cutting out unnecessary meetings, she could probably work a four day week. But...."

Massey pushed his hat back on his head and scooted his chair closer to the table. The prospect of being paid more, added to the chance at controlling or at least contributing to the control of his own destiny, intrigued him, and the others. For the first time in five years, every practitioner at the meeting paid attention to the ongoing conversation. "But what?" Massey demanded.

"I don't want to be director," Dodd stated. "I burnt out the last time. After making all the hard decisions, you lose friends. Neal has no friends because he makes bad decisions. Our last director had no friends because he refused to make any decisions whatsoever. But losing friends because you make good decisions, that put money in their pocket, place free time at their disposal, or lighten their work load is a bum trip I'd rather not re-explore."

"If it's any comfort," von Weintraub suggested, "I

already don't like you." The other practitioners nodded in assent; most did so in jest.

Abramowicz listened briefly to the conversation swirl around him and about him. Realizing he stood in the enemy's camp, he left the conference room without speaking another word. His secretary trailed after him; slamming the door, they departed. Several minutes later the psychiatrist, Persia Summers, sneaked quietly out of the room, unnoticed by the others. They continued their intense discussion. Despite protests and pleading from his colleagues, Dodd remained firm. He would not spearhead the bid to preserve their jobs. If they wanted, he would offer assistance in designing the bid, but someone else would have to be point man. The meeting ended without any firm decisions being made, other than to continue the conversation at a local tavern that evening.

BeeBee dallied in Dodd's office. Dodd quickly slammed the door and locked it behind him, before anyone else saw the raven. "*Mellita, domi adsum,*"[13] the bird said to Dodd.

"How did you get in here?" Dodd demanded.

BeeBee nodded toward the window. "Someone left it open. Obviously, they needed fresh air. The stench is pretty thick."

"What stench? I don't smell anything," Dodd said defensively, "and, besides, ravens are immune to bad odors. Any species that eats maggots can't be too sensitive to scent."

"*Ars longa, vita brevis.*[14] Hippocrates." BeeBee said.

"Doesn't apply. We're talking money here, not patient care," Dodd argued. The bird tilted his head, obviously disagreeing. "Okay," Dodd admitted, "so if this place ran better, we could give better care to more really sick students. But, I'm not the guy to run it." BeeBee tilted his head to the other side, waiting in silence. "I no longer have what it takes, BeeBee. No stamina, no strength; even my clinical skills fade with each passing day of seeing sore throats and runny noses. I can no longer fight city hall; the Don Quixote in me has died."

"*Non est ad astra mollis e terris via,*"[15] BeeBee replied. He hopped onto the top of the bookcase and became stationary. Immediately, a knock sounded at the door. Dodd looked at the bird. Immobile except for an eyelid, he winked at Dodd.

Dodd released the lock, opening the door inward. Massey bolted into the small room, practically pushing Dodd into one chair. He lifted Dodd's briefcase from the other and deposited it on the floor, sitting in the second seat. Out of breath, he asked, "Do you really know a nurse who could replace Neal?"

"Absolutely. My ex-partner fired my previous office manager, Patricia Masters. She would shame Neal within two minutes of taking over. I just have to find out where she is and recruit her."

Massey beamed. "And replace four other people, too?"

"I did exaggerate a little," Dodd admitted. "Maybe three." He smiled, knowing he told the truth.

"You've got to do this, Spence," Massey begged.

"Do what?" Dodd stalled.

"Be our leader. Hell, none of us has ever set up a private practice, except the Nazi. Besides, she's loud and obnoxious, whereas you are just obnoxious."

"Easy as falling off a log," Dodd said. "After you get yourself a couple hundred thousand dollars into debt, the rest becomes second nature. You start with snide remarks and end up nearly killing the guys who used to be your best friends. At first, it's simple. It's you and your partners against the world. After you win the battles and things settle down, you start to wear on each other. I'm not ready for that."

"Okay," Massey agreed. He pulled nervously on his ponytail, centering it over the bald spot. "Then you be chief negotiator; someone else can be director."

"And if you don't like the decisions I make during negotiations, I get ridden out of town on a rail," Dodd countered.

"We'll sign a contract, whatever," Massey suggested.

"So who's going to be the boss? You? A.J.? Hilda? Persia?" Dodd asked, eyebrows raised higher with each name.

"Okay, no winners there," Massey agreed. "We'll hire someone we all can agree on, and sign an oath in blood that we'll live with your decisions."

"I'll think about it."

Massey jumped to his feet. He grabbed Dodd's hand and shook it vigorously. "Thanks, pal."

"I said, I'll think about it," Dodd repeated to deaf ears.

As Massey turned to leave the room, he noticed the huge black bird on top of the bookshelf, just out of reach. He examined it carefully and turned toward Dodd. "Someone did a great job of mounting that bird. It looks alive. That's the biggest crow I think I've ever seen."

"Raven," Dodd corrected Massey.

"What's the difference?"

"American crows are *Corvus brachyrhynchos*," Dodd explained. "Ravens are twice to three times their size, *Corvus corax*."

Massey eyed the black bird suspiciously. "Looks like a damned big crow to me," he said, letting himself out the door. He pulled it shut gently.

"Who's your taxidermist?" BeeBee asked, bounded down, to the desk and took several smaller hops toward the open window. The bird stopped in front of the computer monitor and examined the screen. "You have a full schedule, today, Spencer. It's going to be a busy month."

"Have you always been a pain in the ass?" Dodd asked the bird.

"*Ab ovo*,"[16] he said, climbing through the open window

and dropping to the ground. Dodd looked out, down at the bird on the freshly mowed lawn. BeeBee looked back at him, deep black eyes boring into the physician. *"Dependeto totum,"*[17] the bird said. Strong wings spread, forcing air toward the ground and lifting him into the sky. He disappeared over the top of the closest dormitory, Garrette Hall. Dodd shook his head.

Invictus

Chapter Thirteen
November 1ˢᵗ, One Hour Later

Inside Abramowicz's plush office, with the door closed tightly, the psychiatrist, Persia Summers, and Abramowicz faced one another. Summers screamed at him, "You louse!" How could you tell them about privatization? About all the ways it could be done?"

"I had to," Abramowicz protested, his immense bulk against the door to his office, hoping to smother the sounds of her voice. He did not want his personal secretary to hear them arguing. He prayed the noisy copier covered the scream. "Dean Waters told me I had to." Engulfing the psychiatrist with both arms, the administrator smothered her retort by clamping her head to his chest. "Calm down, Persia," he begged. "Calm down. Dodd is going to drive his comrades right into our arms. They may not like me, but they certainly have no use for a man who criticizes everything they do. I, at least, leave them alone."

Persia Summers relaxed in Abramowicz's arms. She nodded, leading him to think she agreed with him. He relaxed and let her slide slowly backward, out of his reach. "However," he said, "I did enjoy being close to you for a moment. Would you like to continue our conversation on the couch?" He held his hand out toward the two-seat sofa in the back of his office.

Still livid, Summers uncorked a right-handed slap that could be heard through the door and over the copier. Abramowicz's head snapped backward, colliding with the solid wood door. Stunned by both blows, he sank to the floor, moaning.

Terrified she might have seriously hurt him, and

worried she might also be trapped in the room and unable to move him to open the door, Summers knelt close to Abramowicz. She stroked the bright red cheek with the hand that still hurt from the force of the blow. "Oh, Neal, Neal," she cooed, "I'm so sorry. I lost my temper."

Abramowicz opened one eye and looked at her warily. "Damn, Persia," he asked, "why did you hit me?"

"I don't know, baby. I saw red," she lied. "Will you ever forgive me?"

Slowly, Abramowicz rolled to his knees. On all fours he rocked gently until he built up enough momentum to regain his feet. Summers held his arm and led him to his large, coastered chair, where he sat heavily. A knock sounded. J.P. Jones, his secretary, called warily, "Everything okay in there?"

"Fine," Abramowicz said. "Just fine, J.P. Hold all my calls please. Dr. Summers and I have to discuss something vital to the university." The assistant's footsteps backed cautiously away.

Summers eyed her hand print on Abramowicz's face and gave herself a nine for placement. She would like to have packed more power, but had she balled her fist, she was certain it would have broken on the man's jaw or eyebrow. As it was, her hand still stung. Reflexively, she repeatedly opened and closed the hand. The pain subsided.

"Feeling better?" Summers asked gently. Abramowicz nodded. She continued, "Now tell me, how we are going to alienate Dodd? It seems he has lit a fire under the practitioners. They certainly seemed more receptive to working for him than you."

Abramowicz explained, "First, they don't want to work for him. They just don't want to work for me. In their present positions, the state allows them to be autonomous. They are really responsible to no one. Unless, or until, they prove they are incapable of practicing medicine, I leave them alone. Dodd stays after them, makes them defend themselves if they act with less than his own vigor. He's incapable of letting them slide through life, when all they want is to be left alone, to put in their forty hours a week for nine months, and to practice medicine in their own little worlds."

"So, we just make them believe that you will allow them to continue to vegetate?" Summers asked.

"That," Abramowicz agreed, "and make certain they know that he would eliminate their pet projects as inefficient or unnecessary."

"Like the hypertension clinic A.J. runs for the seven hypertensives on campus?"

"And the wart clinic a certain retired neurosurgeon holds."

Summers saw a flaw in the plan. She said, "Some of these preventive medicine clinics have value."

"Damned few," Abramowicz disagreed. "I think we can save at least a hundred thousand dollars a year, a hundred grand you and I can split, dear Persia. For instance, we spent ten thousand dollars last year on the campaign to make everyone on campus aware that testicular cancer occurs in males between the ages of fifteen and forty-five."

"Why is that a waste of time?" Summers asked.

"There are only 7500 cases in the whole United States in an entire year; that's a hundred-fifty in all of Virginia. Dodd was right. If he spent an extra ten minutes with each male patient, he lost two hours of productive time per day."

Confused, Summers asked, "But you disagreed with him and forced them to do it, why?"

"Dean Waters liked it. It made him feel good to be able to tell the parents we practice preventive medicine, even if the United States Preventive Services Task Force thinks this is a crock."

"What about the cholesterol screening?"

"Same thing. Just like Dodd said. But von Weintraub loves the program. It gets her out of the clinic one afternoon a week. She'll hate it if Dodd tells her it has to go because the Task Force says it's a waste of time and money."

"And you'll keep it?"

Abramowicz laughed. "Hell, no. But, I'll make her think I will."

"What can we do to get the nurses on our side?" Summers asked.

"That's the best part. We don't have to do a damned thing. Given the opportunity, they'd string him up in a heartbeat."

"They'd lose the doughnuts he brings to work every Friday," Summers suggested.

"Even if he spends four or five hundred bucks a year on Christmas gifts and doughnuts, that won't save his ass. The Task Force recommends hypertension screening on all individuals; the nurses hate to take blood pressures and vital signs. He's history if he needs their support."

Warming to the plan, but curious how the administration above Abramowicz would receive it, she asked, "What can you tell Dean Waters about what you'll do, so he can assure the parents that we do practice preventive medicine? They certainly don't want to hear that we pass out free condoms and birth control pills."

Abramowicz nodded in agreement. "We'll avoid mentioning the condoms and pills, but our program will fit right in with the public's perceived need to eliminate alcohol from campus and keep tobacco products from juveniles. Those are high profile killers. Everyone is aware of them. Once we're in charge, we'll show Dean Waters the data, and we'll sink our money, what little we will spend on public health, into anti-smoking and anti-drinking campaigns. It'll look good. It'll feel good, but it won't accomplish much. That way we will impress the parents. Of course, the students won't be affected by a cheap campaign that rehashes everything they've heard hundreds of times before, so they won't be upset. The town retailers won't lose income; they'll stay happy. We'll be sitting pretty. Waters will appear successful to the administration. I'll look good here, and with luck everyone moves up a rung on the ladder."

"Except Dodd," Summers corrected.

"Except Dodd," Abramowicz agreed. "He not only moves down a rung, but probably has to get off the ladder altogether."

Coyly, Summers asked, "You do know how to run a medical clinic, right, honey?"

"What's to know?" Abramowicz asked scornfully. "Put patients with the doctors. Physicians have no business sense. They try to do everything they can to help the patients. The trick is limiting the amount of money they spend doing it. HMO's have known for years that they can run their businesses with high school graduates. The less their employees know about medicine and the younger they are, the less empathetic they are to the patient's plight. We're dealing with a mainly healthy population to begin with. The shoestring on which we will run this place leaves a lot leftover for the owners of the contract — you and me."

Summers reached for Abramowicz with both arms. He flinched and then ducked, rolling his chair backwards. "Silly man," she said, wrapping her thin, dark-skinned arms around his neck. "You are a genius. You deserve a reward." Gently, she nibbled on his ear. He purred. Over his shoulder, Summers saw the pictures of the nude women on the monitor. His favorite choices all looked as if they originated with a clan of individuals who qualified for a group discount on stomach bypass surgery. Wincing, she kept her thoughts to herself. Why not ride this fat man's coattails to something more pleasurable than dealing with student drug addicts, those with eating disorders, alcoholics, and psychopaths?

Bill Yancey

The phone rang. Abramowicz waved off the psychiatrist temporarily and answered the phone. J.P. Jones spoke in his ear. "Sorry, boss, Dean Waters wants to speak to you."

"Put him through," Abramowicz said. He placed his thick hand over the mouthpiece and spoke to Summers. "Dean Waters," he whispered, "quiet."

The phone clicked, Waters spoke to Abramowicz in his earthy, southern drawl, "Neal?"

"Yes, sir," Abramowicz said.

"Just calling to see how the doctors liked our idea about making student health a for-profit organization?"

Abramowicz beamed, winking at Summers. "Actually, sir, they loved the idea. All except one man, that is, Dr. Dodd. Of course, no one expected he'd like it."

"He's the outspoken one?" Waters asked. "He's the physician who argues about everything, isn't he?"

"Yes, sir, that's the one."

Waters surprised Abramowicz with a suggestion. "Well, you might listen to some of what he says, Neal," he said. "It never pays to have too many yes men on the staff. Understand?"

"Yes, sir," Abramowicz answered snappily, unaware of the irony in agreeing with his supervisor.

"Oh, and by the way," Waters continued, "the missus and I are going to have a get together after the football game on homecoming weekend. We'd like you to come; bring a guest. You'll have to start calling me Murray, though. President Furneaux will be there. I think we can get a couple of cocktails into him and then lay the plan on him. Will you be ready for that?"

"Yes, sir-ah Murray," Abramowicz responded. "Absolutely, sir. I'll be ready. I will also talk with Dr. Dodd and see what his concerns are. You can rest assured, sir, that his ideas will be given every consideration."

Invictus

Chapter Fourteen
Evening of November 1ˢᵗ and Early Morning of November 2ⁿᵈ

Dodd, on the rolling stool, gazed steadily into the eyes of the student sitting on the examination table. The disheveled patient returned the stare, a sullen look on his unshaven face. Threads and foam padding hung from disintegrating seams of the dirty baseball cap, on backwards. Stone Garrette's unkempt hair sprouted in several directions from under the hatband. Dark bags under Garrette's eyes showed fatigue. Slumped forward, hands twitching unnaturally, the young man wore an inside-out gray sweatshirt, long athletic shorts with the Southwestern Virginia University Black Bear logo, and dilapidated soccer flats, no socks. For a chilly autumn day in the mountains of southwestern Virginia, Garrette wore too few layers.

"So, Stone," Dodd started the conversation, "what brings you in?"

"A red Porsche Targa, my roommate's car," Garrette replied, eyes not leaving the doctor. A pained grin crept across the young man's face.

"Touché," Dodd acknowledged the joke. "Why are you here?"

"I'm tired."

"Go home and go to bed," Dodd suggested, knowing the easy answer would not suffice. "In fact, stay in bed the whole weekend. Looks like it might rain all day today and tomorrow. I know that's what I'm going to do after they lock the doors this evening." Dodd looked at his watch. "In nineteen minutes and twenty-seven seconds, not that I'm counting."

Bill Yancey

"Not sleepy," Garrette explained, "tired of competing with my old man. I've tried, Doc, but I'm not the man he is. I'm so damned tired." Garrette slumped even further on the table, leaning backward against the wall. He pulled one knee to his chest, placing his shoe on the paper on the table. His hands shook; he wrapped his arms around the leg. The paper tore where his shoe rested on it. "Sorry," he apologized.

"No problem. Everyone gets new paper," Dodd told him. "Why do you think you are competing with your father?"

Garrette shrugged. "He's a success. I'm a failure, an alcoholic who can't decide on a major, can't graduate. I have enough credits, but if I picked a major today, I'd still need two years." He wiped a tear from his eye. Dodd waited for him to continue, not wanting to rush him. "Pop dropped out of high school to support his family. His father was killed in the Korean War. He started by selling newspapers. Now, he owns a media empire: three newspapers, nine radio stations, five television stations, all sorts of stuff."

"Have you talked with him about this?" Dodd asked.

Garrette stared at his holey shoes, dirty bare feet visible through the torn leather sides. "Sure," he said. "'Get an education,' is all he says, plus, 'I never got an education.' He wants me to get his degree for him."

"Then what?" Dodd asked.

"Then what, what?"

Dodd elaborated, "After you get a degree, then what? Does he want you to work for him, manage his money, run a radio station, what?"

"We never talk about that," Garrette admitted. "Doesn't matter, I guess. Don't know if I want to be around."

Worried about Garrette's state of mind, Dodd asked the young man, "Are you suicidal?"

Invictus

"I don't want to be around him. I'm more homicidal than suicidal, I think." Garrette laughed. "If I see him in this condition, I'll kill him for the years of torture."

"Which condition?"

"I've stopped drinking," Garrette stated. "Cold Turkey. I'm a little hyper, but I've got it under control."

"You need some help, don't you?" Dodd suggested.

Garrette sat silently staring at Dodd. He pulled his other leg onto the bed and sat cross-legged. Eventually, he hung his head, nodding. The tears flowed. "I've never asked for help before, Doc. It's a sign of weakness in my family. If you can't do it yourself, 'with grit,' as the old man says, then you're not a man."

Dodd placed a hand on Garrette's knee. He said, "Your dad is a rare person, Stone. Not many people can emulate him. In fact, he himself couldn't duplicate his success in today's world, in your shoes. A rare combination of deprivation and drive fueled him. He's like a nuclear breeder reactor, feeding on itself. If he's lucky he will burn out slowly; if not, he may explode. If you are interested, I had a similar experience and survived. My father graduated from West Point. If you listened to him, you'd think he ran the mighty 8th Air Force and won World War II by himself. He flew forty-eight bombing missions over Germany, and commanded a bomber wing in Korea. Retired Lieutenant General. Boy was he upset when I quit the Point."

"You went to West Point?" Garrette asked.

"Briefly. I should have done what my original roommate did and quit the first night. I waited through the summer and one semester, about seven months. I still have bad dreams about the experience. When I enlisted in the Navy, he disowned me. Took him thirty years to admit I wasn't a total failure, or for me to recognize he didn't think I was a failure. That wasn't until after I became a doctor. Although, he never let me forget my shortcomings. His getting Alzheimer's disease was a blessing for me. Now, he can't remember all the ways I disappointed him."

"You know what I'm feeling, don't you?" Garrette asked the doctor.

Dodd patted Garrette's leg. "Absolutely," he said. "Well, some of it anyway. You'd like to drink him under the table, but his liver is bigger than yours. It's a fight you'll never win. Let me call Dr. Summers. We can get you some help. Okay?" Garrette nodded. Tears soaked the thin, white paper between his legs, turning it transparent.

Dodd left him sitting on the exam table. He closed the door slowly behind himself, flipped the door flag to indicate the patient was still in the room, and walked across the hall to his office, where he dialed the five digit code to Counseling. "Hello. This is Dr. Dodd. I need to speak with Dr. Summers urgently," he told the receptionist. "Yes, I know it's Friday afternoon, and no, I don't care what she is doing. I have a psychiatric patient for her to see."

Eventually, Summers came to the phone. The chill in her voice reached through the line and slapped him. "Yes, Spencer?"

"Persia," Dodd said, ignoring her tone of voice, "Stone Garrette is in one of my exam rooms. He's tried to quit drinking. It looks like he's getting ready to go into delirium tremens. He may be a danger to himself or others. I'll have one of the nurses walk him up, if you want."

"I'll come down there," Summers decided. "He'll need a physical exam for admission. Will you do it?"

Dodd thought about asking her if the M.D. after her name stood for medical doctor, massive debt, or manic depressive, but thought better of it. "Okay," he said. "Give me ten minutes. Can you interview him then?"

"I'll be there."

Dodd returned to the exam room. "Dr. Summers is going to come down here and talk with you," he told Garrette. "Slip off your shirt, so I can do a quick physical on you."

Silently, Garrette stood and bared his chest by removing the dirty sweat shirt, after pulling off his hat. He dropped both onto the floor at his feet and sat again on the table, eyes downcast. "They're going to put me in the hospital, aren't they?" he asked quietly.

"Could be," Dodd agreed. "That might be the best place for you. How long have you had the shakes?"

"About six hours."

"Quit drinking when, Monday or Tuesday?"

"Tuesday. That's what's causing this?"

Dodd nodded. "Withdrawal. Any auditory or visual hallucinations?" Garrette gave Dodd a quizzical look. Dodd rephrased the question, "See anything or hear anything you thought didn't exist?"

"Not yet. Will I? That sounds scary."

"It happens sometimes. The medicine Dr. Summers will give you helps prevent that." Dodd touched the long, thin, pink, new scar on Garrette's tanned, muscular back. A very sharp object had sliced his skin cleanly from the middle of his neck to the top of his left shoulder blade. "Been in a knife fight?" Dodd asked.

"Coral," Garrette said. I joined the scuba club last spring. Have to do something with all my free time."

Dodd nodded, placed the stethoscope in his ears, and listened to the young man breathe. "Deeper, faster," he coached.

"A beautiful woman once told me the same thing," Garrette laughed miserably.

"Sorry," Dodd said, removing the plastic tips of the stethoscope from his ears. "What did you say?"

"I'm a quitter, Doc. I took flying lessons and quit after I soloed. Never got a license. Did rock climbing. Quit the club after learning the basics. Caving, same thing. Scuba club, too. Get the basics and quit. No stamina. Drives my old man batty that I quit. He never quit anything.

Just kept pounding until he succeeded or killed his competition." Garrette wiped his dripping nose with the back of his hand.

"Open wide. Say, 'ah,'" Dodd told the young man. "Let me look in your ears. Your father is not perfect. Sounds like the two of you have a difficult time communicating. How well do you get along with your mother?"

"Which one of my four step-mothers are you asking about? He drove my real mother away. Her family thinks she's hiding from him, somewhere in Seattle."

A knock sounded at the door. "That's probably Dr. Summers," Dodd told Garrette. "Be honest with her. Answer her questions." Garrette nodded sullenly. Eyes downcast, he dressed slowly.

Dodd opened the door. He nodded to Summers and then introduced her to Garrette. "Stone, this is Dr. Summers. Persia, Stone Garrette. I'll be in my office if you need anything," he told them both.

He watched Summers reach for and shake Garrette's hand. "Nice to meet you," she said pleasantly to start the conversation. "Dr. Dodd says you want some help with an alcohol problem...." Closing the door softly behind him, he left the two alone.

Dodd walked across the hall to his office. Summers's briefcase sat on his desk, draped with her raincoat. He swivelled the desk chair and propped his feet on the window sill. Between his crossed feet, he watched a short, portly campus cop in a yellow slicker, with a gray handle bar mustache, work the Friday evening quitting-time traffic. With obvious experience, the man motioned to the drivers; but even he could not stop the car that locked its brakes and skidded on the rain-soaked asphalt into the side of a pick-up truck. The closing speed was less than five miles per hour, but there was a long screech before and a dull thump when the two vehicles collided. Dodd dropped his feet and leaned forward, curious if there had been any injuries. Both drivers, coeds, hopped from their vehicles and inspected the damages. At least they have a credible witness in the cop, Dodd thought.

The exam room door slammed behind Dodd. He spun the chair and found himself facing Summers. "He won't go into the hospital," she said, closing the office door behind her.

Rather than stand, as he knew a gentleman would — his father certainly would have jumped to his feet — Dodd pointed to the chair. Summers sat. "Do you think he's suicidal?" he asked.

She shook her head. "Not right now. He's certainly at risk, however."

Surprised that Garrette had changed his mind, Dodd told Summers, "He was willing to go into the hospital when I talked with him, although I didn't explain everything you would do to him. What happened?"

"I had him call his father...."

"Why?" Dodd asked.

"To make certain he had insurance or his father would cover the cost of the admission. Hospitalization is expensive, Spencer."

"You know who his father is?" Dodd asked. She nodded. "He has more money than God."

"But we can't spend it without his permission," she explained.

"So what did he say?"

Summers shrugged. "I don't know," she said. "I never talked with the man. Stone talked with him. Then he refused to go to the hospital."

Dodd stood up. "Well, maybe I can change his mind." He opened the office door. Across the hall the door to the exam room was wide open, Garrette no longer in the room. Desperate, Dodd jogged to the back door of the health center. As he reached the glass door, the large spoiler on the tail of a fire engine red Porsche waved good-bye; the vehicle accelerated quickly from the parking lot. He watched the huge airfoil recede in the distance. Making a fist, Dodd pounded on the glass.

While he beat on the door ineffectively, Summers sauntered toward him. "Don't break the glass," she said sarcastically. In her hands she carried her briefcase and raincoat.

"We missed an opportunity to make a difference," Dodd said, leaning his forehead on clasped hands on the glass door.

***

The phone rang in Dodd's efficiency. He looked at his watch. Just after midnight. Struggling to see in the dark, he found the phone by Braille. "Dodd," he said.

A female voice spoke to him. "Dr. Dodd, this is dispatch at the university. The rescue squad has asked that I contact you. They have a problem. As you are their faculty advisor, they want your assistance at Sykes Hall, the recreational sports and student health building."

"What kind of problem?" Dodd asked.

"This is an unofficial call, Dr. Dodd. I can't say." The dispatcher hung up.

Dodd realized he had not heard the usual beep-beep in the background that meant the conversation had been recorded. His heightened sense of responsibility ('Never explain; never complain,' Dodd's old man had preached.) took over. He pulled on the clothes he had dropped on the floor next to the bed, and slipped his feet into the worn flight boots without socks. Certain that Cody Gray, with his lacerated arm, had been found in the building, he hopped into the Miata, top still down. Cold night air woke him quickly.

It took almost no time to cover the block to campus and the half mile to the recreational sports building. Dodd found a scene reminiscent of his emergency medicine days. Red and blue lights flashed from several different police vehicles. Two ambulances were parked on the grass, also with lights flashing. A group of men, two opposing teams from a rugby scrum, faced one another in the middle of the expansive sidewalk leading to the front of the building. One of the rescue trainees ran to Dodd. Panting between words, he told the physician, "Someone jumped. They won't let us treat him."

"Oh, shit," Dodd said. "Who?"

"Don't know," the pimpled-faced kid answered. "They want us to pronounce him dead, but they won't let us treat him.

Having heard enough, Dodd strode purposely past the young man, and bellowed, "Who's in charge here?" A uniformed officer, in a tightly pressed blue uniform covered by a gray five gallon hat, held up his hand. "Where's the patient?" Dodd asked.

"Body," the officer corrected Dodd.

Dodd stopped walking, inches in front of the officer. He looked the man directly in the eye, noting the gray mustache and the name, Grier, on the bronze name tag. Three chevrons decorated the short sleeve shirt. A muscular chest and arms filled the uniform. Dodd did not flinch when the officer puffed out his chest in Dodd's direction, daring him to challenge the policeman's jurisdiction. He spoke slowly and clearly so the officer would have no trouble understanding the situation. "Sgt. Grier, the injured party is a patient, until someone pronounces him dead. *Then* he becomes a corpse. The State of Virginia gives you the authority to declare a person dead. Since you called the rescue squad, you obviously don't feel qualified. I suggest you and your men get out of the rescue squad's way. If you delay their evaluation any longer, the patient's family may have grounds to sue you for preventing him from receiving medical care. If he dies, your interference may be criminal neglect. Now, where is the *patient*?"

The officer pursed his lips. Not answering, he surrendered the field. He turned and walked toward the front door; the other officers quit obstructing the rescue squad. Three of the squad's medics ran to the building. On the cement walk in front of the door lay the crumpled body. Gently, protecting his neck and back as best they could, they rolled the man over.

"How long ago did this happen?" Dodd asked the group of officers.

One of the policemen replied, "Someone called in a man climbing the stone face of the building about eleven. I searched the building for him and finally found him about fifteen minutes ago. He had climbed the front wall to the cooling tower. He was dancing along the ledge at the second level. About five minutes later, as the squad and other officers were arriving, he slipped or jumped." Dodd gazed at the roughly hewn rock that defined the front of the building. Mentally, he visualized a person climbing the wall, looking for hand holds, placing his feet in precisely the right places, and working his way to the ledge above the second floor.

"Weak pulse, Doc!" a medic called.

"Bradycardia on the monitor," said another.

"One line in; starting the second," a third added.

Dodd knelt next to the young man, afraid to look at the face. When he did, he realized the patient was not Cody Gray, but Stone Garrette. Several large lacerations, massive swelling, and the blue discoloration of his skin distorted his features. While Dodd stared at the young man, the boy opened his eyes. Recognizing Dodd's face, Garrette tried to smile. Painfully moving his jaw, he whispered through the broken, bloody teeth and lips, "The spiders were after me, Doc. Spiders." The eyes closed.

"Start a third line. Try to find a blood pressure. Oxygen. Bag him," a paramedic directed his squad of life savers.

Invictus

Dodd stood up and backed away from the paramedics, arms sweeping the policemen behind him. That allowed the paramedics to do their job without interference from him or the officers. In years prior he would have insisted on helping and probably would have hindered them. He had learned; they do best in the field if left alone. They would ask if they wanted assistance. For thirty minutes, he leaned against the side of his Miata watching the paramedics resuscitate Garrette. Eventually, the ambulance rolled out of sight, toward the helicopter landing zone near the administration building. A Life Flight helicopter from a hospital in Roanoke would be there to meet them shortly after they arrived with their patient.

The officer who had been in charge, Sgt. Grier, walked over to Dodd after the ambulance departed. Chin on chest, hands crumpling his hat, he spoke. "Doc."

Dodd held up his hand, not wanting to hear an apology. Anger raged inside his chest: at Summers, at Garrette, at Garrette's father, and at the officers. Finally, he spoke, terse, mean sentences. "Do you know what a self-fulfilling prophesy is?" he asked rhetorically, then answered before the officer could. "If you had kept us from him for a few more minutes, he would have been dead. You would have been right. These guys are patients until rescue says they are corpses, understand?" The officer nodded. "If you ever keep the rescue squad from evaluating a patient again, I'll sue you myself. If you want to pronounce people dead, fine. Do it. Don't wake us up in the middle of the night to cover up your mistakes." Dodd wanted to say more, to tell him how unlikely it was that Garrette would survive, and that if he did he would probably be a cripple for life. The words stuck in his throat. He slid over the door of his car and dropped into the driver's seat. While the cop watched, Dodd drove away from campus, toward Route 58, Interstate 81, and Roanoke, two hundred miles and several hours away by car.

BeeBee rode on the folded top, leaning into the wind. *"Aegroto, dum anima est, spes esse dicitur,"*[18] the bird said. The car slipped through the dark, cool night. The cold front had passed through the region more quickly than the weatherman had predicted. Stars shone throughout the clear dark sky. Headlights reflected off the moist blacktop made the oncoming traffic doubly bright.

"I hope the university paid its malpractice premium this month," Dodd answered.

"Primum est non nocere.[19] Hippocrates," the bird said.

"No. The *first* thing we do, let's kill all the lawyers. Shakespeare. *Henry VI,*" Dodd corrected the raven. "Then we do no *more* harm."

"Good plan," BeeBee admitted.

Invictus

Chapter Fifteen
November 6th

Downtown Fawsville died after the Southwestern Agriculture College became a university. The abrupt escalation in the size of the student body necessitated a precipitous boom in apartments, music stores, clothing stores, and fast food outlets. Surrounded by the University and the Poor Valley Ridge of Cumberland Mountain, Fawsville had nowhere to grow, except upward. Several attempts were made to build high rise apartments and parking garages. After one new townhouse complex disappeared — fortunately, before being occupied — into a sink hole formed over a huge limestone cavern in the karst topography, the residents nixed further construction.

Real estate developers then snapped up outlying farms, closer to Route 58; strip malls and more transformed the landscape of Lee County. Most businesses escaped the confines of the town to reestablish themselves in the more spacious outlying commercial properties.

For those small businesses forced to remain close to campus, the cramped remains of central Fawsville's three-block-square downtown section barely sufficed. Entrepreneurs paid premium lease prices for floor space in tiny, subdivided buildings. A computer start-up rented two hundred square feet of office space on the second floor of a dilapidated building. Five hundred feet of floor space more went to a compact disc exchange. Twelve hundred square feet became the Bear's Den, a restaurant in what used to be the moldy basement in the home of the first president of the agriculture college.

Dodd sat in the booth in the Bear's Den. Smoke from

burnt food and cigarettes, so thick that asthma patients routinely keeled over at the entrance before they entered the establishment, formed a ceiling-hugging haze that made it difficult for him to see Hilda von Weintraub at the far end of the table. She and A.J. Watson had pulled their chairs closer to join the discussion. In addition to them, the practitioners had packed six people into a four-person booth, with Dodd farthest from the aisle. "If there's a fire, I'm dead," Dodd told Clint Massey, who pressed tightly against him.

"What?" Massey asked. The loud music drowned most of the discussion. Dodd never heard the words to the songs, although his seat vibrated with the bass that reverberated through floor, walls, and furniture. A string puppet resembling Pinocchio, hanging on the wall opposite Dodd, seized with each bass chord blasted through the air. There were times when being half deaf made sense. Of course, the next generation would also be hard of hearing and without having the benefit of military service or spending time listening to the whine of jet engines on an aircraft carrier.

"Who's going to check on the costs of insurances? Malpractice, Workers Compensation, Liability, whatever." Dodd asked.

"Hilda," Massey answered. "Since she already has a private practice, she has access to an agent."

Turning to face Massey, so his friend could more easily read his lips, Dodd asked, "Billing stuff? Computer. Codes. Insurance reimbursement. HMOs."

"Unless your friend, the nurse with the MBA, shows up, I'll do it," Massey volunteered. "Do we have any idea what the budget looks like now? It would be a lot easier to make a meaningful bid if we had that information."

Dodd smiled, revealing the one ace up his sleeve. "It's a public institution. I know all of the university employees' salaries are available in the library. I'll see if the school

Invictus

budget is there, too. Health services should be a part of that. May take a couple days to track down the information."

A.J. stood at the far end of the booth; Von Weintraub had already departed. He threw a ten dollar bill onto the beer slicked table and waved at Dodd. His lips moved; Dodd tried to read words into the movement. He thought the diminutive doctor said something about meeting the wife or getting a life, and work tomorrow. Dodd waved good-bye. A.J. spun his wobbly wooden chair around and slipped it under the table behind him. A passing intoxicated student immediately pulled the chair out and slid it farther down the floor to another crowded table.

Business meeting complete, the group of doctors, nurse practitioners, and physicians' assistants began to disperse. Money fell onto the table between the beer bottles and crusts left over from burnt pizza. Moving away from Dodd to give them both some breathing room, Massey gathered all the bills together. "How much more do we need?" Dodd asked reaching for his wallet.

"I'll get this if you pick up the tip," Massey said. "Ten each should cover it." Dodd handed Massey a twenty, pulling a wet, sticky ten dollar bill from his colleague's hand.

"Thanks," Massey said. Abruptly, he asked, "How's Stone?" He watched Dodd carefully, wondering how the question affected him. Dodd tried to hide his response. Beneath the blond hair, mixed with a touch of well-hidden gray, Massey saw his friend's face blanch. Lips tightened; Dodd's stomach knotted. Facial muscles trembled, then relaxed. Dodd willed himself to take a deep breath.

"He's lucky to be alive," Dodd replied. "His skeleton basically exploded upon impact. They counted thirty-two separate fractures, and those are just the ones they can see. He spent seventeen hours in surgery the first night; they expect he'll have several more procedures before he can go to rehabilitation. That'll take a year, minimum."

"Ouch," Massey winced. "This is going to cost his old man a fortune."

"Which means he probably won't be giving one to the university," Dodd observed. "The finger pointing has already started. Neal wants me to be the scapegoat, I think. My choice would be Summers for not admitting him, but the real villain is his father. The corporate lawyers are likely scouring the country looking for world-class malpractice specialists. Garrette Enterprises might make money in the end, given a big enough settlement."

Skeptical, Massey asked, "What malpractice?"

Dodd explained his interpretation of the American legal system concerning civil law. "Anyone can sue anyone else for anything at any time for any amount of money: the motto of the American Trial Lawyers Association. Even if they don't win the case, the lawyers make money."

"The great American lottery," Massey commiserated. A smirk appeared on the hippy physician's face. "I have my eye on an uneven patch of sidewalk in front of the new bicycle shop in town. Next ice storm, I plan to suffer a crippling back injury."

Dodd smiled. He pushed Massey toward the end of the bench. "Got to go, Clinton. Tomorrow there will be colds, sore throats, and other lives to save."

"Joie will be happy we quit early, unless, of course, I tell her that you may be her boss some day," Massey noted.

"I'm never going to be the boss, but if I were, she'd be the first one fired. Actually, I would probably assign her to be A.J.'s private nurse, just to bug him." Dodd chuckled while Massey paid the cashier. Massey followed Dodd to the door and up the rickety steps to ground level in the middle of Fawsville. Cool, fresh air greeted them. Widely dispersed white clouds cast dark shadows from the bright town lights toward the mountains and constellations above them; Orion hung in the southern sky, seemingly close enough to touch. A low cumulus cloud obscured most of Cumberland Mountain.

Weekends had a way of expanding or contracting depending on the workload of the students. Even though midterm exams neared, some students did less work than others. They celebrated life and freedom from parental constraints from Thursday through Tuesday. Although the pedestrian traffic did not approach that of the nominal Saturday/Sunday weekend, Dodd knew the streets would never completely empty. He shook hands with Massey and walked toward his apartment, three blocks distant. Massey plodded toward his car in the small parking. He played house with LaFlamé, north of town in a rented condominium, in a subdivision populated by faculty and their families.

"Yo, Doc," someone called as Dodd waited to cross the street. Dodd turned his head, then spun on his heels trying to locate the owner of the voice. In front of the Nite Owl coffee shop, Cody Gray waved. Dodd walked toward him along the curb, dodging partying students.

"Out late?" Dodd asked. "Some coincidence running into you at this time of night. Your studies should keep your nose buried in some very technical text books."

"No coincidence. I knew where to find you," Gray said. He lowered his voice and stepped closer to the physician. "I need to show you something, Spence."

"Can it wait?" Dodd asked, exhausted. "I got very little sleep over the weekend, and I've been working overtime this week putting together the contract bid."

Grabbing Dodd's arm, and speaking more emphatically, Gray elaborated, "All your work will be for naught if you don't come back to your office with me tonight."

Dodd shrugged. "I doubt that."

"Seriously, Doc," Gray whispered. "It won't take but a couple minutes to convince you. If I'm wrong, you will miss but thirty minutes sleep."

Bill Yancey

An intoxicated student staggered into the street near Dodd. A driver slammed on the brakes, swerving to miss the young man. The screeching tires startled Dodd. Reflexively, the physician grabbed the drunk's left arm with his left hand and pulled the young man out of the street. "Hey, buddy, how you doing?" Dodd asked the drunk in an exceptionally friendly voice.

"Jesh great," the boy slobbered. Eyes red, he weaved to and fro, having difficulty maintaining his balance. The smile on his face turned to a look of concern. He held up one finger. Bending at the waist, he rotated his body and vomited in the direction of the lamp post, splashing beer and wine onto his own shoes. The stench of stomach acid tainted by alcohol wafted upward, wrinkling Dodd and Gray's noses. The drunk turned around again to face his new friends, big grin on his face. "Buds," he said ebulliently. "How about some Bud for my buds?"

Gray grabbed the drunk's other arm. He looked at Dodd for direction. "Where to?" he asked.

Dodd tilted his head toward the center of town. "O'Toole is nearby," Dodd explained. "I saw the police car. Let's walk south." Arms locked, the trio staggered toward the restaurant district of the tiny village.

They found O'Toole writing a parking ticket for a Vespa scooter. The owner left it parked on the sidewalk and chained to a lamp post. Officer O'Toole had been one of the night watch in Fawsville since he graduated from the agriculture college before it became a university. Over thirty years, he had seen a lot of changes. As retirement approached and he aged, O'Toole took less interest in the students. His eyesight slowly failed, along with his hearing; his reaction time slowed. Shriveled hands and wasted muscles, along with the heavily creased sun-exposed areas of his body, made him look ten years older than his actual age. Working as a farmer during the day and as an officer at night destroyed his once athletic body. O'Toole lived

Invictus

for the last day of the year and his move to a retirement community in Florida.

Unable to tolerate another winter in the mountains, or one more semester of self-indulgent students, his wife had packed and left town before the students returned in the fall. Already entrenched in Fort Lauderdale, she freely spent the real estate developer's money. (A corporation bought their small dairy farm, intent upon building yet another shopping center, College Center Square.) O'Toole hoped some of the money would still be in her possession by the time he arrived in the sunshine state. All around him, underage students stifled laughter and walked upright until they were out of sight. O'Toole ignored them. He had had his fill of inebriated students over the years. Better to let them go home and aggravate someone else. If they weren't dangerous, he intended to leave them be.

"Officer O'Toole," Dodd called cheerily.

The officer ripped the ticket from his pad. After stuffing it under a strap on top of the Naugahyde covered seat of the scooter, he folded the pad and tucked it into his paperwork holster. Dramatically, he slid his well worn mechanical pencil into the correct slot, closed the leather cover, and snapped the clasp. Slowly, he turned to face Dodd; his features mirrored his weariness with his profession and life. "Yes, sir," the older man answered politely.

"Can you give this young man a safe drive home?" Dodd asked. The boy's eyes grew big when he realized he stood face-to-face with a police officer. His head turned rapidly, eyes looking first at Gray, then Dodd. Legs weak, he sagged slightly between them. They caught him by his armpits.

"What's his name?" O'Toole asked. Dodd shrugged.

"Bryan Bliss," the young man blurted.

"Where does he live?" O'Toole asked. Dodd and Gray looked at the soused student. He shrugged.

O'Toole sized up the young man swaying uncertainly

in front of him, He realized that he was probably underage and very, very intoxicated. "If I take him, he has to be under arrest."

"Come on," Gray started, "if we let him go, he'll walk in front of a truck."

Adamant, O'Toole recited, "Sorry, that's the rules."

"It's okay, Cody," Dodd interrupted. Deftly, he reached for O'Toole's handcuffs, hanging on the officer's belt. Before the older man could react, Dodd slapped one end around the drunk's arm and the other on O'Toole's wrist. "Think of this as a learning experience," Dodd told Bliss, and Gray indirectly, slapping the drunk on his back. "We wouldn't want you to leave college without learning at least one real life lesson."

"Hey, you can't do that," O'Toole protested. Dodd shrugged, smiled, and turned to walk away from the officer and his new charge. Gray followed.

"That was low," Gray told Dodd angrily.

"Live and learn," Dodd said. "You said yourself he was a danger to himself."

"Still...."

Dodd and Gray walked swiftly toward Sykes hall, Gray's home. Hands in their coat pockets to ward off the chill, they walked in silence until they passed the cemetery. "Almost died here when I was a student," Dodd said.

"You went to school here?" Gray asked. Dodd continued his stride.

Dodd pulled the zipper higher on his leather coat and shoved his hands deeper into his pockets. Head lowered, he sagged forward slightly. He confessed, "Went to five colleges. I finished my undergraduate degree here at SVU. The day after graduation, we had a party. I drank too much. One of my friend's graduation presents was a new motorcycle. He convinced me to take it for a ride. I had never been on a motorcycle before; but what the hell, they're just like a powered bike, right?" Gray shrugged, not certain. "Wrong," Dodd continued. "After a five minute lesson, I took it out for a spin." Dodd pulled one hand from a pocket and waved it at an invisible road. "Before they built that apartment complex, there was a gentle left curve that followed the edge of the cemetery. I was speeding along leaning into the curve when I realized that a car was headed in my direction. The wheels of the motorcycle were in the right lane, but I leaned into the opposite one. It was either straighten up, or leave my face on the car's bumper."

"What did you do?"

Mentally reconstructing the painful memory, Dodd said quietly, "I straightened up, flew off the side of the road at about fifty miles an hour. If you'll look carefully at the next headstone, you'll see it belongs to a guy named Miles Linkous. He died in 1871, on my birthday, September 21st. That's where I landed. The bike was totaled."

Gray ran ahead and onto the grass. He examined the inscription on the headstone. "Ironic," he called to Dodd.

Dodd continued moving, never slowing his pace toward their objective. "Coincidence," he corrected. "Almost every year since the old agriculture school became a university, at least one student has died from alcohol abuse. No one died that year. I often wonder if I was the guy who was supposed to."

A light shone from Abramowicz's office window. Gray pointed to it and motioned to Dodd. The doctor nodded, understanding they had to move quickly and quietly to get to the third floor apartment without being detected. "You could go crazy thinking stuff like that," Gray offered while Dodd unlocked the door to student health.

"Crazy enough to talk to birds?" Dodd asked, winking at the raven that swooped close to the glass door. He locked it behind them.

"Yeah, I guess," Gray replied absent-mindedly, walking with practiced ease through the dimly lit medical clinic to the back stairwell. "Do you do that?"

Dodd trailed the young man, taking the steps one at a time instead of Gray's two or three. "Just one bird, actually. A black bird; his name is B.B., or BeeBee, for Black Bird."

Gray waited at the top landing, door already unlocked and open. "I hope he doesn't talk back," the student said with a chuckle. He pulled the door shut and locked it behind them.

The two men walked slowly through the dark room in front of the apartment. "Only on special occasions," Dodd replied. "Now, why do I need to be here when I am suffering from sleep deprivation?"

Gray bolted the door to the apartment. Lit only by the computer monitor's screen saver, the room could have seemed spooky, if Dodd had been faint of heart. Gray strode to the monitor quickly, knowing where all the hidden obstructions lay. Dodd followed exactly in his footsteps so as to miss the mines. "This is why," Gray said, sitting on the five gallon bucket and moving the mouse. The screen sprang to life, lighting the room more fully. Dodd stood next to Gray and stared at the email he had sent to Massey earlier in the day. "The meeting is still on at the Bear's Den. 7 p.m. Leave LaFlamé at home."

"You're reading my email, Cody." Dodd observed, unconcerned. "Don't waste your time; it's not at all titillating."

"Actually," Gray announced, "I'm reading Dr. Abramowicz's monitor. I...ah...borrowed the software he uses to spy on you and your colleagues. He's reading your email. Anything he puts on his screen, I can read, just as he can read yours."

Dodd swore, "Shit, he's eavesdropping on us." The screen changed. Rows of numbers appeared. "What's that?"

"A spreadsheet."

"Spread — sheet. That's Spanish for 'disperse the

manure, isn't it?'" Dodd joked. Watching the numbers scroll across the screen, he felt a tightening in his stomach. "Can you record that information, save it to a file?"

Gray's hands flew across the keyboard. A whirring noise clattered from behind the desk. "I'm saving it on my video tape backup. Why?"

"It looks suspiciously like the student health budget. We can use those numbers," Dodd explained. "I'm beginning to think that I will like firing that unethical bastard someday."

"Isn't that information supposed to be confidential?" Gray asked.

"Since this is a public institution, the real budget is a matter of public record," Dodd said. "You're going to save me the trouble of having to find it in the library."

Gray observed, "That may not be the real budget. That might be his projected budget."

A sour expression crept across Dodd's face. "Thanks, Cody," he said. "Now I have to find the real budget anyway, just to compare the two."

Bill Yancey

Invictus

Chapter Sixteen
November 16th

A chill settled on the homecoming celebrations as the sun set behind Cumberland Mountain. The sunlight dimmed; street lamps on campus in the shadows of large buildings began to light sporadically. Soon, they all would be lit. In the huge parking lot reserved for alumni, Dodd stood at the periphery of several intersecting tailgate parties. He had difficulty deciding where one stopped and the next began. The radiuses of the parties varied with the size of the vehicles hosting them, he assumed. All around him, just outside vans, mini-vans, campers, trailers, luxury motor homes, and an occasional dropped tailgate to a classic, antique, or just battered old-fashioned station wagon, hundreds of people frolicked. Homecoming meant revelry. The Black Bear Alumni from the four corners of the world returned to 'The Den' to watch the current Black Bear football team maul a suitably chosen, weak opponent. Outcome rarely in doubt this one week of the football season, the party-goers laid wagers on how big the point spread would be on the final score.

One group of revelers most intrigued Dodd. A short, feisty man with a ruddy complexion, white hair, and a bevy of beautiful women acting as hostesses, stood in the middle of the parking lot closest to the football stadium, Linkous Field. Dodd entered the space carved out by the party, but he wandered the rim, listening to the conversation, in no hurry to approach the host.

The usual banter between young and old alumni assaulted him, loud to even his ears. Every conversation seemed to transpire in the upper limits of the noise level tolerated by the human eardrum. The high decibel level deliberations occurred because the parking lot was crowded with dialogue. Many of the participants had imbibed too much already, even though the nationally televised game would not hit the airwaves for another hour. Television broadcasters demanded the show start after 7:00 p.m. to achieve the highest possible rating. Stone Garrette's father, Murphy Garrette, the tycoon whose fledgling communications empire and network broadcast the football game, held court at the center of the party that Dodd circled warily.

Dodd watched and listened with fascination. An elderly white, wrinkled old man dressed in a letter sweater and leaning on a cane conversed with a younger black graduate, who wore a letter jacket. "Right!" the old man said, "And Eldridge Cleaver was Beaver Cleaver's older brother." The younger man laughed and said something Dodd could not hear. The black athlete had to lean closer to the older man and shout into his hearing aid. The older man responded, "You listen to me, I did everything the doctors said: no alcohol, brushed my teeth, avoided cigarettes, remained true to my wife, and what did it get me? I'm still old, bald, toothless, have emphysema and liver disease. I should have enjoyed myself...."

And been dead twenty-five years ago, Dodd thought. He picked a pathway between hundreds of football fans. Two very old women, evidently widows of graduates from the time before the integration of women and minorities, sipped champagne while sitting at a folding table in the shadow of the huge motor home. "What are you doing now?" one woman asked the other.

"Nothing," the second widow answered, bluntly. "Just sitting around waiting to die. I do spend some of Jack's insurance money to fly here for homecoming every year. He would have wanted me to do that," she chortled. A giggle escaped her lips, lubricated by the tiny bubbles in

Invictus

her glass.

Turning toward the center of the parking lot festival, Dodd passed a heated conversation between several men of different generations. "We outlasted Hitler, Beatniks, Hippies, Punk Rockers...."

"Not Ho Chi Minh," a younger voice interrupted.

"That was your father's generation's fault...."

"Baby-boomers," a second elderly alumnus added, "Their boom is a lot worse than their bite."

Another elder citizen spoke, "I never did trust a generation who thought that love was free." The entire group guffawed.

Dodd moved closer to Garrette, hearing part of the conversation when he neared the central party. Garrette held forth his views on business, "I always say: when participating in a rat race, try not to smell like cheese." He howled at his own joke. Dodd had difficulty ignoring the fact that everyone within earshot laughed also, although some had obviously heard the cliché in the past. "And what is it with the middle name Wayne?" Garrette continued his stand up routine, "John Wayne Bobbit, John Wayne Gacy, Thomas Wayne Akers, Timothy Wayne Snyder, David Wayne Mason, all victims or accused murderers. Do you see a pattern here?" As if scripted, the group roared in unison.

A pleasant looking woman in a tight blouse and short skirt handed Dodd a full beer mug. "Thanks," Dodd said, tipping it in her direction. She smiled and moved into the crowd dispensing more mugs from her tray. He watched her go, swaying to the music blaring from the speakers at the rooftop corners of the motor home. Dodd turned toward Garrette; the conversation had stalled temporarily. He recognized an opportunity to speak. "Mr. Garrette," he interjected.

The older man shifted his gaze from the bosom of the tall young woman standing in front of him and looked at

Dodd. "Yes," he said.

Dodd held his right hand out toward Garrette. "I'm Spencer Dodd," he said. "I know Stone."

Garrette looked into Dodd's eyes for a long time without reacting. Dodd began to wonder if the elder Garrette read his mind. Finally, Murphy Garrette smiled. He took Dodd's hand with both of his. "Stone speaks of you a lot, Doctor," he said. Without letting go of Dodd's hand, Garrette turned to the tall blonde at his side and said, "Honey, tell President Furneaux and his deans that I will be several minutes late." Returning his attention to Dodd, Garrette added, "Please do come inside, Dr. Dodd. I would like a word with you in private. It's so noisy out here."

Dodd nodded. Garrette allowed him possession of his hand once again and then led the way into the motor home. When the door closed behind them, the raucous noise stopped so suddenly that the silence startled Dodd. He spun his head toward the door, to see if someone had quieted the crowd. Through the window he saw that the celebrations continued unabated. Garrette smiled. "This used to be my mobile sound studio, Spencer. The sound proofing is superb, as you noticed. May I call you Spencer?" Dodd nodded. "Have a seat." Garrette pointed to one of the luxurious chairs. Dodd placed his half empty mug on the table next to the chair. He settled into the soft seat, and wished he had a similar one for his apartment.

"I've wanted to meet you for a long time, Spencer," Garrette said. "You can call me Murph."

Dodd nodded. He replied honestly, mindful of Abramowicz's order to apologize to Garrette, "I can't say I've been looking forward to meeting you, Mr. Garrette."

"Murph," Garrette reminded Dodd. The smile faded slowly, uncertain if Dodd joked with him. "Stone thinks a lot of you. He has convinced his doctors that you saved his life."

Dodd chewed on his lower lip. He waited before

speaking, searching for the right words. They never came. During medical school, Dodd had convinced himself that he suffered from situational aphasia; the imaginary disease grew worse with age. The words always came later, after the stress, the anger, or whatever dissipated. "I could have saved him the trip to the operating room, if I'd been a little more astute," Dodd suggested.

"Oh?" Garrette raised an eyebrow.

On uncertain ground, knowing the university's lawyer would have forbidden the conversation, Dodd continued nervously. "He's had a drinking problem for years. I was never able to connect in a meaningful way with him, or to make him see the risks involved with his lifestyle."

"No one ever told me, at least not before you phoned my office several months ago," Garrette offered. He settled into a plush sofa and pulled up the armrest. From the hidden refrigerator, he reeled in a beer can. Popping the top, he took a big swig. "Stone always seemed in control around me. Why didn't someone from the university call me sooner?"

"He's an adult," Dodd explained, "has been since age eighteen, according to the federal government. We get in big trouble if we infringe upon civil rights. I took a chance of causing great embarrassment to the university for breaking confidentiality when I called. Dean Waters certainly was upset with me. My boss thought about firing me when you contacted the dean and offered to have my scalp for accusing Stone of being an alcoholic."

Garrette rationalized his response. "I thought you were out of bounds. Of course, now it seems you were correct. Someone should have contacted me earlier; I do pay his tuition."

"Makes no difference to the lawyers or the government, Murph," Dodd said. "If he doesn't sign a release, we can't legally speak with anyone, unless he is a danger to himself or others. We have to document that belief also. Didn't you ever notice that he was taking an unusually long time to finish college?"

"I thought it was a phase he was going through," Garrette laughed, "like sex, drugs, and rock and roll."

Dodd tried to change the subject, not liking the direction in which the conversation headed. "How is Stone doing?" he asked.

Garrette shook his head. "He almost died in the intensive care unit — went through alcohol withdrawal and recovery from surgery at the same time. Wasn't pretty. They had to do a tracheostomy. Last week they closed the hole in his neck; it left a nasty scar. He's just learning to speak again. But he won't talk to me. He's angry with me, Spence." Garrette's face clouded, hurt by words from his son that Dodd had not heard but could easily imagine. "Why would he be mad at me? I've given him everything, everything I never had."

Dodd stared at Garrette, amazed by the naiveté of the man. He imagined his own father mouthing the same speech. His own life crises would have been that much worse if the retired general had possessed Garrette's money. It was tough enough trying to duplicate your father's success without trying to match his wealth, too. "Everything but the words, 'I'm proud of you,'" Dodd mumbled.

Garrette had been gazing out the window at one of the scantily clad hostesses. His head snapped toward Dodd. "What did you say?" he demanded.

Dodd fleshed out the thought. "Did you ever say to Stone, 'Son, I'm proud of you,' or 'Be yourself; you don't have to be me.'"

"Do you take me for a fool?" Garrette accused Dodd. "That would be tantamount to saying, 'Go ahead, be a failure.'"

"Or the equivalent of 'I love you for who you are; be yourself, not me,'" Dodd hinted. Garrette grimaced, his

Invictus

face became red. Dodd stood, leaving the beer mug on the table. Garrette continued to sit and glare, not standing, not offering a farewell or a hand to shake, or even a fist shook in Dodd's face.

The doctor let himself out of the motor home. Relieved not to have been forced to shake Garrette's hand a second time. Outside, the field lights burst to life, like a bright flashbulb that didn't go out. The loud cheer by the assembled crowd in response to the appearance of the blinding lights deafened him. Smells of barbecued ribs and steak basted in onion sauce assaulted his nostrils. Delighted with an excuse for the moisture in his eyes, he walked toward the stadium. Dodging intoxicated alumni circling the encampment like vultures, Dodd concentrated on his own thoughts, oblivious to their conversations. A huge, full moon hung over the east end of the stadium, as big and orange as a Halloween pumpkin. Garrette's television crew could not have constructed a more beautiful background prop for the game, even had Murphy Garrette ordered one.

Bill Yancey

Invictus

Chapter Seventeen
November 17th

Barefoot, Dodd answered the knock at the door, in long, baggy gym shorts and his favorite exercise shirt. The T-shirt had holes in it older than most of the students attending the university. Having just finished a five-mile jog around campus, sweat drenched his clothing. When the knock came, he had been on his way to a shower. Still holding a towel, he opened the door and found a tall brunette, also dressed casually in jeans, sandals, and an amply filled T-shirt that proclaimed within the outline of an SVU bear: "Bears *DO* do it in the woods. Go SVU." She wore her straight hair pulled back into a pony tail. With high cheekbones and even teeth, her beautiful smile radiated warmth. Dodd rated her one of the best looking women on campus, Miss October, a ten or eleven.

"I kept hoping you'd make a house call," the young woman complained. "But you never did."

Dodd kept one hand on the door, the other on the frame, as if guarding a soccer goal from a corner kick. Drolly, he replied, "I keep telling you, Ms. Rivera, I don't make the kind of house calls you are expecting, especially not to my patients. Since you are still a registered student at Southwestern Virginia University, you are legally one of my charges. It is, therefore, unethical for me to have a personal relationship with you."

"Call me Gerianne, or Geri, please," the young woman corrected. "Have you always been a killjoy?" She leaned heavily against the door with one shoulder.

Dodd held the door firmly in check, preventing it from opening. "My ex-wife thought I was pretty dull. Boring is my forté."

Rivera laughed at the self deprecation. "You're funny, Spencer. May I call you Spencer?"

"Doctor Dodd would be fine, thanks."

Rivera waited an eternity, hoping Dodd would speak. "Aren't you going to invite me in?" she finally asked.

Dodd shook his head. "Hadn't planned on it," he said.

She craned her neck, bobbing her head between his arm and the door, and explored the efficiency apartment. "Don't you watch football games on Sunday afternoon like most men?"

"Only if the Panthers are playing," Dodd answered. "They have a bye this week." In the kitchen, the phone rang. Dodd turned his head toward the sound. "I have to go," he said.

"I want to ask you a serious question," Rivera said, taking advantage of Dodd's indecision.

Dodd looked at the phone. The second and third rings tugged at him; he was too compulsive to let it go unanswered. "Stay right here," he ordered Rivera, leaving the door open and scrambling to grab the telephone.

"Dodd," he said into the handset. "Hello? Damn, whoever it was hung up." Dodd turned to see Rivera between him and the television, kneeling on his couch. She faced him, leaning over the back of the couch with the remote control in her hand. The front door was closed.

"You've got a nice looking butt, Doc, and muscular legs," Rivera said, leaning over the couch, staring at him. Her ample breasts hung on his side of the couch, attempting to escape the low-cut, too-tight T-shirt. "Too bad about the scars on the knees. Did you play soccer or football?"

Self-consciously, Dodd looked down at the faded scars. "Football, and not very well. They used me as a tackling dummy for several years. Four orthopedic surgeries attest to the fact that boys under one hundred seventy-five pounds probably should not play collision sports with Neanderthals weighing over two hundred fifty pounds."

"Where are the other scars?" Rivera asked coyly, "I only see two."

Dodd started to pull off the tattered shirt, thought better of it, wary of her intentions. "Herniated disk and separated shoulder," he said. His face clouded. "I thought I asked you to wait outside."

Rivera ignored the statement. "So, why did you play football if you were so small?"

Dodd shrugged. "To impress my dad and a girl," he said.

"Did it work?" she asked seriously.

Dodd laughed. He told Rivera the old joke he used to cover his wounded pride. "Yeah; she's now my stepmother." Dodd padded toward the front door. Once there, he propped it open widely with a thick, heavy anatomy book. Rivera turned seductively to follow his progress.

"Really?" Watching him test the book's ability to keep the door open, by pushing the door against it, she added, "What are you doing?"

"Just kidding," Dodd admitted, "my girl friend ran off with the co-captain of the team." Answering her second question, he said, "Chivalry never died. Also, I fear for my chastity; I think I'm safer with the door open."

Rivera laughed. "Do you think anyone in this town cares if you have a woman in your apartment? What century do you live in, Spence?"

"Dr. Dodd to you," he corrected her. "The second A.D., I think. Maybe the Victorian. As a paranoid once said, 'I have my enemies.'"

"Really? I would have thought that you'd be pretty well-connected politically. You've been here what, five years?"

"Going on seven. I'm politically as naïve as one can be, I'm afraid. Never liked boot-licking or ass-kissing. If you can't say what you mean, I have no use for you." Rivera leaned forward, elbows on knees, cleavage making Dodd uneasy. He amended his statement. "Let me rephrase that; if someone can't say what he means, I have no use for him. I'm not sure I want to hear what you have to say at the moment."

"Sounds like you got burned, romantically or politically, that is," she guessed, sinking into the couch, disappointed by Dodd's continued reluctance to sit next to her.

"Frequently," Dodd answered. He circled the room, avoiding the couch. Picking up his sweaty socks, he tossed them into the bathroom, then closed the door. "Thanks to politics, I lost my last job."

"Amazing," she said.

"What's amazing?" Dodd asked.

Rivera explained. "One thinks of doctors as people who give of themselves; you'd think they'd be above politics."

"Before there was any money in medicine, that was probably true," Dodd agreed. "Nothing makes men more political than the thought of an unjust reward."

"Money?"

"Exactly." Finally tiring of walking around the sofa in circles, Dodd slumped into the matching stuffed chair.

"Well?" she asked.

"Well, what?"

"Tell me the story," she begged.

"About being fired? I don't know you well enough."

"Pretend you do. Cripes, Doc," she exclaimed, "I'm an MBA student. I like hearing how Machivellian the real world is. I may have to work in it, again, some day. Maybe I'll be offered a job in a hospital."

Dodd frowned. He sat in the chair and played with his foot. He fidgeted, examining the holes in his ancient shirt. "It's not a pretty story. And it may not be accurate. I pieced it together after the fact."

"Try me."

"Okay." Dodd crossed his legs and stared at his toenails, acutely aware of how old his feet looked in comparison to his guest's. "I took a position: the assistant medical director of an emergency department. My first week on the job, one of the orthopedic surgeons introduced himself to me. He offered to take any and all orthopedic cases off my hands if I had trouble finding another surgeon. In fact, he offered this same courtesy from his entire partnership; told me to call them anytime, day or night."

"Was that a big deal?" Rivera asked.

"Yeah, huge," Dodd explained, holding his hands out as if describing a monstrous fish he had caught. "It's always difficult to find someone to admit a patient after midnight, or to do follow-up care for some patients, especially indigent ones. As hellos and offers go, this one was outstanding."

Rivera imagined she understood the significance of the overture. "So far, so good," she said, anxious to hear the remainder of the story, and to encourage Dodd to relax in her presence.

"Well," Dodd continued, "after I had been in the hospital six months, no other orthopedic surgeon had made such an offer, in fact few physicians in any specialty acknowledged my existence. In general, they avoided the ER and emergency doctors." Rivera fondled the remote control. She leaned back into the couch, settling in for a long story. Dodd had difficulty concentrating; he watched her stretch her long legs and rest her calves gently on the stack of magazines on top of the table. The sandals dangled from her long toes.

Determined to shorten the tale, he hurried, "On duty, one holiday, I think it was Thanksgiving, I ran into this same orthopedic surgeon in the doctor's dining room. Like a long lost brother, I greeted him. We sat together for the meal. The two of us had an animated conversation; I can't remember what it was about, but I remember enjoying having someone to talk to, other than sick patients. At the far side of the room were a group of resident doctors and some old curmudgeon. The old guy kept giving the two of us dirty looks. I didn't find out until later who the guy was."

"Who?"

Dodd's face contorted. After ten years, the memory still tightened his stomach. He continued, "Another orthopedic surgeon. In the past, his partnership had owned an exclusive contract with the hospital. For several years they had kept other orthopedic groups from competing with his, by not allowing them to have hospital privileges. The guy I was talking with successfully sued the old guy and broke the monopoly, essentially costing the original partnership hundreds of thousands of dollars in operating and referral fees. They hated each other's guts. Neither said a word about it to me. I was too näive to figure it out."

"So how did that cost you your job?" Rivera asked, confused.

A cold chill radiated down Dodd's spine to his extremities. The memory played inside his head. "The old guy was still a crony of the hospital administrator; he went to him and accused me of sending his private patients to the second, newer group. I got canned in a hurry."

"Didn't they have to prove the assertion? Wasn't there a hearing?"

Dodd shook his head. "When a guy who brings millions of dollars of revenue into your hospital tells you he doesn't like the ER doctor, who, coincidentally, works on a contract for a group from Chicago you don't like anyway, he usually gets his way."

Disbelief crossed Rivera's face. "What did your boss say?"

Recovering, pushing bad memories back into their

hiding place, Dodd laughed. "Sacrificial lamb, anyone? Sure, we can fire him. Anyone else you'd like to let go?"

"No balls," Rivera observed.

"And no integrity," Dodd added. "They replaced me with a doctor who was in treatment for drug addiction and compulsive gambling, who had just gotten his license back. He was a golfing buddy of the older orthopedic surgeon."

"Ouch."

"Mucho ouch," Dodd corrected her.

Empathetic, Rivera asked, "Has that happened often in your career?"

Dodd smiled, "Doing things that are not in my best interest? Sure. I once told the CEO of another hospital that he couldn't use the hospital trauma helicopter for his own personal transportation."

"That makes sense; you never know when it would be needed as an ambulance."

"But he didn't like it since, being the E.R. doc, I had veto over him when it came to dispatching the chopper. I think I had that job less than a year, too."

Smitten with Dodd and his tales of woe, Rivera asked, "Would you like to go out for dinner, Doc?"

Dodd shook his head. "Sorry. I told you we can't have a personal relationship."

"You're going to make me transfer to another school so I can date you?" Frustrated, Rivera's raised her voice. "You can carry ethics too far, Spence."

Dodd shook his head. "You can never carry ethics too far." He added, "I'm going to make you transfer to another school so you will be too far away to ask me out for a date." Dodd laughed, again. "Look, Ms. Rivera, I'm not a great catch. I work for the state government. You'd be much happier with a surgeon closer to your own age, who makes big bucks. They can easily earn four to five times what I do."

"I'm not looking for money," Rivera stated bluntly.

Dodd tried another tack. "There's the age difference, too," he observed.

"So, you look late thirties, forty, maybe. I'm late twenties. Ten years. What's the big deal?" she asked.

"Early fifties for me," Dodd revised her generous estimate.

She blanched. "No way," she said, not certain she should believe him.

"Sorry, it's true," Dodd admitted. "If you want to live forever — if your goal is to be miserable that long — all it takes are good genes, regular exercise, and the avoidance of nicotine and hard alcohol. I look younger than I am."

Standing abruptly, Rivera scuffed her sandals on the carpet, pushing them firmly onto her feet; she headed for the open door. She handed Dodd the remote with her left hand, and shook his right hand weakly. Confidence faded from her face. "Well, I guess I have to be going," she said.

"It's okay, Ms. Rivera," Dodd joked, "I already had plans to watch a television concert: Ashley Black and the Seven Giants." He smiled. The joke sailed over her confused head. Not finished, he added, "Then I was going to finish reading my book. It got good reviews from Clumsy, Snow White's literary dwarf."

"Uh, sure," Rivera replied, flustered. "See you around, Doc." Backing her way out, she fled the bad jokes and the now seemingly ancient, old man. More sensitive to the abundant visual cues she had missed earlier, she noticed Dodd's skin wrinkling, then cratering in front of her when he grinned. By the time she walked briskly away from him, he looked ninety.

Dodd kicked the book holding open the door. It spun out of the way; the door closed quietly. The phone rang again. He walked to the kitchen and picked up the receiver. "Dodd," he said.

"Hey, Spence," Clinton Massey said, "you going to join me for the Washington-Dallas game and a beer?"

Invictus

"Who's this?" Dodd asked.

"Clint."

"Oh, sorry, I didn't recognize you," Dodd said.

"Yeah," Massey teased Dodd, "it's tough to see through those little holes in the telephone."

"Be right over, wise ass," Dodd said. "Give me a half hour to shower. I got interrupted." He told Massey about Rivera's short visit and how he sent her packing.

"I would have lied about my age," Massey told him. He ended the conversation with a piece of advice: "Usually, if I want to get rid of a female patient who has attached herself to me, I mention getting her weight on the medical scales."

"I'll remember that," Dodd said, "but I don't think that would have affected Ms. Rivera. Bye." Later, in the shower, Dodd had difficulty forgetting her pretty face and beautiful body. Had he the strength of youth, he would have kicked himself for throwing her out. The hot water released his tension and stress. Her image washed away, down the drain with the sweat and smells from the run.

Bill Yancey

Invictus

Chapter Eighteen
November 22nd

Abramowicz struggled to climb the spiral stone staircase in the round turret at the west end of Burroughs Hall, the main administration building, known as 'The Castle.' He coveted an office in the citadel; worse, he wanted a key to the elevator. Secretaries and staff running errands squeezed by Abramowicz's bloated frame, their bodies pressed so close to his that he decided he might not dislike walking the stairs after all. That is, until he and an equally large and sweaty woman met near the top of the staircase. She wore the gray work clothing of a university housekeeping employee. More of a gentleman than Abramowicz, she backed up the stairs to allow him to pass. He turned to head down the hallway toward Dean Waters office at Student Affairs. The fat woman pinched his butt. "Meet me in the janitor's closet on the third floor in about an hour," she urged, attracted rather than repulsed by his size.

In reply, he stuck his nose in the air and pretended not to hear the proposition. He heard the ugly, old witch cackle as she rode her swab to a lower floor. "Bitch," he vented quietly.

A full glass door with painted titles led to the secretary's office in front of Dean Waters's suite. Abramowicz saw the secretary's rear end through Waters's office door. She leaned over the dean's desk, ample chest flattened nicely where it met the leather blotter. Her short skirt barely covered the well-proportioned bottom; Abramowicz did not see a slip. Tempted, he almost dipped his head to check for underwear. One of her legs bent at the knee and rubbed suggestively on the other. Abramowicz could not see the Dean's face, but he doubted the old goat complained about having a young woman almost prostrate before him, her cleavage beckoning. Standing in the doorway, trying to think of a subtle manner in which to sidle up to her in a compromising way, Abramowicz cleared his throat.

Nonchalantly, the pretty young nymph stood erect and straightened her clothing. She retrieved a piece of paper from Waters's desk and left the room, impish smile on her face. "Good morning, Dr. Abramowicz," she said lustily, departing.

"Morning, Cheryl," he replied, gloomily, remembering the name engraved on the brass plate on the outer office desk.

Waters motioned Abramowicz toward a chair, thought better of it after visualizing the antique collapsing under the strain, and said, "Have a seat on the love seat, Neal. Sorry to get you up so early. You look a little peaked. Working too hard?"

"No. Some asshole put my name on the internet along with an advertisement for a portable computer. 'Call anytime, twenty-four hours a day,' it said. I had to take the phone off the hook and get the number changed. Hell, I even had calls from Nome, Alaska."

"Must have been a really good deal...." Waters grinned, recognizing the bags under his colleague's eyes. "Can you give me the specs? I might want to buy it myself." The dean chuckled. "Who do you suspect?"

In spite of the little man's irritating giggle, Abramowicz managed a wounded smile. He moaned, "Dodd would be the chief suspect. He's one of the more computer literate of the staff. However, this seems a little beyond his capabilities. Some hacker geek made it appear that I had posted the ad myself, from my own computer." He paused, frowning. "Can we talk about something else,

Murray? Like, what's up?" The administrator filled the small couch completely, which creaked, but withstood the assault.

Waters nodded, smiling. He continued, pushing papers to one side. "I wanted to fill you in on the latest developments concerning student health. President Furneaux, as you remember from the party, has given us permission to explore the possibility of privatizing." Abramowicz nodded. "He wants to accomplish this study without alarming the student body, that means secretly. We don't want editorials in the student-published school paper spilling into the local press and making their way to the House of Delegates in Richmond, at least not until we are certain we can prove the move will save the state and the institution money. In times of financial challenge, we will have the support of the state legislature and the governor, but only if their constituents aren't screaming at them."

"I understand the need for confidentiality," Abramowicz acknowledged, "President Furneaux mentioned it Saturday after the game."

"There's a complication," Waters added.

Abramowicz shifted his weight. The sofa groaned. "What's that?" he asked, raising an eyebrow.

Waters stood. He picked up a single piece of paper between his thumb and forefinger as if it were radioactive. Gingerly, he walked around his desk and dropped it into Abramowicz's lap. Abramowicz jumped, as if he expected the letter to be malodorous or to catch fire when it hit his lap. Silently, he read the epistle. Waters watched the his lips move while he digested the message within the communiqué. "It's not a lawsuit," Abramowicz finally said, "just a request for information."

"I've been through enough litigation to know where this is headed," Waters disagreed. "Next, after a review of the charts and the information they requested, there will be depositions, then testimony. Even if we prevail, our image may be smeared."

Abramowicz shrugged. "What can we...what can I do?"

Waters returned to his seat and sat heavily. A former high school football coach, he primed Abramowicz, hoping the man had a home run or a touchdown hidden within his brilliant mind. "I was hoping you'd tell me," he said.

Energized by the challenge, Abramowicz rubbed his meaty hands together. Wheels spun; gears meshed; a plan developed, in outline, anyway. Finally, he spoke, "How about this? I think we need to send a message to Garrette's lawyers — not openly, of course — but obvious if one reads between the lines. Dr. Dodd, the physician who most often took care of Stone Garrette, is shall we say a man at odds with the way our university is normally run. He has taken it upon himself to practice medicine in a manner...ah, not practiced by his colleagues. Maybe he should be at fault for this bad outcome. You know, if he had followed accepted guidelines and practices, this never would have happened. He's a rogue. The university will be willing to sacrifice, er, terminate him and reach a suitable settlement, say the costs of the younger Garrette's medical expenses, in order to avoid unwanted publicity."

Waters leaned backward in his chair, placing a knee against the side of the polished mahogany desk top. He stared at the ceiling for a brief moment, smiling. He had elicited a splendid response from his subordinate. "I like the general tone of that. Flesh it out for me. Let me see some details next week, after Thanksgiving break."

Abramowicz watched the short, gray-haired dean gaze out his window contentedly. Below them, students tramped across the wide expanse of grass that had been the pass-in-review drill field during the school's original military/agriculture incarnation. Chewing on the end of a pen Waters had apparently forgotten that Abramowicz remained in the office. "One other thing," Abramowicz said, returning Waters to reality.

Invictus

"Yes?" Waters said, eyes widening.

Abramowicz turned on his political voice, a smooth cajoling warble. He said, "As you suggested, I discussed the possibility of privatization with the physicians. And you did tell me to listen to Dr. Dodd's objections. Some of his ideas might be worthwhile. He did have one viable suggestion."

"And that would be?" Waters asked.

"To make certain that no fly-by-night organizations bid on the privatization, maybe we should charge a non-refundable fee, something applicable to the first year's lease on the building, or the cost of processing applications. Say, $100,000."

Waters shook his head slowly, thinking about the suggestion. He pressed both palms together and placed his finger tips under his lower lip, as if praying. Answering, he said, "I don't know if we can do that legally, but I'll check on it. You say this was Dodd's idea?"

Abramowicz nodded. The lie flowed effortlessly from his lips. "Among others," he said. "He rambles so. The man has more complaints than you can shake a stick at."

"Well, maybe he has more business sense than I gave him credit for," Waters allowed. He looked at his watch. "Oh, the time just flies. I have a meeting with Dr. Furneaux, Neal, so I guess we should end this one. You will get back to me with the plan for dealing with Garrette's lawyers?"

"Absolutely," Abramowicz said cheerfully. He grinned. Killing two birds with one stone, a lawsuit and a grackle named Dodd, made him extremely happy. "Mind if I ask you where you found your new secretary?" he asked Waters.

Waters shrugged. He stood and walked from behind his desk toward the door. On his way, he pulled Abramowicz to his feet with a handshake. The two reached the door together. Waters explained, before opening the door, "The secretarial pool. The usual story. Shortly after she started her freshman year, some junior or senior promised to marry her and gave her an engagement ring. So she quit school, went to work to support him, and shacked up with him until he graduated. Then he moved on, leaving her here. The town is run by spurned, lusty young women, Neal. They are the business managers, and/or mistresses, of a hundred absentee owners. Many of them are eager to get back at the men who lied to them in the past. Some are power hungry. It pays dividends to be perceived as powerful within the local community. I understand President Furneaux has quite a harem of girls vying to be the next trophy Mrs. Furneaux. Mildred, his first wife, is probably spinning in her grave." Waters opened the door and led Abramowicz into the antechamber. In front of the secretary, he added, "Play your cards right, Neal, and you could occupy this office if I am promoted." Waters winked at Abramowicz without the secretary seeing; using the opposite eye, he winked at her so Abramowicz could not see, a private joke on each of them.

Abramowicz trailed Waters into the hallway. When Waters turned toward the president's office, Abramowicz turned toward the spiral turret, praying that the cleaning lady had found another stairway to clean.

Invictus

Chapter Nineteen
November 23rd

Catnapping but not sleeping well, Dodd tossed about. Through the open window, he heard the light automobile traffic on Main Street. A cold drizzle pelted the glass and the aluminum window frame. The only traffic light in the middle of town reflected off the wide-open casement window. It cast red, green, then yellow light across the hide-a-bed. A ruffle of feathers rushed toward the window, then stopped. Dodd heard BeeBee shake off the water and the subdued clip clop of his hard feet and claws. They tap danced across the wide oak windowsill. Hopping with spread wings, the bird landed with a gentle thump on a second pillow next to Dodd's head.

Groggily, Dodd asked, "Who's there?"

"*Nemo. Hannibal est ante portas,*"[20] the bird said.

"Hannibal has been dead at least two thousand years," Dodd replied, waking more completely.

"*Barbarus est ante ianuam,*"[21] the bird corrected himself.

"Barbarian?" Dodd asked.

"There's a drunken body at your front door," BeeBee said more plainly to the sleepy Dodd.

"It's too cold for bodies at the front door." Dodd sat upright in the bed, pulled his glasses off the end table, and looked through the lenses without unfolding the frame. In the distance, through the partially fogged window, the First Nation Bank of Fawsville's clock flashed: 32° F, 0° C, and 2:13 a.m.. in quick succession. Sleepily, Dodd said, "Glad I remembered to put the top up on the car." He rearranged the pillow and blanket, lay back down, and turned on his side making himself more comfortable.

"The door," BeeBee reminded him.

Dodd listened. He heard a scratching at the door. He dismissed the bird. "It's not a body, yet. It moved. What's wrong, is the roost too cold for you? Are you and your buddies freezing your tail feathers off? Do you want to spend the night in here?"

"It's too stuffy in here," the bird answered. He hopped to the desk and pecked at the computer until he hit the power switch with his beak. The monitor flared to life; a raucous set of cow bells sounded from the computer's speakers.

Irritated, Dodd sat up in the bed. "Okay, okay, I'll check the door." He fumbled with the blankets, then fitted his glasses to his face. He pulled his long gym shorts over his underwear and slipped into sandals. Retrieving his terrycloth bathrobe from the floor, he wrapped himself tightly against the chill and shuffled to the front door. Placing his eye against the peep hole, he looked out. He saw no barbarians in the open stairway. Sleet swirled past the lens. At the exact moment Dodd had decided to return to bed, a thump sounded at the bottom of the door. Startled, he unlocked the deadbolt and opened the door. A huddled figure rolled from a kneeling position into the apartment. Pushed by a strong whirlwind, frozen moisture blew into the apartment.

Dodd knelt. He turned the body over onto its back. The blue-tinged, pale face of a semi-conscious young man with a ragged goatee stared into space above Dodd's head. Hastily, the physician felt for a carotid pulse, and thanked God when he found it. The man breathed slowly; cold, alcohol-tainted air fogged Dodd's glasses when he leaned closer to listen to the rasping. Standing, he dragged the young man into the apartment and slammed the door.

Leaving him on the floor, Dodd closed the window. BeeBee had already departed. Before returning to evaluate

Invictus

the drunk, he pushed the thermostat higher and pulled the blankets off his bed. Stripping the wet coat and knit cap from the boy, Dodd wrapped the young man's upper body in the blankets, then pulled off the wet jogging shoes and soaked denims. With the sopping clothing removed, he re-wrapped the boy completely in the blanket.

Positioning a towel and pillow under the young man's head, Dodd noticed the drunk's eyes staring at him. "Dad?" the boy asked.

"Nope," Dodd said quietly. "Who should I say is looking for him?"

The young man slurred his speech. "Jared," he said. "It's me, Jared Greenhall."

"Had a bit too much to drink, Jared?" Dodd asked. The boy didn't answer, having drifted back into the nether world of chilled liquor. Dodd checked his pulse and respirations again. Satisfied the boy slept instead of being comatose, he went in search of the electric space heater he kept in the closet. After plugging the machine in and directing it toward the slumbering body, he sat at his desk and stared at the computer screen.

Unable to sleep, Dodd sat in front of the computer. An hour passed while Dodd dispersed the manure, using a spreadsheet to evaluate different scenarios for staffing the student health center. He plugged in alternative numbers of hours per week of operations, different methods and percentages of reimbursement. By any measure, unless there were some very expensive and very hidden expenditures, privatizing seemed to give the students better service: more hours at lower fees. Dodd searched, but he could not find a reason that all the staff should not have raises. They might not like the shift work, however, if student health were to open twelve to fifteen hours a day and six or seven days a week, he mused. Still, Dodd felt that the center should be open long enough to cover all the intramural activities.

Overall, the costs would drop. If they were allowed to bill the students' insurance carriers, and, another big if, managed care groups would give the student health service provider status, the new student health service as visualized by Dodd would be a huge improvement and a success. He printed his projections to show the other physicians later. Rubbing his hands together cheerfully, he looked forward to the day that the staff would have to answer to the doctors' demands and their jobs depended upon keeping the physicians' happy. No longer would he hear the refrain, 'This is just one more day toward the day I retire on a state pension.' Capitalism meant provide a service or look for another line of work.

About the same time, the body on the floor stirred. "Shit," the boy said. "God, where am I?"

"Is that you, Jared?" Dodd asked.

The body rolled over, face upward; the blankets parted. With obvious, great effort, the boy responded, "Yeah," he said. "Who are you? Oh, crap, where are my clothes?" he asked when he looked down and saw his underwear.

Dodd explained. "They were wet. They're hanging in the shower. I'll take them down to the laundry room in a little bit and throw them in a dryer."

Unable to see Dodd while lying flat on his back, Greenhall sat up — too quickly. He lay down again while the vertigo dissipated. "Who are you?" he asked, again supine. Teeth chattering, he re-wrapped himself in the blankets.

"Dr. Dodd."

"Do I know you?" Greenhall asked.

"Have you ever been to student health?"

The boy answered scornfully, "Nah. A bunch of quacks work there. I only go see real doctors."

Dodd laughed. "Then we've never met. Been drinking?"

"Dumb question," Greenhall stated.

Invictus

"Why?" Dodd asked.

"Everyone drinks, man. This is a university. A university in the middle of nowhere...."

Dodd interrupted the drunk, "Not, 'why is that a dumb question?' Why have you been drinking excessively?"

"Broke up with my girl," Greenhall explained, then fell silent. The sobs were gentle at first, then they burst forth in heaves, accompanied by tears. Between sobs, he chanted: "It's my fault. I didn't do the little things. I took her for granted. I was never there for her. I should have paid her more attention. We'll never get back together. It's my fault. I love her. She was my life. I can't go on living. She said she will always love me."

Dodd raised his voice, "Jared!"

"Uh, what?" Greenhall asked, startled, having forgotten Dodd.

"If you recite one more cliché, especially any cliché thought up by a woman in order to make a man feel guilty, I'm going to physically throw you out the front door." A sobbing snore answered Dodd's diatribe. The physician returned to poring over the spreadsheet.

A short while later, Greenhall woke again. "Dad," he said "I broke up with Susan. It's my fault. I didn't do the little things. I took her for granted. I was never there for her. I should have paid her more attention. We'll never get back together. It's my fault. I love her. She was my life. I can't go on living. She said she will always love me." Dodd waited. The youth fell asleep again. He woke and repeated the ritual four or five times more before morning came. As his liver metabolized the alcohol, the soliloquy recurred less frequently.

The smells of bacon, eggs, and coffee wafted through the apartment. Salivating, Greenhall eventually roused himself. He sat upright, in the middle of the floor. Dodd had folded the bed into the couch and replaced the cushions. Next to him, Greenhall found his clothing, fresh from the dryer and warm to touch. From the bathroom he heard the sounds of a shower. Greenhall slipped from the blankets. Too warm, he leaned toward the electric space heater and snapped it off. Then he put on his clothing, except for his shoes, which remained damp, despite the heater. The warm socks felt good; he slid his cold feet into them. Stomach growling, the young man searched the apartment for the source of the aroma that made him drool. On the small table in the kitchen, sat two plates. One held a steaming helping of breakfast, the other was covered with crumbs from burnt toast and smeared egg yolk. Dirty silverware lay in the middle of the used plate; a clean set sat to the side of the full plate.

Uncertain if the feast were meant for him, Greenhall circled the table like a vulture. He finally decided he would starve if he didn't eat something. Gingerly, he stole a piece of bacon off the plate. At the same moment the bathroom door opened. Startling Greenhall, Dodd emerged, freshly scrubbed and shaved, wearing clean clothing. He looked at the boy, who tried to suppress his chewing. "I thought I heard someone bumbling about, Jared," Dodd said. "I'm Dr. Dodd. Go ahead; it's for you. Drink the coffee, too. An old wives' tale says coffee's good for hangovers."

Not needing Dodd to repeat the invitation, Greenhall sat and ate hungrily. "Thanks," he mumbled between shoveling large chunks of food into his mouth. Dodd busied himself straightening the room. Finished that chore, he returned to the kitchen, picked up his dishes, and placed them into the sink. Deftly, he dropped a little soap on the plate, ran the hot water, and filled the sink with soap bubbles. Then he retrieved those Greenhall had used. "Done with those?" Dodd asked the boy. Greenhall nodded mutely. "Something wrong?" Dodd asked, seeing a strange look in the youth's eyes.

"Am I...are you...do we have some kind of relationship?" Greenhall finally asked.

"I don't follow you," Dodd said. "I never met you before last night. If you hadn't...."

"Am I gay?" Greenhall blurted, covering his face briefly when he did so.

Confused, Dodd asked, "You're asking me? I don't think so, given that you have, or had, a relationship with a girl. Maybe you are bisexual? That sometimes messes up relationships."

"You know about my girl friend?"

"You mentioned her a couple times last night," Dodd answered. "But back to your question: why ask me if you are gay?"

Greenhall chose his words carefully. He spoke slowly, as if his lips had been numbed by a dentist. "I never woke up in a man's apartment before. The thought crossed my mind that maybe I had gotten in touch with my feminine side. Suicide also crossed my mind when I thought that. I would much rather wake up in the arms of a beautiful woman."

"Wouldn't we all. Hold off on the suicidal ideation," Dodd suggested. "You're lucky you didn't die of exposure last night. I found you drunk and freezing to death outside my door. Do you live near here?"

"Where's here?"

"Cumberland Efficiencies. Apartment 140."

"Susan lives in Apartment 340. Guess I got lost."

"Guess so," Dodd agreed. "Maybe you and I should have a short talk about the abuse potential of alcohol before you leave."

"Are you a psychiatrist?" Greenhall asked suspiciously.

"No, just one of those quacks from student health," Dodd informed him.

"Being a little judgemental, aren't you,? Not that I'm complaining."

Dodd dried the silverware, shoving it unceremoniously into an open drawer. "One becomes judgemental," he said, "after years of dealing with thousands of immature juveniles."

Greenhall made a face, not liking Dodd's tone. "Anyway, thanks for saving my ass, and for feeding me this morning."

"Yeah," Dodd said, "I could have saved a couple eggs and some bacon if I had let you die on the doorstep."

"Are you always this friendly?" Greenhall asked.

"Most people find my sense of humor intimidating," Dodd allowed. He changed the subject. "What's your major, Jared?"

"English, with a minor in business."

"English?" Dodd smiled. "What was your native language?"

Greenhall squinted at Dodd, not certain he understood the question. "English," he answered uncertainly.

Jokingly, Dodd asked, "Doesn't that give you an unfair advantage? Shouldn't you study a language foreign to you?"

Greenhall returned his attention to the coffee in front of him. "My luck to be rescued by a wise ass," he mumbled through the sips of coffee. Dodd laughed.

Invictus

Chapter Twenty
December 2nd

Inside student health, Dodd stood in the long hallway. He had paced off twenty feet to see where the patients would stand, if and when someone ever installed the eye chart he wanted. Exhausted from a long weekend, he yawned. One of the few nurses still talking to him cheerfully poked him in the ribs with an elbow when she tried to slip past him. "No yawning allowed," she said, "and thanks for the article on muscular dystrophy. My daughter appreciates your help."

"Not only is yawning allowed," Dodd argued, "it's recommended. The new genetic treatments may be of some use to your grandson."

"Well, since you're bored, we'll put you to work." The nurse pointed at the plastic flags hanging above Dodd's exam room doors. "Dr. Dodd has two white flags," she called loudly to her cohorts, indicating that his exam rooms awaited patients.

"That means I've surrendered," Dodd offered another explanation. He pointed to the speaker in the ceiling. "Working here is like playing a continuous game of musical chairs. All we need is some good music, instead of that funeral parlor stuff they play. Our deejay must be on St. Peter's roll. Once the music stops, someone pulls my coffin out from under me." Turning toward the back stairway and trying to ignore a sappy version of 'Tie a Yellow Ribbon,' Dodd almost ran into the physical therapist. She gave him a mean look when he said, "Morning." Ignoring this, Dodd stepped around her and climbed the stairs to the administrative wing and the mail room.

In his box Dodd found a single announcement among the mass of throw away journals from the American Medical Association and other junk mail advertisements. Dodd spent ten minutes deciding to throw it all in the recycle bin. He reread the announcement. The information systems manager had scheduled some maintenance on the pharmacy computer system. Abramowicz, or the chief pharmacist, or both, had decided that the practitioners should dispense medications from a special cart while the computer was down instead of continuing to send patients to the pharmacy. Seeing red, Dodd stormed toward Abramowicz's office. When he arrived, the door opened and the grumpy physical therapist emerged. She again made an ugly face and maneuvered past him without a greeting.

Dodd shrugged and pushed on the door. It opened slowly to reveal the red-faced Abramowicz growling over the telephone. "Well, find him and send him to my office!" Abramowicz snapped at the person on the other end of the phone line; he slammed the handset onto its cradle.

"Find whom?" Dodd asked.

Startled, Abramowicz looked up. Speechless, he stared in Dodd's direction for five seconds. Regaining his composure, he said, "You, Spencer. Close the door and come in here. Have a seat."

Dodd pushed the door until the latch clicked. He walked to the chair nearest Abramowicz's desk and sat. Without waiting for Abramowicz to speak, he started to complain about the pharmacists taking the day off at the practitioners' expense. "They don't need a computer, Neal."

Not listening to the physician, Abramowicz blasted Dodd about the latest complaint. "That woman has breast cancer, Spencer."

"They can work from the cart, or from their own stockpile better than I can," Dodd continued.

Ignoring Dodd, Abramowicz also continued, "We can't

have you callously mentioning death in front of her."

Not listening to the fat administrator, Dodd added, "You're trying to kill us, Neal. I don't have time to write a prescription, get a drug off the cart, write a label, explain the usage of the medicine to the patient, after seeing him and writing a note, too. We can print labels for the pharmacists if they want. There's no reason for them to sit around while I work my butt off."

Abramowicz raised his voice when he realized Dodd was not listening. "She works her tail off. Did you know she's wearing a wig? The chemotherapy cost her her hair," he said.

"The pharmacist?" Dodd asked, confused.

"The physical therapist," Abramowicz explained.

For several seconds the two men stared at one another in silence. At the exact same moment they each asked the other, "What the hell are you talking about?"

Dodd allowed Abramowicz to speak first. He said, "You mentioned funeral music in front of Mrs. Vasquez."

After a minute of memory search, Dodd still had not recalled when. He asked, "When? And so what if I did?"

"She has breast cancer," Abramowicz repeated.

Stunned, Dodd asked, "I'm supposed to know that? Was there a memo? There are memos for everything else: parking, birthdays, garage sales, everything. I throw most memos away without reading them."

"No, there was no memo," Abramowicz said, frustrated that he had to explain the situation again. "You have to be sensitive to these things."

Now angry, Dodd exploded. "I'm supposed to know when someone has cancer? They give off radio waves I'm supposed to pick up? How am I supposed to know, Neal?"

"You're a doctor...."

Dodd interrupted, "But not a mind reader. If someone wants special consideration, for instance if she is handicapped and wants a reserved parking space, she should have to fill out a request and then get a special sticker. That's it, Neal! Just like the handicapped sticker you get for being fat (or is it mentally deficient?), cancer patients should all wear special name tags. Bring back the scarlet letter; make it an L for leukemia. Might work for the handicapped, or whatever challenged, too. D, for deaf. S, for stupid. You have a real idea there, Neal. I'll see if your secretary can promulgate that memo. I'm glad we had this little talk. You've finally solved a problem during your tenure at student health, not only for us, but for the entire country — if not the world."

"I'm going to ignore that remark," Abramowicz said stolidly.

"Good," Dodd said. "I'm going to ignore your insinuation that I would purposely hurt someone else's feelings. Other than yours, of course."

"She's undergoing cancer chemotherapy, Spencer. You can't mention death in front of her."

"Neal, no one told me she was losing her hair because of chemotherapy. I thought she liked wigs. If she wants extraordinary consideration, maybe she should tell *everyone* that she has cancer. Better yet, maybe a person who is worried about dying shouldn't work in a medical clinic, where the possibility of dying comes up everyday!"

"You are so callous," Abramowicz observed.

"I'm a doctor, Neal. Do you really want me going to pieces and weeping every time someone mentions death? If nothing else, your Kleenex budget will double." Dodd climbed onto his soapbox; he rambled, "This is a medical clinic, or have you forgotten? We mention death here, routinely. It's one way of getting the patient's attention. We also ask questions about bodily functions, diseases, and body parts people don't normally mention in polite society. Not only that, Neal, but we examine patients, we even touch forbidden parts of their bodies. Outside of this building, we would be considered perverts. Inside of

Invictus

it we are healers, by God." Warming to the soliloquy, Dodd finished with a flair, "If doing those things, or failing a medical test embarrasses a patient, then so be it!"

Not seeing that the argument had any effect on Abramowicz, Dodd stood and strode to the door. "And," he said, opening the door dramatically, "it will be a cold day in Hell before I'll dispense drugs while a trained pharmacist sits on his or her ass in the pharmacy because the computer is down."

Halfway down the steps Dodd passed Abramowicz's personal secretary, J.P. Jones, going in the opposite direction. "Oh, Dr. Dodd," she called after him when he did not slow down. "Dr. Abramowicz would like to talk with you in his office."

Unkindly, Dodd told Jones, "Tell Neal that the school mascot is looking for someone to mate with and have his litter."

The morning passed slowly. Most students were unlikely to rise from bed before noon, unless they had classes to attend. Consequently, appointments went begging or students failed to show for them. The afternoon rush crushed Dodd. Not only did every appointment show, but every student who woke at noon with a sore throat thought he faced death and demanded to be seen. Those few patients that the nurses tried to push into appointments the following morning threatened to have their parents call President Furneaux. They would demand to know what the hundred dollars they paid for student health bought, if not immediate gratification.

Eventually, the torture ended. Someone locked the front door and escorted the students from the building. After all the patients departed, the nurses began to celebrate, by playing with the intercom system. Dodd heard, "Calling the bald eagle," a reference to Massey, from the overhead speakers. Every room contained a phone and a link to the intercom; it was therefore impossible to tell from where the calls were made. "The eagle has landed," Massey's voice announced to everyone.

Dodd wondered if Massey had landed on the moon with Apollo 11, or on top of his favorite nurse. He picked up the phone and dialed the intercom system while sitting with his door cracked slightly. "Attention on deck, attention on deck," he declared. "All hands aft go forward; all those forward go aft; all those amidships mill around or direct traffic." His broadcast was a parody of navy announcements he had heard on the aircraft carrier during his enlistment.

From the office next to his burst retired United States Navy Commander A.J. Watson. The little man looked furious. Balding head a bright red and teeth clenched, he marched to a position in the clinic where he could see the nurses' station. From there he made rapid, repetitive hand signals: back edge of his hand and fingers moved across his throat, which Dodd assumed meant, 'Cut the noise or I'm going to cut your throats.' Holding a patient's chart in his hand, Watson alternately pointed at it and his office door, apparently indicating that while they may have finished, he still had a patient in his office. White coat tail trailing after him, and madder than the last hog to the slop trough at feeding time, he stomped back into his office and slammed the door. A few minutes later a student patient emerged carrying a prescription slip. Not wishing to face the angry Watson, Dodd picked up his briefcase, closed his door, and left the building.

The autumn days shrank. Darkness, aided by the shadows from Cumberland Mountain, enveloped Fawsville earlier and earlier in the evening. Dodd left work at about five-thirty. Taking advantage of the warmer than usual autumn day — a gift from El Niño , he folded down the convertible top and pointed the nose of the Miata in the direction of Kentucky. Red and gold leaves interspaced with evergreen filled the windscreen. The smell of pine sap tickled his nose. Cool, crisp air filled his lungs. He drove north and west until darkness rendered the view invisible and the chill required that he turn the heater on high. Tucking himself lower into the canopy to avoid the wind chill from the fifty-mile-per-hour blast of air, he resisted raising the top or surrendering to the nature he wanted to experience.

When he slowed for a curve in the road, BeeBee appeared out of nowhere, landing on Dodd's briefcase in the passenger seat. "*Invictus*,"[22] the bird said.

"Undefeated?" Dodd asked, unsure of the meaning of the word.

"In your case, unsubdued," BeeBee explained.

"Because I left the top down? How many Roman chariots had tops?" Dodd asked. He grinned, amused by the vision of a convertible chariot.

"More to the point: you are unsubdued by life in general or its rules," BeeBee explained. The raven rode with Dodd, returning to Fawsville and the parking lot in front of Cumberland Efficiencies. He appeared to enjoy the view of the stars under the moonless and cloud free night. Dodd raised the top; the bird flew away.

"*Amicus verus est rara avis*,"[23] Dodd called after the departing raven.

"*Pessimum genus inimicorum laudantes*,"[24] BeeBee replied, disappearing into the darkness.

The phone rang as Dodd finished in the bathroom. He picked up the receiver and shoved it under his chin. Walking away from the phone base allowed the long cord to dangle the length of the small kitchen. "Dodd," he answered. No response. "Hello?" he mumbled, opening the refrigerator.

Hesitantly, a distantly familiar voice asked, "Spencer?"

"Vanessa? Is that you?" Dodd asked. He turned a clear plastic container over in his hand. Whatever he sealed inside had turned a bright green on the bottom. The smell wrinkled his nose. Certain the container held no vegetables, Dodd dropped the entire object into the garbage can with a loud thump.

Vanessa Grant's voice wavered. "Yes. I need a favor."

"Well, I need a favor, too," Dodd said. "We could use a nurse of your caliber in student health. Why don't you get that MRI and come back to work?" He referred to a remark he had made to her three years earlier. He had been convinced that she had become psychotic or had developed a brain tumor. Two years before that she had left her husband of sixteen years and two pre-teen children, in order to run away from life with her 'soul mate.' Unlike her family, student health never recovered from her abandonment. Had she remained at student health as the head nurse in place of LaFlamé, nursing problems would have been non-existent.

"Sorry, Spence," she said. An awkward silence hung in the kitchen while Dodd searched the fridge for enough leftovers to combine into one edible meal.

"Where are you?" Dodd finally asked.

"Albuquerque. If it's a bad time, I'll call later."

Dodd chuckled. He sniffed at the edge of another plastic container, then laid it on the counter. "If by bad time you mean the nurses can't follow directions, or when I tell people to do things they say that they can't and their supervisors won't, or no one will take responsibility for their actions, or the new director thinks it's more important to think about eating five fruits per day than quitting smoking, or the students still think that antibiotics cure everything, then, yeah, it's a bad time. But since those things will never change, I guess it's a good time. What favor do you need?"

"Still tilting at windmills?" Grant asked.

"Don Quixote was my hero," Dodd admitted.

"I need a reference."

Dodd closed the refrigerator door. "Another one?"

he asked. "How many jobs have you had in the last three years?"

"This makes nine," she said.

"Worse record than me," Dodd observed. "Why do you change so often?"

"It's Barry," Grant explained. "He can't keep a job."

Dodd sighed, understanding the challenge. "Well, tell him to stay at home, be a house husband."

"I tried. It offends his manhood."

Dodd avoided calling her insignificant other a loser, at least out loud. He knew how the label could hurt, having been branded himself. Making trouble for arrogant assholes, whistle blowing, believing in himself above all others, and maintaining his integrity meant more to him than keeping a job. Maybe it did for Barry, too. "No problem, Vanessa," he said. "Who's paying for the call?" Dodd dumped the contents of three plastic bowls onto a single plate, then covered it with a paper towel. Placing it into the microwave he prepared to nuke any surviving bacteria.

"It's free, a promotion by a drug company."

Settling into the kitchen chair after setting the timer on the microwave, Dodd smiled. "Good. Who else have you called?"

"Ted Brooker. He's still mad at you."

"About what?" Dodd asked, never having been on the wrong side of the congenial general surgeon.

"Something about April Fool's. God, Spence, if there is anything I do miss, it's your April Fool's jokes. Remember the rectal adapter? What did you do this year?"

"He didn't tell you?" Dodd asked. He placed a glass on his small table and scrounged through the drawer for some silverware. Opening the fridge again, he searched for iced tea.

"No."

Dodd described the prank to Grant. "I sent a letter

around the clinic via email. It said that I had participated in a study to implant hair into bald guys, using a sophisticated new machine that attached a carbon fiber hook onto individual hairs and implanted them with a computer directed nitrogen powered gun — sort of like a semi-permanent wig. The letter implied that we were looking for investors. He and three other doctors in the clinic believed it. They came to my office with open checkbooks in hand. Ted only wanted to invest in the company, but A.J. Watson and Clint Massey wanted treatments. You don't know A.J.; he's balder than a bowling ball."

Grant laughed. "Have you heard from Denise?" she asked.

The microwave beeped. Dodd opened the door and pulled the hot plate from the machine while cradling the phone with his head tilted. "Ouch. That's hot," he said. He told Vanessa what he knew about Denise. "She moved to Indiana or somewhere in the mid-west. Dave's Ph.D. is employable in only three universities in the country. IU was one. She was here about nine months ago. The kids are grown. She's got a part time job in a nursing home. What a waste for such a talented nurse."

"You should leave, too, Spencer," Grant offered advice she knew Dodd would ignore. "Why stay where you aren't appreciated?"

"What are my other choices?" he asked. "Work for managed care? See a patient every ten minutes and get screamed at for both the things I do and the things I refuse to do? Set up my own practice? That's very expensive. Go back to the ER? Then I have four people to keep happy: the patient, the administrator, the patient's real doctor, and the guy who owns the contract. No thanks. I'll get out of medicine, again, first. Maybe I'll try a new medical field: computers, informatics for instance."

"So do it," Grant challenged him.

Invictus

"Not until I beat these guys at their own game. There has to be a way of getting things done without being pummeled for trying."

"Why worry about it?" she asked. "No one else seems to care — not the students, not the administration, not your colleagues. Leave the red tape to strangle those who produce it. Denise and I don't miss the bureaucracy. Why should you? We were happy to leave."

Dodd popped a too hot potato into his mouth, had to spit it out. Between sips of tea to cool his tongue, he said, "I think the students deserve more, if they're sick. Less, if they are not. I guess my happy medium is different than most people's. There's a chance that student health will be privatized. Are you interested in a real job?"

Grant declined; she said, "I don't see how we can leave the crystals, the rocks, or the stone formations here in the desert, Spence. And the pyramids seem to be so much more powerful out west than in Virginia."

Dodd shook his head in amazement at her words. "How is it that you can have a job in a scientific field and espouse such nonsense?" he asked.

She retorted, "Spencer, how can people be scientists and still believe in God? One doesn't exclude the other. There are forces in the universe more powerful than anything humans can understand."

"Maybe," Dodd allowed. "Where do you want the letter of recommendation sent?"

"I gave Ted the address."

Bill Yancey

Invictus

Chapter Twenty-one
December 3rd

Frost covered the car windshield, inside and out. Dodd had left the top down overnight, again. The seats, too, were covered with the spidery weblike remnants of frozen moisture. He spent several minutes scraping both sides of the window, and wiping the driver's seat. After pulling up the top and clamping it in place, he crawled into the vehicle and zipped shut the rear window. Opening the heater vents, Dodd started the engine and turned on the heat. He set the defroster and fan to run full blast. Then he backed out of the car, leaving the engine running. He stood in the nearly empty parking lot, between the open car door and the idling Miata. Waiting for the ice to melt and then evaporate from his seats, Dodd leaned across the top of the car.

Arms extended and hands clasped together, he scanned the sky. On the clear, crisply cold late autumn day, visibility was unlimited. A faint, nearly full moon hung near the ridge of Cumberland Mountain in the west. Above him in the stratosphere contrails, crystalline, concise footprints left by huge passenger jet aircraft, painted white streaks across the deeply blue sky. This day the trails were short, to him no more than the distance from his thumb to his wide-spread index finger at arm's length. On more humid days they had been much longer, the length of his arm and, sometimes, from horizon to horizon. With those contrails, he could easily have plotted the position of the local vortac. Aircraft on their way to New Orleans, Miami, Atlanta, and New York, changed directions overhead. They bent their routes 35,000 feet above the invisible radio beacon, which originated on top of Cumberland Mountain. "Lucky bastards," Dodd called after the pilots, resenting their exalted position: the few who passed the physical and mental rigors necessary to fly jets.

BeeBee landed on the roof of the Miata near Dodd. "Jealous?" he asked.

Dejectedly, Dodd answered, "I often wonder if I had the ability to fly fighters. I never had the chance to find out."

"Bad eyesight eliminates a lot of candidates," BeeBee reminded him. "You have to do the best you can with the hand dealt you."

"Too bad life's not a card game," Dodd responded bitterly.

"Maybe it is," BeeBee offered. Dodd heard the bird's raucous caw-caw laugh as he flew away in search of breakfast. He folded his lanky frame and crawled into the small car. Gunning the engine, he steered it out of the parking lot toward work.

The electric doors to student health swung outward, toward Dodd. He waited patiently for them to open completely, puffing steam from deep inside his lungs. The moisture froze in front of his face when it hit the cold air. The very warm air inside the building quickly warmed Dodd's nose and chin. Two employees stood in the hallway inside the doors. Continuing their conversation, they turned toward him. Dodd nodded in their direction. "Morning," he said quietly. They stared at him, not returning the greeting.

When he turned the corner near the nurses' station, the four nurses chatting noisily suddenly quieted. In unison, they swivelled their heads to watch him walk past. "Good morning, Dr. Dodd," one said. Concerned by their sudden silence, Dodd did not respond. He waved and continued toward his office.

His normal level of paranoia heightened by the

encounters, Dodd expected something bad had happened. The note on his office door confirmed his suspicions. "Your schedule has been cleared. Come to my office. Neal," the hand-written scribble read.

"Shit," Dodd said out loud.

The three men sat in a semicircle in Abramowicz's office. Dodd leaned forward, elbows on both knees, buttocks on the edge of the stuffed chair. Abramowicz filled his chair to overflowing. Fat rear end and thick thighs elevated him skyward, preventing his short legs from reaching the floor, a Humpty-Dumpty in search of a fall, Dodd thought uncharitably. Trim and confident, the third man, Phillip Scollick, leaned backward in his seat and crossed one leg, exposing a knee length sock stretched taut by a garter.

Scollick, university lawyer, also a state employee and ostensibly on Dodd's side, spoke accusingly, "Your notes are rather cryptic, Dr. Dodd," he said. "'Normal physical exam. Patient refuses to enter rehabilitation program for alcohol abuse,' leaves a lot unsaid."

Dodd nodded. "True," he admitted.

"Shouldn't he have asked if Garrette were suicidal?" Abramowicz inquired, needling Dodd in the process, and enjoying it. The pleasure would have been much greater had Dodd squirmed some. Dodd seemed too tired or too depressed to care.

"I did," Dodd said. "He wasn't. He mentioned the possibility of killing his father, but that seemed more in jest than sincere."

"You didn't document either comment," the lawyer repeated.

Dodd explained his lapse. "I called the psychiatrist to evaluate the patient. I thought she'd document his mental status better than I could. Did you read her note?"

The lawyer, neatly dressed in three-piece pinstripe suit, crew cut black hair, and nails manicured and coated with clear nail polish, slipped his left hand under his tie nervously. He balanced the yellow legal pad on his right knee with his right hand cradling his pen. Looking at Abramowicz, he asked, "Neal, do you want to address that?"

Abramowicz cleared his throat. He spoke slowly, driving each word deeper into Dodd's chest. "Dr. Summers says the patient was gone when she reached the clinic."

Dodd sat upright, stiffly. Hands on his knees, he glared at Abramowicz. "That's a lie. We talked about this before, Neal. Persia had him talk with his father. She's the one who let him walk out of the building."

"She denies seeing him. There's no note in his record indicating otherwise," the lawyer said.

"My word against hers?" Dodd asked hollowly.

"Seems so," the lawyer agreed.

"Well, you'll have to talk with Stone Garrette then," Dodd suggested.

Abramowicz could not resist smiling. "As part of the discovery process, we have been given access to his hospital records. In it, his surgeon says he has amnesia from twenty-four hours before the event until about twenty-four hours after recovering consciousness. Not unusual, I'm told, for severe head trauma. Dr. Summers remembers you calling for a consult, but that the patient had departed before she arrived. Do you have any other witnesses, Spencer?"

Dodd shook his head. The lawyer reached behind him. From Abramowicz's desk he hefted a six inch stack of paper. He leaned forward, handing it to Dodd. "These are the records for the case, Dr. Dodd. I suggest you review them before your deposition. We have tentatively scheduled that for early next semester. I'll go with you, unless you prefer to hire your own attorney."

Dodd stood. With leaden hands he grasped the five pounds of paper. Assuming the interview to be over, he began to walk toward the door, head bowed. "One more

Invictus

thing," Abramowicz called after him, cheerfully.

Dodd turned; he squinted in the obese administrator's direction. "I can hardly wait to hear what that is," he said.

"The top piece of paper on that pile is a letter from an attorney representing a Ms. Geriann Rivera. She plans to sue you for sexual harassment. Something about touching her inappropriately during an office visit. We'll have to address that situation when we get more information from her attorney." Stunned, Dodd looked at the paper. Unable to focus his eyes, he nodded and backed out the office door. Dodd heard Abramowicz address the lawyer as the door closed, "First time I've ever seen him speechless," the fat man said. The solid wood door almost hid the glee in his voice.

Massey spotted Dodd when he emerged from the back stairwell. The look on Dodd's face qualified him for an antidepressant, or electro-shock therapy. Massey followed him to his office. "What's up?" Massey asked. Dodd dropped the load onto his desk.

"Morton," Dodd said.

Having heard the expression from his friend before, Massey understood that Dodd referred to the salt company. "When it rains, it pours," Massey quoted Dodd. "Well, what did Neal dump on you this morning?"

"Two lawsuits," Dodd groaned. "Actually two possible lawsuits. A deposition for a possible suit by Garrette's family, failure to commit, or wrongful injury, something a million and a half dollars of malpractice insurance won't cover, I'm sure. The State of Virginia has deep pockets here, so they are involved, too." Dodd fell silent, staring at the bookshelf. Raped, he thought. I'm about to be raped. A random act of violence is about to happen to me and there's no way to fight back. Post traumatic stress syndrome, here I come.

"And...." Massey said.

"Oh, and a coed has accused me of perverting my

physical exam. We have to wait for her attorney to give us the particulars."

"Who?" Massey asked.

"That same broad who invited herself into my apartment last month."

"Shit," Massey whistled between his teeth. "I can help you with that. I'll go dictate a letter to Neal. I'll tell him what I remember you told me later that morning."

"Do that, but don't give it to Neal," Dodd suggested. "He's looking for ways to serve my head on a platter. Write it down and save it for your deposition. I plan to have you called as a character witness. And this is all confidential, right?"

"Fair enough." Massey agreed. He looked at his watch. "I've got a patient waiting for me in the treatment room. Got to go. Hang tough, Spence. Oh, did you do any more work on the proposal?"

"Looks like you guys will have to proceed without me. Can't think of anything that would lose the contract for you faster than having my name associated with it," Dodd told the second physician.

Massey stopped in mid-stride toward the door. He spun toward Dodd. "You keep working on it," he commanded. "It'll be good therapy for you, Spence, take your mind off this crap. We might take your name off of the proposal, but you'll still be here if we have anything to say about it. We need a guy who is assertive. The rest of us are pushovers." Without waiting for Dodd's response, Massey rotated on the balls of his feet, and let himself out.

"I think that's what Neal is counting on," Dodd said to himself. A tapping sounded from the window. BeeBee sat on the stone ledge outside the glass. "Go away," Dodd said, waving his hand and turning his back toward the bird. The tapping continued.

Dodd relented. He turned the crank and opened the

window, just a crack. BeeBee stuck his beak inside the office. "*Femina aut amat aut odit: nil est tertium*,"[25] the bird said.

Before Dodd could respond, the phone rang. "Dodd," he said when he answered it.

"Dr. Dodd," an unfamiliar voice said, "this is Dr. Wendall Lockhart from the biology department. One of my students, Heather Evans, saw you last week."

"Yes?"

"She brought a slip of paper to me that says she was seen in the student health center, but I want proof that she was too sick to take this exam."

"I'm sorry, Dr. Lockhart," Dodd started politely. "Without her written consent, I can't discuss her medical care with you or anyone else."

"Well, I need to see her medical record, then, or I can't postpone her exam...."

Lockhart's words opened another seething wound in Dodd. The emotions from the morning session with the lawyer and Abramowicz erupted through the seemingly small aperture. "Look, you little piss ant," Dodd exploded, "you can't see that chart without a subpoena! Not only that, asshole, it's a waste of my professional time to write notes for the likes of you, so that you can feel good about giving students the benefit of the doubt. If you had any common sense at all in your pea-sized, Ph.D. brain, you'd figure out a way to tell when students were lying to you, rather than have them come lie to us, too. All we do is formalize the fib. Which one of us, or even her private physician, is going to tell you, 'No, she wasn't sick.'? You moron! How the hell are we supposed to know if they are too sick to do their school work? We have a hard enough time taking care of the truly ill students without having to weed through the extras you send here looking for written excuses. Take that note you got from us and shove it where the sun don't shine!" Furious, Dodd slammed the receiver onto the cradle. Lockhart had long since hung up. The phone line from Lockhart's office to Abramowicz's office nearly melted when Abramowicz answered.

BeeBee looked at Dodd. He said, "*Ira furor brevis est. Medice, cura te ipsum.*"[26]

"*De recta non tolerandum sunt!*"[27] Dodd yelled, still emotional.

"*Nil desperandum!*"[28] the big black bird said and hopped to the ground.

A knock sounded on the door. "Dr. Dodd," the pregnant nurse, Virginia Strahan, called through the door. "Are you going to work today? You have patients in both exam rooms and more waiting. They'd like to get to class some time today."

"Be right there," Dodd responded. He cranked the window shut and unplugged his phone.

Invictus

Chapter Twenty-two
December 4th

Clinton Massey, A.J. Watson, and Dodd sat in the dark booth in the depths of the vast, upscale restaurant. Between special events, like proms, ring night, or homecoming, few students patronized the establishment. The prices kept the riff-raff to a minimum; the doctors thought they could speak freely without fear of eavesdroppers reporting their conversation to administrators. It was certainly quieter and the atmosphere less toxic than the Bear's Den.

Cobbled together from boxcars and cabooses abandoned over the years by small southwestern Virginia coal mining railroads as they went out of business, the restaurant emerged a complicated maze. Frequently, guests spent many minutes trying to find their way to their booths, especially after leaving their table in search of a restroom when drunk. Knowledgeable patrons, like the three physicians, experienced no difficulty navigating the labyrinth, not until they became inebriated.

Referring to von Weintraub, a tipsy Massey asked, "Where's the Nazi?"

"She called me at home;" Dodd allowed, "she can't make it."

"Is she siding with Abramowicz, or did that no good husband of hers beat her up again?" Watson asked. "Someone should shoot that bastard."

Dodd shrugged, not knowing the answer. Massey snarled, "She can run everyone's life but her own...."

Watson swayed at the end of the table. He had consumed three times the amount of alcohol that Dodd and Massey drank, combined; but he had had more practice imbibing during his long navy career. "Where does the extra money go?" he asked again.

Dodd shook his head. Watson had asked the same question three times already. "We don't know, A.J. Unless it is into this investment fund. See this number. There is $772,000 in there."

"Why does he need that much money invested?" Watson asked his second most common question. "What's he planning to do, run off to Venezuela with the funds?"

"Certainly looks like he could afford to give some people raises, or to pay for our continuing medical education," Massey suggested, slurring his speech slightly. He never overlooked a challenge to out-drink a friend. "You look like you need to make a trip to the bathroom," he told Watson.

"Wonton," Watson replied without batting an eyelash. His massive, trained bladder had room for at least one more pitcher of beer.

"What?" Massey asked. "Chinese food?"

"Not now — backwards — won ton," Dodd interpreted for the hippy physician.

"Well a half million dollars can't just disappear," A.J started onto a different tangent.

Massey disagreed, after belching like a Norseman at a feast. "Apparently, it can."

"We discussed that already, too," Dodd reiterated. "It costs half a million dollars to pay the mortgage for the new building."

"I thought the legislature paid for that," Massey said.

"They floated a bond," Dodd explained one more time. "We have to pay it back. It would have been nice if the architect had listened to us when they designed the building, so we could have gotten our money's worth. But since we share it with recreational sports and counseling and they have more political clout, they called the shots."

"Even though counseling rents space from us?"

Massey asked. "Because they can't afford to pay their share of the debt?" Dodd nodded.

"Damn ass-kissers," Watson growled. He scanned the menu. "Do you suppose they have any caviar pizza here?" he mused. "The prices are high enough."

Overhead, an ancient speaker crackled and buzzed. Words, sounding like, "Do we love her," filtered down to their level for the third or fourth time.

"Hell, yes, we love her," Massey replied, too loudly. He poured more beer into his glass from the pitcher, spilling a little onto the polished table. "One question though, who is she?"

The two other physicians ignored their colleague's fantasy. "Why are there so many categories of income?" Watson continued, trying to stay on track. He shuffled the papers Dodd had copied in the library.

"Apparently, the health center enjoys a special status," Dodd explained. "It is auxiliary funded. In other words, the state makes no provision for the operation of our clinic in their budget. It has to be run solely with the fees collected from students. It does harvest some money — that's called revenue on the third line," he pointed for Watson, "with the few drugs we sell, special splints, x-rays, and medical services not covered by the basic fee."

"What's E & G?" Massey asked, rejoining the conversation and focusing on another line in the budget.

"Education and General Funds, tuition and grants from the general assembly," Dodd said. "Counseling gets most of its money that way."

"Recovery?" Watson asked.

Dodd explained what he had learned from poring over the manuscript. "Services we provide to other university divisions, like tetanus and rabies shots for the veterinarians."

"Can the administration be skimming money? And, if so, what would they be doing with it?" Massey asked.

"It's no secret that the state budget is tight," Dodd said. "Burroughs Hall takes at least six percent off the top just for handling charges. That's $180,000 each semester, and $60,000 in the summer, or $420,000 per year."

"Just for providing a bank account for the money?" Watson asked.

"They'd say they do 'administrative stuff,' too, I'm sure," Dodd said. "That's Neal's favorite line. They could be taking more. If so, they can use it in any way they choose, support women's athletics, political action committee funds, whatever. The governor is sensitive to the charge that tuition has risen during his tenure. He'd show a blind eye to using fees, other than tuition, for balancing the books."

"That would be legal," Watson observed. "If this half million went for legal stuff, it should show up in the budget. It just disappears. Where does the extra money go?" he asked, again.

Massey summarized the thought, "I think the questions are these: is it really missing, i.e. is it a bookkeeping error? If it is not a bookkeeping error, who knows about it? If we know who approved the budget, then we can find it."

Dodd nodded. "The problem is that we used two sources for our information. The public budget is precisely correct, to the penny. Only Neal's version shows this excess, more taken in than the published budget accounts for. Maybe it's his mistake."

"How do we find out?" Watson. asked. "Or do we care? The really important issue is this: if we privatize, can we live within our own budget? Do we have to bill the students' insurance companies? Boy, that's a hassle."

Dodd placed both elbows on the damp, sticky table top, his rolled sleeves nearly touched the mass of paperwork. "I think," he said cautiously, "that we should plan on taking the fee and living within its constraints, at first. We should let the students know that we will start billing their insurance companies eventually. As soon as we learn how to adapt to the real world, and capitalism, we can start refunding a portion of their fees. When we are on our feet, we will stop taking it altogether."

"I think I know how the Russians felt, after the collapse of communism and the Soviet Union," Watson offered. "This is scary."

Dodd laughed. He did his best to be a cheerleader. "You have to remember that there are hundreds of thousands of doctors doing this already. We'll make some mistakes, but docs don't usually go bankrupt. We can do it."

"Managed care will be a problem for us," Massey suggested.

"We're big enough, and have enough of a population, that we should be able to negotiate with managed care," Dodd suggested. "In fact, it may pay us to set up our own PPO."

"Oh, Jesus," Massey observed, washing down Dodd's words with a swig of beer and making fun of Dodd, "he's one of them, A.J.! Spencer speaks that foreign tongue: alphabet soup."

"Speaking of unusual enterprises," Dodd expanded on the opening, "we may have to advertise, do some marketing."

"Why?" Watson asked.

"If we are going to compete with the local physicians and the two hospital systems, Carilion and HCA-Columbia, then we need to be visible to our patrons, the students," Dodd said.

"We should at least let them know that we have new hours and are under new management," Watson added.

"I favor a *Heaven Can Wait* campaign," Massey said, again slurring his speech.

"A what?" Dodd asked.

"It was a movie in the late seventies, starred Warren

Beatty," Massey explained. "I loved the advertising. It started on billboards with just a pair of wings. Every week they added a little more, until the whole angel and the title appeared. It was great. I started out a communications major, thought about being in advertising until I switched to pre-med. Wrote a term paper on movie marketing."

"Well, we found our marketing department chairman," Dodd told Watson

"What's Neal planning?" Watson asked.

"From the numbers on his spreadsheet...." Dodd started to say.

"Where did you get that?" Massey asked.

"I can't reveal my sources."

"Bet you're humping the stiletto," Massey accused Dodd.

Confused, Watson asked, "Stiletto?"

Massey explained the terminology, "Abramowicz's personal secretary, J.P. Jones, the one who delivers bad news for him. She stabs everyone in the back." Directing his comments to Dodd, he added, "I hope you didn't tell her anything; she can't keep a secret. Her other nickname is 'Town-crier.'" Dodd shook his head.

"Hatchet-man, or hatchet-woman," Watson suggested; he asked Dodd, "You're in bed with *her*?"

Dodd made a face, gagged on his beer. "No way," he denied the suggestion, "but I can't reveal my sources, under penalty of death. Anyway, it looks like the bookstore scenario. He goes private, writing a contract between himself and the university. All the employees are fired from state jobs, with their expensive pensions and benefits packages. Those who don't know any better are rehired, or replaced, as wage people with almost no benefits. Saves a bundle. He skims that, and pays the university a kick-back from the profits so no one squawks too loudly."

"He's shrewd," Watson suggested.

"Wile E. Coyote," Dodd acknowledged. "We just have

to be his Roadrunner."

"Can we learn all this stuff in time to put together a competitive bid?" Watson asked the others, "like corporation types, accounting, marketing, budgets, wages laws, OSHA rules, all that stuff. I don't want to dig a hole I can't climb out of later."

Neither Massey nor Dodd knew the answer. "Let's look at the rest of the budget, try to figure out what these abbreviations stand for," Dodd said. "Maybe there's a hint in there. Each of us should take a third of this home and plug through it over the weekend. Fair enough?" The others nodded solemnly and gathered the papers Dodd handed to them.

After they visited the men's room, they followed the maze to the cashier in order to pay their bills. Dodd pointed to the tall, male cashier's name tag for Massey. 'Dewey Glover,' he read to Massey, "as in, 'Do we love her?'"

"Nope; I don't," Massey answered, changing his mind when he saw the young man.

Bill Yancey

Invictus

Chapter Twenty-three
December 6th

The too frequent announcement that the pharmacy computer was 'down,' again, and that the practitioners should fill their own prescriptions from the rolling drug carts flitted from the clinic's overhead speakers. A collective groan emanated from the medical offices. Dodd waited only a couple minutes before climbing the back stairway to the administrative suite in search of Abramowicz.

Through the open door, Dodd spied the administrator leaning over his desk, poring over a set of papers. His administrative assistant evidently ran errands; her desk sat empty. Dodd mused that no one manned the machine gun nest to cut down those seeking an audience with the Pope of Kilocalories. He strolled into Abramowicz's office and closed the door noisily. Startled, Abramowicz sat upright, eyes large. He shuffled papers clumsily. "Ah, Spencer, what can I do for you?" he eventually asked pleasantly.

As casually as he could given the rage festering inside him, Dodd said, "Pharmacy has decided that we should fill our own prescriptions, again. I thought you agreed that they would fill them by hand and then update the computer when it came back on line?"

"I did, but the pharmacists complained...."

"Now the practitioners are complaining. We outnumber them four to one."

"I guess I should walk down to the pharmacy," Abramowicz offered. Clearly nervous about something, he turned the papers on his desk face down. He stood and walked toward Dodd and the door. "Is there anything else I can do for you, Spence."

Surprised by Abramowicz's congeniality, Dodd said, "Yeah. For some reason the nurses have stopped recording respiratory rates on patients who come through the cold clinic. Colds are respiratory illnesses, Neal. A respiratory rate is a *vital* sign for respiratory illnesses, if you catch my drift."

Surprising Dodd with his instantaneous and forceful, apparent agreement, Abramowicz said, "Well, I can take care of that."

Also startled by the fat man's apparent sincerity, Dodd almost blushed, embarrassed that he had been so sarcastic. "Gee, that's great, Neal," Dodd said.

"Fine, fine. Will I see you at Jane Shore's party tonight?" Abramowicz said, shooing Dodd from the room.

"I'll be there," Dodd replied, barely missing having his fingers closed in the door when Abramowicz hustled him out of the office. He heard the door lock behind him.

At the end of the day, the pharmacy had yet to fill its first prescription. Additionally, the nurses voted not to take blood pressures on students who had had a blood pressure taken at least once during that semester.

***.

The retirement party for Jane Shore took place in the university's Faculty Club, the faculty hotel, recreation, and meeting building, on campus near the drill field. A previous structure, the performing arts building, once occupied the same location. Many years before, during an anti-Vietnam War rally, some over-zealous protesters started a fire in a trash can, assuming the fire department would respond quickly and put it out. They underestimated the flammability of the one hundred year-old structure. Luckily, no one died in the blaze. A new, larger, performing arts building, badly needed anyway, now stood a block away on the opposite side of the drill field. When the faculty grew tired of fighting students for parking and stationary bicycles in the Memorial Gymnasium, they induced the administration to build a castle they could call their own. Strict rules determined who entered the building. Without a faculty identification card, or a guest pass, an interloper soon found himself on the street. The building was the last bastion for faculty; there, they retreated to hide from students, and the administration.

Someone, obviously a state employee with too much time on his hands, thought that Jane Shore's retirement party should have a theme, as if retirement were not theme enough. Each guest had been asked to dress to remind the ancient nurse practitioner of an incident that took place during her tenure. Since she was older than dirt, and had been in the old building since before World War II, that allowed a lot of possibilities. Dodd had thought about going as Death, complete with scythe, but decided against it. Shore had been present during the meningitis outbreak. Although only two students died; the mention of the panic on campus still brought tears to her eyes. She had spent twenty-three hours a day for a week trying to figure out where students were, in which classes, living in which dorms, all before the advent of computers.

Dodd eventually decided that the overriding impression he had of Nurse Shore was her lack of height. The feisty red/blue/white/silver-haired (depending upon who did her hair that month) woman tipped the scales at a mere ninety-two pounds and stood only four feet ten inches tall. In celebration of her diminutiveness, Dodd wore a dress and knee pads. He had a pair of woman's shoes duct-taped to his thighs. Once inside the Faculty Club, he intended to walk on his knees and impersonate a very short, ugly woman. Even on his knees, he remained only slightly shorter than the lilliputian nurse. The blue wig, the dress, and shoes, he bought at the local Salvation Army Store. He fully intended to re-donate them after the

Bill Yancey

party.

The Faculty Club operator hired school athletes to man the front door of the building. This evening, a huge young man wearing a yellow pin-striped suit with wide lapels, purple shirt and tie, and black and white spats guarded the entrance. A matching wide-brimmed hat lay on the counter with the sign-in log. When Dodd approached, he recognized the Hispanic defensive lineman as one of his patients. Leon Luz, nicknamed 'Neon' for his choice of clothing, stood at attention with his arms folded, blocking the door. Directly in front of the football player, a young woman pouted. Dodd noted that her skin color was a shade darker than Luz's. She faced the young man, her hands on her waist. Weight on her back leg, her leading foot pawed the top step like a bull preparing to charge. With each word, her high heel shoe slammed into the metal tread on the step with a loud crack. Every motion of her legs highlighted her shapely figure, creasing and re-creasing her tight skirt. "Why can't I go in?" she demanded. "I was personally invited to this party by Nurse Shore. She said, 'Anna, come to my retirement party.'"

"Sorry, Miss Mueller," the polite young man responded. "You are not on my list. Graduate students are not allowed in The Faculty Club. It's the rules, ma'am."

"I am adjunct faculty!" she yelled.

"Not according to my computer," Luz said, evenly. Many students tried to break the rules and enter the building over the course of the year.

Distracted by the motion of her body within the blue silk skirt, Dodd almost missed hearing the shapely young woman's name. Interrupting the argument, Dodd slipped his arm between her arm and waist. She turned toward him, a surprised expression on her face. He smiled and said, "Anna! So glad you made it to the shindig." To the football player, he continued, "Leon, Ms. Mueller is with me."

Invictus

The lineman's stern look turned to a smile. Recognizing the physician in spite of the outfit, he asked, "May I see your identification, Dr. Dodd?" After taking Dodd's identification number for billing purposes, he wrote Dodd's and his guest's names in the log book and handed Mueller a guest pass.

Dodd folded his wallet, covering his identification card. He placed the wallet inside his matching handbag. "Just add it to my bill, Leon," he said, grinning. He walked arm-in-arm with Ms. Mueller into the club.

Inside the front door, in the large foyer, Mueller halted and pulled her arm from Dodd's. He also stopped, and turned to face her. Aware he was an unusual sight, broad shoulders in a dress and carrying a purse, not to mention the shoes hanging above his knees, he shrugged. She confirmed his suspicions. "Are you a pervert?" she asked, speaking with a slight British accent.

Dodd smiled through the made up rosy cheeks and lipstick. "Am I a cross-dresser? No. Do I detect an accent?"

Still undecided about their relationship, she answered. "I'm from the Netherlands. I studied in England."

"Of Indonesian descent?" Dodd asked.

"How did you know that?"

"Made sense," Dodd said. "You look Asian. Indonesia used to be a Dutch colony."

"Not many Americans know that," Mueller observed.

Dodd explained, "My father was in the United States Air Force. I grew up in Europe and the Far East. I probably know more about the Dutch and Indonesians than your young American peers because I lived through the colonial wars after the end of WWII." Uneasy about being seen with a man dressed as a woman, Mueller edged away from Dodd as he spoke. He saw the worried look on her face. Sensing her discomfort, Dodd smiled; he said, "Go ahead and take off. Hang on to that guest pass, though."

Bill Yancey

Relieved, she turned to flee from the apparition. Dodd laughed. "Thanks for your help," she called over her shoulder.

"No problem. Enjoy the party," Dodd said, waving with one hand. He watched her go, wistfully, and then wandered toward the check-in counter. A bevy of students in school colors, light blue blazers with gray ties over white shirts, signed in and checked out hotel patrons. A Civil War conference had just ended. It featured author Jake Laughlin and his latest information on Stonewall Jackson, a thousand page treatise that covered Stonewall's life from birth to age sixteen.

Other alumni and fans of the football team, dressed in school logo clothing and expecting the undefeated football team to earn a bowl bid by whuppin' the hated nearby rivals from Virginia Tech, stood in lines waiting for room assignments. The Virginia Tech Hokies had reverted to their 'chokie' ways from pre-Coach 'Bunk' Franklin times. After becoming famous as coach of the College Football National Champion Hokies, Franklin took the head position with the recently renamed Washington Redskins. Some wags suggested the team be renamed the Martians, so as not to offend anyone occupying this planet. A more mundane mascot won the ballot. Under Franklin's tutelage, the Washington Presidents were politically correct and confidently marched toward a team record third in-a-row Super Bowl appearance.

Standing behind a fan who wore a beanie with bear ears that wiggled when she pulled a string, Dodd waited patiently, collecting stares. Someone tapped Dodd on the shoulder. He turned to face the man who had to reach up to make contact with his shoulder. It took Dodd a second to recognize 'Worm' Thornton. The physician's assistant wore a paper-maché bedpan costume. A small man, the P.A. filled the pan, his head and most of his body inside the construction. Dodd rolled his eyes. "You are in an appropriate place," he told Thornton. "Feel at home?"

Thornton spoke with a slight lisp. The speech impediment and his effeminate mannerisms belied his heterosexuality. He had earned his nickname by being Abramowicz's 'yes' man. The brown nose occupied a fitting location. "I just came to tell you that we will miss your dry wit and dissent when you leave," Thornton said.

"I'm not going anywhere...." Dodd started to deny his departure. Then he saw the look of horror on Thornton's face. Grabbing the man by the throat, Dodd pulled him away from the crowd and into an empty stairwell. "What have you heard, Worm?"

"N-n-nothing," the little man stammered.

"That's a lie," Dodd observed coldly.

"Don't tell Neal, Spence. He'll kill me."

"I'll kill you first. What's going on?" Dodd asked.

"He and Dean Waters have decided not to renew your contract."

"In January?"

"No," the little man shook with fear, intimidated by Dodd's size and strength. "The rule is you get a year's notice, but they figure you will quit before the year is up." Emboldened by Dodd's sudden paleness and apparent knee weakness at the news, Thornton continued, "They think you lack intestinal fortitude and will leave, rather than play by their rules."

Dodd's pallor passed quickly, replaced by bright red rage. His grip tightened on the frightened little man. "If you tell another soul about this, I will personally string you up, from the goal posts. Got it?"

***

Massey found Dodd in the small basement gym of the Faculty Club. He had stripped the costume, washed off the make-up, and put on gym shorts and an SVU Bears T-shirt. Sweat stained him front and back. It poured from his scalp, obscuring his vision. He had finished riding the stationary bicycle after an hour. Presently, he pounded a punching bag, enjoying the thought that it could have been Abramowicz. "Well, I can take care of that," Dodd repeated Abramowicz's words from earlier in the day, over and over, again. "Well, I can take care of that. Is this how you take care of things, asshole?" he blurted, unaware that Massey stood behind him. "You fire people who question your ability?"

"Careful," Massey warned, "you don't want to have a heart attack."

Dodd recognized the voice. He spit back, "Maybe I do," never taking his eyes off the sand-filled punching bag. It reverberated with each punch.

"You missed a fine party, Spence. Where did you learn to box?" Massey asked.

"Required physical education for plebes at the Point," Dodd said, slamming his fist into the bag. "One of my best friends broke my nose in class. We both got A's for the day. The more blood the instructors saw, the higher your grade."

"Unique grading system," Massey offered, then observed, "Well, it's better to leave on the bus than in a pine box."

"Who told you?" Dodd asked, continuing to throw punches at the defenseless, leather bag.

"A.J.," Massey answered. "He wants your office. Says it's six inches wider than his."

"Sharks after chum," Dodd wheezed, lungs burning and heart pounding. "No one's upset?"

"You don't expect us to stand up for you, do you?" Massey asked, voice betraying his surprise at the question. "At one time or another, you have castigated each of us. Some more than others, I realize. I still carry the psychic scar of having missed the appendicitis in the woman with a urinary tract infection."

"Deservedly criticized. You now do an abdominal exam

Invictus

on every female who says it hurts to pee, don't you?" Dodd gasped, then pounded the bag ten more times in quick succession, counting each hit. He stopped, allowing his heavy hands to fall to his side. Turning to face Massey, he said, "You guys don't understand, do you? You, individually and as a group, lack a voice and are unassertive. Neal will drive you all.... Hell, he'll herd you like the sheep you are. If he wins the contract, you'll suffer and work; he'll make an enormous profit, get fatter and lazier."

"Sorry, Spence." Massey stared at his own feet. He spoke slowly, almost apologetically, "I took an informal poll. You've used up all your goodwill currency. You'll have to fight this one on your own. We're all spent. And we're tired of trying to figure out who's going to win the power struggle. If you are interested, the odds are a hundred to one that Neal is still here in twelve months, and you aren't. If our bid wins, we'll let you stay. But, we don't think the contract stands a chance with your name on it. We voted to remove your name — only for show of course."

"Then you won't mind if I put in a bid of my own?" Dodd asked angrily. He watched his own feet; the sweat poured off his face and dripped onto the dirty mats between his jogging shoes. Rage surged within him that the practitioners changed allegiances to suit the situation. It was a defense mechanism he understood, but the cowards lacked loyalty to even their own thoughts and ideas. He could not look Massey in the eye. Had he, he would have allowed his rage to spill over and engulf the spineless physician, too. Friends, even fainthearted ones, were in short supply. The smell of sweat and fear co-mingled in the gymnasium, flaring his nostrils in response. Dodd wished some of the fear were not his own.

Massey shrugged. "Guess not. You'll have to hire us to work for you, or you'll have to recruit a new set of docs if you win."

Bill Yancey

A motion, caught out of the corner of his eye, stopped Dodd. Anna Mueller strolled into view from behind a set of lockers. She traipsed across the gym mats, stunning body in the tight, low-cut blue dress briefly reflected an infinite number of times between the parallel mirrors covering two walls. Slowly, she approached the men. "It is a nice gymnasium, Clint, even though it is very small," she said to Massey. She averted her eyes from Dodd. "Who's your friend?"

Massey brightened. "Anna, this is Spencer Dodd, one of my colleagues. Spencer this is...."

"We've met," Dodd and Mueller said simultaneously.

"You have?" Massey asked Mueller.

She nodded, turning and smiling at Dodd, with her right hand extended. "You look so much more masculine without the dress. Taller, too," she said, admiring Dodd's muscular physique. "In addition to knowing more history, you also appear to be in better physical shape than most of my contemporaries."

Dodd allowed the sweat to pool in one spot beneath him. "Working out helps me deal with the frustrations of employment at SVU," he said holding her hand within the boxing glove longer than necessary. He looked at Massey. "For the next couple months I'm going to need a lot more exercise, it seems. After that, my aggravation should end dramatically."

Massey felt out of place, seeing Dodd's and Mueller's eyes lock onto each other's. Warily, he said, "Anna is an exchange professor in the school of health sciences. She is a friend of Joie's, and has a masters degree in nursing. She's from...."

"The Netherlands," Dodd finished for his friend.

Invictus

Chapter Twenty-four
December 14*th*

Dodd abhorred hospitals. He despised the smell; he detested the looks. He disliked the sounds; he hated the people — personnel and patients. He took offense at the feel; he loathed it all. Memories of multiple surgeries, his knees, his back, his shoulder, and more, flooded his brain. He struggled to remind himself that as a doctor he should identify with the surgeons, not the patients.

Silently, he waited for the elevator door to open on the sixth floor, location of the University of Virginia Hospital Neurointensive Care Unit. Alone on the spacious elevator, he hummed to himself in an attempt to maintain his courage. The door rolled open slowly, revealing a wide corridor. Dodd stepped out of the metal box; the door slid silently closed behind him. A piece of cardboard hung over a wet floor sign. "Trip Hazard," someone had written on the cardboard. "Do not remove until repaired." The bright yellow, plastic, bivalved contraption straddled a large rip in the carpet directly in front of the elevator door. The first guy to catch his foot in the carpet is probably a head trauma patient, Dodd mused. Deftly, he skirted the open seam in the carpet, spotting a sign on the far wall. One arrow pointed to the waiting room, the other to the intensive care unit.

Dodd pushed open the door to the waiting room. A huge picture window gave those family members visiting critically ill patients a panoramic view of the Blue Ridge Mountains visible to the west of Charlottesville. The room itself held several knots of people, each a core of support for one of the victims struggling to survive in the next room.

They kept to themselves, looking up only briefly when he entered. Dodd did not see Murphy Garrette. He did recognize the cortege of beautiful women that usually accompanied the man. They sat in one corner conversing quietly among themselves. Dodd left the room without interacting with them.

He walked to the door in front of the intensive care unit. While he read the rules concerning visitors, both doors swung outward. A janitor pushed his wheeled bucket through the doors with his mop. Dodd picked up the phone that connected him to the nurses' station. "Yes," a voice said.

"Uh, this is Dr. Dodd," he said uncertainly. "Is Stone Garrette's father with him?"

"I'll check," the voice said. A soft hum sounded from the handset; the owner of the voice placed him on hold. Dodd stood at the phone, holding it to his ear, waiting for the person on the other end to return. Minutes passed. Dodd squelched the urge to hang up and call again. Both the double doors opened. Murphy Garrette walked out of the intensive care unit. Dodd hung up the phone.

Garrette held his right hand out to Dodd. "Doctor," he said, "thanks for coming." Pulling Dodd by his hand, he directed him into the intensive care unit. "Please, come in."

Dodd swallowed hard, initially resisting. "Are you sure?"

"Absolutely. Stone would want you to come in." Garrette dropped Dodd's hand and the physician followed Garrette into the spacious ward.

Individual rooms, enclosed in glass, approximately twelve by twelve feet in size held single patients and multitudes of medical equipment. Dodd heard respirators hiss, monitors beep, and intravenous machines call for attention. He kept his eyes on Garrette, in an effort to allow the patients and their families some privacy and to avoid seeing the horrors who recuperated, comatose, in their beds. Garrette led him to the far room. Outside the smaller window, Stone Garrette would have enjoyed the same view as the visitors, had he been conscious. "What happened?" Dodd asked Murphy Garrette. They took positions at the foot of the younger Garrette's bed. "I thought he was doing well."

"He was," Garrette agreed. "At the rehab hospital, he tripped using the crutches. He fell and hit his head. He had a concussion. They examined him and told him to sit out the rest of the day. The next morning they couldn't wake him."

"Subdural?" Dodd asked. His eyes examined Stone Garrette. The young man lay partially turned on his right side. A large bandage covered his head. His face was puffy. Dodd could not have identified him; he had to take Murphy Garrette's word that his son lay in the bed. The young man had bilateral black eyes. His eyelids remained closed, glistening with an antibiotic ointment the nurses used to prevent eye infections. The wide, accordion-like respirator tubing connected to the smaller diameter tube taped securely to Garrette's mouth. The machine wheezed. It inflated the young man's lungs occasionally; a puff of vapor exited near Garrette's mouth. Stone seemed to be breathing on his own most of the time. Four intravenous solutions hung from the metallic shelf above his head. Two lines of medication ran into each arm. A clear plastic tube carried urine to a plastic bag hung on the side of the bed.

"Some kind of big blood clot in his brain." The older Garrette explained what Dodd already knew. "They had to drain the clot. He's been comatose for twenty-four hours. Several hours ago they stopped his sedation and paralysis medications. His doctor expects him to wake up any time. At least that's the hope."

"MRI? CT scan?" Dodd asked.

"Both show no permanent damage. Just a little

swelling," Garrette said. He stroked his son's arm. The hand opened and closed, making a fist. The patient's feet began to move, pushing the sheets with a soft pedaling motion. Stone Garrette opened his eyes.

Dodd watched Stone search the room without moving his head. Eventually the young man's eyes locked onto the respirator in front of him. He blinked several times then closed his eyes again, in recognition and resignation, Dodd supposed. Looking at the color computer monitor hanging from the ceiling, Dodd saw numbers and graphs indicating that Stone's blood pressure rose; his respiratory rate increased, and his hemoglobin oxygen content increased slightly.

A nurse entered the room. "Alice," the elder Garrette said, recognizing the woman, "this is Dr. Dodd, from Southwestern Virginia University, where Stone goes to school."

"Nice to met you, Doctor," the nurse said perfunctorily, shaking Dodd's hand. "I'm afraid I'm going to have to ask you two to leave, though."

"Why?" Garrette asked.

It was Dodd's turn to pull Garrette by the elbow. "Stone's waking up, Murphy. They want to rearrange things to make him more comfortable."

"Get him off the respirator?" Garrette asked.

"Possibly," Alice responded. She shooed them from the room, closing the wide, glass door after them and pulling the curtain to seal the room.

Dodd led Garrette to the waiting room. Wordlessly, he deposited the man among his assistants, then meandered to the window to take in the view. In the distance a hawk flew, harassed by two ravens. Dodd watched the birds wheel through the sky in a misnamed 'dog fight,' knowing the ravens either chased the hawk from their nest or taunted it because it carried food. The scavengers loved to steal food from raptors, as well as lead them to a victim and then

Invictus

swipe a meal after the bird of prey made a kill. The aerial duel continued for many minutes, eventually disappearing behind a taller building north of the hospital.

Vicariously engrossed in the birds' adventure, Dodd did not hear Murphy Garrette until the man stood next to him. Garrette placed a hand on Dodd's shoulder. Dodd jumped slightly. "Sorry, Spencer, " Garrette said. "Didn't mean to startle you. The nurse said we can go back in."

Alice met them at the door. "He's still very groggy. Try not to wear him out," she scolded.

The young man lay in the bed on his back, eyes closed. Fresh sheets covered him from the waist down. The bandage on his scalp had been changed. Without the respirator tubing, Dodd saw all of his face. He looked more like the Stone Garrette Dodd remembered, if a little thinner and paler. Murphy Garrette knelt on one knee at the bedside. He touched Stone's hand. Instantly, Stone's eyes opened. He raised his head slightly, looked at Dodd and his father, and then let his head drop onto the pillow. He grimaced when his head touched down. "Dad?' he whispered.

"Yes, Stone," the elder Garrette said. Dodd watched the father weep, sobbing quietly.

Eyes closed, Stone spoke, "I've got one hell of a headache. Thanks for coming, Doc. What happened?"

"Seems you are clumsy with crutches, Stone," Dodd said. Tears fell onto the sheet from Murphy Garrette's eyes; he continued to clasp tightly his son's hand.

"Dad?"

Murphy Garrette sniffed, drawing tears into his nose. He cleared his throat. "Yes, son?"

"When you woke me, I was having a dream. St. Peter stopped me at the Pearly Gates. He said, 'Stone, you're not half the man your father is.' I said, 'That's not quite true, St. Peter. I am *exactly* one half the man my father is.'"

The elder Garrette laughed, wiping tears from his face. "What did St. Peter say to that?" he asked.

Stone paused. Dodd watched him swallow hard several times; he knew his throat hurt from the respirator tube. Finally, he spoke. "St. Peter said, 'Go back and try again.' Will you let me, Dad?"

Dodd left the room, after patting Stone on the hand. Neither Stone nor Murphy seemed aware of his presence or pending absence. Returning to the parking deck, Dodd found the aging Miata. He unzipped the rear window and let the top down. In order to find the exit from the deck, he drove two circuits around it. BeeBee landed in the passenger seat as he left the ticket booth. The bird said nothing while Dodd piloted the automobile through Charlottesville and south to Interstate 64 West, then to Interstate 81 South.

Lost in his thoughts, reminded of his past failures by Neal's recent notification that his contract would not be renewed, Dodd drove on autopilot for hours. He paid little attention to the traffic, instead dwelling on his failings, running vignettes through his mind: the seaman named Green with whom he fought on the carrier; reading comic books on his first date in Newport News; the girl who wanted to marry him and put him through medical school; the fight he lost in grade school; Brandy, the married woman; another fight he won at Boy Scout camp. The scenes washed across his psyche eroding his self-confidence, digging deeper, hurting more with each replay.

"Lookout!" BeeBee shouted.

From the right, lower corner of his visual field, Dodd saw the huge buck climb the hill. It never slowed. With a single bound it cleared the railing between it and the highway. The second bounce placed it directly in the path of the red car in front of the Miata. Dodd slammed on his brakes and pulled to the right side of the road, knowing

Invictus

what would happen next and powerless to prevent it. The small red car in front of him swerved to the left, too late. The deer tried to jump again. The car cut its legs from under it.

In slow motion the deer flew upward and to the left. It flipped one and a half times in the air, legs straight out, having gained momentum from the collision with the car. Unable to take his eyes off the deer, Dodd watched it land on its back on the lefthand side of the highway. It rolled forward three times, tumbling into the median. Briefly, it tried to stand, collapsed, and, Dodd assumed, died from its injuries.

The red car screeched to a halt, pulling onto the left shoulder of the road. Dodd bolted from his car and, dodging traffic, ran to the driver's door. He expected to see carnage, blood from the deer, a shattered windshield, blown airbags, injured driver and passengers. He found a startled teenage girl with no apparent injuries. "You all right?" he asked incredulously through the side window. Numbly, she nodded.

Dodd examined the front of the car. The headlights shattered on impact. Pieces lay all over the highway. The hood of the automobile had been flattened on top of the engine. It was jammed shut. There was no other visible damage. Kneeling, Dodd looked under the front of the vehicle. No fluids drained from the radiator or the engine. He stood and returned to speak with the driver, who had managed to open the door and stand next to the car. She took repeated deep breaths, fighting the urge to vomit.

"A deer?" she asked.

"About a twelve point buck, I'd say," Dodd told her. "It's dead, I'm pretty sure." He pointed to the animal on the grass about a hundred yards behind the car. The carcass lay immobile; she made no effort to look at it. Turning his attention to her vehicle, Dodd asked, "Does the engine run?"

Bill Yancey

The young woman sat in the car and started the engine. She raced it several times while Dodd searched for leaks, smoke, or other signs of something wrong. It seemed to be okay. "What do I do now?" the girl asked.

Dodd thought. "Best thing is to notify the police so your insurance company will get a report. Need to have someone check the car to make sure it's not too damaged to drive, too. I don't want to check the engine here. If I get the hood open, I may not be able to close it again. How about this? I'll follow you to the nearest gas station; you can call the police from there."

The girl agreed. Dodd watched her ease the vehicle onto the highway. He followed her in the Miata to the next exit and left her with a mechanic and the highway patrol. BeeBee had disappeared during the interlude. Dodd returned to the interstate. As he started up the on ramp, the bird dropped into the passenger's bucket seat, flaring its wings and tail, matching speeds perfectly.

"Nice landing," Dodd said.

"Nice good deed," BeeBee returned the compliment.

"As good deeds go, that one was unimpressive," Dodd answered. "What do you suppose got into the deer?"

"It's rutting season," the bird explained. "His thoughts were scrambled by pheromones, estrous odor from some doe. Deer are so dumb."

"Yeah and ravens are so much smarter; humans, too, when it comes to females," Dodd said.

"I don't know about humans," BeeBee said. "The genus Homo has only been around for four or five million years. Birds have been evolving since the time of the dinosaurs, at least a hundred-forty million years."

"Are all corvids a pain in the ass?" Dodd asked the bird.

"*Besia asinum meum*,"[29] BeeBee replied.

Dodd laughed. "Where did you go while I followed her to the gas station?"

Invictus

"To let my brothers know about the fresh roadkill. Do you suppose you could go back and skin it?"

"Yuck! Why?"

"That makes it easier to get at the meat. Otherwise they will have to wait for the coyotes and badgers to rip it open. If the dogs don't find it soon, they will be forced to eat maggots — a delicacy, of course, but it takes awhile. We are scavengers, you know." BeeBee stood upright, throwing back his shoulders and strutting left and right along the front edge of the car seat. He expanded his throat and chest feathers, increasing his apparent size by fifty percent. Ear feathers raised, he lifted his head. His white nictitating eyelids slid forward and back several times.

"Proud of yourself?" Dodd asked.

"We hunted with wolves, cats, and bears before humans learned to hunt," BeeBee explained. "Before your species became extremely dangerous, we helped other predators track down your ancestors, then shared in the spoils."

"You're making me sick to my stomach. I couldn't be a scavenger."

"You're a doctor;" the bird said, "*blood and guts* is your business."

"You're a ghoul," Dodd responded.

"It's in our genes. We scout. Then we partake of the remains. It makes no difference if you bring down a buck with a gun or an automobile. It's all food."

"I'll try to remember that when next I eat crow," Dodd said gloomily.

Ignoring the pun and the insinuation, BeeBee said, "Quit feeling sorry for yourself, Spencer. You don't have to punish yourself because Abramowicz is an asshole. So he sucker-punched you. Get up. Fight back. Go work for someone else. Or yourself. You don't need him to run you down. You've got me to do that." Dodd laughed again. The ancient failures slipped from his consciousness and retreated to their dungeon in the depths of his mind. There he chained them again and slammed the door, locking it tightly, if temporarily. In silence, BeeBee preened for the remainder of the trip to Fawsville.

Invictus

*Chapter Twenty-five
December 15th*

Cody Gray sat on the bucket. He watched Dodd enter the apartment, "So what's up with the Wizard of Gauze?" he called, back to the computer monitor.

"Not much, Lord of the Files," Dodd replied amicably.

Going directly to the small fridge, Dodd retrieved a beer. He sat on the edge of Gray's bed. He had been there every night the previous week, watching Gray beta test the GoKart Web Site. For hours, it seemed, Gray manipulated his joy stick. His fingers danced across the keyboard faster than Dodd could see them. Jumbled video of an indoor, dirt race track and small racing vehicles filled the screens with a constantly changing perspective. Despondent, Dodd sat silently and drank beer after beer, afraid to interrupt his young friend and destroy his concentration. He waited patiently, if not soberly.

Through blurred eyes, he watched the student manipulate the image on the screen. A camera in a go-cart showed, to Gray and Dodd, what a driver would have seen if one had been present: directly in front of the little vehicle another, similar car flipped into the air after hitting the wall of old tires. Two other go-carts slammed into the crashed one; wheels and other parts flew through the air in all directions. Deftly twisting the joystick, Gray turned his go-cart into a sideways skid and hit the brakes. His vehicle closed rapidly upon the upside-down, crashed vehicles. Gray pushed the joystick forward. The go-cart accelerated, narrowly missing the pile-up.

"See that, Doc?" Gray asked excitedly.

"I saw all the parts. This could be an expensive hobby,

Bitman."

Gray kept his eyes on the track. "Nah," he said. "The carts are designed to fall apart on contact. Great visual effects; little real damage. Takes a couple minutes to put them back together." Pushing the buttons on the joystick allowed him to see the track beside him and behind him. The side and rear view mirror projections appeared in small, auxiliary windows at the top and sides of the computer screen. The front view continued to fill the major portion of the monitor. Gray's vehicle inched closer to the two go-carts leading the race. In the distance, he and Dodd could see the black and white checkered flag that marked the finish line. Out of the last turn, Gray accelerated into the straightaway, but no faster than the two carts in front of him increased their speed. His vehicle finished behind them.

On the screen, the view of the track slid off the monitor, replaced by words too small for Dodd to read from his position ten feet behind Gray. "We finished third," Gray told Dodd. "Better than I thought. Not bad for ten dollars worth of entertainment. I think we'll be a hit when we go online for real."

Dodd leaned backward onto the bed. "Where did you get the money for the equipment, Cody? That can't be inexpensive."

"Benny the Mooch, the bookie in Vegas," Gray said, "He thinks he can eventually give odds on who is driving and their chances of winning. If that happens, he can then make book and bucks, if you know what I mean."

Despair evident in his voice, Dodd replied drunkenly, "Evidently, I am wasting my time working for a living. Mooch is probably a millionaire. I'll be lucky to get social security when I retire."

"You'll find a new job, Doc."

"Fat chance," Dodd said waving a hand in the direction of Gray. "I'm too old to start my own practice. It'll take

Invictus

thirty years to pay off a loan for that. Urgent care positions are rare, especially in this end of the state. Who wants to live in a big city? A lot of docs can do that kind of work, whether they trained for it or not. I don't think I can stand to go back into the ER; I hated it while I was there. Besides I pissed off a lot of people...."

Gray laughed. "Not you," he said.

Too drunk to catch the sarcasm, Dodd nodded. "They either loved me or hated me. Didn't seem to be much middle ground. The great majority, I got along with. The few that detested me were a vocal lot. They were similar to Abramowicz: mousy, unassertive, secretive, unreal expectations because of who they thought they were. They wrote letters to Abramowicz, to Furneaux, to their Congressmen, too, I think...."

"And they could tell that you were not impressed with them," Gray suggested cautiously.

"Evidently," Dodd agreed, angrily. "And that I wasn't going to be their lackey. 'I have a sinus infection,' they'd whine, the first or second day of their cold. 'Sure,' I'd say, 'but it's a *viral* sinus infection. You'll have it for two weeks. It'll go away, most likely. And, if you'd stop smoking, stop sleeping on a feather pillow, stop letting the cats sleep with you, or change your sheets more than once a semester, you'd have less trouble with your allergies, and get fewer colds and sinus infections.' 'But make me well, now! Give me antibiotics, now! Or, I'll call President Furneaux, or Neal.' 'Drop dead,' I'd say."

"Bet that made you a lot of friends."

Dodd lay on his back on the bed and stared at the empty beer can in his outstretched hand. It dangled over the edge of the bed. "Six to ten real enemies per year. You should have read some of the trash they, or their parents, wrote: 'ashamed to be a physician,' 'inadequate care.'"

"Well, Doc, the first time I saw you, you pissed me off, too."

Dodd rolled onto an elbow and stared at Gray through half open eyelids. "Yeah? How's that?"

"That little spiel you gave me about warts."

"Let's see," Dodd said returning to his back. He stared at the pipes and supports in the open ceiling and recited from memory, "A wart is caused by a virus. If we burn, cut, or freeze it off, you may get a scar that will be a bigger problem than the wart. The wart will eventually go away on its own. That means your immune system has learned to recognize the virus and it will never come back. In addition, if it's frozen, cut, or burned then you will not be immune to the virus and you can be infected again. Use this solution to irritate the skin and it may speed up how quickly your immune system recognizes and kills the wart. Thirty-three seconds for the spiel, five minutes for the appointment. Next!"

Gray laughed. "Word for word. I hated it at the time, but it worked. Now, I assume, I'm immune to plantar warts. My sister has had hers frozen off six or seven times. They keep coming back."

"See?"

"But it ticked me off. I'm sure it upset others."

Dodd shrugged. "Sure it did. It may not have been politically correct, but it was the honest thing to tell you. I can't help it if people expect to receive worthless treatments. I spend hours talking people out of unnecessary treatments or tests. Everybody's an expert these days, whether they went to medical school or not. How many people in the world do you think have hypoglycemia, Cody?"

"Millions?"

"Hundreds. Maybe ten people in the whole state of Virginia. But every fourth coed on this campus thinks she has it. Doctors get in ruts; they get caught up in a 'I'm next to God, so I should be able to diagnose anything' mentality. Instead of telling patients that they just don't know for sure why the patient is tired, or dizzy, or weak, because nothing showed up in the history or physical exam, they start to order tests, do procedures. Costs be damned. Eventually, the doc'll do a glucose tolerance test, to rule out diabetes. This test was never designed to test for hypoglycemia, only hyperglycemia; so the results are suspect. No one in a natural setting ever ingested that much sugar. And *no one* knows what the normal response to that big a sugar load is — so *almost every patient* gets labeled hypoglycemic. It's a worthless diagnosis, unless you have a pancreatic islet cell tumor or use too much insulin; then it means something."

Gray needled Dodd, "Really? HMOs must have helped save a ton of money."

Dodd missed the jab, he made his usual counter argument. "Except they went too far in the other direction. No tests unless the patient is dying. Oh, what the hell, since he is going to die anyway, no tests."

"Is a lot of medicine like that?" Gray asked.

Tongue looser than normal because of the beer, and anger boiling inside, the depressed Dodd let the rage out in a rambling soliloquy. "Medicine has done a disservice to the public, Cody. It touted its cures. It told people it could fix everything, when it can't; it led people to believe that there would be a pill to cure every disease. Now, don't get me wrong. When we do understand a hell of a lot more, and start to genetically rearrange life on this planet, that will be true. Right now, though.... Right now, we know little more than the quacks who sold snake oil, or the surgeons who trephined for headaches last century."

Dodd bent his knees, pulling his feet onto the bed. "In the old days, we helped people in need because we believed in ourselves and in the inherent goodness of mankind. That was beautiful. We made honest mistakes, and we sometimes did help people. Then someone realized you could make money off the fears of the common man.

Prolong life! Cure all ills! A little snake oil, for a lot of money. Hell, once the AMA made the common man scared of his own shadow, the voters convinced Congress that it was their God-given right to have medical care and that the government should pay for it."

Raising his head briefly, Dodd looked in Gray's direction. The boy typed on the keyboard, watching the monitor. Dodd continued, "The lawyers liked that. If no one else understood the underlying problem, they did: the doctors didn't know as much as they claimed. There were going to be a lot of bad outcomes. Why not make a living pointing out docs' mistakes? And there were really a lot of mistakes. The biggest blunder was to dangle immortality, beauty, perfection, or improved function in front of some poor slob and then not deliver. No wonder John Q. Public got mad and sued...."

"I don't think I followed all of that," Gray said.

"That's okay," Dodd answered, dropping his head onto the bed. "It needs work, or a soap box. Got another brew?"

Gray slipped from the five gallon bucket seat and sat on the floor within arm's reach of the half fridge. Opening the door only a crack, he peered in. Three beers stared back at him. He closed the door. "Sorry, Doc. All out." He climbed back onto the bucket seat.

"Just as well," Dodd said. "I'm a little too plastered already. BeeBee will be pissed."

"Who is BeeBee? Your new girl friend?"

"That would be Anna," Dodd said wistfully. "I wish she'd dump that jerk boy friend of hers in Amsterdam."

"Then who's BeeBee?" Gray reminded Dodd.

"My conscience," Dodd answered.

"The little voice inside your head that tells you when you've screwed up?"

Dodd nodded. "Like that. He speaks Latin. B.B. stands for Black Bird."

"You call your conscience Black Bird?" Gray asked,

confused.

"No, I call him BeeBee. He *is* a black bird."

Gray suspected Dodd of being too drunk to think clearly. "Why does he speak Latin?" he asked the physician.

"That was the first language he learned, over two thousand years ago," Dodd said.

"And you understand him?"

"Certainly. After eight or nine years of Catholic schools, and innumerable drills in declensions and conjugations, anyone could. *Mea culpa*.[30] Catholics are the best at passing out fault and guilt." Dodd placed his right hand over his heart and bent his neck, trying to bow his head.

"You're the one who's drunk, Doc," Gray observed, "but I'm the one who's baffled."

The empty beer can slipped through Dodd's fingers and landed with a hollow 'bonk' on the carpet. Dodd ignored it. "When I was thirteen, I shot a black bird. By accident. Well, on purpose. I aimed the gun at it. I pulled the trigger. I didn't think I'd hit it. It died, regardless of what I thought. The big brave hunter. Shot a defenseless bird. Robbed it of its only possession, life. I started to cry. That really angered the old man, which ticked me off. I broke the stock off a two hundred dollar rifle wrapping the barrel around the tree. Then I ran home. He never took me hunting again."

"Whatever you say, Doc." Gray moved from the bucket to a position on the bed near Dodd. Picking up the remote control, he turned on the small color televison directly in front of him. Leaving the sound muted, he asked, "So, whenever you screw up, you think of that, and your conscience bothers you?"

Dodd shook his head. "BeeBee is real, or I'm psychotic. By the way, if anything happens to me, I want you to have him. No one else I know qualifies. He is a raven, a corvid. Problem is that he says he's been around for about three thousand years. He's smart as a whip. I think he lies, though. Speaks several human languages. The first language he learned was Latin. When I was in medical school, he used to sit on the railing of my balcony and listen to me sound out Latin and Greek medical terms. Finally, he got so frustrated, he corrected my pronunciation. Talk about shockers. He's been hanging around ever since. These days, he corrects my ethics, although he continues to give me lessons in Latin."

"Well, what kind of stuff does he say?" Gray asked.

Dodd's eyes searched his surroundings, finally stopping on the beer can on the floor. "Maybe he'd say, *'Da mihi sis cerevisiam dilutam,'*"[31] the physician mumbled.

Gray raised his eyebrows, "And that means?"

"A light beer, please."

"He likes light beer?"

"*De gustibus non est disputandum.*[32] Or, there's no accounting for tastes, he'd say," Dodd said.

A smile crept across Gray's face. His eyes lit. "Does this bird know anything about computers?" he asked, anticipating another joke and pointing toward the monitor. A multicolored screen saver roiled across the monitor's face.

"*Purgamentum init; exit purgamentum,*"[33] Dodd suggested.

"Garbage in; garbage out," Gray made his own interpretation, guessing correctly. "I love it." He grabbed a piece of paper and a felt tip marker. "Spell that for me, Doc."

Dodd repositioned his legs. "Just like it sounds: P...u...r...g...a...."

When Dodd finished spelling the Latin phrase, Gray pushed up the pillow behind his head. He stared at the televison, avoiding Dodd's eyes. Dodd stared at the ceiling silently. His eyelids closed slowly, then snapped open, repeatedly while he attempted to remain awake. Gray asked, "And what does BeeBee have to do with the bird you shot?"

"I haven't figured out the connection, yet," Dodd replied.

Gray waited several minutes, then increased the volume on the television. Someone broadcast a collection of old commercials. He watched bearded women sitting around a barroom drinking beer. The subtitle on the video read, "1960 East German Olympic Women's Track Team." He wondered out loud why that was funny.

Dodd tilted his head up and peeked at the advertisement. He said, "That's my all-time favorite commercial. We all knew they were on steroids or testosterone. You know, I always wanted to start a cable channel that showed only commercials, the good ones, the funny ones. Eventually, someone would pay me to show their commercials among the entertaining ones. Then I'd get rich, because no one would know." His eyes closed one last time; he lapsed into silence. His breathing changed to a slower and deeper rhythm.

"Know what?" Gray asked. A snore answered his question. Gray laughed. "I guess I shouldn't bother to ask you who you think will win the bowl game, Tennessee or SVU? You have to stop treating your body like an amusement park and start treating it like a temple again, soon, Doc," the boy lectured the sleeping Dodd. "You're not much company when you're drunk and depressed."

Bill Yancey

Invictus

Chapter Twenty six
December 19th

Dodd set the parking brake on the Miata. His eyes scanned the sky, already dark at 5:00 p.m. The winter weather threatened precipitation, probably rain. Sleet and snow occasionally surprised Fawsville residents in the middle of December, being more common in February. He groaned raising the top to the convertible and latching it in place. After rolling up the windows, he locked the doors. An icy wind cut through his weatherbeaten bomber jacket and leather gloves as he walked toward the apartment building.

Several ravens, from the communal roost in the open foyer above the third floor, hung out on the roof of the building. All bachelor birds, male and female, there appeared to be two juveniles and three or four full-grown adults. Dodd couldn't tell which one was BeeBee, but he knew he was there, somewhere. Dodd tipped his right index and middle fingers to his right eyebrow, saluting the birds. "Caw, caw," came the reply. Dodd smiled.

After unlocking the front door to the apartment, Dodd opened the door slowly. The usually neat apartment looked as if a cyclone had hit a laundromat and dumped the result in his single room. Clothing hung from every piece of furniture. It even lay on the counter and dangled from some of the kitchen appliances. Shaking his head, Dodd closed the door behind him, locking it. Nearly tripping over it, he skirted the open suitcase that lay on the floor in front of the closet. Stuffing his worn gloves into the pocket of his jacket, Dodd hung his coat from a brass hook on the inside of the closet door.

He surveyed the room, looking for a place to sit. A

Bill Yancey

light shone under the bathroom door. Steam hovered just outside of the room and near the ceiling. "Spence, is that you?" a voice called from inside the bathroom.

"None other, mon cheri," he replied. For one of a very few times in the previous two months, Dodd smiled. *Bene vita est. Et luna*,[34] he reminded himself. Behind the door, Anna Mueller stood, he surmised, possibly naked, probably in her underwear. She preened for him. They were going out on the town for dinner with Clint Massey and Joie LaFlamé. Then they would spend a quiet night at home, just the two of them. The sadness came tomorrow when he had to drive her to the airport at Kingsport, Tennessee and put her on a plane to New York City. From there she would catch the non-stop, Christmas-vacation flight to Amsterdam. They had talked little about what would happen when she returned in January for the second semester — even less about her visa expiring on July first.

"Your brother rang," she called through the closed door. Dodd shuddered. He had an unpleasant vision of Bob, his older brother and surrogate father during his father's mental absence, finding out that Dodd had a female professor — a foreign, darker-skinned female, at that — living with him. "I didn't answer the phone," she continued, "just listened. There's a message on the answering machine."

Dodd sighed, thankful not to have to explain the situation to his demanding sibling. He stabbed at the play button on the machine. His father's voice talked to him through the first born's larynx. "Spence, this is your brother, Bob. Give me a call as soon as you can. Mother's feeling poorly. Use this number: (202) 555-6910." Dodd did not recognize the telephone number, but his brother changed portable phone service frequently, in search of the cheapest rates. 'Mother is feeling poorly' could mean anything from a high fever to a heart attack. Even more stoic than his father, his mother never complained. She had undergone bypass surgery only after the treadmill test indicated that she should have already been dead. Never did she complain of chest pain, only a minor ache in her back. He shook his head and dialed the number left by his brother.

When the voice on the other end said, "Washington Hospital Center, Neurosurgical Intensive Care Unit," Dodd understood the gravity of the situation.

Anna Mueller stepped from the bathroom, stunning in a slinky dark red dress that highlighted her gorgeous figure. Slowly, she waltzed in silk stocking feet to a position directly in front of Dodd. Silently, she smiled warmly at him and wrapped her arms around his neck. "How was work?" she purred, pulling his lips to hers. The kiss was far more passionate than any Dodd had experienced during the last ten years of his marriage. The scent of her perfume raised goose bumps on the back of his neck. Her right calf rubbed the back of his left, sending intense messages to his heart, which thundered like the piston of a steam locomotive out of control.

Gently disengaging himself from her clutches, Dodd held both of her hands. He delighted in the tactile sensation her moist palms gave him. The contrast between his pale skin and the olive tones of hers amused him. "Are you mad at me?" Mueller asked, surprised at his reticence.

"I have to break our date," Dodd said. "I'm sorry. It's my mother."

"The call from your brother?"

Dodd nodded. Letting go of her right hand, he picked up her underwear from the couch and laid it on the chair. Positioning her seated on the couch, he sat next to her, facing her, still holding her left hand with his right. "She's had a massive brain stem stroke. They don't expect her to live through the night."

Mueller's head dropped; her eyes stared into her lap. She bit her lower lip. "I'm so sorry, Spencer. Is there anything I can do?"

Dodd shook his head. "No. Well, yes. You'll need to be understanding about tonight. I have to drive to Washington, D.C. As soon as I pack, I have to leave."

Nodding in agreement, Mueller remained silent. She leaned forward. Placing her right hand on his cheek, she kissed him tenderly on the lips. Alighting from the couch, swiftly, she started clearing her clothing from the room, throwing it into the gaping maw of her huge suitcase.

Dodd walked into the kitchen and lifted the telephone receiver. He dialed and waited for Clinton Massey to answer.

"Yeah, hello," Massey said.

"Clint, this is Spence."

"Long time no see," Massey said affably, having walked Spencer to his car when they left the student health center less than twenty minutes before.

Mueller closed her suitcase and scooted it away from the closet. "I'm afraid the double date is off, Clint. I have to go to D.C. My mother had a stroke."

"Gee, Spence. I'm sorry. Is there anything I can do?"

"Well, yes, there is. Anna needs a ride to the airport tomorrow. Her flight to JFK leaves at 7:15 a.m., from the Kingsport. Do you think you could take her?"

"Absolutely. When are you leaving?"

"In about five minutes. I'll tell Anna to expect you, here at my place, at about 5:00 a.m. She'll call you, if you aren't here by then."

"If she wakes Joie, there will be hell to pay."

Dodd laughed. "Then don't be late," he said. "Thanks, buddy."

"No problem," Massey said, hanging up the telephone.

Thirty minutes later, Dodd thought he had everything he would need for two or three days away from home. He never took any more than that, because no more fit into the sports car's tiny trunk. As it was, his only suit lay draped across the passenger seat.

On his final trip to the apartment to retrieve his toiletry bag, Mueller stopped him just inside the front door. She held his hand with both of hers. A worried look on her face, she made a big frown. "Spence," she said uncertainly.

"I'll drive carefully," he said, cheerfully as possible. "The car practically knows its own way up Interstate 81; it's been so many times. I'll see you when you come back second semester. You have a safe trip, too. Enjoy Christmas in Amsterdam. Skate one canal for the Gipper."

She shook her head. Tears flowed from her eyes. Briefly, she looked him in the face. He saw how red her eyes were. The shoulder-length, straight black hair seemed askew. Her slightly flattened, brown nose wrinkled involuntarily. She returned her gaze to the floor. "I wasn't going to tell you until tomorrow...."

"Tell me what?"

Her voice broke; the words flowed unevenly. "Next semester.... I'm not coming back next semester. Jon and I have decided to marry."

Dodd's chin dropped. His mouth moved; no words emanated from his paralyzed vocal cords. Too hurt to speak, he sat in the chair, leaving Mueller standing, like a school girl being punished. Realizing she was embarrassed, he reached up and took her hand. He pulled her into his lap. She collapsed in his arms, her head on his shoulder. Tears ran down his neck; she sobbed. Eventually, he recovered. He spoke softly, "It's okay, Anna. Really, it's no big deal. You don't need two fathers."

"Never say that, Spence. It's not that you are too old," she blurted, then stalled briefly. "It's just that I have certain sexual needs...."

"That a fifty-plus year-old man can't satisfy," Dodd finished for her. "You don't need to sugar coat it; you can say what you mean.".

"That's not what I wanted to say...."

"Yes, it is," he countered. She sobbed harder. Dodd continued with a litany of clichés he had learned from other failed romances, some his own, "But, it's okay. You need to grow old with someone. To have kids. Jon's a lucky man. I'll miss you. I may even love you. It's better this way."

"I love you, too," she wailed. "Oh, I'm so confused." She stood suddenly and ran into the bathroom, locking the door behind her. Dodd followed her to the door, unsure what he would do to comfort her if she opened it. He knocked anyway. "Go away!" she shouted.

Meekly, he replied, "I have to leave. I'm sorry, Anna. I have to leave...."

"Go!" she shouted.

Dodd left, locking the front door behind him. Sullenly, he walked through the parking lot. BeeBee awaited, sitting on the black, vinyl top to the little car.

Irritated, Dodd asked the bird, "What do you want?"

"*Estne volumen in toga, an solum tibi libet me videre?*"[35] the bird asked.

"*Fac ut vivas.*"[36]

"Actually, I thought you could use some company," the raven said. "*Mobilior ventis...femina.*"[37]

Dodd nodded. He opened the door, holding his arm out. The bird hopped from the vinyl top to Dodd's arm, and then into the interior of the automobile. It settled onto Dodd's suit, tucking it's feet underneath itself. "*Quod non dedit Fortuna, non eripit,*"[38] the bird whispered. "*Nemo in amore videt.*"[39]

"*Labra lege. Vescere bracis meis,*"[40] Dodd replied. He drove in silence, replaying his last conversation with Mueller over and over in his mind. Finally, he turned his head toward BeeBee and asked, "You know what she's going to say about America when she gets home, don't you?"

"*Veni, Vedi, Visa,*"[41] the bird replied. They both laughed until tears fell from Dodd's eyes.

Invictus

Chapter Twenty-seven
December 30*th*

Fawsville in December reminded Dodd of the England he had lived in for two years as a child: cold, dreary mists; intermittent freezing rain; and frequently cloudy skies. The permanent population took a collective sigh of relief when the students went home for the combined semester and holiday break. Over the first seven days, in fact, everyone celebrated. The second week the residents observed Christmas and the New Year, for the most part. Fawsville had become an international community. Its inhabitants practiced more different religions than almost any other community in the state, with exception of the suburbs of the District of Columbia, and the home towns of other state universities. Boredom set in during the third week. After that, shop owners began to worry. They wondered if they would survive without the monetary input of the students. By the end of the month, townies were ready to celebrate the return of the students and their newly cash-lined pockets.

Dodd avoided celebrating the departure of the students. Trying to keep his usual tight rein on his emotions, he stood near the apartment picture window staring at the gray clouds rolling overhead. Anna's farewell crippled him emotionally. Her loss added to his mental burdens. His mother, her intellectual powers effectively isolated from the rest of her body by the midbrain stroke, remained alive but comatose. She had been transferred from the hospital and acute care to the same nursing home that housed his father, not that Robert F. Dodd, Sr. cared. His Alzheimer's had worsened. Their living deaths haunted Dodd, aware that he shared genes with them. Robert, Jr., his older brother, seemed blissfully unaffected by his parents' plight. With the exception of his complaint about the two using up any possible inheritance to pay their medical bills, he seemed unperturbed by their circumstances.

Dodd possessed a limited number of friends. Clinton Massey had left town; he and Joie LaFlamé had decided to tie the knot. To announce the pending nuptials, they left on a month long tour of his and her extended and widespread families. They planned a July wedding. The school and town chapels had been booked solid for the next six months by students soon to graduate. Planning one's life around the presence or absence of students seemed second nature after so many years of doing so.

Plopping onto his couch, Dodd pulled his day planner from the end table. He opened the book to the last page. There, he kept his list of prospective projects for break times and the summers. He scanned his list, looking for something he could accomplish in less than a month, if he put his mind to it. He realized that if he remained idle for too much longer, his depression would deepen, possibly with disastrous consequences. Lifting his feet onto the coffee table, he leaned backward into the soft cushions. He read the list out loud to himself, "Learn Linux, maybe. C++, better choice. Update my pilot's license and medical, too expensive. Learn to rollerblade, too cold. Start Tai Chi, nah. Install a CD player in the Miata, three days tops. Maybe I should install the new shocks and wiring harness, too. Clint did leave me the key to his garage...."

The knock on the door ended his review session. Dodd laid the planner on the coffee table with the Popular Science and MIT Technology Review magazines, rose, and went to the door. Taking a quick peek through the peephole brought a smile to his face. Eye level for him brought him even with the sternal notch of the huge black man standing outside the door. Without seeing his face, Dodd knew who

Invictus

waited. He opened the door, with a big grin. "Mr. D, come in!" he exclaimed, holding his right hand out to the young man. "Back in town to practice for the bowl game?"

Dodd had difficulty remembering that the huge football player standing outside his door was really a boy, a mere teenager, no less. 'D' stood for Mr. Defense, or Devon Dixon Danners, depending upon on which side of the football scrimmage line one stood. The young man smiled. His grin revealed perfectly even teeth. Massive right hand engulfed Dodd's, gently. Effortlessly, he pulled Dodd to his chest with his left hand. He smothered Dodd in a gentle bear hug reserved for close friends, all of whom were smaller and did not play football. Not accustomed to touching people, except under professional circumstances, Dodd initially fought the hugs. He gave in after he sensed that he had hurt the boy's feelings months before. "Okay, okay," Dodd's muffled voice emanated from Danner's chest. "Don't suffocate me or break my neck."

Laughing, the six-foot, seven-inch Danners released Dodd. "Good to see you, Doc. Merry Christmas," he said. The big, sophomore, defensive end plowed into the small apartment, nearly filling it. Making himself at home, he walked straight to the refrigerator. Leaning forward, his long, intricately braided, dreadlocks swung toward the floor, covering his face. He reached down to open the refrigerator door; his big hand snatched two beers from the top shelf, handing one to Dodd. Dodd closed the front door.

"You're going to get me arrested for contributing to the delinquency of a minor, D," Dodd told the giant. "Put mine back, please. I've given them up until my depression clears. Alcohol adds to my doldrums. Sit — on the couch. Tell me what's going on."

The gentle giant padded slowly toward the couch. Muscular frame curling efficiently, Danners sat, ignoring screams from the hide-a-bed springs. "I need your help, Doc," he said.

"How's that?" Dodd asked, settling into the matching stuffed chair.

Danners sipped the beer. He explained, "During exams, I was taken from practice to the hospital with a concussion. Couldn't study for my calculus exam. The professor said I could make up the test, so long as I did it before the bowl game."

"There are some inconsistencies with your story, D." A big grin appeared on Dodd's face. Danners squinted at Dodd and pursed his lips, puzzled. "First, who is big enough to give you a concussion? Second, a defensive lineman taking calculus? Come on!"

"Doc," Danners pleaded, "this is serious. I need three days to study for this exam. Next Monday, we fly to New Orleans. The latest I can take the test is Friday."

Still teasing Dodd said, "But if you miss practice, our chances for a national title diminish. I don't know, D. I've got a hundred bucks riding on the outcome."

Finally realizing that Dodd teased him, Danners said, "Don't make me hurt you, Doc." He sipped at the beer bottle slowly, more conservatively than Dodd would have.

Dodd laughed. "Okay, we need a disease. Flu?"

"Had the shot. Whole team did."

"Strep throat?" Dodd asked.

"Just treated for that last week."

"Has to be a virus then, " Dodd decided. "Something ghastly. Did you have your immunizations as a child?"

"Everything except the mumps shot. My older sister had a nasty reaction to it. They thought it would be better if I got the disease."

"Did you?" Dodd asked.

Danners shrugged. "I think so."

"Doesn't matter; you can have it twice. What's Coach Halloran's telephone number?" Dodd asked. Danners told

Invictus

him, then returned to the refrigerator in search of food. Dodd assumed the lineman burned five to ten thousand calories per day. He dialed the coach's office. A vision of the boy wandering, from friend's refrigerator to friend's refrigerator to friend's refrigerator, ad infinitum, entertained Dodd while he waited for someone to answer the telephone. Head varsity football coach, Lee Halloran's secretary answered for him. "Athletic department. Coach Halloran's office. Miss Montgomery speaking."

"Good morning, Miss Montgomery," Dodd said. "This is Dr. Dodd from student health, is Coach in?"

"Can I tell him why you are calling?" she asked pleasantly.

"D's sick," Dodd said simply.

Coach Halloran knew well that his big, fast end anchored his nationally ranked defense. Recruited from the ghetto and a dysfunctional family, Devon Dixon Danners managed to overcome his handicaps. With hard work, and a work ethic seemingly borrowed from Quakers or Asian Americans, Danners had become indispensable to the defense, and the team. In less than ten seconds Halloran spoke to Dodd. "Dr. Dodd, this is Lee Halloran. Kathy says you mentioned Devon?"

"He may have the mumps, Coach," Dodd said. The telephone line became instantly silent. Dodd listened to see if he could hear the thump when Halloran's body smacked the thick pile carpet in his office overlooking the coliseum and the football stadium.

No thumps were forthcoming. "Wh-wh-what exactly does that mean?" the coach finally sputtered.

"Well, if he does have the mumps, he's going to miss the bowl game, Coach." More absolute silence greeted Dodd. Halloran kissed his defense, the bowl game, a national championship, possibly his job, and maybe his ass, good-bye.

"Gawd-d-d," Halloran finally groaned.

"I need to run some tests, Coach," Dodd said, winking at Danners. The young man settled onto the couch again, balancing a plate of two-day-old fried chicken.

"You mean there is a chance he doesn't have the mumps?" Halloran asked.

"There's a possibility that a parotiditis can be caused by the flu, a bacteria, or even a parotid stone," Dodd agreed.

Halloran added, "I thought all the kids got shots for mumps these days."

Dodd explained. "Devon's sister had an allergic reaction to the shot. A bad one. He never got it, or the disease, apparently," Dodd said, crossing his fingers and showing them to Danners. The boy grinned.

"How long until we know?" Halloran asked anxiously.

"Usually, it takes six to seven days," Dodd ad-libbed. Halloran groaned even louder, "but I think, if we can get the lab to cooperate, I can find out by practice Friday afternoon." Dodd raised his eyebrow, looking at Danners. The boy smiled and nodded. "He has to be quarantined until then."

"Can one of my assistants talk to him?" Halloran asked.

"I don't think so, Coach," Dodd said. He added the information he knew would get Halloran's attention. "Adult mumps sometimes affects the testes, Lee. Epididymo-orchitis is really unpleasant. Your balls swell to twice normal size, turn blue, and sometimes die. The worst result is sterility, of course, but the pain is almost unbearable while it is going on. We don't want anyone else exposed. People rarely get mumps twice, but the consequences are disastrous. I don't think any of the assistant coaches want to risk that."

"I understand, Doc," Halloran agreed. Listening to his voice, Dodd could almost see the coach reach for his own genitals, a pained expression on his face. "Where is Devon going to stay?"

Dodd improvised a scenario; Danners listened

intently. "Student health is closed this week. Instead of putting 'D' in the hospital, I've elected to let him stay here, at my apartment. The school pays me to take these risks. If he gets worse, I'll drive him to the hospital myself."

Halloran asked anxiously, "You'll let me know as soon as possible?"

"Absolutely," Dodd promised.

"And, Doc?"

"Yes?

The coach tried to bribe a virus. He begged, "If you have him ready to play next Thursday, you can sit in the box with President Furneaux, my guest at the Sugar Bowl."

Dodd smiled, "Thanks, Lee," he said. "I can't guarantee anything. It's not up to me. Mother Nature has this one, one-on-one, so to speak." Dodd threw a sports analogy into the conversation to make the coach feel good. "Good bye."

"Bye," Halloran said glumly.

Dodd hung up the receiver. Danners clapped his hands together mightily, big smile on his face. "Bravo, bellisimo, Doc. You're a miracle worker."

"There's not a lot of difference between miracle workers and magicians," Dodd countered, "a little sleight of hand...."

Danners asked, "You don't mind my staying here?"

"Absolutely not," Dodd said. "I'm going to publish a paper in the medical journal *Sportsmedicine* on the caloric intake of defensive linemen. I'll have to write down everything you eat." Dodd headed toward the door. "I've got to go buy a month's worth of groceries so I can feed you for the next four days. Anything you want?"

"Could you stop by the athletic dorm and pick up my books, please?" Danners asked. Dodd nodded. "What do I do if one of the coaches sees me in the math building Friday morning?"

"Grab your nuts and scream like you're in terrible

pain," Dodd replied. He opened the door. Danners threw him a set of keys. "What are these?" Dodd asked.

"Keys to my room and Coach Jackson's car; it's a BMW. I don't think he'll mind if you drive it. In fact, he may want to give it away without ever sitting in it again, especially after he hears what Halloran has to say about the mumps." Danners laughed. Dodd laughed louder.

BeeBee landed on Dodd's shoulder as he negotiated the parking lot, looking for the BMW. He never found it. Instead, he headed toward the Miata. "Practicing your lying?" BeeBee asked.

"Jeez, BeeBee, you'd think I'd stolen the Sears Bowl Trophy. Devon's here to get an education. Even though he'd like to play in the NFL someday, he's realistic enough to understand that he'll need an education to survive after his career ends. And if he gets injured or doesn't make the pros, a degree is even more important. I can't turn my back on that kind of dedication."

"You just taught him that it pays to manipulate you and the coach. *Exitus acta probat,*"[42] the bird suggested.

Dodd nodded. "A dangerous thought, indeed. I'll have to discuss it with Devon, to make certain he understands my motivation. If I want to be manipulated, I'll go see a chiropractor."

Invictus

Chapter Twenty-eight
January 5th

Thanks to the university's computer power and the ethernet card in Dodd's computer at work, the web pages flashed onto and off the screen quickly, saving him valuable time. Doing the same research from his apartment would have taken weeks over the telephone line with a modem, versus hours from his office in the health center at Sykes Hall. Outside Dodd's window, the western sky and Cumberland Mountain came to life as the sun rose in the east, behind the recreational sports building. High clouds, similar to thunderstorms during summer, continued to dump snow on the campus at a high rate. Dodd estimated that an inch an hour had fallen, a guess confirmed by the local radio station playing on the worn transistor radio sitting on his desk. The weatherman said a foot of new snow had fallen since 6:00 p.m. the previous night, when Dodd started his project.

A burst of rapid footsteps sounded in the hallway. Dodd heard the runner make the transition from carpet to vinyl floor, footfalls louder and headed in his direction. They stopped outside his open door. Dodd looked up to find Cody Gray panting, out of breath. "Well, hey, Cody. Happy New Year. I thought you went to the bowl game?"

"Flight leaves at noon, Doc, but I might not be on it." Gray glanced nervously out the office door. Both men heard the clip clop of hard-soled shoes in the hallway. "Mind if I come in?" Gray asked, stepping into the room and pushing the door closed behind him without waiting for Dodd to respond.

"No. Come in," Dodd said. "Someone looking for

you?" he asked.

Gray nodded. He sat quickly in Dodd's second chair and pulled off his shoes. "Doc," he said, "do me a favor and take off your shoes."

"Why?"

"No time to explain," Gray said. "Hide them under your desk." Bounding out of his seat, Gray put one foot on Dodd's desk, his second on the tall bookcase. Pushing up a single panel of the suspended ceiling, he pulled on the steel framework above the ceiling and climbed into the empty crawl space between the false ceiling and the second floor. The square, sound-absorbent tile dropped back into place. Tiny powdered fragments of the material fell onto Dodd's desk. He wiped and blew them away after pushing his shoes out of sight. A knock sounded at his door.

Casually, Dodd responded, "Come in." The door opened slowly revealing a campus police officer. Innocently, Dodd asked, "Can I help you?"

The cop stared at Dodd, recognizing his face as that of a faculty member, but not remembering his name. Moving his head slowly, he allowed his eyes to absorb the contents of the cramped room, ending with the wet shoes next to the second chair. Snow on the tread had begun to melt, puddling on the floor. "These yours?" the officer asked.

Suffering a sudden attack by his conscience, Dodd refused to lie outright. Moving his body in an effort to exaggerate the motions, he looked first at the shoes and then down at his stocking feet. Sarcastically, he asked the officer, "What do you think?"

"May I see your campus identification?" the man asked. Dodd stood. He pulled his leather jacket from the coat hook on the back of his door, and his key chain from one pocket of the coat. Along with the keys dangled his picture identification. He held it out to the officer. "May

Invictus

I take a closer look?" the officer asked. Dodd nodded, dropping the collection of keys, can opener, and small knife into the man's hand. The policeman examined the picture and then Dodd. "You shaved your beard," he observed.

Dodd rubbed his chin absentmindedly, nodding again. "Yeah?" he said.

"You know that you're not supposed to punch holes in campus IDs?"

"Seemed to be the only way to hang it on the key chain," Dodd said.

"If you were a student, I'd confiscate it."

"I'm not a student," Dodd stated the obvious, voice rising with his anger. "Did you want something, or are you just trying to spread misery for the holiday season?"

Seeing that Dodd was not intimidated, the officer shrugged. He handed the identification card back. "Seen anyone else here this morning."

Dodd smiled. "We're closed," he said honestly. "No one else is allowed in the building."

Unhappy with the response, the officer grunted, "And what are you doing here, Dr. Dodd?"

Dodd pointed to the computer monitor. "Research. Web prices for office and medical equipment. I'd love to talk, but I'm busy. Close the door on the way out, will you?" he answered, rudely dismissing the officer. The physician swivelled his chair away from the policeman and sat facing the monitor. Using the mouse, he scrolled through several pages of WebOfficeSales.com. Having no reason to continue the conversation, the officer departed. Gray waited ten minutes before lifting the ceiling panel and climbing down from his perch.

"Mind if I see if he left the building?" Gray asked as his feet touched the floor.

"No," Dodd said. "How can you do that?"

Gray leaned over Dodd. The web page disappeared from the monitor. The student moved the mouse and clicked on an obscure icon. A yellow striped tic tac toe board divided the screen into nine equal rectangles. Within each there was a video sent by a security camera. Gray pointed to the parking lot pictured in the right lower box. The officer trudged through the snow toward his white police cruiser. Together Gray and Dodd watched him start the vehicle and drive away.

"That was close," Gray said, slumping into the second chair.

"What happened?" Dodd asked.

"Don't know for sure. I think he followed my tracks in the snow."

Dodd looked at the monitor. "I didn't know I could watch the security cameras."

"It's part of my web page. I connected your computer to it," Gray said, stretching. He leaned over Dodd again, fingers flying across the keyboard. "You'd be amazed at the stuff you can find online. For instance," he hit 'Enter' and a black and white picture of Abramowicz's office filled the screen."

"Why does he have a security camera in his own office?" Dodd asked.

"Damned if I know," Gray responded. "Maybe he's paranoid. Then, maybe, he realized I had been in there. I've searched the security system's video tapes; I'm not on any of them. In any case, security has gotten tighter recently. It's tougher to get in at night and out in the morning for my early class. There always seems to be a patrol car nearby."

"Did you steal anything?" Dodd asked. Gray smiled. He shook his head. Dodd decided the questioning had to be more specific. "What, exactly, did you do to Neal's office?"

"Nothing," Gray responded innocently.

"Nothing?" Dodd asked.

"Well, I did add his name to some web sites, servers,

Invictus

clubs, and stuff."

Dodd turned to face Gray. "Tell me all of it, Cody. I have a feeling I'm going to get blamed for this. I may as well know what's coming."

"I didn't do it to get you in trouble, Doc," Gray protested. "I just don't like the fat man either. Never have."

"Stand in line, Cody. What did you do?" Dodd demanded. "His paranoia has gone overboard. Do you know he has the docs carrying charts back to medical records and double signing everything? He must think people break into student health to read medical records."

Gray grinned broadly; he added, "And to sign him up for liposuction at a discount, several health and fitness clubs, and every diet web site available. He gets about two thousand pieces of junk email a day now." Gray looked at his wet stocking feet. "Most of it is for diet pills. That's harmless, isn't it?"

Dodd laughed. "I guess so," he admitted.

Sitting in the second chair, Gray shoved his feet into his wet shoes, and began lacing them. He told Dodd, "I've got work to do, Doc. And a flight to catch. You want to see what's going on?"

The physician shook his head. "I've been up all night, Cody. Sleeping seems to be harder for me now that Anna's gone. Maybe some other time."

"Okay. See you later." Gray said. He left the door to Dodd's office open when he departed. Dodd heard his squishy wet shoes walk down the hall and enter the back stairwell to the third floor.

In need of sleep, Dodd shut down the computer and left the health center. He waded through two and a half feet of snow. Leaning into the frigid, gusty wind, he trudged the three quarters of a mile to the apartment. He had left the Miata parked in the apartment parking lot, certain that the light, rear-wheel-drive automobile would slide on the icy streets. Buried by snow, the sports car was invisible from the street. When Dodd neared the apartment, he spied BeeBee playing with another raven.

Side-by-side, they hung upside down from a telephone wire. While upside down, the big bird spread his wings. A gust of wind pushed him upright. At that point, the bird folded his wings, and dropped, completing a single rotation around the wire. Repeating the sequence, the bird spun, faster and faster. Dodd counted, three, four, five revolutions. Finally releasing his grip on the wire, the dizzy bird spiraled downward, spreading his wings and pulling out of the dive just above the snow. The second bird tried to duplicate the trick. Too dizzy to pull out of the dive, it flopped, with wings spread, into the snow. With a loud squawk, it stood and shook its wings and head. BeeBee flew to Dodd's shoulder. "Dumb bird," he said and laughed a raucous, "Caw, caw."

"I'm impressed," Dodd told the bird.

"Better than being compressed, suppressed, depressed, or just pressed," the bird suggested.

"It's not nice to play tricks on your friends," Dodd reminded him.

"*Solum inimicos tui?*"[43] BeeBee asked, then flew away.

Invictus

Chapter Twenty-nine
January 14*th*

The return of the students for the second semester in the middle of January meant, for Dodd, that entering the recreational sports side of Sykes Hall would no longer be easy. Over the break, on the few days the building opened its doors, there were no student monitors present at the controlled entrances to check identifications. The students who filled those low paying work-study jobs languished at home enjoying Christmas presents and turkey. While they were away, Dodd experienced no difficulty sneaking into the 'students only' haven and using the only indoor track on campus and the exercise equipment. He would have to modify his strategy to thwart the administration's rule that only students were allowed to use the building, now that they had returned.

Dodd disagreed vehemently with the provost's position that, somehow, the hundred or so faculty members (out of nineteen hundred) who exercised on a regular basis would overwhelm a facility built for use by thirty thousand students. The omnipotent 'they' refused to acknowledge the merits of his arguments. In addition, the administration also knew that only five thousand students exercised regularly. They inflated the numbers to make themselves feel good that they had supplied an alternative outlet to the heavy drinking done by the students, because so little other entertainment existed in their isolated, backwoods corner of Virginia.

At times, it seemed to Dodd that the majority of students disparaged exercise; they seemingly lived to binge drink in the bars in town. He knew neither generalization accurately described the student body. Most wanted an education; they rejected both the party life and the rigors of constant body building. They hit a happy medium, playing some intramural sports, partying occasionally, but keeping their eyes on the real prizes: an education and employment after earning a degree. Those required hard work and study, leaving little time for excessive recreation, organized or otherwise.

The recreational sports and student health building, a gothic glass and stone monument to a previous president of Southwestern Virginia University, sat in the southeast corner of the campus, within the confines of an active dairy farm. The building housed the recreational sports department, student health services, and student counseling. That President Sykes had died of complications from smoking and drinking: emphysema, heart disease, and cirrhosis of the liver, only six months into his first term, at the grand old age of fifty three, Dodd initially found ironic. Eventually coming to terms with the idea, Dodd decided: who better to inspire the student body to exercise and practice moderation in diet than a man who died because he refused to do so?

Within the eastern flank of the building, Dodd sat in a plush chair, next to an oak table on which lay several body building magazines. Plush carpet covered the walkway from the entrance to where he sat in front of the control desk. The vaulted ceiling space above his head opened all the way to the steel girders supporting the roof of the three story building. A wall of glass protected him from the snow outside. It towered over his head, from his feet to the third floor ceiling. Clearly visible through the glass wall, the early morning sun rose behind the football stadium. Pink clouds and sunrise reflected from the melting snow. Nearly solid puddles of ice water warmed and began to coalesce, draining the intramural soccer field lying between Dodd and the practice football field. Rivers of water flowed over the granite and marble steps, into the parking lot. The unseasonably warm morning brought a gush of water toward the storm sewers. By that evening, Dodd knew the snow would be gone, except for the deep piles in the corners of the school parking lots. Those might hang around until the middle of spring, being made from tightly compacted ice, snow, and gravel.

"Bonjour, Doc," a familiar voice rang out. A tall, thin student, a former university basketball player, called to Dodd. The athlete had quit the team; he had not liked the brusque, foul-mouthed demeanor of SVU's resident varsity basketball coach.

The physician stood and held his right hand out to Jean Luc Bekalé, an exchange student from Gabon. Bekalé studied biochemistry; his brother earned an advanced degree in geophysics at the University of Virginia. The two of them would be the entire science department in a small Catholic city college in Ndjolé, Gabon after they graduated. "Jean," he asked, "did you go home for break?"

The seven-foot, four-inch tall black man shook his head. "Non," he answered, high-pitched, French accent in full force. The African's sweet mixture of languages and accents almost sang in Dodd's ears, "I met some nice ladies from New York City. We went there. I love the city. I think I will return after I graduate." Looking down on Dodd, Bekalé asked, "Why are you here, Doctor?"

Dodd shrugged. "To run. It's too wet outside for these old bones. I need an ID card to get in. I was hoping someone would lend me his."

Without hesitation, Bekalé pulled his wallet from his pocket and his ID card from the worn, tri-folded piece of leather. He handed the picture ID to Dodd. "I will come by your office later and get this back, non? Do not touch the Bear dollars and do not put it near a magnet. Ne c'est pas?" the giant cautioned Dodd and laughed. He referred to the magnetic strip on the back side of the card. Students used the information encoded there to access virtual bank accounts in order to download and spend 'Bear Dollars.' Without the proper personal identification number, no one could get at the money.

Dodd examined the photograph on the card carefully. He had hoped to find a student who resembled him, at least superficially. Not only was Bekalé more than a foot taller than he, he was black and had a beard, differences hard to hide. But, if Dodd did not exercise soon, he would have no time to shower or eat breakfast before going to work at the health center. Dodd eyed the student sitting at the control booth at the entrance to the gymnasium. At the early hour, the young woman had difficulty keeping her eyes open. "It's worth a shot," he told Bekalé. "Thanks."

As Dodd approached the guard, he rehearsed his answers: well, I shaved the beard; the tan *has* faded quickly, hasn't it? Fortunately, the picture only showed Bekalé from the shoulders up; the fourteen inch deficit in height was not obvious. Holding his thumb over the picture, Dodd flashed the card at the woman, and ran the edge through the electronic reader. He tried to leave the vicinity quickly, before the woman woke up.

"Mr. Bekalé," she called after him.

Too late, Dodd thought. He stopped, ten paces away from her. Turning slowly, he answered, "Yes, ma'am?"

"Your towel fee expires this month," she said, scanning the monitor in front of her and not looking at him.

"How much is it?" he asked edging away from her.

"Ten dollars a semester," she said, pointing at the fee on the screen.

"I'll take care of it later," Dodd replied, quickly turning and running up the stairs to the elevated track that encircled the three full-sized basketball courts. Seven laps to the mile, he reminded himself.

"Didn't I already tell you that, earlier this morning?" the coed asked, looking up and turning toward him. Dodd

Invictus

had disappeared. "Oh, well," she said, shrugging.

For twenty-seven minutes Dodd ran in tight circles above and around the basketball courts. Huge, picture windows made up the walls of the building and gave him views unsurpassed on any other campus he had ever visited. To the south, he saw the varsity baseball and softball fields, intramural fields, varsity soccer field, outdoor track, and the connecting field house. Clockwise, a quarter of the way farther around the track sat the coliseum and football stadium under the rising sun. The north end of the building housed the Olympic sized pool; humid air trapped by huge glass panels between it and the track steamed the glass wall. On completing a lap, Dodd looked westward and saw the greenhouses and fields of the broad expanse of the dairy farm. The farm was huge, despite losing some acreage to Sykes Hall. Single file, cows ambled along a muddy trail from the dairy barn toward the pastures, the areas of brown grass spreading as the snow melted. They were accompanied by a young woman, probably a pre-veterinarian student earning brownie points for her resumé and veterinarian school application, he assumed.

Below him, basketball raged. Half court, pick-up games surged back and forth on four of six possible sites on the three full-sized courts. The squeaking shoes, thuds of bouncing balls, thundering feet, and grunts and groans of the players entertained Dodd as he ran. He wondered where the students found the energy at seven in the morning to push themselves. The answer came to him later; it was simple. He reminded himself that some of them probably had not been to bed, yet. Several students rode stationary bicycles and trod on stair climbers in the alcoves surrounding the track and on the bridge between the two straight-aways. There were more exercise machines and televisions in just one corner of the track than existed in the entire Faculty Club, making Dodd extremely jealous. These machines frequently sat idle while Dodd and other faculty fought over the four machines in their club. The causeway also housed the stairs and the open shaft from which Dodd could see a portion of the weight room in the basement. Glass walls kept basketballs and players out of the wide chasm. Also on the bridge were the water fountains, juice machines, and soft drink dispensers.

Finished running three miles on the cushioned rubberized track, Dodd sneaked down the back stairway, away from the woman at the front desk. Once inside the weight room, he slipped into the quadriceps machine and adjusted it for his leg length. Superbly equipped, the weight room stocked almost every type of weight machine and free weights known, and then some. It easily shamed the gym in the Faculty Club. The four walls of the room had been covered with mirrors. Months before, after some initial disorientation, Dodd had taught himself how to keep track of everyone in the room by finding them in the mirrors. Occasionally, really good looking women frequented the weight room — eights, nines and an occasional ten, although never an eleven or twelve on his scale. Two foxes, in fact, good-naturedly harassed a weight lifter in the corner behind him.

Closer to the physician, several people worked out. Most were older and participated in the free cardiac rehabilitation program, guinea pigs for the graduate students in physiology. Metal weights clanged together; men and women strained; the smell of sweat, skin lotions, liniments, and balms permeated the atmosphere. While Dodd watched in the mirrors, the young women with the weight lifter laughed and giggled and pointed at the young man's bulging biceps, triceps and chest muscles. He, apparently, said something to them that they did not like. The laughter died swiftly; an icy chill filled the air.

Ignoring the women, and with an extreme effort, the young man bent at the waist and snatched a great weight from the floor, lifting it over his head. The barbell sagged

Invictus

at both ends, bent by the massive iron discs hung there. As his muscles bulged, balancing and sustaining the weight, one of the petite young women reached forward and yanked downward the young man's pants, out from under his wide leather lifting belt. The shorts fell to the floor. Straining to support the weight and unable to respond, the weight lifter's face turned pink.

The second young woman looked disdainfully at the man's sexual equipment, also clearly visible to Dodd and others in the mirrors. "See, ya, Tiny," she said loudly. The two women turned and exited the weight room. At 7:30 a.m., there were fewer than ten people in the room. Their laughter rocked the entire building. Crimson, the weight lifter replaced the weights on the floor, gently. Elevating his shorts quickly, to conceal his anabolic-steroid-shrunken testicles, he skulked out the door toward the men's locker room.

Done with his knee exercises, Dodd walked over to the small side room that housed more aerobic equipment. No one else used the stationary bicycles. He reached up and turned on the televison, flipping the channel to a news network, in order to catch the latest worldwide information. No sooner had he climbed onto the seat of the bike than a young female student entered the room. She walked to the television and flipped the channel to a rock video station. "Excuse me!" Dodd shouted over the noise of the flywheel spinning between his legs.

The co-ed turned and looked at Dodd. She stood about five-foot, three-inches tall. Her biceps matched his, and her legs were even more muscular. Impatient, she asked, "Yes?"

"I'd appreciate it if you'd put that back on the news."

"That's boring; it will put me to sleep!" she complained.

"Music videos, especially rap, are violent, sexist, and have no redeeming social value. They'll rot your brain," Dodd lectured her.

Sullenly, the woman reached up and returned the channel selector to the news. She stomped out of the room. "...damned graduate student pukes," was all Dodd heard when she left the room.

"And the horse you rode in on," Dodd called after her, but not too loudly, certain she could kick his ass if she wanted. "Damned spoiled students," he mumbled to himself.

Invictus

Chapter Thirty
February 12th

Dodd endeavored to avoid looking at the woman's face. He had struggled to avoid her for nearly two hours, and had also failed miserably. Drawn like a moth to a flame, or a rubber-necking driver to a traffic accident, his eyes returned repeatedly to her soft features, full lips, deep, azure eyes, and perfectly-coiffured, short, blonde hair. Even her fingernails, with their shiny clear polish and perfect cuticles, fascinated him. She wore a somber gray suit, over a pale yellow blouse and matching, large, flowing bow tie.

He had found his eleven, maybe a twelve — he'd have to ask her out to decide which. And Massey was right; he had not found her among the students. She was a decade older than most students, thirty-one, maybe thirty-five years-old, tops. Shame was, she made up part of the legal team that sued him and SVU for malpractice in Stone Garrette's case. In fact, as the attorney taking his deposition, Susan Norton would have enjoyed nothing more than having Dodd confess to her while the tiny reels spun on the cassette recorder that lay midway between them on the polished oak table. Mesmerized by the vision across the table, Dodd would have been happy to spill his guts, but not to lie. Therein lay the rub.

"Your contention," the female lawyer repeated for the second or third time, drawing Dodd's attention to her perfect teeth and slightly upturned nose, "is that Dr. Persia Summers interviewed Stone Garrette after you did. You realize that she vehemently denies this alleged meeting with Mr. Garrette?"

Bill Yancey

Dodd continued to stare at the woman after she asked the question. Phillip Scollick, his attorney, sat next to Dodd, amazed at the change in Dodd over the course of the deposition — from drown-trodden, desolate, and depressed to intent, feisty, and, at times, humorous. Obviously the presence of a beautiful woman had great effect on the physician. Scollick waited as long as he could stand the silence, then kicked Dodd in the leg under the table. "Ow!" Dodd said, eyes darting to Scollick.

"Answer the question, Spencer," Scollick said.

"Question?" Dodd asked. He glanced at Norton. "I thought she made a statement. Would you mind repeating the question?"

In clipped, terse words, squeezed between clenched teeth, the female attorney rephrased the query. "Do you realize that your testimony directly conflicts with Dr. Summers's sworn testimony?" Scollick reacted to her tone of voice. He realized that Dodd's interest in her had an effect on her also. In the past, he would have assumed she had adjusted to such attention by now. He believed that beautiful women in any predominantly male profession developed thick skin and horns, or changed jobs.

"Are you aware that she is lying?" Dodd asked the woman. Within the bare walls and wooden floor in the small conference room near the university counsel offices in Burroughs Hall, a frost hung in the air. The stone walls warmed slowly after being chilled by the long, frozen winter. Small, north-facing windows saw little sunlight during winter months. Scheduled to arrive in less than six weeks, spring always seemed reluctant to thaw the campus.

"Can you prove that?" the woman demanded. Norton bit her lower lip, trying to remain composed. She glanced at Scollick while Dodd thought about his answer to the question, her eyes rolling. Scollick offered no assistance. His task was to protect his client. So taken with Norton was Dodd that his inability to concentrate played in his favor. Scollick smiled and shrugged, as if to say, 'What can I do?'

Dodd finally spoke. "Can we force Persia to take a lie detector test? Listen," he added, "do you always bite your lip like that when you concentrate? It's a very becoming habit spasm. Might lead to an inclusion cyst in the lower lip mucosa, but it is still very becoming." He searched her hands again. He did not see a wedding ring.

Norton clamped her teeth together and pursed her lips slightly, highlighting her dimples. Dodd smiled, delighted by the dimples and unaware that he frustrated the woman. "Are you willing to take a lie detector test, Dr. Dodd?" she asked tersely.

"My client will not...." Scollick began.

Dodd interrupted his attorney. "I will be more than happy to take a lie detector test," he said. Scollick kicked him under the table. Dodd flinched, but did not change his expression. "But I won't, unless Persia agrees to take one also. I'll even go first."

Norton smiled, tilting her head toward Scollick. "You had an objection, counselor?"

"Withdrawn," Scollick said. "Persia will never take the test. I know her attorney."

Dodd placed his left elbow on the table and his chin in his left hand. With his right hand, he bounced a pencil repeatedly on the table, eraser first. Love sick, he gazed into the blonde's eyes. She ignored him, flipping through a legal pad, marking her notes with big backward, left-handed check marks.

"You've had a checkered career, Dr. Dodd?" Norton invited.

"Yes or no questions only, please," Scollick intoned. "My client's previous career is not open to question."

Dodd saw anger flash across her face. The woman's cheeks flushed slightly. "Parts of it are," she snapped. "Dr. Dodd, are you board certified?"

"Short answer: no. Long answer: I was. The certification in emergency medicine is not for life, like some specialties. It requires retesting every ten years. I haven't worked in an emergency room in over a decade. I contemplated taking the test, but I've grown tired of being tested. Do your cheeks always flush when you are angry?"

"So — no," she said, making an extremely large check mark in her notepad. "How long have you been at SVU?"

"Seven years last month," Dodd answered. A chilled whiff of an exotic perfume wafted through the air. Dodd wished he could identify it.

"Your position here?" She reached across the table and abruptly snatched the pencil from Dodd's hand. The soft thumping stopped. Scollick smiled, thinking she rattled easily.

"Sorry," Dodd apologized. "nervous habit. I do acute care. It's like an urgent care center, except the hours are limited, from 8:00 a.m. to 5:00 p.m."

Coldly, she asked him, "What do students do, if they get sick or injured but not during bankers' hours?"

"You know," Dodd said, leaning forward, both hands clasped together. His hands slid across the table until they lay within an inch of her well-manicured fingers. He felt warmth radiate from them. "I have the same complaint. Neal, the director — that's Neal Abramowicz — is against extending the hours."

"Do you have a lot of conflict with Dr. Abramowicz?" Norton asked, pulling her hands closer to herself and away from Dodd.

Dodd rolled his eyes. He asked the attorney, "How much time do we have?"

Scollick chuckled. If his opponent spent time trying to sort the differences in opinion between Abramowicz and Dodd, the deposition would take three days. "Did you say something, counselor?" Norton asked Scollick.

Scollick cleared his throat. He placed his right ankle

Invictus

on his left knee and began to tug at his sock. "In the interest of saving time," he replied, "I think you should avoid the topic of disagreements with the director of student health. It's an unrewarding field of endeavor, believe me. Either one of them could talk your ear off for several hours. At the end you still would not know who was right."

Dodd grimaced at the remark. "*I* know who's right," he growled at Scollick, taking his eyes off Norton for the first time in many minutes. "That stupid s.o.b. couldn't run a medical clinic if someone shrank it to matchbox size, and gave it four wheels and a rubber band motor." Dodd's voice rose as he spoke.

"I see what you mean," Norton told Scollick. She flipped her legal pad pages back to the first page. "Let me reiterate," she said to Dodd. "You interviewed Stone?"

"Correct." Dodd nodded.

"You thought he was going through withdrawal from alcohol?"

"Correct."

"You wanted him admitted to the hospital?" she asked.

"Correct."

"Why didn't you admit him?" Norton repeated a question they had discussed an hour before.

"I do not have hospital privileges at Lee County Hospital," Dodd told her, again.

"Is that unusual?" Norton asked.

Dodd shrugged. "We have an outpatient practice. Having patients in the hospital is a hassle and hard work. In addition, it requires a lot of time. As underpaid civil servants, we elect to let someone else, a hospitalist, admit the patients."

"So you asked an internist with hospital privileges to admit Stone?" She displayed her superficial knowledge of medicine.

"No," Dodd admitted. "I asked Dr. Summers for a second opinion, believing he would be better off on a psychiatric ward than a general medical one."

The attorney probed, again; she asked, "And when she did not show up, you called someone else?"

"She did show up," Dodd repeated forcefully.

"But, according to you, she did not admit Stone to the hospital. Why didn't you then call someone else?"

Dodd explained, again, probably for the fourth or fifth time, "He had already left the building. Persia told me his father refused to pay for the admission. Stone is an adult; he was capable of making his own decisions."

"Only if he was competent, Doctor. Did you think he was competent?"

"I wasn't sure. That's why I called Persia. She let him go. I assumed she thought he was competent."

Norton turned pages in the copy of Stone Garrette's medical record. She said, "Your note doesn't mention competency."

"Persia's would, if she'd let you read it," Dodd offered.

"So, you didn't call another physician to admit Stone?" she asked.

"I told you, he left the building before I could do anything."

"You had his home phone number and address?" the attorney badgered Dodd.

"They are in his chart," Dodd agreed, pointing to the phone number on the progress note in front of her.

"Why didn't you call the police? Why not have him admitted against his will?"

Dodd sat, numb. After two hours of nearly idle conversation, of tapping the fortress with a tack hammer, she had hit the nail on the head — with a ten-pound sledgehammer. He stared at her, his lips pressed tightly against one another. His foot jumped nervously on the bare floor, tapping an unrecognizable rhythm. "I should have," Dodd admitted. "I should not have trusted the bitch. I should have followed him home and called the cops."

Invictus

Convinced she had the testimony she wanted, Norton relaxed. She leaned back in her chair and exhaled slowly, savoring the victory. Cautiously, she managed a smile. Too distraught to notice and devastated by the memories, Dodd relived the confrontation with the campus police, the resuscitation, and the long weekend in the Roanoke hospital. He sat mute in front of her, staring at his own hands. His shoulders and face drooped in resignation.

"Spence?" Scollick asked, "are you alright?" The physician slipped quickly into his previously depressed persona, slouching, head sagging. He stared at his lap.

"I have no further questions," Norton announced suddenly. She reached across the table and pressed the stop button on the tiny recorder. "I'm sorry, Dr. Dodd, I really am," she said. Taking her time, she stood and pulled a brushed aluminum briefcase from the floor to the table top. Snapping it open, she packed her recorder, notebook, and pen inside. Silently, she laid her business card on the table. "I'll be in touch, Phillip," she added turning to leave the room. "You can proofread the transcript after I get it back from the typist." Stopping just short of the door, the well-proportioned attorney spun and gave one last glance at the pitiful Dodd. "If it's any consolation, Doctor," she said, "to Murphy Garrette, this is not personal; it's just business." She turned and disappeared through the door.

"Isn't everything *just* business to him?" Dodd asked the ghost of her perfume.

Several minutes later, Dodd took a deep breath and sighed. He stood up and placed his hands on the back of the uncomfortable wooden chair. He looked at Scollick. Scollick sat, both hands clasped in front of him on the table. The attorney stared at the far wall. "Not good, eh?" Dodd asked. Scollick shook his head. Dodd picked up the blonde attorney's business card from the table and examined it carefully. "Do you think she'd go out with an older man?" He laughed a hollow, gallows laugh.

"She does already, Spencer," Scollick replied. "She dates the senior partner and CEO of her legal firm, William Cassel."

Dodd frowned. "Thanks for that, asshole. For a minute, there, I thought you were on my side," he said.

Anguished by Dodd's answer to the last question, Scollick said, "We talked about that specific query, Spencer. We even prepared an answer for it. What were you supposed to say when she asked it?"

"What I was supposed to say was a half-truth, Phillip. What I said was what I truly believe. If I had only followed him home...."

"If you had followed him home, you would have been arrested for making a public nuisance of yourself," Scollick explained.

"But he would not have fallen off the roof."

Scollick disagreed. He and Dodd had had the conversation before. He stated his position, again, futility apparent in his voice, "They would have let him go. The cops wouldn't be able to tell he was a danger to himself or others, if you couldn't. You would have been in jail, and he would have fallen off the roof anyway. Then he would have died, because no one would have forced the campus cops to back off so he could be treated."

"Maybe, but I wouldn't feel so damn guilty about it. I would have done everything I could have. I was tired, Phil. You can't be tired and practice good medicine. Weariness leads to mistakes."

"Everyone makes mistakes," Scollick said.

"Not ones that cause severe morbidity and mortality to others." Dodd's head hung; he stared at the back of the chair.

Scollick began packing his briefcase. He asked, "So, only supermen should practice medicine?"

Weak, Dodd sat back down in the chair, defeated by the logic. "No. You're right. I knew I wasn't Superman.

Invictus

That's why I asked for some help from Persia. No one believes me, though."

"I'm beginning to," Scollick suggested.

"Bullshit," Dodd said.

Bill Yancey

Invictus

Chapter Thirty-one
March 14th

Clint Massey leaned his shoulder on the door frame, watching Dodd unpack his briefcase. Dodd had arrived four hours late to work, just in time for lunch. Ceremoniously, he ignored the other physician. Following his usual ritual, he turned on only one set of overhead lights. He slipped his lunch bag into the small refrigerator, being careful not to expose the beer to Massey's prying eyes. Then he laid his date book on the desk, opening it to the correct date and perusing his 'To Do' list.

Sitting, he reached under his desk and turned on the computer; the monitor snapped audibly as it came to life. A picture formed on the screen. Dodd had scanned the cover of his favorite book and used it for background: *Elvis Saves*, the title read, a bumper sticker on the rear of a red '67 Mustang. Peanut Press and the author's name appeared below the car.

"Can we talk?" Massey finally asked, convinced Dodd would not speak first.

"About what?" Dodd asked morosely.

"A lot of stuff," Massey replied. He stepped into the room and closed the door behind him. "For instance, I represent the support staff...."

A pained smile crossed Dodd's face; he said, "You look like a supporter, an athletic supporter to be exact. Actually, you look more like something an athletic supporter might support."

"No need to get nasty, Spence, unless that was an awful attempt at humor."

"No humor intended," Dodd admitted, staring straight

ahead at the computer monitor.

Massey continued, trying to ignore the insult. "Do you know what day this is?"

Dodd looked up from his computer, after typing in his personal code. The screen flashed messages; the computer checked for viruses and unauthorized meddling. He shook his head. "No. I give up. What day is this?"

"It's Friday," Massey said.

"TGIF to you, too," Dodd replied contemptuously.

"Spencer. You haven't bought donuts for the nurses in almost two months. They grew to expect that every Friday; you spoiled them."

"Well, pardon me, Clint," Dodd sneered. His long-suppressed sailor's vocabulary overwhelmed the physician's, almost inciting a seizure in his left temporal lobe. "The nurses can buy their own *fucking* donuts."

"You never speak to them, except when required professionally, either."

"They are prone to misinterpreting what I say...." Dodd said, anger increasing. "They're a big part of why I'm leaving, Clint. They're always running to Abramowicz. 'Dodd said this; Dodd did that....' What crap!"

"There is still a chance you will stay. You, or we, might get the contract," Massey offered.

"There are exactly three chances of that happening:" Dodd enumerated the choices, "slim, fat, and no chance."

Pained expression on his face, Massey nodded in agreement. He felt sorry for Dodd, but he knew no way to feel empathetic. The demons Dodd dealt with seemed trivial to him, but they apparently drove the man to alienate even his closest friends. Being right, and maintaining his personal standard of honor, meant more to Spencer Dodd than friendship, marriage, love, and probably life, Massey thought. He knew his friend was miserable, but he reasoned it was Dodd's own fault, or the fault of his formative environment and genes. Massey could not possibly change

Dodd's personality, without destroying the man. "I'm worried about you," Massey said.

"How long have you been worried?"

"A couple weeks, I guess, ever since that awful email you sent to the entire staff."

Dodd rubbed his chin and looked at ceiling, rolling his eyes upward. "Let's see, if you were a student, that would mean one day last week and the first day of this week: two weeks. As in, 'Doc, I've had a cold for two weeks, Friday and Saturday of last week and Sunday and Monday of this week."

"That's not funny, either, Spence. You're depressed."

"No shit," Dodd spat. "I'm surprised you could make the diagnosis. Then, again: *Coniecturalem artem esse medicinarum*.[44] Maybe you got lucky."

"And you're getting paranoid," Massey added.

"I've always been paranoid, Clint. However, it's not paranoia if someone truly is out to get you."

Massey explained his observation. "The nurses say you give them dirty looks if they are talking or laughing in the hallways. Spence, they aren't necessarily talking about you."

"They aren't working if they're hanging out in hallway talking. Besides, they're not upset that I'm leaving, either," Dodd observed.

"Well, they aren't celebrating, yet," Massey offered. "Although, if you don't snap out of it and start showing some of that patented Dodd dry sense of humor, they are going to throw one hell of a going away party — about an hour after you leave the building for the last time."

Dodd shrugged. "Like, I care. They wouldn't feel that way about me if you guys were consistent. Or if Neal had said to them, 'Your evaluations center on the preparation of patients for the doctor to see. That's one third of your job. If you can't do that properly, you need to look elsewhere for employment.'"

Massey shook his head. "It's a bureaucracy, Spencer. You didn't have to take it upon yourself to correct the situation."

"Well, who the hell was going to do it, Clint? You? You're in bed with the biggest dingbat of them all. A.J.? Hilda? Give me a break. You guys were here for at least three years before I arrived. The nurses never got off their asses to do vital signs before I insisted. The first week I was here, every — not most, every — student asked me why he should get undressed so I could listen to his chest. What were you guys doing? Not listening, or listening through four layers of clothing during the winter. Come on, Clint, this wasn't a medical clinic; it was a health food store run by a chiropractor. You guys are lazy; you have no backbone. Stand up to the nurses; put them to work. If you hadn't been dealing with a basically healthy population, there would have been deaths, lots of them, and lawsuits." Dodd caught his breath. He continued, "And not lawsuits because a psychiatrist refuses to admit she made a mistake."

"But, we *are* dealing with a healthy group of patients. Is that all that's bothering you?"

Spinning his chair to face Massey, Dodd pointed his hand at the second chair. "Do you have an hour or two?" he asked. "My mother recently had a stroke. She's comatose. My father's Alzheimer's is worse. My older brother is an idiot. My sister is on an island in the Pacific communing with God knows what and talking to rocks. My ex-wife let my dog get hit by a car. There's a good chance he'll die. Even though she has her own business, she's petitioning the court for alimony because I make a paltry ten thousand dollars more per year than she does. She's living with a guy who is unemployed. I guess he wants a big screen television for his birthday. At least losing my job will fix that. Maybe she'll have to pay alimony to me. Oh, and by the way, I am the defendant in two lawsuits, malpractice and sexual harassment. Do you want to hear about my kids, too?"

Massey declined to sit. He began to inch backward toward the door. His right hand behind him, he groped for the door handle. "Sorry," he apologized, "I can see that this is a bad time...."

"Do you know what that asshole, Neal, had the guts to ask me to do today?" Dodd continued to rant. Massey shook his head, hand searching for the door knob. Dodd continued, "He wants me to write a list of recommendations for improving the efficiency of patient flow. I'll show him efficiency. I'll have the nurses doing throat cultures on every damned patient. The secretaries and receptionists are going to give those God awful cold questionnaires to everyone that walks in the door, even pregnant women and students with obvious injuries. On the bottom of the form, the student will be reminded to ask for his antibiotic, regardless of his illness. In addition, every patient that returns with the same complaint will have to see a different practitioner — for a second opinion. You guys are going to spend your lives sorting through that shit. I'm going to suggest that he open up a triple booking system, to make certain every student who has even the most minor complaint is seen immediately or is in the building before the doors are locked. Only one secretary, Neal's, will be allowed to make schedule changes. You'll be lucky if you get home before midnight!"

Massey stared at Dodd, convinced he had become a madman. "He won't do any of that stuff, will he?"

"He's an idiot, Clint!" Dodd shouted, referring to Abramowicz. "Of course, he'll do it! He'll do all of it! His latest motto is this: *'Don't confuse the patients with facts. Send them away happy. I don't want any complaints.'* He'll think I used reverse psychology in suggesting the changes. He knows nothing about the practice of medicine. Your colleagues and you won't complain. You're wimps. He won't listen to you, anyway. You know it. His chief source of information, Persia, is also clueless. She hasn't done a physical exam in the last nine years. How would she know what makes sense? How about some more 'feel good' clinics? Asthma; change the regimen the students' doctors have them on; wart clinic, don't tell them they go away by themselves, scar them for life instead; preventive medicine clinic, for a basically healthy population; life styles clinic; gay and lesbian clinic; diet clinic; orthopedic.... Are there enough of you to go around, Clint?"

Massey found and grasped the door knob, knuckles white. Afraid to turn his back on Dodd, he pulled the door open wide, ensuring room enough for him to back out of the office without looking behind him. He began to inch out, facing Dodd. "You'd do something different?" Massey asked in an attempt to appease Dodd.

"Damn right, I would!" Dodd bellowed. "You guys don't understand. The majority of patients don't need doctors. The doctors need the patients. Ninety-five percent of all diseases resolve without medical intervention."

Finally a safe distance in the hall, Massey held his palms out, toward Dodd, to indicate he had heard enough. He turned smartly to his right and marched toward the nurses' station, convinced Dodd had experienced a break with reality. As he departed, the group of nurses in the hallway convulsed as one. A collective laugh assaulted Dodd's ears. Dodd slammed the door. After locking it, he reached into his refrigerator and from it pulled a beer. Twisting off the bottle cap, he chugged a third of the malt liquor rapidly. Pulling the paper bag from the refrigerator, he yanked his plastic sandwich bag out, ripping the brown paper bag in the process.

BeeBee sat on the window sill. Apparently, he had witnessed the exchange with Massey. He tapped on the glass with his beak. Dodd cracked open the window. "Tough on your friends, aren't you?" the bird asked. "Might not have any if you keep it up."

"Friends?" Dodd asked. "You mean like that pansy, Brooker? He won't back my appeal to reinstate my contract. He refuses to write a letter to President Furneaux confirming that the present director of student health is a worthless individual."

"He's hoping to retire in a year," BeeBee offered, "Or he doesn't agree with you and is using that as an excuse...."

"Oh, he agrees with me!" Dodd bellowed. "He's too much of a wimp to say so. A letter wouldn't affect his retirement! 'But these are my friends,' he says, 'I have to live in this community after I retire. Besides, I have enjoyed working here, even though Abramowicz is useless, or even detrimental. But I get to retire soon, if I keep my nose clean.'"

A louder group laugh shook the building. Dodd turned and stared at the door, seething. "They're enjoying themselves, Spencer," the bird said. "Does that bother you?"

Dodd sat in the chair and stared into space. "I feel dead," he said. "I'm a ghost walking the halls of student health. I can see and hear them, but not affect them in any way. No one cares what I feel. The pain. The loss. And all because of that asshole, Abramowicz."

BeeBee agreed, "It *is* like being dead, Spencer. You isolated yourself; they can't feel your isolation or loneliness. For them, life goes on. They don't have time to invest in your causes, to mourn you, or to waste on your memory. And after the grief you caused them, why would they want to? Life's too busy nowadays."

Angry with himself for caring what others thought, Dodd tore open the zipped clear plastic bag and shoved the roast beef and lettuce sandwich into his mouth, biting off a huge chunk. "Crap!" he said spitting the mouthful of sandwich into the trash can.

Examining the sandwich in Dodd's hand, BeeBee asked, "Mind if I eat that?".

"It tastes awful, really bitter," Dodd said. He rolled the sandwich over in his hand, showing BeeBee the white mold he had missed while making it earlier. Green mold he could find easily; the white fungus looked like flour and blended with the bread.

"Not to me," BeeBee said. "It will go great with a fat maggot or two." Dodd threw the sandwich out the window, onto the manicured lawn. The bird hopped down from the ledge onto the grass. Dodd closed the window.

Invictus

Chapter Thirty-two
March 25th and 26th

Immobile, Dodd sat on the wooden slats of the cement bench. Late March meant spring everywhere in Virginia, except in the mountains. It would take the higher elevations two more weeks to warm up. In the blustery wind, Dodd shivered slightly in his beat-up leather jacket. He had left his leather gloves and knit SVU Bears cap in his apartment. Overhead, cumulus clouds raced northeast through the sky, along the Blue Ridge, pushed rapidly over the horizon by the gusting wind. The ground alternated with patches of light and dark; shadows hurried to keep up with the clouds.

Canada Geese waddled closer toward him, then pecked at the tidbits of food left on the ground by the previous visitors, a class of grade-school-aged children. Dodd ignored the birds, as he had the children and their chaperones. He wondered how the kids would remove from their shoes the thin coating of goose feces that covered every horizontal surface surrounding the 'Duck Pond.' Years before, when Dodd had been a student, the pond had been a favorite place for lovers to wander. Splendid oaks and maples, grassy lawns, cedars and pine surrounded the small artificial lake. Students, infatuated by their new freedoms and the objects of their desires, roamed or sat, or rowed in one of the rented boats. Then the geese took over; scum covered the water. Fish suffocated. No one came to the smelly sewer-like pond any more, Dodd realized, except the younger children of the graduate students, and then only to dispose of stale bread.

Clinton Massey found Dodd slumped forward on the

bench seat, elbows on knees, face in his hands. He stared at the opposite shore, not aware of his friend's arrival. Massey sat next to Dodd, eliciting no response. "Are you sick?" Massey asked.

Shaken from a profound mental voyage, Dodd turned his head and looked at Massey. "No," he said. "Are you disappointed?"

Massey studied Dodd's face. The wrinkles in the weathered skin seemed deeper. His usual frown appeared more convex than usual. "You're several hours late for work. Is something bothering you?"

Straightening his back and placing his hands on his knees, Dodd shook his head. "Not much. Not if you consider as less than remarkable the revelation that my best friend for the last ten years has been a dog."

"Man's best friend...."

"Not man's. *My* best friend, a yellow Labrador Retriever named Refrigerator." Dodd stared across the pond. Tears welled in his eyes. Seen from the side by Massey, the nearly spherical balls of salt water balanced on Dodd's lower lids; surface tension kept them from bursting and sliding down his cheeks. Dodd swallowed hard, holding inside the whimper. He said, "Fridge was so curious. Just a dumb dog, really, for Christ's sake. When we first got him, he'd stand in the laundry room and listen to the garage door go up and down when one of us left. He'd be waiting there when we returned. I saw a spark in his eyes one day. Then I realized that he thought we spent eight or ten hours in the garage and the screech the door made indicated we wanted to come back into the house."

Dodd shoved his hands deep into his pockets and leaned back against the bench. He put his left ankle on his right knee. Continuing, he told Massey, "So one day, I let him into the garage. He walked around for about five minutes, nose to the floor, smelling everything. Afterward, he sat in the middle of the floor and stared at me, as if to ask, 'What the hell do you do in here all day?' Later, I let him into the garage, after Sherry had gone to work. It was empty, of course. That's when he figured out the truth: the garage was the transporter room. People went into it and, during the noise, were teleported elsewhere. The second time the noise occurred meant they had returned. He enjoyed Star Trek a lot more after making that connection."

Massey sat through the explanation, head tilted to one side like a puppy. "He watched Star Trek?"

"Well, for a while," Dodd said. "He liked the science part; didn't care much for the monsters and fantasy stuff they wrote into the scripts occasionally in the later episodes."

"You're weird," Massey said.

"Not me," Dodd argued. "Refrigerator was weird. And wonderful."

Massey gave Dodd the message he had been commissioned to deliver. "Abramowicz is pissed that you didn't show up for work. Not only that, he has the information systems guy taking your computer hard drive apart. He thinks you're responsible for placing the message on the digital bulletin board at the end of the last semester about wanting to buy textbooks that the school bookstore didn't want. Did you know he finally had to have the cops remove about thirty unruly students from his yard at 2:00 a.m. one morning?"

Dodd shook his head and waved his hand, knowing he had not been responsible for that practical joke. He did envy the creative genius who thought of placing the note, with the addendum to bring the books in person to Abramowicz's home, after 11 p.m., because the buyer 'worked the evening shift.' Smiling at the thought of Abramowicz answering his front door time and again after midnight, getting angry, and turning away student after student with an armload of books, he replied, "This is a mental health day, Clint. I can be sick for one hundred and eighty days before I have to start using my vacation time. If he's not careful, I might be gone that often. Tell him I'm depressed."

"About work?"

"No. About the fact that my dog — *my best friend* — died. Tell him that if I could have arranged it, he would have been the one run over by a car and put down by the veterinarian."

"He wouldn't like that," Massey decided. "I'll just tell him you're depressed."

"Well, what's he going to do, Clint, fire me?" Dodd asked. He stood. Pulling his hands from his pockets, he stretched. "I'm going to walk home now, Clint," he told Massey. "Give my regards to Fatman and Robin."

"I know who the fat man is. Who's Robin?"

Dodd smiled, holding his right hand about five inches above and parallel to his left palm. "Brown bird, about this tall, red breast. You'll recognize him when you see him. It is March 25th, you know."

Massey stood. He watched Dodd start down the path, "Spring. Almost April Fool's Day," he called after Dodd.

"I'll see what I can do about that," Dodd turned his head and said. Leaving, he walked on the gravel path that followed the edge of the pond.

***

Dodd hummed as he printed the forgeries. He wore latex gloves so as not to leave his fingerprints on the pages, just in case. Pulling the latest color copy from his printer, he re-read the letter on the bogus letterhead:

**Carrion Health System
101 Peachtree Avenue
Atlanta, Georgia 30303-1906
Telephone 404/555-3277**

Invictus

Robert L. Thomasson
President

Ms. J.P. Jones
Executive Secretary
Student Health Center
Southwestern Virginia University
Fawsville, Virginia 24271

Dear Ms. Jones;

I have recently been informed by my superiors that in the near future I will begin to manage the day-to-day operations of the student health center at SVU. The transition to private enterprise can be tricky. I already possess a map of your little cow town, but I need more information.

Could you please send to me a copy of the floor plan to the second floor of the health center? I am particularly interested in the dimensions of Dr. Abramowicz's office and the space just outside his office. I have to decide on an entire suite of furniture and color coordinate it with my vestibule.

Also, please send to me the addresses and phone numbers of the closest four star hotels and restaurants. This is to be a temporary assignment (until a permanent director is recruited) and I could not possibly live near rowdy students in an apartment.

Thank you for your time.

Sincerely,
Reginald P. Overstreet, III, MBA

Bill Yancey

P.S. Please be so kind as to enclose an application for reserved parking and the erection of a temporary fabric garage to cover my Rolls Royce.
RPO/frg

CARRION: The Final Solution For Failing Medical Practices

Dodd smiled to himself. Still wearing the latex gloves, he opened a new box of legal sized envelopes. After pulling one from the middle of the pack, he laid the box next to the new binder of printer paper, from which he had taken a single sheet from the middle of the stack. He ran the envelope through the inkjet printer to be addressed. Carefully folding the paper into thirds and creasing it neatly, he placed the letter inside the envelope. Not licking the envelope to ensure none of his DNA transferred with his saliva to the glue, he ran the edge of the envelope under a stream of water in the kitchen sink, then sealed it.

Dodd placed the legal envelope inside a Federal Express Overnight package and mailed it to his accomplice in Atlanta.

***

Drained, Dodd lay on the couch. He had been too exhausted to open the hide-a-bed the night before. Lying on his side, he stared into the open closet door ten feet in front of him. A voice called to him from the box that held his father's service pistol. The box sat on the shelf above the hanging clothes. It would be so easy to end this misery, the weapon said. One bullet; no more pain....

I couldn't shoot Abramowicz, Dodd thought.

Who said anything about Abramowicz? the gun asked.

Too depressed to respond to the suggestion, Dodd continued to lie on the sofa. Finally deciding on a course of action, he thought about getting up. Before Dodd could react to the message from the voice, the telephone rang.

Invictus

Dodd turned his head and eyes toward it. A stabbing pain in the back of his neck, punishment for sleeping with his head on the armrest. He waited; the phone continued to ring. Eventually, it stopped. Easing himself into a sitting position, Dodd rubbed his neck. He stood, intending to retrieve some aspirin from the bathroom when the telephone began ringing, again.

Detouring around the dinette, Dodd plodded into the kitchen and picked up the receiver. Weary from the exertion, he answered the phone, "Dodd."

"Dr. Dodd, this is Linda, from Doctor Nguyen's office. Can you hold for the doctor?"

"Sure," Dodd said, rubbing his neck, eyes closed in pain.

"Spencer," the wiry Vietnamese physician spoke to Dodd. "How are you feeling?"

"Like I slept doing a headstand, Mark. Maybe I have seasonal affective disorder. I always hated February and March; my depression is always deeper during this part of the year. What's up?"

"I have good news and I have bad news," Nguyen said.

"Let it rip," Dodd invited the internist.

"The condition is treatable."

"What condition?" Dodd asked. "I was kidding about the seasonal affective disorder. I get lots of sunlight jogging."

"You have pernicious anemia," the doctor explained. "Vitamin B-12 deficiency in your case. Your symptoms are due to that, I believe. I need you to start today with some weekly B-12 shots. In four weeks we'll have you start getting them monthly. You'll need an endoscopy eventually."

Listlessly, Dodd asked, "Lovely. And I'll feel better when I raise my serum cobalt level?"

"You should have more energy," Nguyen agreed. "You'll make better red cells and faster, also intestinal cells."

"Anything else I should know?"

"Knowing you as well as I do, I hesitate to mention this, but you might be a little more irritable until it is under control...."

Dodd laughed. "Not likely," he said. "I'm about as irritable as one person is legally allowed to be."

"...and possibly more depressed than usual. You haven't had any suicidal or homicidal thoughts, have you?" Nguyen asked, laughing nervously.

"No," Dodd said calmly, not mentioning the conversation with the automatic pistol. "I'll be in later today for the first injection."

***

In front of the full length mirror screwed into the back of the closet door, Dodd buttoned his shirt. Finished, he tucked the light blue shirt into his gray trousers. Depressed and angry, but still reining in his anger over the upcoming hearing, he mentally reviewed statements he or Abramowicz might make. Not paying attention to his choice of belts, his hand fell onto a brown one hanging in the closet.

BeeBee sat on Dodd's shoulder. He looked downward at the polished black shoes, then at Dodd. "Under the circumstances, I think a black belt would be better," the bird said.

Dodd smiled, realizing the raven was correct. "Sure," he agreed, "and if it's a black belt in karate, so much the better." He moved his hand to a black belt and pulled it from the belt rack. The telephone rang as he slipped the stiff, rarely worn leather through the first belt loop on his trousers. Dodd ambled to the kitchen, lifting the receiver on the third ring.

"Dodd," he said into the handset.

"Dr. Dodd, this is Marcia, in Phillip Scollick's office."

Invictus

"Yes, Marcia." Dodd held the phone to his shoulder by tilting his head away from BeeBee. He continued to thread the belt through the loops. "I'll be on time," he assured her.

"That's why I called, Doctor. The hearing has been postponed."

"Why?" Dodd asked, irritated that no one told him until thirty minutes before the scheduled meeting time.

"President Furneaux went to Washington, D.C. on a fund raising mission. At the last minute, Phil asked to go with him. The university's jet just took off from the local airport."

"Crap!" Dodd exclaimed. "You know, communications really suck around here. Sorry about the language, Marcia. There is a lot of mental preparation that one goes through in readying oneself for an execution. It's tough to do over and over, especially when the reason I have to is that my attorney wants to brown nose the university president on his mission to Congress begging money."

The young woman responded, "I didn't say he went to keep Dr. Furneaux company, Dr. Dodd. He just wanted a ride to the Washington, D.C. area on the university's Lear Jet. He's doing his own research on...ah...a different subject."

"Whatever," Dodd snapped unhappily. "This reminds me of the poor communication at student health. Abramowicz treats us like mushrooms; he keeps us in the dark and feeds us...."

"I know," the secretary finished, "manure. The whole university is like that; it's a bureaucracy."

"Right," Dodd agreed. "When do they suppose the hearing will be rescheduled?"

Dodd heard the secretary flip the pages of a desk calendar. She said, "Looks like next Monday, or, maybe, the first Tuesday in April. Sorry, Doc."

Annoyed, Dodd rationalized the time lost in preparing

himself for mortal, mental combat. He decided to take the day off work anyway and do some reading — anything to irritate Abramowicz. "It's not your fault, Marcia," he said, "but you can tell Phillip what I think of his.... Never mind, I'll tell him myself when he gets back." Dodd hung up the receiver. "First, we kill all the lawyers," he reminded BeeBee.

Invictus

Chapter Thirty-three
Morning of March 31ˢᵗ

Seated in the conference room on the top floor of the north turret attached to the administrative building, Dodd ignored the bustle around him. Several people entered and found seats. Long, thin, pointed shafts of light fell across the huge oval conference table. The mirror-like polished oak surface reflected the Gothic windows. Dodd could see the wrinkles in the hand-blown, leaded glass cut to fit the narrow openings. He sat in the heavy oak chair, awed by the room. King Arthur's round table must have been in a chamber like this, he thought.

Surrounded by stone walls, castle-like archery slits, pointed arched windows, and ornate decorations, Dodd eyes took in the exposed beams, the hand-cut glass windows, the huge conference table surrounded by at least twenty chairs, and the tapestries that insulated the cold walls. A sobering insight slipped along his cerebral neurons: in a room like this, Robespierre choreographed the French Revolution until he lost control. The thought of Dr. Guillotine's invention sent a tingle across the back of Dodd's neck.

Provost Gregory G. Marshall sat heavily in the chair at the head of the table. No stranger to proceedings, informal or formal, Marshall had spent his life since age eighteen on the campus of Southwestern Virginia University. In the previous thirty-five years, he had earned degrees: a B.S. in business; an M.S. in management; and a Ph.D. in communications, and worked at SVU. For thirty-one years he had been a part-time and full-time employee. He had worked in the athletic department as a recruiter, the alumni association as a fund raiser, assistant dean of student affairs, vice president of Development and University Relations, and eventually Provost. While a Senior Vice President and Provost, he had proven his political ability to swim with the sharks, wrestle SVU Bears, and survive. He not only survived, he flourished in the academic setting. His people skills, his intellect, and his ability to put the university first in every venue enamored him to everyone on campus. The joke ran that if someone cut Marshall, he would bleed blue, gray, and white blood: the school colors. Dodd pulled his chair toward the table, closer to Phillip Scollick, his attorney. He muttered to himself.

"What's that?" Scollick asked.

Dodd repeated his words, and added to them. "I'm dead meat. First, they give me you for a lawyer; then they appoint Marshall to oversee this hearing. Just point me in the direction of the shower. I wouldn't want to contaminate the room when I slit my wrists."

Not certain if Dodd were serious or expressing gallows humor, Scollick smiled. "Sit tight. Marshall's all SVU Bear," he said, referring to the school mascot, "but he's fair."

"I have some opening remarks," Marshall started bluntly, silencing the groups of people huddled around the edges of the huge table. "First, this is not a legal proceeding. It is an information gathering forum. The material presented here is strictly confidential. It will help me make a recommendation to President Furneaux. He will have to decide whether SVU defends this pending malpractice suit, or tries to settle out of court. For argument's sake, Phillip Scollick, Dr. Dodd's university appointed defense lawyer, will argue that the university should spend resources to refute the malpractice claim made against Dr. Dodd. Kendrick Whitaker will take the opposite position. Phil will defend Dr. Dodd and try to

Invictus

sell me on the realistic possibility of winning his case in court. Kenny will attempt to show why we should cut our losses and settle."

Marshall adjusted his seating. He continued. "This is not a court of law. Even more than the judicial system, we are interested in the truth. But, having learned the truth, our decision may be to save the university embarrassment or financial loss, regardless of what that truth is. Gentlemen, I expect you to remain polite. I want no courtroom shenanigans here. Is that understood?" Both lawyers nodded. "Okay, I assume you have digested all of the testimony given during the witnesses' depositions. Phil, where would you like to start?"

Dodd tried to get a mental feel for the loyalties around the table, by seeing who sat close to whom. Abramowicz and Persia Summers sat near Whitaker, the second lawyer, two seats closer to Marshall and on the opposite side of the table. He labeled them the main antagonists, most likely to push for settling out of court and not defending his honor. The Provost's secretary, charged with maintaining the recording equipment, changing tapes, and monitoring the recording levels on the microphones, sat in the seat next to Marshall on the same side of the table as Dodd. Efficient, and dressed in a severe dark blue suit, with hair in a tight bun, she never allowed her eyes and Dodd's to meet. Bad news, Dodd decided. Several seats around the table remained empty. Dodd knew that witnesses might be called upon to give opinions during the hearing later, and they would sit there. The remaining seats were filled by the lawyers' secretaries, Abramowicz's personal secretary, J.P. Jones, and other lower ranking administrative staff.

Remaining seated to emphasize the informal nature of the hearing, Scollick responded to Marshall, "I'd like to start with Neal Abramowicz, if that's okay, Doug."

Abramowicz shrugged, then looked at Marshall. He

smiled his political, bland, blameless smile. Marshall nodded his assent to the attorney. "We have to start somewhere," Abramowicz conceded.

Scollick pointed to the notebook in front of Abramowicz. "We'll get to your deposition later, Neal. How long have you been director at Student Health?"

"Two years, in June."

"What did you do before that?" Scollick asked.

"Ran the Buildings and Grounds Department for eighteen months."

"And before that?"

"I was the administrator of the Counseling Department, for thee years; before that the assistant administrator in the Athletic Department, fund raising."

"What does Counseling do?"

Surprised by the question, Abramowicz looked at Whitaker and then Marshall. Neither offered any assistance. He answered the question, "A lot of stuff. Mainly it tests for students weaknesses and strengths, helps them choose career paths. Advanced placement. Adjustment to college life. Support groups for women, men, attention deficit syndrome, sexual assault survivors, eating disorders."

"And what did you do?" Scollick asked pointedly. "Your degree's not in psychology, is it?"

Abramowicz smiled his biggest grin. "No. My advanced degrees are an MBA and a doctorate in education."

"So you?" Scollick prodded.

"Administrated," Abramowicz replied testily. "I ran the department. I solved managerial problems, interacted with the higher administration, made the budget, that kind of thing."

"Neal doesn't need to explain his previous life," the other attorney, Whitaker, finally interrupted, tired of his colleague's line of questioning.

"I agree," the Provost added.

Invictus

"In addition to clarifying some things, Doug, I'd like Neal to get a feel for how a plaintiff's attorney might approach this," Scollick explained.

"I think," Abramowicz chuckled, "that I saw plenty of that during my deposition."

"If we go to court, the give and take will be much more intense," Scollick explained. Great, Dodd thought. Even my attorney doesn't want to defend me. Scollick continued questioning Abramowicz, "Did you have a psychiatrist working with your psychologists?"

Abramowicz repositioned his wooden chair. The glued joints groaned. He pointed to Persia Summers. "Of course," the obese man replied, "Dr. Summers."

"She did what, exactly?"

Abramowicz smiled, turning his head toward Summers. "She handles all the pathology, at least initially. After she evaluates students with, say, eating disorders, she makes a treatment plan and turns over the patient's care to one of the psychologists."

"The problems those students have might include psychoses, drug abuse, alcohol abuse...." Scollick suggested.

"In general, anything that might require medication," Abramowicz finished for the attorney.

Scollick paused. He looked at Summers and nodded. "I'm not ignoring you, Persia," Scollick explained, smiling at Summers. "I just want Neal to be certain of this information in his own mind." Summers returned the smile. Scollick asked Abramowicz, "Did you have a good working relationship with Persia?"

"The best."

"Okay," Scollick sighed, finished building a foundation Dodd did not understand. "How did you come to be the administrator of both Counseling and Student Health?"

"The previous director of student health took a job in California," Abramowicz explained. "As an M.D., he could command a much higher salary than the state would pay him here. With the hiring freeze imposed by the governor, the directorships of Counseling and Student health were combined. When the previous director of counseling and student health passed away, I was chosen to replace him."

"And how has it gone?" Scollick asked, tilting his head and frowning.

"Very well, I think." Abramowicz shrugged. He looked at Marshall for support. Marshall remained poker-faced.

"Even though you have no medical background?"

"Well," Abramowicz smiled and turned his head toward Marshall, "I think I'm a quick study. A lot of medicine is like psychology, getting the right bodies together at the right time. Budget is important, of course. I let the doctors practice medicine, I just administrate."

Dodd lost his temper. He exploded from his chair. Jumping to his feet, he shook his fist at his rotund nemesis. "Bullshit!" Dodd shouted. "You interfere with everything, you son of a...."

"Christ, Spence, shut up," Scollick said, grabbing Dodd's arm and pulling him back into his chair, "and sit down." Red-faced, Dodd sat, staring at Abramowicz.

"Dr. Dodd," Provost Douglas Marshall spoke quietly, "one more outburst like that, and you will have made up my mind for me. If you can't control your temper, your defense will suffer. Rather than embarrass this institution in public, we will settle tomorrow for the full amount. Do you understand my position?"

Dodd looked at Marshall, chin on chest, sullen. "Yes, sir," he said apologetically. Abramowicz gloated. Persia snuggled closer to the fat man. Dodd turned his head and glared at Abramowicz. He imagined Abramowicz sticking his tongue out at him, placing his thumbs at his temples, and waving his hands. Childish, Dodd told himself silently, both of us.

"Evidently, there is some disagreement on that last

point," Scollick said. Dodd sulked, but kept his mouth shut. "Have there been any complaints, Neal?"

Abramowicz chuckled. "Most of my complaints come from, or are about, Dr. Dodd. Everyone else seems to be happy."

At the head of the table, the Provost repositioned his chair and suppressed a yawn. "This line of questioning is going to connect to our case at some point, Phil? We have reserved the room for only two days," Marshall intoned, making a not too subtle suggestion to speed up the process.

"Right now, Doug," Scollick replied. "In your deposition, Neal, you painted Dr. Dodd as somewhat of a maverick. I can understand trying to distance yourself from him under the circumstances, but was that justified?"

"Maybe now would be a good time to review Dr. Dodd's deposition," Whitaker recommended, before Abramowicz could answer.

Initially surprised by the request, Scollick stopped and thought for a minute. "I have no objection to that," he said, eventually.

"Great," Dodd whined. He whispered to Scollick, "Let's sink the ship with the first torpedo, why waste a perfectly nice spring day by staying inside?"

Scollick ignored the remark. "Okay, Kendrick, your turn," he told the other attorney. While the second attorney re-arranged the papers in front of him, Scollick whispered to Dodd, "A little give and take, Spence. Give me some room to operate. I promise, I won't disappoint you."

"That's what my wife said before the divorce," Dodd replied venomously, under his breath.

"Spence," Whitaker said to get Dodd's attention.

"Yes, Ken," Dodd responded sourly, rotating his body within his chair to face Whitaker. Forcing himself, Dodd turned his attention from the reflection of the attorney in the huge table to the man himself.

"You've had an interesting career," the attorney

suggested.

"Glad you think so," Dodd replied.

"Kicked out of the Air Force early."

"Honorable discharge," Dodd corrected.

"Ineffective officer; may not rejoin," Whitaker elaborated. Dodd shrugged. Whitaker continued, "Made them mad, did you?"

Dodd shrugged, again. "They insisted on practicing medicine like it was practiced in 1940. I thought they should at least move to the sixties, since that was before I went to medical school. The *administrator*," the word slipped from his lips like a curse, "there was useless, also."

"Dr. Dodd," Marshall said, maintaining his composure. "This may surprise you, but we are actually on the same side here. You need to maintain the appearance of civility, even if you don't feel that generous." Dodd returned the stare silently.

Whitaker continued, commanding Dodd's attention. "You then bounced around at several ERs and urgent care centers, before partnering with another doctor to open your own practice. Why did you leave that practice?"

Dodd turned to his attorney and asked loudly, "We can't ask about Neal, but he can drag my life through the gutter?"

"Neal isn't named in the suit, Spence. You are," Scollick answered quietly.

"Oh yeah, I forgot," Dodd said. Regaining eye connect with Whitaker, he replied, "My partner was a crook. He stole from patients and insurance companies. He threatened my life. When we split up, his accountant tried to stick me with the tax burden. My accountant fixed that by sending the IRS after them."

"This is documented?" Whitaker asked, eyebrows raised.

"Out of court settlement. No documentation available; it's all confidential."

Invictus

"Or fantasy," Whitaker added.

"You could call my accountant," Dodd suggested.

"Might do that." Whitaker wrote a note to himself. "You've been here, at SVU, how long?"

Dodd looked at his watch. "Seven years, three months, six days, four hours, and eleven minutes. Not that I'm counting."

"Enjoy your stay here?" the attorney asked, unperturbed by the sarcasm.

Dodd nodded; he answered, "Until they appointed Neal the director."

"You've been unhappy since then?"

"To put it mildly."

"Why?" Whitaker asked.

Dodd responded in clipped, terse phrases. "Every decision he makes is political, calculated to offend the fewest people. He knows nothing about medicine. Whoever advises him, if someone does, knows less or is not insistent that good medical care be practiced."

Whitaker scratched his chin. He lay his papers on the table in front of him and leaned back in his chair. Crossing his arms in front of himself, he asked, "What sorts of thing constitute bad medicine or bad decisions, as far as you are concerned?"

Dodd relished listing Abramowicz transgressions. He fired his first salvo, "He has never made it clear to the nurses that they are *support* staff, that they should take vital signs on every patient on every visit, undress every patient, or undress all wounds and injuries, for one thing."

Whitaker turned his head toward Abramowicz. "Neal," he asked, "what's your opinion of that accusation?"

"None of the other physicians insist on this level of assistance," Abramowicz answered.

"Why?" Whitaker asked Abramowicz.

Dodd answered for him. "Because Neal controls their purse strings, their CME time and money, their time off.

He wants no conflict with the nurses, so he leans on the doctors," Dodd said.

"I asked Neal," Whitaker said pointedly.

Abramowicz smiled. "They just don't see it as a priority, I guess. It's not that important."

Dodd gritted his teeth; he stared menacingly at Abramowicz; his face turned red and he blew air between his clenched teeth, but he kept his temper. There are sixty employees at student health hoping I'll kill this bastard, Dodd told himself. Then they would be rid of both of us. Later, maybe.

"Anything else, Dr. Dodd?" Whitaker asked.

Dodd pulled a folded list from his shirt. Slowly, he unfolded the lined notebook paper. He read through the titles. "I have examples of each of these, if you'd like to hear them: Ineffective patient appointment system. Lack of leadership skills. Waffling on all decisions. Inability to promulgate or enforce reasonable rules about chronic medicine prescriptions or the treatment of patients with chronic diseases. No consistency in enforcing rules or regulations. Inability to accept constructive criticism. No effective triage system. Refusal to back up physicians who have conflicts with patients over who gets or doesn't get antibiotics and other issues." He looked the page over, turned to the back side to emphasize that it, too, was also filled. "More stuff than you can shake a stick at."

Marshall interrupted. "I think we should take a break, before Dr. Dodd loses his temper again. We'll meet again after lunch, say 2 p.m."

"That's three hours from now," Dodd protested, waving the piece of paper in the air, toward Marshall. "We have a lot of stuff to cover."

"Or nothing at all to discuss, Spencer, if you don't control your temper," Marshall reminded him.

Invictus

Chapter Thirty-four
Early Afternoon of March 31st

Finally, at 2:30 p.m., Provost Doug Marshall returned to his seat at the head of the table. "Sorry," he said, "President Furneaux wanted an update. Phillip, let's let you start, again. Shall we try to keep it civil this time?" He looked at Dodd warily.

"Certainly," Scollick replied for his client. "Neal, you've had a lot of complaints about Spencer?"

"Absolutely," Abramowicz intoned solemnly.

"How many, say, in an entire year?"

Abramowicz rolled his eyes, looking at the ceiling. He guessed, "On average, ten."

"How many patients does Spencer see in the course of a year, fall semester, spring semester, and summer sessions, combined?"

"I don't know," Abramowicz said, shaking his head and shrugging his shoulders.

Dodd answered for him. "Four hundred a month for about ten months. Four thousand, in round figures."

"Does that sound right, Neal?" Scollick asked.

The corpulent administrator tried to shrug his shoulders, again. As a result, his entire body quivered. He answered evasively, "I'd have to check my statistics."

"Good administrators know this stuff," Scollick suggested.

"Uncalled for," Whitaker shot back, trying to protect his position. He thought defending the malpractice case was futile, and he intended to prove it, given the chance. As for Abramowicz, the lawyer did not care one whit about him; but, he did want to win the argument, and that meant protecting the chubby man from being portrayed as incompetent.

"I agree with Phil," Marshall told Whitaker, indirectly chastising Abramowicz. Whitaker nodded, agreeing in principle to the assertion. He slid farther back, into his seat.

Scollick calculated rapidly in his head. "So, Neal," he continued, "ten complaints in four thousand interactions. What's that? One quarter of one percent?"

Abramowicz leaned forward. Hands clasped together, he stared at Scollick. He blustered, "I don't have any complaints about anyone else."

Unmoved by the argument, Scollick reminded the rotund administrator, "Neal. You're going to be under oath in a courtroom."

Abramowicz nodded, conceding the point. He relaxed, and sat back in his chair. "Okay, maybe three or four per year for the others. Dodd has two or three times as many. You should read them. The people who complain really hate him. They write long letters defiling him. Besides, only one in ten customers who are disappointed take the time to write. So there were probably a hundred patients upset with him."

"In your MBA classes, did they also tell you that only one in a *hundred* satisfied customers bothers to write something nice?" Scollick asked sarcastically.

"Maybe. I don't remember."

Scollick rubbed the stubble on his chin. The flight from Washington that morning with President Furneaux had been delayed. Scollick had no time to return home before the hearing. In the airport he had used an electric shaver. He disliked the closeness of the shave and he frowned at Abramowicz. Continuing his line of thought, he asked, "So how many letters of commendation did Spence get, Neal? Remember, you'll be under oath in court."

"Maybe four, five tops per year."

Scollick scribbled on his legal pad, he spoke as the numbers appeared under the point of his pencil. "A hundred dissatisfied customers, four to five hundred very satisfied customers, and thirty four hundred students who had no strong feelings either way? Is that a reasonable summary?" Scollick asked. Abramowicz nodded. "By the way," Scollick continued, "I did read all of the complaints, and I got permission to pull the charts of those people who complained. Did you read those charts, Neal?"

"Of course."

"Didn't it strike you as odd that half of the complaints against Dr. Dodd occurred months to years after he saw the patients who complained?"

"No," Abramowicz said bluntly. He stared at his belly, bored by the conversation.

"How would you characterize Dr. von Weintraub's care of patients?"

Surprised by the question, Neal looked up from his lap. "Excellent," he said. "She's one of the best. She mothers her patients."

"As opposed to Spence?" Scollick asked.

"He's abrupt."

Scollick turned his head toward Dodd, "Spence, your take on that?"

"I don't get emotionally involved with students. I can't. In order to be objective about the seriousness of a patient's illness, a physician shouldn't become psychologically involved. Some of this reticence is my emergency medicine training and background. Personally, I don't have the emotional stamina to invest in both a clinical and a psychological investigation, much less the treatment of both." The physician paused. His mouth squirmed for several seconds; he tried to think of a better way to continue, then gave up. "I admit it; empathy is not my strong point. Making good clinical decisions is. Unfortunately, some patients don't care how much you know until they feel they know how much you care. I'm not very good at revealing those feelings. In fact, I avoid doing so."

"I don't think your perceived lack of empathy is due solely to your training, Spence," Scollick said, staring at Abramowicz, then Summers.

"What do you mean?" Dodd asked, not understanding Scollick's question, but worried about the implications.

"You father spent his life, from age eight until he graduated from college, in military boarding schools and academies. Public display of affection or emotion was anathema to him; he considered it a weakness. That ideal probably rubbed off on you. You mother spent half her childhood in an orphanage. Her father could not afford to keep her, after his wife died of cholera. I doubt either of your parents was very good at expressing their emotions. You just weren't given the emotional tools by your parents to respond in the same way that Dr. von Weintraub does."

Impressed by the attorney's preparation for the hearing, but annoyed by his accuracy, Dodd asked, "How do you know those things about my parents?"

"It's my job to know," Scollick replied. He allowed his eyes to drift from Dodd to Abramowicz and Summers. He added, "about every facet of the case. I spent some time with your brother when I was in Washington. Are those accurate descriptions of your parents?"

Face placid, Dodd recited something he had never admitted before to anyone else. He stared through Marshall, out the window at a cumulus cloud that floated left to right in the light blue afternoon sky. He nodded in agreement. "My parents had complete mastery of their emotions. I have no doubt that they watched beheadings in Saudi Arabia and births in Bangladesh, and that if you watched only their faces, you could not tell which."

"A good psychiatrist, or even a mediocre psychologist, probably could have picked up on that, wouldn't you say?"

Invictus

Scollick asked rhetorically. His head tracked around the room, making eye contact with each person seated at the table. He summarized for those present, "You might say that Dr. von Weintraub becomes emotionally involved with her patients, and Dr. Dodd does not. She assumes the patient to be in need of psychological support, as well as ill. She babies those in need of close supervision, whether they desire such treatment, or not. Whereas, Dr. Dodd's approach might be characterized as treating the illness or injury with a minimum of medical or psychological interference and allowing the patient to run his own life. Dr Weintraub might be seen as taking charge of the patient's psyche." When he finished, the attorney's eyes locked onto Abramowicz. "Neither method is wrong; they are just different approaches to the same problem. Correct?" The corpulent administrator stared at the attorney, confused by the question. Marshall's head nodded, ever so slightly. Rewarded, Scollick continued without waiting for an answer. "Does Dr. von Weintraub get along with Spence?"

"I suppose," Abramowicz offered.

"She hates my guts," Dodd whispered. Scollick nodded.

Scollick persisted, eyes boring into Abramowicz. "Neal, as administrator, it's your job to recognize conflict between your employees. Did you notice that many of the complaints about Spencer — all of those that mentioned a visit more than six months prior — just happened to be submitted on the same day, or the day after, the patient visited with Dr. von Weintraub?" Abramowicz blushed. His body seemed to flutter. No sounds left his larynx although his mouth moved. His pupils shrunk to pinpoint size. Scollick exposed another of his failings. He said, "Looks like you missed a major conflict within your sphere of influence."

"Is that true?" Dodd whispered. Scollick nodded. "I'll kill her," Dodd said. Scollick shook his head. He smiled at Dodd.

Directly behind Marshall, a large black bird landed on the outside ledge of the pointed window fitted into the carved stone opening. It peered into the room, tilting its head, seemingly eavesdropping on the hearings. Unaware of the visitor, Marshall stared at Abramowicz. Abramowicz shrank into his seat. He hid behind Summers, avoiding the Provost's glare. Dodd smiled. He remembered BeeBee's last words before Dodd left him at the apartment. *Mendacem memorem esse oportet.*[45] He had one friend nearby, anyway; possibly Scollick made two. Dodd saw the wheels turning behind the provost's furrowed brow.

Finished glowering at the cowardly mass of flesh that occupied the chair next to Summers, Marshall turned and spoke to Scollick, "I'm not sure this will affect the malpractice aspect of the trial. Do you have anything else?"

Scollick nodded. He spoke in level tones betraying no anger or resentment. "I picked one of the most inflammatory of the letters about Dr. Dodd from Neal's stack. He received this one about five months ago, days before he recommended that Dr. Dodd's contract not be renewed. The author, a student's mother, also sent a copy to President Furneaux. Neal, you talked about this letter in your deposition. It was one way of showing that Spence's practice of medicine was below the standards you set for the group, correct? You'll find it on the tenth page in your deposition folder."

Abramowicz opened the binder in front of him. Summers edged away from the fat man, scooting her chair closer to Marshall and Whitaker. Abramowicz reviewed the letter silently.

"Let me read some of this out loud," Scollick offered. "She opens the letter with, 'I anticipate that you will be aghast at the account of the rude, unprofessional, and inadequate treatment my freshman daughter received from Dr. Spencer Dodd....' After these inflammatory remarks, she goes on, to complain that Spence asked her daughter about the chance of being pregnant, to suggest that he might have lowered her daughter's self-esteem when he questioned her about tattoos and skin piercings. At the end she suggested that Spencer could not be a licensed doctor since he did not give her baby antibiotics for a viral infection. Are you reading the same page, Neal?"

"Yes." Abramowicz's confidence rose; he realized that Marshall did not like hearing the parent's description of her child's interaction with Dodd. Boldly, he sat more upright in the chair. Summers leaned her body slightly closer to him.

"Where was it you got your doctorate, Neal?" Scollick changed the subject suddenly.

"Marshall University," Abramowicz answered, startled look on his face.

"Undergraduate degree and masters?" Scollick asked the massive man.

"Old Dominion, and the University of Virginia," he answered, less surprised by the second question.

Scollick smiled, seemingly recognizing something for the first time. "You're a Virginia boy?" Scollick asked, seemingly amazed.

"Yes, suh," Abramowicz replied, emphasizing his southern accent audibly.

"From which high school did you graduate, Neal?"

"Wakefield, in Arlington."

Scollick elbowed Dodd, to make certain the physician paid attention. He asked Abramowicz, "That's in northern Virginia, near the nation's capital, right? And the same high school that Spencer's older brother attended?"

Abramowicz nodded. "We talked about that once. We graduated the same year. I was only there one year. My mother and I moved to Arlington after my parents divorced. We lived in Norfolk prior to that; my father was a sailor. He met my mother in the Philippines. There, I went to

Norview High School. The Washington Presidents' quarterback, Heisman Trophy winner, Victor Mercer, also went to Norview. Many years later, of course."

"Of course." Returning to the letter in the deposition, Scollick said, almost off-handedly, "I see where the plaintiff's attorney asked you if you knew the lady who wrote this letter. That's on page fourteen, Neal; it's underlined."

Abramowicz turned the pages slowly. Persia saw sweat bead on the back of his neck. The wide expanse of his skin visible to her slowly reddened. From behind, his red jowls hung around his tight collar. Persia watched the collar move up and down rapidly when he tried unsuccessfully to swallow. "Yes?"

"You said, 'No.'"

"Apparently," Abramowicz agreed, reading the highlighted paragraph. His lips moved while he read.

"Let me ask you, again," Scollick said. "Do you know this woman, Cynthia Christopher?"

"I talked with her on the phone," the heavy man admitted.

The lawyer cleared his throat. Leaning forward in his chair, he almost stood, then decided against it. "Let me more specific," he said. "Did you know this woman before she wrote the letter condemning Spencer?"

"No, of course not."

"Even if I asked you that question under oath; and, I remind you, you were asked under oath during your deposition."

Abramowicz swallowed hard. "Even under oath," he said. "I never heard of Cynthia Christopher until she phoned to complain about Dr. Dodd."

Scollick stretched his body. He leaned over the side of his chair and pulled his soft leather briefcase to the table. Unzipping the side pouch, he pulled a battered Wakefield High School yearbook from his bag. Dodd recognized his brother's name, written in magic marker along the spine of the volume. Opening it to a page marked with yellow lined paper, he slid the book across the table toward Abramowicz. "This photograph, I believe, was taken at your senior class prom. Who's this standing next to you, Neal?"

Abramowicz never leaned forward to retrieve the book. Unclaimed, it lay in the middle of the table. Summers bent and reached for the picture album. Abramowicz slapped her hand. She pulled it back rapidly and elbowed Abramowicz. "Neal," she cried, feelings and hand hurt.

"Neal?" Scollick asked, again. "Who is that person standing next to you?"

"Cindy Young," Abramowicz answered slowly.

Scollick stood. He slid the book farther up the table until Marshall had a clear view. "Cynthia Young was Cynthia Christopher's maiden name," he explained, sitting, again. "I think the secret referred to in the yearbook is the fact that Neal and she planned to live together at ODU during their four years of undergraduate schooling. They broke up just before graduation. Neal went to U.Va. and then to Marshall. She married and moved to Richmond."

"I...I didn't know the lady who called was Cindy, until after she complained about Dr. Dodd," Abramowicz whined. "I found out later who she was."

"And you didn't push her to write a complaint?" Scollick asked.

"Never. That was her idea."

"And sending a copy to President Furneaux was her idea, too?"

"Absolutely," Abramowicz said forcefully.

With obvious disdain and contempt for Abramowicz, Scollick reached inside his black briefcase one more time. "I won't have to show these to you, Neal, since you wrote them." He stood. Leaning over the table, he handed a sheaf of papers to the Provost. He explained to everyone in the room while doing so, "Neal obviously doesn't know this, but every email written and mailed through the campus network is archived on CD-ROM. It is held in storage, essentially forever. If you look at these, Doug, you'll see a marked similarity between Neal's email to Mrs. Christopher and the wording of her letter to Neal and the copy she sent, *at his request*, to President Furneaux."

Abramowicz sank into his chair. Summers's chair, distancing itself from his, made an audible and long scraping sound on the polished wooden floor. Even Whitaker inched away, not wanting to be near the lightning bolt when it struck.

Marshall sucked air in through his nose, seemingly forever. His nostrils collapsed inward. Dodd watched the muscles in the Provost's face and temples flex over and over. After several minutes, he spoke to Abramowicz, "Neal, we will address these violations of ethical conduct at a later date. I suggest you retain an attorney." Red-faced, the fat man's chin slipped deeper into his chest. He said nothing, keeping his eyes on his vast stomach.

Addressing Scollick, Marshall added, "We still have the malpractice question to decide, counselor. Does any of this have bearing on that?"

Scollick sat again. He replied, "I'm afraid not."

"Great," Dodd said, glumly "fried anyway." He placed his head in both hands with his elbows on the table.

"But," Scollick added, "I do have some additional information that might."

Turning to Whitaker, Marshall asked the other attorney, "Do you have any comments or suggestions, Ken?"

Whitaker raised his hands in mock surrender. He answered, "At this point, Doug, I'm just hoping to leave the room with my scalp. Let him go on."

Marshall nodded. "Your show, Phil," he said.

"Persia," Scollick said.

Invictus

So wrapped in Abramowicz's fall from grace that she had forgotten the reason for the hearing, the sound of her name surprised Summers. She jumped. "Oh!" she said.

"Sorry to startle you," Scollick apologized to her. "You have your deposition in front of you. Correct?" She nodded. "Under oath, and in direct conflict with Spence's testimony, you stated that you never spoke with Stone Garrette the day he fell from the recreational sports building roof. Would you care to change that testimony?"

Summers looked at Abramowicz. She saw him shake his head subtly, even though he never made eye contact with her. "No," she answered unsteadily. "That's the truth. He had left the health center before I arrived from counseling. I really don't understand why Spencer would lie about such a thing." She attempted to don her psychiatrist's hat and smooth the difference in opinion. "He has been under a lot of stress lately, the divorce, his father's Alzheimer's, his mother's stroke...."

Dodd rolled his eyes. He glared at Summers, livid over the lies. His face flushed with anger, but he gritted his teeth and swore unintelligibly under his breath. Marshall refrained from asking him what he had said, knowing it might lead to another outburst.

"May I have an outsider invited to our hearing?" Scollick asked the Provost.

"Who?" Marshall and Whitaker asked as one.

"Oh, Murphy Garrette," Scollick said calmly.

Every person in the room turned his head toward Scollick. Whitaker recovered first. "Are you nuts?" he asked. "His attorneys are suing us. He could use our discussion against us in court."

"I agree," Marshall said.

Scollick insisted. He explained, "Murphy came without his attorney, voluntarily. Even though he is suing the university, he has been a great benefactor to it. In addition, nothing he will tell you is admissible in court, unless subpoenaed."

Reluctantly, Whitaker conceded. He signaled his concession by leaning back in his chair and raising his left palm, open, to Scollick. He spoke to Marshall. "If you can live with this, Doug, I can."

"I hope you haven't given away the farm, Phillip," Marshall said. "When can he come?"

"He's downstairs, waiting in the parking lot. We met at lunch." Scollick pulled a portable phone from his breast pocket. He flipped open the case and punched ten digits. Waiting several seconds, he said, "Murphy. They agreed. Come on up."

In dead silence, the entire room awaited Garrette's arrival. Dodd noted the raven had returned to pace the window sill. Eventually, the door to the conference room opened. Only Scollick stood. He pulled out the empty chair next to his and motioned for Garrette to sit there.

Garrette nodded to Dodd, then to each familiar face in the room. He arrived alone, no entourage accompanied him. "How's Stone?" Dodd asked quietly.

"Fine," Garrette said. "He told me to say hello to you."

"Did you bring the tape?" Scollick asked Garrette.

Garrette reached inside his coat pocket and withdrew a mini-cassette tape. He placed it on the table. Scollick pulled a cassette recorder from his briefcase. After checking buttons, dials and battery strength, he inserted the cassette into the case. "The headquarters of Mr. Garrette's media company is located in the suburbs of Washington, D.C. In Landover, Maryland, to be precise. Mr. Garrette routinely, and automatically, records all phone calls to his office. It helps him remember the details of agreements he makes over the phone. This practice is technically illegal and thus not evidence permitted in court. His machinery recorded the call from Stone on the day that Stone saw Spencer in the health center."

Summer's eyes widened. She started to speak.

Invictus

Abramowicz kicked her under the table. She closed her mouth. Seeing her lips move, and expecting her to panic, Scollick asked, "Did you want to say something, Persia?" She shook her head, no. Scollick continued. "To refresh everyone's memory, Dr. Dodd claims that Dr. Summers had Stone call his father to ask if he would pay for the admission to the hospital. Dr. Summers denies ever talking to Stone Garrette. Stone has no memory of the meeting or the telephone call. He has complete amnesia for a long period before and after the fall. You might find this portion of the conversation interesting."

Dramatically, Scollick leaned forward and pushed the play button on the tiny recorder. Stone Garrette's voice reverberated through the conference room as clearly as if he stood among them. "Are you sure you don't want me to go to the hospital, Dad?" he said, voice quaking with uncertainty. "Maybe you should talk with the psychiatrist. Dr. Summers is standing right here. She doesn't agree with Dr. Dodd, but she's willing to admit me if you say it's okay."

"I don't need to talk with no nut doctor," Murphy Garrette's gruff voice replied on the tape. Scollick's hand snaked across the table to push the stop button. At the conference table, Garrette's head slumped into his folded arms. Dodd heard him moan. "If only...." Garrette said quietly.

First to recover from the shock, Marshall asked Garrette, "Did you say something, Murph?"

Shaken, Garrette stood. He looked initially toward Dodd and smiled; then he glared at Summers and Abramowicz, neither of whom returned the stare. Finally, he stiffened and turned to face Marshall. "First, I want to apologize to Dr. Dodd for not remembering my son's reference to Dr. Summers during our conversation until Phil Scollick forced me to admit there was a tape and then to replay it. I guess I blocked the memory after the accident." Dodd nodded silently.

Garrette continued, "Second, I understand that this is only a preliminary hearing, but I have an offer to make to the university. I won't say this in a court of law, if we end up there, but I feel partially responsible for my son's accident. I think, had the point been driven home sooner and more forcefully that he had become an alcoholic, I would have responded differently. I am willing to drop the lawsuit, provided no adverse sanctions are taken against Dr. Dodd, and the University splits the medical bills with me. I don't know enough medicine or psychiatry — hell I don't know anything about either — to decide if Dr. Summers has committed malpractice. I think she should be punished for lying under oath, however. Doug, please have the senior university counsel call my attorney, Bill Cassel. Let them work out the details of the compromise." Without waiting for an answer, Garrette spun on his heels and marched out of the conference room.

A minute later, Scollick's telephone beeped in the quiet room. He answered the call. "Yes, I'll safeguard the tape, Murphy," Scollick said.

Invictus

Chapter Thirty-five
Late Afternoon of March 31ˢᵗ

Elated, Dodd left the hearing when dismissed by Marshall. Maybe we shouldn't kill *all* the lawyers, he told himself striding down the granite steps toward the grass, we'll keep Scollick around. One down, one lawsuit to go, he thought. As he started to cross the drill field, he heard his name called. Turning, he saw Murphy Garrette marching toward him. He stopped in the crosswalk closest to Burroughs Hall. Dodd held his hand out to the shorter man. "Mr. Garrette," he said, "I have to admit that I was wrong about you. You're a much better man than I thought. Stone's lucky to have you for a father."

Garrette shook hands with Dodd. "No, Doctor," he said. "You were absolutely correct in your assessment. It took me a long time to realize that I have shortchanged Stone — in a lot of ways. We have many things to catch up on."

"Well, thanks for coming today," Dodd continued. "You certainly saved my butt, at least from your lawyers."

"You saved my son's life," Garrette reminded Dodd. "I can never repay you for that. I would like to try." He reached inside his jacket coat for his checkbook.

Dodd grabbed Garrette's wrist gently, preventing him from completing the gesture. "Look, Murphy," he said. "Thanks, but I don't want any of your money. I don't help people for the money." Dodd laughed. "Obviously. I guess that's why I work here. Virginia doesn't pay well."

Garrette relaxed his arm. Dodd released it, convinced the man would no longer pull out his wallet. Garrette pushed both hands into the front pockets on his trousers.

Bill Yancey

His tie hung loosely around his neck and his shirttail dangled below his sports coat. The millionaire looked more like the street urchin Dodd suspected he had been as a child: a wily, cunning survivor, tough as Kevlar. Except for his eyes, that is, they mirrored the stress from the previous five months. "You deserve to run student health, Dodd. I heard about the move to privatize it. That Abramowicz fellow's a joke. He doesn't know anything about medicine, and whoever has been giving him pointers is obviously more worried about not upsetting him than telling him the truth."

"I think the Provost is going to take care of Neal," Dodd observed, "and Summers."

"In any event," Garrette continued, "Dean Waters said that you may have to withdraw your bid for privatizing student health."

"Yeah," Dodd agreed. "My bank account's a lot lighter than yours."

"*Stone* and I," Garrette said, emphasizing his son's name, "wish to grub stake you to the contract. We'll put up the money so you can submit the bid. You can give it back to us when you win the contract."

Dodd's mouth opened, then closed. No words came out. He stared at Garrette. Stunned, he waited for his emotions to subside. Then he shook his head. "No," he finally told Garrette. "Please thank Stone for me. It is very generous of you both; but if I won the contract, I'd have to be boss. I don't have the temperament for that. I'll work for Massey and the group, or find another job in a clinic somewhere else. I've moved around a lot. I'm getting used to it and I don't mind."

Garrette stared at the taller Dodd, gaze boring holes into the doctor's forehead. "You sure?" he asked.

More certain that the decision was the correct one, after thinking for a moment, Dodd nodded. He held his right hand out to Garrette. "Absolutely, Murphy. It's nice to know I have friends, though. Give my best to Stone."

Garrette grabbed Dodd's hand in an iron grip. "Doctor, if you ever want a job in the entertainment industry, give me a call. I can use a man of your caliber." He released the physician's hand and spun to return to his car. A chauffeur held open the door on the stretched Lincoln, parked in Furneaux's reserved parking spot and three others.

Dodd began the leisurely hike across campus to the recreational sports and student health complex. He had skirted the duck pond and started across the women's soccer field when he heard his name again. Without turning his head, he waved his hand in the air. "*Good-bye*, Murphy," he called. The person calling his name persisted, growing louder by the second. Dodd turned around, and was almost flattened by Cody Gray. The student had his head down, pedaling a rusty bicycle as fast as it would go. Looking up, he realized that he had passed Dodd and slammed on the brakes. Just managing to maintain his balance, he slid sideways to a stop and jumped off the bicycle, letting it crash to the ground.

Running to Dodd, Gray wrapped his arms around the physician and squeezed. "We did it, Doc!" he screamed loudly enough to hurt Dodd's eardrums. "We did it!" Unable to contain his excitement, Gray ran circles around Dodd until he became dizzy; he tripped and fell onto the grass. There, he rolled around until exhausted. Dodd watched in amazement until Gray settled down, lying on his back, gasping for breath, and sweating.

"What did we do?" he asked suspiciously.

"Benny the Mooch and me," Gray corrected Dodd, "we sold the virtual race track. We made a fortune!"

Dodd pulled Gray to his feet, and wrapped his arm around the boy's shoulders. "Great. We need to celebrate. I get acquitted and you make a bundle, all in the same day! What was your take, a couple thousand?"

Gray's laugh became insane. His legs buckled and he fell to the ground, this time dragging Dodd onto the grass with him. "A couple thousand?" he asked, giggling. "Doc! Benny and I each took in 2.3 million dollars, after taxes, after fees. We cleared 4.6 million."

"Jesus," Dodd whispered.

"And it was your idea, Doc," Gray continued. "I can stake you to the privatization bid, if you'll let me."

Without hesitation, having already decided that issue once, Dodd shook his head. He sat up in the grass, hands planted behind him. Gray crossed his legs; he faced the doctor, grin too wide for his face. "Thanks, Cody," Dodd said, "but no. It's been an amazing day: Two offers to back my bid; I am excused from a career ending lawsuit; someone else agrees with me that Neal is a joke as a medical administrator, and you...." His voice trailed, dying.

"What?" Gray asked.

Dodd jumped to his feet. "Joke. Shit," he said. "The April Fool's Day joke." He started to jog toward Sykes Hall.

"Catch you later, Doc?" Gray called after him. "We'll celebrate at the Night Owl." Dodd waved a hand over his head, eyes staring at his goal, three quarters of a mile in the distance.

Abramowicz and his personal secretary had used the automobile leased from the motor pool to go to the hearing; they would get back to Sykes Hall before he could, possibly a long time before. Dodd hurried, hoping the duo would stop somewhere to collect their thoughts. Getting to the far side of campus meant a constant grind, uphill and against the prevailing wind. Despite the chilly March temperature, his face flushed red and sweat dripped from his armpits by the time he reached student health. Walking as quickly as possible, he strode through the back door, toward the stairway to the administration. The staff huddled at the nurses' station, arguing loudly, pointing to a

Invictus

piece of paper. Dodd stopped short of the stairwell. Shit, he thought.

He walked hurriedly to the knot of LPNs and medical assistants. "What's going on?" he asked, hoping he did not know the answer.

Astonished that Dodd spoke to them, after weeks of pretending that they did not exist except when professionally necessary, several of the women stared at him opened mouthed. One handed him a piece of paper, a copy of a letter addressed to Abramowicz's secretary. For show, Dodd scanned the paper; he already knew what it said.

Forcing a laugh, he handed it back. "It's a joke. Look at the date, April 1st. April Fool's Day," he said. "That's not Carilion Health Systems, it says *Carrion* — dead meat, road kill. If you don't believe me, call the number. It probably doesn't exist."

"We're going to be privatized," one nurse lamented, not listening to Dodd.

"I'm going to lose my job," another wailed.

"What will we do?" LaFlamé asked when she joined the group.

Realizing he wasted time, Dodd spun and walked away. He climbed the back steps, taking them two at a time. Once on the administrative floor, he headed for Abramowicz's office. J.P. Jones blocked his way. Gently, he pushed her to the side. "Haven't you done enough?" she yelled. Dodd leaned into the door; it opened easily. Abramowicz lay in the middle of the room, on his back. Next to him lay the letter, blue letters on the counterfeit letterhead screamed *Carrion* at Dodd.

"Neal!" the secretary screamed.

"Call 911," Dodd told her. He knelt at Abramowicz's side, checking for a pulse. "Neal, Neal," he said, slapping the obese man's face. Abramowicz did not respond. Dodd listened for respirations; he saw and heard none. Pulling on the corpulent administrator's tie, he yanked it loose and threw it across the room. Grasping the man's collar, he ripped the buttons off the shirt, exposing Abramowicz's pendulous breasts. The doctor laid his ear on the wide expanse of Abramowicz's chest. He heard no breathing, no heart sounds. Abramowicz's color, normally a brilliant sweaty red, took on a bluish tint.

Dodd turned Abramowicz's head to the side. Pushing open the cold, blue lips, he rammed his fingers into the pudgy mouth and checked for foreign bodies. Not finding any, he started CPR. After giving Abramowicz four breaths, he began chest compressions. He called to the secretary, "Get Massey and Watson up here. Where's the rescue squad?"

Out of sight and crying, she called back, "They're on their way."

"Do you know CPR?" he asked.

"No." Her sobbing echoed within Abramowicz's huge office.

Continuing the workout begun on the far side of campus, Dodd thoroughly drenched himself in sweat compressing the meaty Abramowicz's chest repeatedly. Average response time for the campus rescue squad was five minutes. It seemed like forever before they arrived. Two paramedics Dodd knew well, Karl Wallenstein and Chris Parsons, carrying the drugs, monitor, and endotracheal tubes, arrived first. Dodd assumed that the EMT trainees rode the elevator with the stretcher.

Wallenstein slapped the breathing mask over Abramowicz's face. Repositioning the fat man's head, he began to force oxygen into his lungs. The blue tinged skin turned a pale pink. Parsons set out the endotracheal tube for Wallenstein to use when he felt ready, then offered to relieve Dodd. "Thanks" Dodd said, leaning back on his haunches. While Parsons compressed Abramowicz's chest, Wallenstein attempted to intubate the huge man, to no avail. Dodd watched Abramowicz's skin turn a darker blue around his mouth. "Let me try," he said to the paramedic as the stretcher and the two EMTs arrived.

Using a skill honed in ERs and on hundreds of ambulance and helicopter rides, Dodd shoved the tube unerringly into Abramowicz's throat, pushing it into his trachea. "Tape this down and bag him," Dodd told one of the EMTs. He then stepped back from Abramowicz and sat in one of the plush chairs, thoroughly exhausted. Wallenstein listened with his stethoscope to both lungs while the EMT aerated them. After also listening to Abramowicz's stomach to insure Dodd had placed the tube correctly, he took over bagging for the EMT. The fat man's skin color became pink once again.

The second EMT looked critically at Dodd. She asked him, "Are you all right, Doc?"

Out of breath, Dodd held one finger up. "Okay," he said when he had erased his oxygen debt.

"Can you tell us anything about him?" Parsons asked, while his comrades performed CPR. He listened carefully to Dodd while he attached the monitor electrodes to Abramowicz's chest.

"Late-fifties, obese, white male. History of arrhythmias. Stressed. Found unresponsive about ten minutes ago. I don't think he is on any medications," Dodd told the paramedic.

"Is this compression effective?" the EMT pushing on Abramowicz's chest asked his team leader.

Parsons attempted to find a radial pulse and found nothing. Brachial pulses also were nonexistent. He looked for a central pulse. The carotid arteries were out of reach with the bagging technique Wallenstein used. "I'll have to check his femoral pulse, Doc."

Dodd nodded. "Just do what you normally do, Chris. Pretend I'm not here."

"V. Fib.," the female EMT recognized the rhythm on

the monitor.

Parsons reached for the paddles. Deciding against checking for pulses, for the moment, the paramedic charged the defibrillator. "Clear!" he yelled. The defibrillator downloaded electrical energy into Abramowicz's chest. Clint Massey and A.J. Watson arrived from the clinic. The controlled jolt of electricity caused the huge man's chest and arms to spasm. Pectoralis muscles flexed, lifting the fat arms off the carpet. They rose about a foot into the air, then dropped flaccidly onto the plush pile. "Keep pumping," the paramedic told the EMT. He recharged the defibrillator to its maximum capacity. "Still in ventricular fibrillation," he said, calmly reading the monitor screen. "Clear." Another lightning bolt coursed through Abramowicz's chest, lifting his arms and torso off the carpet. He flopped down, again.

"Start an intravenous," Wallenstein told the male EMT. A female EMT took his place pounding on Abramowicz's chest.

Parsons added, "He has a normal looking QRS complex. I'll check to see if he has pulses with it." Pulling the heavy duty scissors that all paramedics referred to as 'penny cutters' from his belt holster, Parsons cut Abramowicz's belt and pants. He yanked down on Abramowicz's pants, ripping them and exposing Abramowicz from the waist down. The obscenely obese abdomen hung down pressing tightly against his fat thighs, almost to Abramowicz's knees. Squeezing his hand between stomach and thigh, the paramedic had difficulty finding a pulse among all the fat and flesh.

Parsons took another tack. He slit the side of Abramowicz's pants to the cuff and divided the administrator's underwear. The paramedic yanked Abramowicz's right leg outward to expose the femoral area, and a lot more, to everyone in the room. For several seconds, no one moved, stunned. Dodd lifted himself from the chair to get a better view. The paramedic pressed on the femoral artery. "Strong pulse," he said. "Stop compressions. Still strong. You can stop compressions. Keep bagging, Karl. Let's get *her* covered up and to the hospital."

Massey and Dodd stared in disbelief. Watson fainted, falling backward and sliding down the wall, unconscious. The EMT turned her attention to Watson.

Five minutes later the stretcher strained under the weight of Abramowicz. One EMT tended Watson. The other gathered equipment in preparation for the trip to the hospital. After they pushed the gurney onto the elevator, Parsons turned to Dodd. "Doc," he said with a huge grin on his face, "where you went to medical school, didn't they teach you the difference between boys and girls?"

Bill Yancey

Invictus

Chapter Thirty-six
April 21st

Feet propped on top of his desk, Dodd stared out the window. A surprise late-April sleet storm coated it with ice. Lights from passing cars refracted unevenly through the irregular surface adhering to the glass. The natural prisms made by the icicles gave a Christmas look to the view, turning headlights green and red. Hanging over Cumberland Mountain, dark, thick, massive storm clouds in the southwest presaged a long storm. The flow of students through the clinic died with the bad weather. He mulled over the possibility of reading a medical journal, decided against it, and leaned back in the chair, arms behind his head and staring at the ceiling.

Dodd heard A.J. Watson's shoes in the hallway, hard leather soles unique among the staff's preference for jogging shoes. Without looking up, he called, "*Ecce homo!*"[46]

A.J. Watson's voice announced his arrival. "Depressed?" he asked Dodd.

"Haven't decided," Dodd lied. He dropped his feet to the floor and swung the chair to face Watson. Watson stood in the door, already seemingly weighted down by the duties of temporary administrator. The little man wore a long white coat; he clasped his hands together in front of him below his waist. Head bowed so that Dodd could see the top of his head while seated, he looked at Dodd through the tops of his bifocals and upper eyelids. Dark bags hung where the lower lids had been in the past. Dodd did not envy Watson the stress of his new position.

"I have some bad news," Watson said, wasting no words

on generalities, but gathering in the melancholy appearance of his colleague and storing the information for later use.

"I hesitate to ask what could be worse," Dodd said morosely. His chin dropped; he stared at his hands in his lap. "It's been a bad year for me, A.J., as you well know."

"Nellie's dead. She died about an hour ago," Watson announced, stepping gingerly several inches inside Dodd's office. Dodd had so radiated animosity over the previous three months that Watson felt threatened in his presence.

Too melancholy to look up, Dodd asked indifferently, "So, who's Nellie?"

Watson grimaced. "Sorry. Neal's real name was Nellie Lois Abramowicz. Mark Nguyen, her internist, got a pretty thorough history from her. She changed her name between her high school junior and senior years, when she decided to become a man. That's what caused her parents' divorce and their estrangement."

"Sorry," Dodd ventured, raising his eyes to look at Watson. "I didn't recognize her name. When did you say?"

"She died about an hour ago. Last Friday morning she suffered a second, more massive heart attack in the hospital. Nguyen is trying to track down her family. I doubt he will find one. Apparently, she was disowned by both parents many years ago. They'd be in their eighties; they may no longer be alive and she had no siblings."

Dodd's head sank further into his chest; he closed his eyes tightly. Even though the bizarre was commonplace in medical practice, it always surprised him when he discovered it. "Could we have done anything more?" he asked.

"Nguyen says no. She did well after your initial resuscitation until Friday. Then she suffered the second heart attack. Nguyen was surprised she survived the last five days. She never regained consciousness after the second one. Autopsy will give the final details, of course, but he thinks there is ample physical evidence of probable

Invictus

coronary artery disease: her weight, a prescription for testosterone. Add that to the stress she experienced leading a double life, and the hearing...."

"Not to mention an April Fool's joke by yours truly." Dodd beat the desk with the edge of his fist; he ground his molars together loudly enough to make Watson cringe. "Damn! Make sure you order the automatic defribrillator he refused to buy; it might have made a difference." He still could not think of the administrator as a woman.

"It's not your fault, Spence," Watson tried to console him. "She chose her lifestyle; she lived the way she wanted, ate what she wanted. She may have been in denial, but she had to have been aware of the possible consequences. I do have some good news, also."

Dodd lifted his head, wry grin on his face. He asked, "What's that? They're going to charge me with manslaughter instead of murder?"

Watson chuckled at the crisp humor, caught himself and covered his smile with one hand. Standing near the open door, he glanced both ways into the hallway, to make certain no one else saw or heard his indiscretion. Gleam fading from his eyes, he said, "The administration has decided to renew your contract after all."

Dodd held his right index finger toward the ceiling and cut small circles through the air. "Whoopee," he said, anger directed at himself.

"I'd want to try to keep Neal's, ah, Nellie's secrets confidential, Spencer," Watson said.

Dodd nodded, agreeing. *"De mortuis nihil nisi bene,"*[47] he said.

Watson turned to leave the tiny office. He stopped outside the door and turned toward Dodd, a big grin on his face. "Also, that Geriann Rivera woman, the one who threatened to sue you for sexual harassment?" Dodd nodded, glumly. "She says that was a joke. Seems she faked the letterhead of a non-existent legal firm. She laughed herself silly when university counsel contacted her to find out why she hadn't proceeded with the inquiry."

"Jesus Christ!" Dodd exclaimed, "what kind of moron would counterfeit a letter from an attorney...." He stopped speaking in mid-sentence, knowing just such a moron. His eyes grew large and he shook his head. "Guess I deserved that," he added. "Anything new on privatization?"

Watson looked into the hallway, again. Not seeing anyone, he stepped back into Dodd's office and closed the door securely behind him. Sitting uncomfortably on the front edge of Dodd's second chair, he said, "This is privileged information, Spence."

Dodd nodded, accustomed to the drill. With Watson, everything was classified. His military background made it impossible for him to understand the First Amendment to the Constitution. Without a specified need to know, no one knew anything. The military so ingrained secrecy into him that he sometimes forgot to publish the times of his committee meetings. "Top secret. Not to be dispensed without decoder ring," Dodd intoned.

"Privatization bids will be ranked next week. Neal's, uh, Nellie's, has been discarded. Your bid, our group bid, one from the internal medicine group in town, and another from an ER group in Kingsport, Tennessee, are still in the running. Everyone will still have to show a hundred grand in capital and another half million in assets before the contract can be let, however. For some reason, Furneaux liked that rule."

"That rules me out," Dodd said. "Can you guys come up with a net worth like that?"

"As a group, we can."

"They'd be stupid not to take you. You're a known and proven entity."

"We'd like you to stay on, Spence," Watson said quietly, nervously, "if we get the contract, that is. You'd have to tone down the criticism. We're afraid the nurses would jump ship."

"Let them!" Dodd said, warming to the task. "Geez, it would be nice to hire someone who was thinking about making my life easier instead of retirement and a state pension."

Bill Yancey

Invictus

Chapter Thirty-seven
May 9th and 17th

Dodd sat in the passenger seat of the Miata, back pressed against the door. He had both legs draped across the driver's seat, right knee hooked around the gearshift. His left thigh lay on the papers confirming Massey and Watson's contract with Southwest Virginia University to provide medical services to the students.

Top down on the convertible, Dodd had an expansive view of the latest spring morning of the year. A glorious sunrise colored the sky to his right, draping the university football stadium and coliseum in orange, interspersed with the school colors: blue sky, gray and white clouds. He fumbled with the automatic pistol, releasing the clip from the handle and snapping it back into place repeatedly.

A rush of feathers announced the arrival of BeeBee. The raven landed and sat, well balanced, on the top edge of the windshield. One foot grasped the rearview mirror. "Careful," he said. "You might hurt someone with that."

"Precisely my intention," Dodd answered, eyes downcast, not looking at the bird.

"Why? You won!"

Voice a low growl, Dodd responded, "I didn't want to win that way."

"It wasn't your fault that Abramowicz kicked the bucket. Think about it; she had been taking massive doses of testosterone. She was at least two hundred pounds overweight. Surely, the stress of being found out and the revelations at the hearing contributed to her demise. The surprise was that her heart didn't blow a gasket years ago."

"The letter was the final straw. If I hadn't sent it, she

might have lived."

BeeBee turned his head, examining the pistol more closely with one eye. "You're right," he said. "She would have kicked the bucket in July, instead of April. Are you going to shoot anyone I know?" the raven asked, then preened his left wing with his black beak.

"You."

Fearless, BeeBee raised his head and looked Dodd directly in the eyes. "You can't miss from this distance. Mind if I ask you why?"

With great effort, Dodd said, "I'm tired."

"It's a coward's way out. What will your family think?

"What family? My father has Alzheimer's; my mother's comatose. The ex-wife is gone for good. My dog is dead."

"Self pity didn't used to be your major failing. What about the boys?"

"They're grown." Dodd shrugged. He added, "They can take care of themselves."

"If they overcome the shame," BeeBee suggested, then added, "Shouldn't you worry that they might also make this choice, given your example?"

"They're stronger. They inherited their mother's fortitude and intellect — rock solid, imperturbable."

Bobbing his head, the bird argued, "Still, it's a coward's way out."

Dodd disagreed; he shook his head and said, "The real question is: Do I have the courage to pull the trigger?"

"No," BeeBee objected. "The real question is which takes more courage: to pull the trigger, or to live with the consequences of not pulling the trigger?"

"Don't try to confuse me," Dodd scolded the bird.

"Well you did contribute to the death of another human being. An eye for an eye and all that...."

"My thoughts exactly," Dodd agreed.

"What will the Church say? Eternal damnation for a

Invictus

mortal sin? Doesn't that worry you?"

"I'll claim to be Japanese," Dodd suggested. "Häri-käri is an honorable way of paying one's debt to society."

BeeBee tilted his head, not certain what Dodd meant. "Just one final thought," the bird offered, "death *is* the last great adventure for any living creature."

Dodd leveled the weapon at the bird. Undaunted, BeeBee stood upright, spreading his shoulders. He flared his ear, throat, and chest feathers defiantly. Turning his head, he stared directly down the barrel of the weapon and into Dodd's eyes. "*Mortem non timeo*,"[48] he said.

"*Vale, mi amice*,"[49] Dodd replied. He pulled the trigger.

The loud explosion deafened Dodd, stabbing painfully at his eardrums. Instantaneously, he saw a excruciatingly blinding, searing, white light that obliterated everything in his field of vision. The white flare cooled; he saw the tips of impossibly tall trees hanging over him. A tiny speck of a black bird sat on one of the branches, seemingly miles away. The black point exploded; feathers scattered in every direction. One large, inky black feather floated downward, winding its way to earth. As it neared Dodd, his field of vision became gradually dimmer, like the setting sun; a blackness as dark as the white light had been brilliant closed over him. *Acta est fabula, plaudite*,[50] Dodd thought.

***

Joie LaFlamé watched the rescue squad personnel work methodically in the parking lot. She stood just inside the back entrance to the health center, staring through the glass door. Clint Massey stood next to her, hand on her shoulder. They conversed in quiet tones, surrounded by silent colleagues. A hundred feet in front of them, A.J. Watson traipsed back and forth in the parking lot between Dodd's automobile and the ambulance, keeping his back toward the building. LaFlamé and Massey saw only the back of A.J.'s neck; his head drooped nearly to the asphalt.

"How?" LaFlamé asked.

"His father's service pistol," Massey answered. "One shot to the head. Instantaneous, I'd guess. Certainly, he did not have pain long, if he felt anything at all."

They watched the paramedic wheel the stretcher, loaded with the body and covered with a sheet, slowly from the Miata to the back of the ambulance. The head of the sheet and stretcher dripped liquid crimson. LaFlamé covered her face.

Behind her, von Weintraub spoke bitterly, "He won't be missed. Bastard."

Massey did not turn, unable to take his eyes from the grisly scene. "Maybe not by you, Hilda. There are a lot of students on campus, and, I daresay, some of his colleagues, who loved him."

"Bull," von Weintraub spat.

"Why?" LaFlamé asked.

Massey shrugged. "I guess the stress finally got to him. When you tilt with windmills, you have to be aware of the blades."

The rescue squad EMTs slid the bloodied stretcher between the gaping doors at the back of the ambulance. The body disappeared into the dark interior; the stretcher wheels collapsed upward, into the frame. The last paramedic visible to the crowd gave a waist-high half-wave to A.J., then slammed the rear door to the compartment. He walked around the ambulance to the passenger door and climbed into the vehicle. Backing slowly from its position, the van moved unhurriedly out of the parking lot. The lights on the roof remained dim, not flashing; there would be no mad dash to helipad or hospital.

When it moved away, the vehicle revealed more clearly the two police cars parked behind it. Red lights and white strobes flashed. Blue-suited officers took pictures and collected evidence from the small sports car and the asphalt. A long, silver tow truck, yellow lights on the cab

Invictus

flashing slowly, made its way ponderously into the parking lot. It wove its way between the emergency vehicles and curious students. Shortly thereafter, the blue Miata, windshield covered in gore and hoisted by its rear end, receded from the parking lot. A lone employee from the buildings and grounds department opened the valve on the nearby fire hydrant. Dragging a brass-tipped, red hose, two inches in diameter, the man scoured the parking lot with a continuous blast of water. He flushed oil, gasoline, anti-freeze, and any remaining evidence down the nearest storm drain.

Class called the students, work the employees. The crowds dissipated, leaving the damp spot on the parking lot to evaporate, taking Dodd's soul heavenward with the water vapor.

***

At midnight, Cody Gray leaned against the small U-Haul trailer, finished with loading. Sweat poured from his forehead and armpits. The SVU Bears T-shirt clung to his chest, sopping wet. He finished the soft drink in one gulp, then crushed the can within his fist. Stepping away from the trailer, he chucked the aluminum container into a nearby fifty gallon drum overflowing with graduation paraphernalia and trash.

Inside the coliseum parking lot, the trailer was only one of a hundred rented vehicles used to unload the dorms of the students' possessions and transport them home. Battered, his trailer had seen better days. It had been the last one on the rental lot, and about one third the size Gray thought he needed. Hitched to his new pickup truck, the weight of his paraphernalia within the trailer pushed the truck bumper closer to the ground. Over the previous week, he had surreptitiously removed his belongings from the Sykes Hall attic and stowed them inside. All his possessions now lay packed into the trailer, under the tarp covering the bed of the pickup, or crammed onto the passenger seat of the new vehicle. The cap and gown he had worn that morning at graduation covered the books in the front seat. The tassel from his cap hung from the rear view mirror.

Dodd's suicide numbed Gray. A single tear dribbled down his sunburned cheek when he wished Dodd had been in the football stadium for the sun-baked ceremony. "Son of a bitch!" he said out loud, to himself. He walked toward the student health center, intent upon retrieving the piece of plywood that kept the back door from closing and locking. When Gray bent to pick up the wood block for the last time, he changed his mind and left it in the door jamb.

Walking quickly to Dodd's office, he opened the door, turned on the light, and stared at the space. As of that moment, no one had come to claim Dodd's possessions. The books sat in the same places; a chart lay on his desk, probably the last patient Dodd saw. Gray looked at the name: Alexander. Appropriate, he thought. Tears fell more quickly; Gray stifled a whimper. He turned to leave. As he did so, he saw something that had escaped his notice every previous time he had sneaked into Dodd's office to steal food or drink. A huge stuffed raven stood on the top shelf of the tall bookcase. Mentally, Gray heard Dodd's voice repeat a message he had almost missed many weeks before, "I want you to have him if anything happens to me."

Climbing onto Dodd's desk chair and balancing precariously when it tried to roll out from under him, Gray retrieved the bird. Holding it under one arm, he turned off the lights to the office and closed the door. He left the office unlocked as Dodd always had. At the back door to the building, he kicked the plywood chunk into the parking lot. Freed to close, the door slammed behind him, locking when it did. Gray never looked back. He balanced the bird on top of the graduation gown in the passenger seat and climbed into the truck.

Gray drove one last circuit around the drill field. Holding his left hand out the window and high in the air, he presented his middle finger to the institution as a salute, screaming the entire time, "So long, you bastards! Yahoooo!!" Two hours later, he pulled onto Interstate 81, headed north towards Washington, D.C. Goosing the accelerator, Gray revved the engine. The pick-up shot quickly to cruising speed, merging with the heavy 18-wheeler traffic on the six lane super-highway.

"Where are we going?" a voice asked.

Gray snapped his head to the right. BeeBee balanced himself on a computer manual wedged between a box of books and the dashboard. "Jesus," Gray said, "you're alive. And you spoke!"

"Would you rather I wrote notes?" the bird asked.

Stunned, Gray stared at the highway and the myriad of truck lights ahead on the interstate for several minutes. Eventually, he spoke, smile creasing his face. "You're Doc's bird, BeeBee."

"I prefer to think that he was my person," BeeBee replied.

"What happened?"

"He lost his ability to distinguish between reality and fantasy. In your case, as an entrepreneur, that could be an asset."

"You already know where I'm going, don't you?" Gray asked.

"Absolutely," BeeBee replied. "After we get A.C.N.E., All Commercial Network Enterprises, launched, I have some more ideas...."

"Me, too."

Bill Yancey

Invictus

(Endnotes)

[1] What's new, Spence?

[2] I have this compulsion to speak Latin.

[3] You are a rare bird.

[4] Hail, two-legged animal without feathers.

[5] Time flies.

[6] I hate Astroturf.

[7] Honk if you speak Latin.

[8] Don't let the bastards wear you down.

[9] Don't let the bastards wear you down.

[10] I will either find a way or make one.

[11] Which was to be demonstrated

[12] Get out of here you fat bastard! Not worth a rat's ass!

[13] Honey, I'm home.

[14] The skill or art (of medicine) is long, the life (of patient or doctor) is short.

[15] The journey from the Earth to the stars is not easy.

[16] From egg.

[17] Let it all hang out.

[18] It is said that for a sick man, there is hope as long as there is life.

[19] First of all, do no harm.

[20] No one. Hannibal is at the gates.

[21] A savage is at the door.

[22] Undefeated, unsubdued, unconquered, unconquerable, invincible

[23] A true friend is a rare bird.

[24] Flatterers are the worst type of enemies.

[25] A woman either hates or loves: there is nothing in between.

[26] Anger is brief insanity. Physician, heal thyself.

[27] No assholes will be tolerated!

[28] Never despair!

[29] Kiss my ass.

[30] My fault.

[31] A light beer, please.

[32] There's no accounting for tastes.

[33] Garbage in; garbage out.

Invictus

[34] Life is good. And crazy.

[35] Is that a scroll in your toga, or are you just happy to see me?

[36] Get a life.

[37] Woman is more changeable than the winds.

[38] Fortune does not take away what she has not given.

[39] No one in love sees.

[40] Read my lips. Eat my shorts.

[41] I came, I saw, I did a little shopping.

[42] The end justifies the means.

[43] Just on your enemies?

[44] Medicine is the art of guessing.

[45] A liar needs a good memory.

[46] Behold, the man!

[47] Nothing but good about the dead.

[48] I don't fear death.

[49] Good bye, my friend.

[50] The play is over, applaud.